DANGEROUS

BOOK ONE

Therapy

O'CONNOR BROTHERS

RHONDA BREWER

Dedication

This book is dedicated to my husband. He gives me the encouragement to follow my dreams. Thank you for your love and support. I love you.

Acknowledgments

So many people made publishing this book possible, and saying thank you doesn't seem like enough.

I want to thank Golden Czermak, the Furious Fotog for the fantastic model photos, Chase Ketron for posing for the image on the cover, and Majeau Designs owned by Cory Majeau, for the cover design.

I also want to thank the many authors who helped me along the way with advice, experiences, and the pep talks to make this possible. Becky McGraw, Abbie Zanders, Susan Stoker, Kathleen Brooks, Rhonda Carver, Candace Osmond, Kate Robbins, and Lynn Raye Harris. They are amazing authors and fabulous ladies.

A very special thanks to these other special ladies for taking the time to read and help me make this book happen. Amabel, Daniels, Michelle Eriksen, Karie Deegan, Jackie Dawe Ford, and Nancy Arnold Holloway.

Last but certainly not least, I want to thank my two children. They both pushed me to follow my dreams of being an author and stood by me through every step. I'd also like to thank my parents because nobody could have a better mom and dad.

Chapter 1

The dispatcher sent another cruiser to an accident on the Outer Ring Road, and Constable John O'Connor shook his head. Icy roads claimed two more lives because careless drivers thought they could speed on the highways in winter weather.

Idiots.

Before he could think about the families who would have to deal with the horrific loss, horns blared, tires squealed, and John made a quick right into the university parking lot. In the rearview mirror, he witnessed a white Hyundai Accent blow through a red light and barely missed an oncoming truck.

"Jesus Christ." He took a quick U-turn as he flicked on the siren, and to his relief, the driver pulled in quickly.

Traffic stops were the worst since some people argued that they did nothing wrong. It was worse in the cold January wind because while he tried to explain the reason he pulled them over, he'd feel the chill right down to his bones.

John called into the dispatcher with the license plate number and waited for her to respond before he exited his vehicle. The cold winter wind swirled snow around him, and the ice pelted him in the face felt like knives piercing his skin.

John yanked the collar of his jacket around his neck, but it did very little to block the gale of the icy wind. When he neared the rear of the small automobile, an ear-splitting scream caused another type of chill to skitter down his spine. Without a second thought, John gripped his holstered Magnum as he guardedly crept toward the driver's side window.

The petite blonde in the driver's seat lowered the window, but all her focus was on her passenger. As John moved closer, he saw the reason for the screams. Another woman sat in the passenger seat doubled over, with her hand pressed against her swollen stomach.

"Breathe, Rina, you can do this. Just breathe, honey," the driver coached, but her voice sounded terrified.

"Are you freaking kidding me, Steph? I can't breathe with this…Oh. God, no," the passenger snapped then groaned.

There was no way to mistake the situation, but John didn't need this woman giving birth in the middle of a fucking snowstorm. Not to mention they were pulled to the side of one of the busiest streets in the city

Shit.

"I'm so sorry, officer, but my sister's in labor, and she's in a lot of pain, and she screamed just as the light changed, and I hit the gas. I'm sorry," the driver rambled but seemed to recognize she was, then stopped.

2

John nodded and gave an understanding smile. He blessed himself and said a little prayer before hurrying to the other side of the car. It appeared as if he had another crazy John O'Connor traffic stop at the end of his shift. At least once a week, he'd end up with some freaky traffic stop to tell his coworkers.

John yanked open the passenger's door and bit his tongue to keep the curse from escaping. Sweat covered the woman's lovely face, and she gripped the dash with one hand while her other lay pressed against her enormous belly.

He didn't know much about pregnant women, but he knew enough to see the woman was ready to pop. Why didn't he go to medical school like his father and younger brother, at least he'd know what to do here?

First thing's first.

"I need an ambulance on Prince Phillip Drive, in front of the Confederation Building ASAP. I've got a woman in labor." John kept his voice calm and professional as he spoke into the radio clipped to his shoulder.

The woman needed to see him calm and collected. If he appeared nervous, things could get out of control. John pulled out all the lessons he'd been taught by his uncle Kurt to control his breathing and heartbeat. If he showed any uncertainty, the woman would possibly panic, and it could mean real trouble.

When he received confirmation from dispatch the ambulance was on the way, John pulled off his peaked cap and jacket. He stooped next to the car and tossed his things on the floor of the

3

vehicle. John tried to give her what he hoped was a reassuring smile. To his relief, she returned his smile, and it helped ease his anxiety.

Breathing is good, and not just for the pregnant lady. Stay calm.

John repeated the words over and over in his mind like a mantra. He tried to keep his breathing slow and steady so he wouldn't alarm the two women. Yeah, that was easier said than done.

"An ambulance is on the way." John focused on the panting woman. "What's your name, Miss?"

"I can't do this," she wailed and grabbed John's arm.

It made him feel like a wimp when he flinched. His father once told him a woman in labor had the strength of ten men, and the vice-like grip she currently had on his forearm was evidence it was true.

"Her name's Marina," the driver practically shouted across the vehicle.

"Okay. Good. Marina, I need you to take short, shallow breaths, like this." John demonstrated by inhaling and blowing out with short pants.

He encouraged her to do the same by breathing with her. John didn't know if the breathing worked, but he remembered it from a movie and asked his brother about it. Ian told him it helped to decrease the woman's anxiety and helped them to calm during active labor.

"I need to push," Marina wailed through gritted teeth, and her nails sunk into his skin.

Fuck, that hurt.

Why women needed long nails was beyond him. It was a good thing he had a good poker face because she'd think he was a wimp and couldn't handle a little discomfort. John had to stop worrying about nail prints, probably permanently pressed into his forearm, and focus on the task at hand.

"How far along are you?" John asked.

"No. More. Questions," she growled through clenched teeth as she doubled over with a scream so shrill his ears rang.

John sent up a silent prayer, practically begging someone upstairs to keep the baby inside until the paramedics arrived. He wasn't squeamish over the woman giving birth, but it was too damn cold for a baby to be born outside.

"She's full term," the driver answered for her sister. "Rina, you've got to breathe like the officer told you." She brushed Marina's hair back from her face with a shaky hand.

John tried to remember if his twin brother's wife had such intense labor. Marina's contractions seemed hard and frequent, which could be in trouble if the ambulance didn't hurry. What was worse, it meant, he may have to deliver the baby himself. John trained to help with a routine delivery, but if there were complications, he was screwed.

Damn it, where's the fucking ambulance?

"What's your name?" John asked the driver when he noticed her knuckles turn white as she gripped the wheel.

"Stephanie….um, Stephanie Kelly." Her eyes darted back and forth between him and her sister, but she eased her hold on the wheel.

It wasn't hard to see the concern on Stephanie's face, even if she tried not to show it. Before John could say another word, flashing lights lit up the front of the car, as the ambulance pulled in front of the vehicle. When he saw the paramedics hurry toward him, and it relieved the stress in the situation.

"Stephanie, the ambulance is here." His voice remained calm. "I need you to come over here with me. The paramedics need room to take care of Marina."

He grabbed his things and was about to step back when Marina grabbed his arm. Her tear-filled eyes seemed to beg him to stay with her. John's heart went out to the frightened woman.

"It's okay. They'll help you now. Your sister and I will be right next to the car." He hoped his smile reassured her.

Marina released his arm reluctantly, and John turned to speak with the paramedic. Once he'd given all the necessary information, John stepped back next to Stephanie.

Stephanie stood with her arms wrapped around herself, shivering. It was the first time John noticed she wasn't wearing a coat. The petite woman barely came to his chest, but at six foot two, it wasn't unusual for him to tower over most women. He stood stiffly reluctant to put his arm around her, but she trembled, and it

6

killed him. After a few seconds, John decided to hell with it and wrapped his jacket around her shoulders.

"Thanks," she said softly.

He could barely hear her quiet voice over the howling wind, and he had to lean down to make sure he knew what she said. Stephanie's gaze never left the paramedics and her sister.

With her full attention on the ambulance, John took the opportunity to study her profile. She had what his mother would call a button nose, and her long blonde hair swirled around her face like a cascade of gold silk. When his gaze dropped to her mouth, all he could think about was how her bottom lip appeared a little fuller than the top. It made him want to nibble on that lip.

Kissable.

Like a quick gut punch, he realized it was precisely what he wanted to do to the beauty next to him, a woman he didn't even know. He'd never wanted to kiss anyone so much in his life, but he knew better, which was why he stepped away from her and put some distance between them.

"Did you want my license, so you can write the ticket before I go?" She turned to him.

Her green eyes stared up at him, and it was the first time he realized why he'd pulled her over in the first place. With all the commotion, it completely slipped his mind.

"I'm not giving you a ticket." John chuckled when her eyes widened.

Gorgeous.

It was suddenly hard to breathe, and it wasn't because of the frigid air. How was a stranger affecting him in such a way? It was beyond ridiculous.

"Oh, my God. Thank you so, so much." She wrapped her arms around his waist, and her vanilla scent wafted around him.

Having her pressed against him was a whole lot of wrong, but damned if it didn't feel like the best thing in the world. Stephanie stepped back, and he felt the loss of her warmth deep inside.

"Thank you." Her lovely face flushed pink as her gaze met his. "I appreciate it so much."

John's mouth went dry. He needed to say something, but forming words seemed impossible. Time appeared to slow as he gazed into her eyes. John took a step forward, but before he made a complete fool of himself, the ambulance door slammed and broke the spell.

Stephanie slipped his jacket off her shoulders and practically threw it at him before she ran to the other side of the vehicle. She yanked open the car door and stopped.

"Thank you again," she said then jumped inside her little Hyundai.

John didn't know how long he stood on the road staring in the direction of where she disappeared. It wasn't until a horn honked behind him that he was brought back to reality. His reaction to a simple hug was insane. John mentally slapped himself out of the stupor and jogged back to his cruiser.

Maybe his self-imposed celibacy was the reason he reacted to a simple hug. His annoying but well-meaning brothers were probably right. John needed a date, but getting one wasn't the issue. John didn't trust his judgment with women, not since he'd made such an error with his ex.

John yanked open the door to his vehicle but stopped when something on the road caught his eye. He quickly closed the car door and approached the object.

A woman's purse.

John snatched it from the snow-covered pavement and shook the snow off it. The wind carried a scent of sweet vanilla to his nose, and his dick twitched. It had to be Stephanie's.

He cursed the icy wind that seemed to want to freeze his ears off as he hurried back to his cruiser. The stinging sensation reminded him of exactly why he hated winter. January weather sucked in Newfoundland because it was either snowing, raining, or a combination of both.

John jumped into the driver's seat and tossed the purse on the passenger's side. He eyed the bag next to him as he rubbed his hands together to get them warm and help the blood circulate again as he debated with himself what to do.

To search through the bag seemed as if he was invading Stephanie's privacy. He was probably apprehensive because his mother always told him and his brothers, a woman's purse was her secret, and for her private view.

Kathleen O'Connor had dozens of little pieces of wisdom she bestowed on them and probably created the stories to keep seven mischievous boys out of her things. Still, it stuck with him.

What's the big deal?

It wasn't like he hadn't searched through people's belongings before. John participated in several search warrants and searched countless vehicles, houses, and closets over the years. Why did this feel so different?

With a muffled curse, John snatched the bag off the seat, unzipped it, and pulled out the wallet.

The contents confirmed it belonged to Stephanie, but the picture on her license didn't do her justice. Her heart-shaped face and sweet smile caused his heart to race. He didn't need this.

John dropped the wallet into the purse and placed it on the seat again. Thinking about her only wasted his time because he'd never see her again. He'd take the lost item back to the station and let them contact her. That was the procedure.

An hour later, John's shift ended, and he'd completed all his reports for the day. Once he dropped off the paperwork, he wanted to go to the hospital to visit his sister-in-law. The thought put an idea into his head.

John could drop the purse off himself. She was probably worried about where she'd lost it. John couldn't think of a better excuse to see her again, and he shrugged as he tossed the purse into his car.

It didn't make any sense, but he felt a deep need to see Stephanie. Almost as if he wouldn't be content until he did, and the feeling wasn't familiar. He'd never felt the magnetic pull toward anyone in his life. Less than five minutes with this woman, and he was desperate to be near her again.

John pulled into the Health Science Centre parking lot. The large building was one of the two major hospitals in St. John's. The only downfall with the place was finding a place to park. He probably should have kept the cruiser because he could have parked in one of the designated parking places for police. Since he drove his car, he'd entered a game of *seek and find* a parking spot. After a few minutes, a spot finally opened, and John quickly pulled into it.

When he jumped out of the vehicle, John glanced down and realized he still wore his uniform. He forgot to change into his civilian clothes because he was in such a hurry. He didn't want to miss her in case she left the hospital before he could give her back her purse.

Once he'd entered the door, he headed straight to the elevators. He stood back to wait for the arrival of the elevator but felt eyes on him. An older woman eyed him but looked away when he glanced at her. It probably seemed a little odd for a man to carry a purse, and his cheeks warmed at the thought of what the poor woman must think.

After several moments of uncomfortable silence, the doors of the elevator opened. John's twin brother, James, stepped off and

11

gave him a forced smile. James' ordinarily bright blue eyes were dull, and the dark circles were evident he hadn't slept in days.

Jesus.

Who could blame him? Sarah, the love of James' life, was fighting breast cancer, and worst of all, it was a battle she wasn't going to win.

James and Sarah hadn't even been able to enjoy their new baby. Her diagnosis came three months after Mason was born. Now, two months later, she'd had a full mastectomy, but her cancer spread. She was undergoing rounds of chemotherapy, but the doctor said her prognosis was not good.

It killed John to see the couple go through it. They were supposed to raise a family and grow old together. It was difficult to understand how such a sweet woman could be stricken with such a horrible disease.

For the first time in his life, John felt helpless because he couldn't fix it. All he could do was be there when James needed him. The five other brothers, Ian, Keith, Mike, Nick, and Aaron did their part as well. They took turns watching Mason or stayed with James to make sure he took care of himself. Their parents and Sarah's family spent time with Sarah at the hospital, when James had to get away and take some time for himself.

At least three times a week, John dropped by with coffee for James and to visit with Sarah. It was his day to visit, but since James was on his way out, John knew she was probably getting treatment or asleep. The last time John saw her, he could barely contain his shock. The beautiful woman James married was pale, thin, and her voice barely audible at times. Still, she wore a bright, infectious smile when anyone walked into her room. It amazed John how she could always keep a smile on her face in her situation.

"Hey." John stepped back to allow people to get onto the elevator.

"You didn't have to come here today," James replied.

"I know, but I'm just returning a purse someone lost." John glanced around, averting James' eyes.

"Why are you returning it here?" James narrowed his eyes

"Long story," John explained.

He wasn't about to have that conversation with James because, as a cop, his brother knew the protocol. Not that they all hadn't broken it once or twice over the years.

"How's Sarah today?" John quickly changed the subject.

"She's okay." James took a slow deep breath and shoved his hands into his jean's pockets. "She's in good spirits, but you know Sarah, she never lets anything get her down. I honestly don't know how she's keeping it together."

At the sight of the tears in James' eyes, John gave his brother's shoulder a gentle squeeze. The tension in James' body only got worse with his level of frustration. It had to be gut-wrenching to watch the love of his life slowly fade away, but the good thing was Sarah appeared to accept her possible fate.

"Sarah may not be an O'Connor by blood, but she fights like one." John forced a smile. "You need to keep the faith, bro."

13

"I'm trying." James sighed. "Ian was here earlier."

Ian was the only one of the seven brothers to follow in their father's footsteps. As a doctor, Ian worked in the emergency department and would spend lunch breaks with James and Sarah. He also kept the family up to date on any changes with Sarah's medical condition.

"That's good." John shifted and glanced down at the other reason he'd come to the hospital.

"Yeah," James whispered.

John waited for his brother to speak again, but instead, James' eyes glazed over as he stared out through the entrance. James told John every time he left the hospital, he was terrified she'd pass away before he returned.

"Where are you going?" John asked after a moment of silent support.

"To Mom and Dad's place. I need to check on Mason. Sarah's mom is with her now, and I wanted to give them some alone time." James blew out a slow breath.

"Be careful on the drive. We had some snow earlier. When you get home, hug that nephew of mine for me." John pulled James in for a quick man-hug, then released him.

With a wave, James trudged out of the hospital. John watched with tears forming in his eyes. They weren't identical twins, but there was still a connection, and John felt his brother's pain like it was his own. John was pissed because cancer was an enemy the O'Connor brothers couldn't bring down. None of them could lessen

14

James' pain one damn bit. All they could do was pray James could carry on if Sarah lost her fight.

John pulled himself together and stepped on the elevator when it arrived. He drummed his fingers against his leg nervously as he watched the elevator lights flash as it passed each level. It was insane that the closer he got to the unit, the more his heart raced, and when he stepped off the elevator, it pounded.

This is fucking ridiculous.

John pushed the buzzer for the case room nurse and glanced through the small window in the door. The place looked deserted, except for the loud shriek that suddenly echoed through the door.

Damn, how did women do this? Why did they do this?

"Can I help you?" A woman's voice crackled through the speaker.

"I'm looking for Marina Kelly." Better to ask for the woman in labor.

"Are you the father?" Her tone sounded clip.

"No," he practically shouted. "I mean, I actually need to speak with Ms. Kelly's sister. I found her purse." John sighed and plowed his hand through his hair. "It's a long story, but she dropped it in all the commotion."

The buzzer sounded, and he pulled the door open. Another scream echoed down the hall, as a short, plump nurse walked toward him and smiled wider when she noticed his uniform.

"Wait here, officer." She nodded, glancing over her shoulder and scurried down the corridor toward the screeching.

15

John gained new respect for his mother and winced when he heard a woman shout that she wanted to castrate her husband. Yeah, Mom deserved a day at the spa. John had to call his brothers about a day for mom, especially since February was her birthday.

The nurse returned and motioned for him to come further down the hall to a waiting room. A man about his father's age glanced up from a book when John entered. The gentleman's eyes moved to John's hand, and he smirked before he returned to his book.

As if it wasn't embarrassing enough, another man entered the waiting room, but at least the younger man gave him a sympathetic smile. At twenty-nine, John never stepped foot on the delivery floor of the hospital. Even when Sarah delivered Mason, he only visited the day after, and by then, Sarah was in a regular room.

John scanned the walls of posters, but they didn't help his discomfort. Signs of pregnant women and new mother do's and don'ts covered the waiting room. He didn't need to know why pregnant women weren't allowed to shave before giving birth or the best way to stimulate milk production.

I need to get the fuck out of here.

John bolted out of the room and hurried toward the exit, but the sound of a soft voice halted him in his tracks. When he turned, Stephanie stood in the corridor dressed in blue scrubs. The top hung from her delicate shoulders, and the pants dragged on the floor. They were too big on her, but she looked incredible.

"Hi." she twisted the ring on her finger and appeared as nervous as he felt. "The nurse said you were looking for me."

John couldn't find his voice and had to swallow against the dryness at the back of his throat. Her eyes hypnotized him, and he struggled to remember how to form words.

What is wrong with you?

"Did you change your mind about giving me the ticket?" She clasped her hands in front of her.

"No." Was that really his voice? He held up her purse as he cleared his throat. "This must have fallen out of your car. I found it after you drove off and thought it would be less of a hassle for you if I returned it right away."

"I didn't even realize I'd lost it. With everything that happened, my head was spinning." She laughed nervously, and it sounded like music to him.

"Completely understandable." John shoved his hands into his pants pockets after he handed her bag to her. "How's your sister doing, by the way?"

"Better than I'd be in her condition." She snorted, and it was the cutest thing he'd ever heard. "She's close, so I need to get back to her, but thank you so much for returning this." She held up her purse.

"No problem." John tried not to sound disappointed with the short conversation.

He felt like a teenage boy who just tried to talk to his biggest crush. There had to be something seriously wrong with him. Before he could escape through the exit, he heard her voice again and turned to see her hurry toward him.

"I'm sorry. I didn't get your name," she said.

"John," he croaked out the name.

If she asked his last name, he wasn't sure he could remember it at that moment. Stephanie held out her hand, and John managed to not make a fool of himself by forgetting what the motion meant. The softness of her tiny hand sent a wave of desire through his body like a lightning bolt, and he dropped her hand as quickly as he'd taken it.

"Thank you for everything today, John," she said. "I appreciate it."

He locked his eyes on hers, and the array of beeps and screams from the rooms seemed to disappear for a moment. John felt as if he were inside a fog, and the only thing in clear view was Stephanie.

Breathe.

"I guess I'd better go." She broke the gaze and hurried back down the corridor.

He couldn't stop his eyes from dropping to the sway of her hips. The scrubs were big, but it didn't hide her firm round ass. If there was one thing John loved, it was a great behind. She turned, and his eyes jumped to her face. She waved to him, and as he returned the gesture, he prayed she didn't see where his eyes were focused.

"Jesus, you're acting like a horny teenager," John mumbled as she disappeared into the room.

The tightness in his groin only proved he was an asshole. Okay, Stephanie was cute. Well, that word didn't do her justice. Gorgeous would be a better word. The fact her sweet little body had a way of bringing his back to life without even trying pissed him off.

It also made him a hypocrite. All the times he gave his three youngest brothers shit over the way they ogled women, and he did the same thing. Much to his mother's and grandmother's dismay, it didn't look as if any of the O'Connor boys were into long-term relationships. Except for James. Was he like Aaron, Nick, and Mike, or did he miss Kim?

Hell no.

Then why was a woman he spent no more than fifteen minutes with, making his heart pound and his dick ache? Attractive women were everywhere, but no woman ever turned him on without trying.

"Get over it." He sighed.

John wasn't even sure he wanted to see her again. Who the hell was he kidding? He never wanted anything more, but it wouldn't happen, and he had to forget about her.

That should be easy. Right?

Chapter 2

Stephanie smiled at the tiny bundle in her sister's arms. Daniel Douglas Kelly fed on Marina's breast while she stroked his soft brown hair. The whole scene was so beautiful it had Stephanie on the brink of tears.

She didn't know where Marina got the strength to go on after her ass of a husband left three months earlier. Marina insisted she didn't need Marc O'Reilly, and she could do it on her own. Stephanie didn't doubt her sister's strength, but she wouldn't allow her sister to do it all alone.

When Marc left, Stephanie insisted Marina move in with her in a small three-bedroom bungalow she'd rented close to the university. She originally planned to lease the other two rooms to students, but plans changed when Marina needed her. Stephanie didn't want her sister to deal with a new baby by herself. At first, Marina was against the idea, but with a little push from their parents, Marina agreed.

"Isn't he perfect?" Marina smiled as a tiny hand wrapped around her finger.

"He's beautiful, Rina." The baby was the only good thing to come out of Marina's doomed marriage.

"Thank you for everything, Steph." Marina's eyes filled with tears, and Stephanie did her best to keep her emotions in check. "I don't know what I would do without you."

"I'm glad I was here." Stephanie hugged her. "Besides, how many people can say they saw their first nephew being born?"

"True, or get pulled in by a beefcake in uniform." Marina wiggled her eyebrows.

"Rina," Stephanie gasped. "How did you notice that while you were in labor?"

"I didn't lose my eyesight or my sense of touch." Marina sighed and fanned herself. "His arms were all muscle, and believe it or not, something was soothing about his gorgeous blue eyes. He was calm and made me feel safe."

"You didn't seem very calm. I think the man was scared to death." Stephanie snickered. "At one point, I thought he'd jump up and run."

John was gorgeous, and those blue eyes were intense, not to mention those dimples. Dimples were her weakness. Not that she didn't notice his body. *His body.* The only thing to say about it was, God was kind to the man.

Then there was the scent. A man's smell had never aroused Stephanie so much, but when he wrapped his jacket around her, she almost had an orgasm right there. Maybe it was a bit of an exaggeration, but whatever body wash the man used was

21

intoxicating. He smelled of sandalwood with a hint of spring. It was arresting.

While Stephanie and Marina discussed the assets of the sexy police officer, the door to Marina's room slammed open, bringing their giggles to a sudden stop.

"Oh, sweet heavens. Look at him, Doug." Her mother ran into the room with her hands pressed against her chest.

Stephanie's mom kissed the baby's tiny feet and ran her hand over the top of his head. Stephanie couldn't help but grin at her mother's fussing over the little boy. A grandmother seeing her first grandchild would make anyone smile.

"We finally have our boy, Janet." Stephanie's dad said.

Her father beamed with pride as he wrapped his large arm around Stephanie's shoulder. The scent of old spice surrounded her, and it comforted her, as it always did. He was the only man throughout her whole life who never broke her heart. He was her rock.

As the father of two girls, it was evident to anyone her father was ecstatic to have a boy in the family. He'd always wanted a son, but he never made Stephanie or Marina feel they were a disappointment to him. If anything, he always told them how proud he was to be their father.

"Such a handsome boy," her mother cooed.

"I love my girls, but it's good to have another male to fight against all that estrogen." Her dad winked at her.

"You finally have a fishing buddy, Dad," Marina handed Danny off to her mother.

"I guess we can stop trying to have one of our own, honey." Her father grinned at her mom.

"Dad, you're too old to have babies." Stephanie rolled her eyes.

"It's always fun to practice." He chuckled and squeezed Stephanie gently.

"Ugh, Dad," Stephanie and Marina groaned together.

"Just look at him, Princess." Her father grinned. "Such a big healthy guy."

"He's definitely a Kelly." Her mom swayed with the baby in her arms.

"Marina did great," Stephanie said. "I was terrified."

"I would've fainted." Her dad kissed the top of Stephanie's head, and she glanced down at her watch.

Damn.

She needed to get some sleep because she worked the night shift for the next three nights. If she sat with a patient in the hospital all night without sleep, Stephanie wouldn't make it through the first hour.

She hugged her family and kissed her nephew on his little forehead before she hurried out of the room. Stephanie clutched her purse close, and her heart fluttered.

He touched it.

What was she, ten years old? She acted like a silly schoolgirl with a souvenir from her favorite celebrity. It was stupid, but the thought of his hands on something belonged to her was erotic.

Pathetic.

Stephanie's mind wandered while she waited for the elevator. How would his lips feel against hers, or his hands on her body? She was lost in the fantasy when her mother's voice brought her back to reality. She tried to hide her embarrassment as her mother hurried toward her.

"Something wrong, Mom?"

"I wanted to tell you how proud you've made us, Stephanie." Her mother smiled.

It wasn't strange to hear her mother tell her she was proud, because she said it all the time to both Stephanie and Marina. What didn't make sense was why her mother felt the need to say it now.

"I didn't do anything, Mom," she replied, and her mom cupped Stephanie's face between her hands.

"You were there for Marina when that sleveen walked out on her." The dislike for Marina's husband was evident in her mother's tone.

Also, her use of the word sleveen, a term only Newfoundlanders understood, made it clear precisely what she thought of Marc. Her mother basically called him an asshole.

"You pushed back your heartbreak to help your sister." Her mother always knew when either of her daughters hurt, even when they tried to hide it.

24

"Thanks, Mom." Stephanie blinked back the burning tears in her eyes.

"I love you, Stephanie." her mother kissed Stephanie's cheek and winked as she walked back down the hall.

A tear trickled down Stephanie's cheek as her mother entered Marina's room. Stephanie wiped it away angrily because she wasn't going to cry over him again. Brad King wasn't worth any more of her heartache or tears. With a deep breath, she turned and bolted for the elevator.

Stephanie needed to compose herself before she could drive out of the hospital parking lot. It was the last time she'd shed a single tear over Brad. She wanted to move on with her life. Like her father told her the day Brad left, there were plenty of fish in the sea. John's handsome face flashed in her brain far too quickly.

Lunchtime traffic was terrible. How were so many people on the road in the middle of a workday? Shouldn't everyone be at work? The lack of sleep and the adrenalin rush of the early morning started to get to her. By the time she turned onto her street, Stephanie wanted to scream.

Stephanie arrived home exhausted. Dead on her feet was a more accurate description of how she felt. Her shift started at midnight, and it was already after one. She'd need at least five hours of sleep to get through the night. Her plan earlier in the morning was to get her laundry done by noon and sleep for the rest of the day. She'd been in the middle of sorting her clothes when Marina screamed, and all hell broke loose.

Things weren't any better when she opened her bedroom door and saw the piles of laundry still where she left them. She groaned at what resembled the aftermath of a tornado. As a personal care attendant at The Janeway Children's Hospital working twelve-hour shifts, her time for housework was limited.

"Another day isn't going to matter." She was too damn drained to care about the mounds of clothes.

Stephanie changed into her usual sleepwear, a tank top, and lounge pants. She wrapped her favorite homemade quilt around her like a cocoon and flopped down on the bed with the hope sleep would come quickly.

Stephanie struggled to relax, but considering the events of the day, it wasn't surprising. The only thing she could think to do was to try the relaxation techniques she suggested to some of her patients. It wasn't working entirely because her body relaxed, but her mind was another story.

The entire day flashed through her mind like a movie. Frantically running around when Marina's water broke, and then speeding down Prince Phillip Drive while Marina screamed bloody murder. Of course, she couldn't forget barely missing a truck because she ran a red light, and there was no way she could ever forget getting pulled over by him.

John.

He was the best-looking man she'd ever had the pleasure to meet. It was hard to concentrate on Marina when he stood next to her. She could still smell his scent of sandalwood and spring. The hug was spontaneous because he had no intention of giving her a ticket. A huge mistake on her part, because the feeling of his hard body pressed against her was startling.

When he showed up at the hospital to return her purse still in uniform, she wanted to rip off his clothes. Men in uniform made her panties wet, but John made her feel as if she'd ignite into flames. His smile and those damn dimples made him so striking she could hardly breathe.

Argh.

It wasn't fair a stranger could make her feel this way. She didn't even know his last name because she was in such a whirl she forgot to ask. The thought to check his name tag didn't occur to her until he left. It was unnerving because she'd never had such an intense attraction to a man she just met — not even Brad. Then again, the ass probably saved his charm for the other women he screwed.

"God, what the hell's wrong with me?" She flopped over onto her stomach.

Sure, he was easy on the eyes, but all she had to do was think about what Brad did to her, or what Marc did to Marina. Neither she nor her sister had great luck with men in the recent past.

Good looks didn't mean he was a decent man. Brad proved it. Still, something told her John was nothing like Brad or Marc. Stephanie closed her eyes and sighed.

"He's just a guy," she mumbled as she drifted off to sleep.

An irritating buzz jolted her from a deep sleep. Stephanie snatched her phone from the night table and cursed the time. It felt as if she'd just fallen asleep, and the energy to move didn't appear to exist. The thought of a twelve-hour overnight shift twisted a knot in her stomach.

She enjoyed being a private personal care attendant, but the long hours were monotonous, and it wasn't what she wanted to do. Physical therapy was what she loved to do, and Stephanie wished she could get a full-time job in the field. She'd only added the personal care attendant course to give her resume a boost.

The problem was physical therapist positions were few and far between. So, until she could find something in the field, she had to take what she could get to pay the bills.

Heaven knew the rent for her beautiful house was steep, and with Marina still in school, what little money her sister received had to go to Danny. Marina needed her, and Stephanie wouldn't let her sister down. She couldn't afford to miss a shift, and it motivated her to drag her ass out of bed and get ready for work.

Children were her favorite patients. It could be heartbreaking to care for the ones who wouldn't leave the hospital, but those kids always seemed to be stronger than most adults.

Stephanie's assignment for the night was a little boy named Tristian. He was six years old with William's Syndrome and had the sweetest disposition of anyone she'd ever met. She didn't know much about it, except he was born with the genetic condition. He had medical problems, too, including cardiovascular issues and developmental delays with learning disabilities, but he had the sweetest smile and loved listening to music.

Most of the time, he'd sleep through the night, but someone needed to be there twenty-four hours a day just in case. Her favorite part of caring for Tristin was when he'd wake up in the morning. He expected a hug as soon as he woke, and always had a song to sing for her. When his parents arrived in the mornings, he would get so excited. Tristian was the reason Stephanie talked her father into making a regular donation to the children's hospital.

"You look tired, Steph." Donna Green sat behind the nurse's desk.

Donna was one of her closest and oldest friends. They'd met in high school and remained close through university. They didn't get the same shifts very often, so when they did it, they would catch up.

"I'm exhausted. Marina had the baby this morning." Stephanie flopped down in the chair next to Donna.

"I'm guessing Marc hasn't come back." Donna turned in her chair to face Stephanie.

"No. The asshole better not." Stephanie tried to cover a yawn. "I think there's more to the story, but Rina's not ready to tell us exactly what happened."

"I'm sure she'll tell you when she's ready." Donna handed her a bottle of orange juice. "By the way, I applied for a position with the place I told you about last week."

"You did?" Stephanie wasn't surprised.

Donna didn't enjoy the hospital shifts. At the beginning of her career, Donna worked as a private nurse. When her client passed away, she took a position with Eastern Health, but she still wanted to go back to what she loved.

"Yeah, and they're hiring at least six registered nurses." Donna held up her crossed fingers. "They're looking for full-time personal care attendants and physical therapists as well. You should apply."

"Why?" Stephanie was too frustrated with applying for jobs she never got.

"It's only eight-hour shifts, and you only have to do four-night shifts a month." Donna handed her a piece of paper with the website.

"It would be perfect." Stephanie swiped her time card. "Is the pay good?"

"The place pays almost double what you're getting here," Donna informed her. "The nurses' salary's about the same, but it's better hours."

Stephanie couldn't remember the last time she worked an eight-hour shift. All the positions she'd taken over the previous few years were always twelve-hour shifts. Working a standard eight-hour day sounded wonderful, but dreams didn't always come true.

Stephanie was tired and spent her entire shift fighting to stay awake. Applying for that job sounded better and better by the minute. It would be a change, and she'd be home more often to help

Marina. She pulled out her phone and opened the website Donna gave her.

Nightingale's Private Care and Therapy catered to people who needed around the clock home care. They also provided physical therapy for people who preferred to complete their treatment in the comfort of their own homes or were unable to leave their house.

She scanned through more than a hundred reviews and comments left on the company Facebook page. None were less than four stars. It was also Newfoundland owned and operated, which Stephanie considered a plus. What did she have to lose by submitting her resume? Nothing, because if she got the job, she'd have better hours, more money, and do what she loved.

Although it was a long night, Stephanie wanted to see Marina before going home. Thank God, the children's hospital and the maternity ward were in the same building. She clocked out and made her way to her sister.

When Stephanie walked into her sister's room, she found Marina curled up on the bed with tears streaming down her cheeks. Stephanie's stomach tightened at the sight because her sister rarely cried. Something was wrong.

"Rina, what's wrong? Is the baby okay?" She rushed to the side of the bed and wrapped her arms around her trembling sister.

"I... I t...told him to leave, Steph. I had to." Marina sobbed into Stephanie's shoulder.

"Who? Marc? Was he here? I left instructions with the nurses that he was not permitted to come in here." Stephanie tried to stay calm at the thought of her brother-in-law upsetting Marina.

"No, he wasn't here." Marina sniffed. "He didn't leave me, Steph. I kicked him out."

"What? Why, Rina?" Stephanie handed a box of tissues to her sister.

"Because I found drugs under our bed." Marina sobbed.

"Marc was on drugs?" Now it all started to make sense.

Marc's personality changed drastically over the last several months. He seemed on the verge of rage, and Marina always appeared nervous. Stephanie wasn't Marc's biggest fan from the beginning, but she tolerated him for Marina's sake.

"Yes. He was injecting himself with something, but I don't know what it was. When I saw it, I knew why he'd changed so much. He said such horrible things, Steph. He told me he never loved me and getting pregnant was the worst thing to ever happened to him." Marina sighed and wiped her nose. "I started to scream at him, and he slapped me across the face."

"He hit you?" The news did not help Stephanie's temper.

Stephanie would love to have Marc next to her for five minutes. She so angry she would probably rip his head off and spit down his neck.

"It wasn't the first time," Marina's voice was a whisper. "I couldn't tell anyone because I didn't know why he started acting so different."

Stephanie couldn't believe what Marina was telling her. The idea of Marina's asshole husband abusing her infuriated Stephanie.

"I knew when I found the drugs. I couldn't bring a baby into a house with someone so violent. I should've left the first time he hit me, but I was shocked and embarrassed, and he apologized afterward. The last couple of occasions, though, he didn't care." She grabbed another tissue and blew her nose.

"You did the right thing, Rina." Stephanie missed all the clues of her sister's abuse.

"I know, but I'm not sure if I can do this on my own." Marina wiped her eyes. "I'm terrified."

"You're not doing this alone. You've got me, Mom, and Dad." Stephanie hugged her. "You won't ever be alone, Rina. Never."

"What about if you meet someone?" Marina forced a smile after a few minutes. "You know I didn't see a wedding ring on Officer Hunky."

"I'm sure Danny will be in college by the time I meet someone." Stephanie chuckled. "And as for Officer Hunky, I don't plan on going through any more red lights."

"Thanks, Steph. I needed to get all that off my chest." Marina sighed. "I haven't told Mom and Dad yet, but I will."

"I'll let you tell them, Rina." Stephanie pushed Marina's hair back from her face. "But I'll be there for you if you need me."

She stayed with Marina for a little while, and once she got some snuggles from her adorable nephew, she headed for home. On the way out of the hospital, she decided to push her luck and see if she could get a few of her shifts switched. Everything needed to be ready when Marina got home, and since Danny didn't have any issues, the doctor would probably release her the next day.

Although her boss didn't appreciate the short notice of the schedule change, he managed to switch shifts with another attendant. Stephanie didn't like the idea of working six days in a row, but Marina needed her. An employer change sounded better and better.

Exhaustion started to set in by the time she arrived home, but everything Marina told her made her more determined to apply for a position with *Nightingale's Private Care and Therapy*. Stephanie wanted to support her sister until Marina could get on her feet.

As soon as she opened her bedroom door, she groaned. She'd forgotten the mess piled on her bedroom floor. She didn't worry about it and grabbed her laptop. Before she set to writing her cover letter and ensuring her resume was up to date, she opened her email inbox.

She scrolled through the heaps of messages and deleted all the junk. She was about to exit the email program when a new message popped up, and it made her heart pound. An email from Brad sat in her inbox. No contact in six months, then suddenly an email out of the blue. The temptation to delete the stupid thing without reading it was intense, but curiosity taunted her to see if it was an apology.

The cursor hovered above the email, blinking like a beacon. Was there more heartache in the email? Did she want to go there again? Stephanie couldn't take the curiosity and clicked the mouse button. She closed her eyes, and after a deep breath, opened them and began to read.

> *Stephanie,*
>
> *I know I'm probably the last person you want to hear from, but I needed to tell you I'm sorry. With my shifts at the fire hall and yours at the hospital, we drifted apart. I was lonely. I shouldn't have cheated, I know that, but you were never around, and Erica was. You have to admit this was as much your fault as mine. You weren't there when I needed you. By the way, the money you said I stole was mine. So, call off the lawyers. I don't owe you anything. I took what was mine. Have a good life, Stephanie. I know I will.*
>
> *Bradley*

"You've got to be kidding me." Stephanie clenched her fists and started to tremble with rage.

This was his apology for screwing around and taking all the money she'd put away for the bills? Not him, her. He never put one red cent in the account. He wasn't getting away with it, and she certainly wasn't calling off the lawyer.

Stephanie yanked her phone from the night table and made the call to her father's lawyer, Fred Dinn. Fred agreed to help her get back the money Brad had taken. After all, Brad never paid toward anything. Well, except for his precious car. She never understood why he'd spend so much for a car, and not be able to pay even five dollars on a light bill.

Asshole.

A few minutes later, her rage had calmed to mild anger. Fred guaranteed he would handle everything, but she probably wouldn't get the money back. The good news, she was entitled to half of the property in their apartment. Although everything she wanted, she'd taken with her the night she left. Stephanie forwarded the email to Fred, but she didn't care what happened anymore.

She sat back on her bed with a huge sigh, and as much as she tried to stop it, a tear ran down her cheek. It would be a long time before she'd trust another man. Stephanie knew all men weren't like Brad, but she didn't know if she could ever open her heart again.

Her body shook as she reread the email. Brad wasn't the same man she fell for three years earlier. His words seemed different. In all their time together, he never called her Stephanie, nor did he refer to himself as Bradley. He told her once he hated his full name.

She flopped back on the bed, pressed a pillow to her face, and screamed into it for a few seconds. Once the aggravation dissipated, she tossed the cushion to her side and smiled.

"Damn, that felt good." She snickered to herself. "Today is the start of a new chapter in my life."

Brad King could rot in hell for all she cared, and he could take his new girlfriend with him. She didn't need any man.

Chapter 3

The beer bottle in his hand was still full and had gotten warm. John gazed through the patio doors in his brother's kitchen and tried to make sense of what happened. Sarah was gone.

How James got through the last three days was a mystery. John's heartfelt as if someone ripped it out of his chest, and it wasn't even his wife who passed away. It wasn't right. How could someone so young and vibrant be gone because of a stupid fucking disease? It wasn't fair to James or baby Mason.

John squeezed his eyes shut to stop the hot tears from spilling out. The whole day John waited for the moment when James would fall apart, but James was rock solid. At the funeral home, he greeted people as they gave condolences. At the church, he sat in the front pew holding Sarah's mother's hand as Mrs. Mason cried, but James didn't shed one tear. Was James in shock? Was he trying to keep it all together until he was alone? Either way, John was concerned for his twin.

"Mom wants to know if you want a sandwich?" Aaron asked as he walked up behind John.

"No, thanks. I'm not hungry," John answered, then quickly cleared his throat before he turned.

Aaron, or as most people called him A.J., was the youngest of the seven O'Connor brothers, was completing his second last year of Police Studies at the university. Once he graduated, he wanted to join the Police Academy. Aaron was also the biggest horndog John knew.

Hopedale had to well-known dance clubs, and Aaron frequented both of them. He'd walk in, and within the first hour, he'd have at least one woman hung all over him. All Aaron had to do was flash a smile, and girls came running.

Aaron stood quietly for a few minutes. It appeared as if he was searching for something to say. It was weird to see him without the mischievous grin or a sarcastic remark. The only other time he acted like that was when their Grandfather had died, and the same week his girlfriend dumped him. As easy-going as his little brother was, he was uncomfortable when it came to serious things.

"I still can't believe she's gone," Aaron finally said.

"I know. It doesn't seem real." John took a swig of his warm beer and forced it down. "I honestly don't know how James is holding it together."

"Me neither." Nick sauntered into the kitchen, leaned against the kitchen counter and folded his arms across his chest. "Christ, she wasn't even my wife, and I feel as if I'm going to explode."

Only thirteen months separated Nick and Aaron. Nick was twenty-two, and Aaron was twenty-one. The two of them looked more like twins than John and James. They were also very close.

Nick attended law school and already had an internship with one of the best law firms in the city. John wasn't sure his younger brother wanted to be a lawyer. Nick also liked to play the field and had a different girl on his arm every week. They were still young, but John couldn't understand how they could do it.

"We all knew this was coming, but I guess I didn't want to believe it." Aaron crossed his arms over his chest.

"Losing someone is never easy whether you expect it or not," Nick returned.

"Did I leave Mason's diaper bag in here?" James appeared in the doorway of the kitchen and glanced around the room, but when nobody answered, he stared at them. "Hello?"

"Are you ok?" John needed to ask.

It wasn't normal for James to be able to function. John recalled the day the doctor told James and Sarah her cancer had spread, and they were out of options. James had completely fallen apart when he got home.

"Nick, grab the other three before I start." James walked next to the kitchen table and motioned for the others to join him. "I only want to repeat this one more time, because I've already told Nan, Mom, and Dad."

Nick left the kitchen and returned a few seconds later with Keith, Ian, and Mike behind him. It was the first time in a few years all seven brothers were in the same place at the same time. Keith recently moved back from Yellowknife, and Mike just returned from Ontario. John was glad they were all home for good, but wished it was under better circumstances.

"What's going on?" Mike turned one of the kitchen chairs around and straddled it.

Ian sat next to him, as Keith leaned against the wall close to the door. Nick grabbed another of the chairs while John and Aaron sat on the other side

"I know you're all worried about me. I see it in your expressions, and I understand why." James leaned his fists on the table. "When we realized Sarah would lose her battle, I was devastated. I knew from the beginning of her diagnosis, it was a possibility, but there was always part of me hoping for a miracle."

James dropped his head, and John placed a hand of support on his twin's shoulder. The crack in James' voice made it hard to believe he was okay, but without a word from either of the brothers, James lifted his head and continued.

"The day the doctors told us there was nothing else they could do, I spent the night with Sarah. I was awed by her strength. She didn't shed a single tear, or at least not in front of me. I can't say the same for myself. She held me in her arms for an hour while I cried like a baby." James dragged in a long slow breath and went on. "When it was out of my system, we talked. She said she made her peace with everything. You see, she knew she wasn't going to make it before the doctor even told her. She said she accomplished everything she wanted to in her short life. All I kept thinking was, how the hell did she accomplish anything in twenty-seven years?" James walked away from the table and stood next to the counter with his back to his brothers.

"Bro, you don't need to...," John began, but James turned and ran his hands down his face.

"You know she used to scare me sometimes. Sarah always knew what I was thinking. She told me the only thing she ever wanted in her life was to marry the man of her dreams and have a baby." James chuckled at the memory. "She smacked my arm when I asked her if she was going to introduce me to her dream man."

The six brothers smiled, but no doubt forced for James' sake. Sarah had been part of their family, and they all loved her. John was about to say that when James walked back to the table and sat down.

"She told me she could leave this world knowing Mason would be loved and raised with the best father he could have. There were a few things she wanted me to promise her." He stopped, and for the first time in three days, John finally saw the tears in James' eyes.

"What did she want you to do?" Mike vocalized the question John was about to ask.

"First, she wanted me to promise I wouldn't close myself off to everyone. The only thing she was afraid of was I would turn everyone away. Second, she wanted me to find love again. Can you imagine? My wife wanted me to find another woman to make me happy. I tried to argue, but she told me she knew it would be a while, but she didn't want me to be alone for the rest of my life. Mason needed a mother in his life. Third, she wanted to make sure Mason knew how much she loved him, and she'd always be watching over him." James leaned back in the chair and looked up at the ceiling. "The next one involves all of you."

"What?" Ian seemed as confused with the statement as John did.

"She said all of you are terrified of commitment, and if there were any way possible, she'd make sure the six of you found a woman to put you in your place." A chorus of laughter filled the kitchen.

Since the day Sarah married James, she told all of them she was going to find wives for them. According to Sarah, the O'Connor brothers needed to settle down. She'd said several times she needed some more women in the family to help with all the testosterone. She was probably right.

"Sounds like something she'd say." Aaron snorted.

"She said if I see any of you run from a woman who Aunt Cora says is for you, I'm supposed to kick your asses." James grinned.

Cora O'Connor Nightingale was his father's younger sister. All the brothers grew up hearing stories of the family Cupid, and her gift. Cora knew when two people were meant for each other.

"Sarah told me she was the right person for me for a short time, but I needed to find the right person for the rest of my life." James' voice dropped to a whisper.

"She was an extraordinary woman, James," Keith said.

"Yes, she was, but what keeps me going is the last thing she said to me." James smiled. "She said part of her will always be with me in Mason."

James walked to the counter and pulled open the cupboard. When he turned around, he held seven shot glasses in his hands. John knew what was coming. Sarah's favorite drink was Newfie Screech, and she'd always make everyone take one shot with her when they would drink together. It was also their grandfather's go-to drink. James pulled the bottle of dark rum from the fridge because nobody liked warm Screech. He poured seven shots and brought them to the table.

"Now, let's drink a toast to my beautiful wife?" James pushed the glasses to the center of the table, and each brother grabbed one.

"To Sarah," the seven brothers shouted together then tossed back their shots.

"I got a feeling she's up there laughing at all of us and making devious plans." John chuckled.

Knowing James made peace with everything helped John feel more at ease. John certainly didn't think he would be so strong, but there grandfather taught them one thing, and God never gives you more than you can handle.

The numerous visitors had dwindled an hour later, and John found James on the back deck. The strained expression told John, James wasn't holding up as well as he wanted everyone to believe.

As he stepped out onto the deck and closed the sliding door, John moved behind his brother and squeezed his shoulder. James' entire body stood rigid and tense. Nothing would make all this ok. Sarah was gone, and nobody could change that.

"Where's Mason?" John broke the silence.

"I put him down for a nap." James cleared his throat.

"You want to get out of here for a while?" John suggested. "It's a lovely afternoon we can take a drive up to the cabin."

Maybe getting away from all the family and friends continually streaming into the house would give James a chance to catch his breath. If John felt overwhelmed with it all, James had to feel it as well.

"Sounds good, but I think I'll take a nap." James yawned. "I'm exhausted."

"I understand. You get some sleep," John said. "Mom and Nan are staying here tonight, so you sleep as long as you want."

"Yeah, sleep sounds good." James headed back inside the house, but as soon as he stepped inside the door, he turned and wrapped his arms around John. "Thanks for being here, bro."

"Since conception, bro." John hugged him back and swallowed the lump in his throat.

The words he replied to James was a phrase they used between them ever since he could remember. Since they were twins, it made sense. It finally hit James that Sarah was gone and John could see it. When James finally released John, he made his way to the stairs and stumbled up. John wasn't sure if James was drunk or exhausted. All John knew was his eyes burned with unshed tears. Tears he wasn't sure were for Sarah or James. Maybe for both.

John loved his family, but three solid days together were starting to get to him. A drive to the cabin sounded like the best way to clear his head and feel a little closer to his grandfather. It hadn't been long ago the family lost him.

Nanny Betty's Irish lilt met him as he walked into the living room. The scene looked amusing, and John decided to put his drive off for a few minutes to enjoy the show.

Elizabeth Power O'Connor, otherwise known to everyone as Nanny Betty, was originally from Cape Broyle on the Southern Shore of Newfoundland. Most of the people from the community spoke with an Irish dialect.

When Jack O'Connor died three years earlier, Nanny Betty moved in with John's parents. Of course, she didn't agree right away. She insisted she was more than capable of looking after herself. It took everyone in the family to convince her to move to Hopedale.

When Nanny Betty was pissed, or someone harmed one of her family, she was a force of nature. Only four foot ten and a hundred pounds, she could still send the biggest man running with *the devil's glare*. Even his six-foot-two father and his six-foot uncle, backed off when they knew she was on a rampage. All Nanny Betty had to do was lower her head and narrow her eyes, and it was enough to have all of them snapping to attention.

"Sean Thomas O'Connor, if ya don't stop tellin' me, I needs a nap. I'm gonna duff ya in da arse."

Here we go.

"Mudder, you've been up since six this morning. You've got to be tired." John's father tried to reason with the stubborn woman, but trying to reason with Nanny Betty never went well.

John's grandfather used to say it would be easier to reason with a brick wall. If Nanny Betty set her mind to something, no amount of discussion would change it.

"Lord, dine, Jesus, if I needed a nap, I'd bloody well take one. Now ya get before I takes ya over me knee and busts yer arse." Her bony finger pointed at his father.

"Mudder, when are you going to realize we're grown men and not little boys?" Kurt O'Connor chuckled from the other side of the living room.

"Ya might be bigger den me, but I can still swing up at ya." She pointed her finger at Kurt.

John coughed to cover a chuckle as his Uncle Kurt clamped his lips shut. John glanced around the room and saw he wasn't the only one trying to stifle laughter. His mother, his aunt Cora and Kurt's wife, Alice, quickly headed to the kitchen, covering their grins. Kurt's daughters Jess, Isabelle, and Kristy, followed behind them. Thank God for Nanny Betty, she was at least making a dark day a little easier, even if she didn't realize it.

"Where's Jimmy?" Nanny Betty looked toward John.

"He went upstairs to get some rest," John replied once he'd cleared his throat.

"Good. He needs some rest after t'day." She stood up and headed toward the kitchen. "I'm gonna help da girls clean up da kitchen."

"Mudder, you …." Nanny Betty slapped his father's arm, and John laughed.

"Don'cha Mudder me," she snapped as she marched out of the room.

"That woman has got more energy than all of us together." Kurt chuckled.

"Damn right, I do." Nanny Betty yelled from the kitchen. "And better hearin' too."

The room erupted into laughter, but John wanted to get out by himself for a while. It seemed wrong to leave, so he flopped down on the couch next to Ian and let voices around him fade into a soft chatter.

John hadn't realized he'd zoned out until a knock on the door stopped all the conversations. From what John could see, the entire family was already in the house, and most of the family friends had already been there earlier. His father headed toward the door, but Nanny Betty hurried down the hallway with a wave to say she would get it.

The familiar voice floated into the room, and John cringed. What was she doing here? She was the last person he wanted to see, and James certainly didn't need the drama. All eyes turned to John as he stood up and made his way to where his grandmother glared at his ex.

Kim Newman. Fuck.

"Johnny, haven't ya got rid a dat streel yet?" Nanny Betty was anything but quiet or subtle with the use of the Newfoundland term for an untidy woman.

Kim wasn't untidy, but Nan didn't care. Everyone knew what happened between John and Kim, and it was the reason his grandmother disliked her. Kim's expression showed her annoyance, but at least she wasn't stupid enough to say anything to Nanny Betty.

"I'll take care of it, Nan." John kissed Nanny Betty's cheek as he walked around her.

"Ya better, or I'll do it. She's not welcome here. She's a jinker," Nan warned with a Newfoundland word meaning bad luck.

After giving Kim *the devil's glare*, Nanny Betty turned and scurried back to the kitchen. John closed the front door behind him and turned to face Kim. His mood wasn't the best to deal with the woman who cheated on him, but he didn't have a choice.

"What are you doing here?" John managed to keep his voice monotone.

"I wanted to offer my condolences to James and your family." She reached out to touch his hand, and he stepped out of her reach.

"You could have sent a card." He snapped.

"I know, but I wanted to talk to you." Her voice lowered to the seductive way she used to try and get him into bed.

"Kim, I don't know how many more times I've got to tell you, but it's over. I don't want to talk to you or see you anymore." John glared at her.

"You won't even let me explain," she whined.

"There are no explanations that'll make what you did right. I'm done. You're the one who screwed someone else before we even slept together." He didn't care that he'd raised his voice and could probably from inside the house. "Stay away from my family and me."

"I was drunk," she began as the front door opened, and Nanny Betty stepped out on the porch.

"Now ya listen here young lady, and I use dat term loosely. Johnny's had enough a yar shenanigans, and Jimmy don't need ya here yappin'. He's tryin' ta rest. Now ya get," Nanny Betty grumbled as she all but pushed Kim off the step. "And doncha go botherin' Johnny again."

Nanny Betty grabbed John's elbow and practically dragged him back inside the house. John got a quick glimpse of a slack-jawed Kim as Nanny Betty closed the door and turned to face John.

"Young man, ya needs ta grow a backbone," Nanny Betty told him and then glided down the hall to the kitchen like a miniature tornado.

Kim's arrival was the last straw; John needed a little peace. His family probably thought he left to catch up with Kim, but he didn't care. John said his goodbyes but didn't get away free and clear because he received another lecture from Nanny Betty about finding a nice girl to marry.

With the lecture, Stephanie's beautiful face flashed in his thoughts. Even after a couple of months, John couldn't get her out of his mind. She'd appear in his thoughts whenever he was alone, and she consistently starred in his dreams. It was insane to be infatuated with a woman he spoke with for fifteen minutes.

The slight chill from the air didn't make him roll up his windows on the Southern Shore Highway. The sky was clear, and the bright sun made it seem as if spring was around the corner. It was April, and except for the cool breeze, it was a beautiful day.

The O'Connor's were originally from Cape Broyle. The house belonged to Nanny Betty and Grandda Jack, and his father grew up there. After Grandda passed away, his father convinced Nanny Betty to move to Hopedale to be closer to the family. She refused to sell the house and kept it as a family summer home.

Nobody had been at the house since October. Since he was in the area, it was probably a good idea to make sure the place was okay. Besides, he always felt closer to Grandda there.

Jack O'Connor was a big teddy bear and always had a positive attitude. No matter how bad your day was, he still found a way to make you feel better. There was a silver lining in everything, according to him. A self-educated man, and successful businessman, he worked hard for everything he had.

Grandda started as a fisherman in his late teens, and by the time he was in his forties, he owned several fishing boats. He was well respected and loved by everyone who worked for him, and anyone who met him became an instant friend. When Grandda retired, he sold the boats to the people who worked for him.

The O'Connor's weren't millionaires, but Grandda made sure Nanny Betty would never have to worry about money for the rest of her life. When he died, it was difficult for the whole family. Nanny Betty especially. They were together for over fifty years.

The night he passed away, Grandda told everyone to be happy for him. He lived a wonderful life with the most wonderful woman in the world, but John missed him.

John pulled into the unpaved driveway of the navy blue bungalow. His legs were stiff after almost an hour's drive, and it was euphoric to unfold himself from the car. As he stretched his arms over his head, he scanned the horizon across the road. The view of the ocean was John's favorite part of the area. Much like Hopedale, on a clear day, you could see the whales jumping next to the small islands scattered around the coast.

The house hadn't changed much over the years. The hooks where his grandmother's porch swing had once hung were still there. As well as the fence his grandfather placed around what used to be the vegetable garden. On the side of the house were several fishing nets once used by his grandfather on his fishing boat. The sight of everything calmed his frayed nerves and always made him feel closer to Grandda.

John pushed open the heavy wooden door to the cottage. The musty smell was evident nobody had been inside for the last few months, but with the coming spring, the family would start to make frequent trips for fishing and family fun. They'd had a lot of fun times over the years, but John never got to go as much as he wanted. He opened the windows to air everything out. He couldn't stay long, but it was nice to look around.

"Grandda, I miss you." John sighed as he strolled around the small house.

As children, John and James spent a lot of time with their grandparents during the summer. Grandda would take them fishing, and they would help Nanny Betty in the garden. The five younger boys didn't enjoy the work as much as John and James, but they would still help out when asked.

On the mantel over the fireplace sat a picture of Grandda and Nanny Betty at James' engagement party. It was the last photo taken of him before he got sick. John lifted the photograph from the shelf and stared at it. Sarah's death brought out his emotional side, and he couldn't keep the tear from spilling down his cheek.

"Grandda, you take care of Sarah up there, and we'll take care of James and Nan down here." John choked out before he placed the picture back in its place.

John spent the next hour wandering around the house or daydreaming on the front porch. By the time he locked up, he felt relaxed. He should've taken an overnight bag and stayed the night, but when he left James' house, he just wanted to escape. Staying overnight wasn't an option, and he needed to get home before nightfall. The scenic drive was great, but when night fell, the roads could be treacherous this time of year.

He was about thirty minutes outside of Hopedale, a light drizzle and dense fog settled across the road. He could barely see a foot in front of the car's hood, but at least it wasn't snow. The road straightened, and he increased his speed a little. Daylight quickly disappeared, and he glanced at the dash clock to check the time. His gaze moved back to the road, just as a large dark object appeared directly in front of him.

A moose.

Shit.

John slammed on the brakes, but the road had become slick with the drizzle, and the car fishtailed. He heard a heavy thud, screeching tires and shattering glass. The airbag deployed with a pop, and a surge of pain shot through him.

Then everything went black.

Chapter 4

It took almost three months, but Stephanie finally got an interview with *Nightingale's Private Care and Therapy*. It took so long to hear back from them; Stephanie didn't think she'd get a call. The interview went well, and she tried to be optimistic. The lady who interviewed her was nice enough, but something seemed strange in the way the owner stared at Stephanie. The questions she asked weren't typical interview questions either, but she blew it off as Mrs. Nightingale being a little eccentric.

Stephanie arrived home in time to hear her nephew making his presence known, and he didn't sound pleased. Little Danny certainly had a healthy set of lungs, especially when he screamed the roof of the house at four in the morning. Stephanie didn't regret her decision to have Marina and Danny live with her, but it would be nice to sleep through the night once in a while. Danny however, had other ideas.

Marina spoke in soothing tones to the baby, and it always seemed to calm him. Only three months and Marina was a pro at figuring out what her son needed. According to Marina, Danny had different cries. One for when he was hungry, one for when he was tired, one for diaper changes and one for when he wanted to cuddle. It all sounded the same to Stephanie. Loud.

"Hey." Stephanie walked into the living room.

"How was the interview?" Marina lightly bounced Danny in her arms, and the cries began to subside.

"Good. The lady who owns it interviewed me." Stephanie flopped down on the sofa.

"Why do you look so unsure about her?" Marina could practically read her mind.

"I don't know. She was nice enough, but she kept giving me the strangest looks and asked a lot of personal questions," Stephanie explained.

"Like what?" Marina moved Danny to her shoulder but didn't slow the light bounce.

"Well, she asked me if I was seeing anyone, and if I'd rather live in town or outside of town." Stephanie shrugged. "Oh, and the best one was if I believed in love at first sight."

"Weird." Marina snorted.

"Yeah, but I guess she was a little distracted. She attended a funeral this morning." Stephanie felt awful that Mrs. Nightingale had to perform an interview after going to a funeral.

"I'm surprised she just didn't postpone it." Marina placed Danny in his swing and turned it on.

"I know, but this job would be perfect." Stephanie sighed. "I wouldn't be stuck in a building; I'd be doing a lot more physical therapy as well as personal care."

55

"And the money is great," Marina stated the number one bonus of the job.

"That too." Stephanie laughed.

Her stomach rumbled, reminding her she hadn't eaten all day. She stopped on her way out of the room and cooed to her nephew for a few seconds before she continued to the kitchen. As she could open the fridge, her phone vibrated in her pocket.

"Hello," she answered pleasantly.

"Can I speak with Stephanie Kelly, please?" A female asked.

The woman had a slight Irish lilt to her voice, and it Stephanie thought it might be Mrs. Nightingale. She was afraid to get too excited in case she was mistaken.

"Speaking," Stephanie replied.

"This is Cora Nightingale." The woman replied, and Stephanie crossed her fingers.

"Oh, hello, Mrs. Nightingale." She waved her crossed fingers at Marina.

"Call me, Cora, please. I wanted to let you know I'm very impressed with you. You're what we need for our family. I've called to offer you a position." Cora sounded professional, but all Stephanie wanted to do was scream.

"Thank you so much, Cora." Stephanie danced around but managed to sound calm and collected. "I'd love to work with your family, and I accept your offer."

"That's grand, Stephanie." Cora sounded relieved. "You can come by tomorrow to get the necessary paperwork completed."

"I'll be there first thing in the morning." Stephanie pumped her arm in the air.

"Wonderful. I'll see you then." Stephanie ended the call and squealed as she hugged her sister.

"Did you get the job?" Marina chuckled.

"Yep." Stephanie grinned. "I'm so happy right now."

"Gee, I never would have guessed." Marina feigned surprise.

Stephanie immediately called her parents to give them the news. As usual, they decided a celebration supper was in order, and her mom demanded they arrive by six. Her mother thought any good news was a family mealtime, which wasn't a bad thing because nobody cooked like Janet Kelly.

A little after five, Stephanie pushed open the door to her childhood home, and the mouth-watering aroma of salt beef boiled together with potatoes, carrot, cabbage, turnip, and split peas pudding had her salivating. The meal was what Newfoundlanders referred to as Jigs Dinner, and it was sometimes paired with a roast or turkey. From the smell, her mother had chosen beef, which was Stephanie's favorite.

She hugged her mom and joined her dad in the living room when he sat watching the news. He seemed focused entirely on the screen, and when she sat down next to him, it was clear why. A mangled car flashed across the screen with what looked like a moose on the hood of the vehicle.

"My God. What happened?" She covered her mouth at the horrific sight.

"Somebody hit a moose on the Southern Shore Highway," her father explained. "The reporter said the guy is in rough shape. He's in critical care at the Health Science Center."

"How awful." Stephanie felt a chill run down her back.

"Yeah, a lot of fog and drizzle out there today," her dad said. "It doesn't matter what speed you're doing on that road when it's foggy. You'll be on top of it before you even realize it. I hope the young man's gonna be okay. He's only twenty-nine."

The knowledge of the man's age made Stephanie's stomach clench. He was only two years older than her, and she couldn't imagine what his family was going through. There were far too many people hurt or killed on Canadian roads due to moose jumping in front of cars. Stephanie hated the highways and would always find another route to get.

During supper and even after, she couldn't get the memory of the accident out of her thoughts. She tried to listen as her father talked about business picking up. Construction was slow in the wintertime, but her thoughts kept returning to the accident on the highway. She couldn't shake the feeling she knew this person, but maybe it was because the victim was so close in age. All she hoped was the poor man would be okay.

For the rest of the evening, she did her best to shake the foreboding feeling she had. Her mother noticed her distraction and asked several times if she was feeling alright. What could she say? She couldn't get the thought of a stranger hurt in an accident out of her mind. It was ridiculous. Still, something told her there was a connection.

The next morning, Stephanie sat across the desk from Cora. While Cora explained the policies and procedures of *Nightingale's Private Home Care and Therapy*, she kept glancing at the phone on her desk with the screen up. Again, Stephanie got the same feeling from the previous night. What the hell was wrong with her? Cora was probably expecting an urgent call.

Cora passed Stephanie some papers to fill out, then excused herself. Cora returned a few minutes later, with watery eyes and blotchy cheeks. Stephanie was naturally curious, and she hated to see anyone upset, but she didn't think it would be appropriate to ask Cora what was wrong.

"I'm thrilled you'll be part of our family, Stephanie." Cora held out her hand.

"Me too." Stephanie shook her hand.

"Stephanie, because of your background and experience, your salary will reflect that. We'll be utilizing all of your skills," Cora continued as she slipped a folded piece of paper in front of Stephanie.

"What's this?" Stephanie picked it up.

"That's your yearly salary." Cora handed her a piece of paper.

Stephanie unfolded the paper and gasped because it was almost double what she made with her current job. Stephanie glanced up, and Cora smiled, but it seemed forced.

"You've come to us at the perfect time. I've got a couple of clients set up for you already." She handed Stephanie two files. "Their schedule is in the folder, but they're only short term. I'm hoping to have a long-term one for you soon."

"That's great." Stephanie began to smile, but it faltered when she noticed Cora's eyes filled with tears. "Cora, are you okay?"

"Don't worry about me, Ducky, it's just allergies." Cora wrapped her arm around Stephanie's shoulder as she walked her out to the reception area.

Allergies? Stephanie knew tears when she saw them. Whatever was bothering Cora, she didn't seem to want to talk about it. Stephanie hated to see people hurt, but what could she do.

Stephanie walked out of the office and glanced back several times to see Cora watching her. It should have made her feel uncomfortable, but for some reason, it didn't. Stephanie climbed into her car and pulled out of the parking lot. Her thoughts drifted back to Cora, and she wondered why her new boss seemed so concerned. Stephanie got distracted and almost ran another red light.

"Damn it. Why do I keep letting my mind wander while I'm driving?" At least this time she didn't go through it.

Stephanie couldn't stop the smile from forming at the memory of the last time she ran a red light, and Officer Hunky pulled her over. The same hot sexy cop who invaded her dreams every damn night since the day her nephew was born. Visions that made her wake aching for him.

The thoughts of this man started to concern her. She met the man for all of fifteen minutes and hadn't seen him since. Maybe she had built him up to be her fantasy man. The perfect guy who would never hurt her, but he was just that — a fantasy.

Stephanie pulled into her driveway and pressed her head against the steering wheel. Sure, John was sexy as hell in his uniform, but so was Brad. Her ex was a fireman, and in his uniform, he was sex on a stick. Too bad the asshole turned out to be a cheating bastard. It would be damn hard to trust another man, especially one in uniform.

Chapter 5

The low voices sounded muffled and hard to understand with the constant beeps of something else in the background. John's eyes felt as if they were weighed down and made it almost impossible to open them. Something pressed against his nose, and a strong odor burned his nostrils. There was a heaviness in his body, and when he tried to move, pain shot through his body like a bolt of electricity. Where was he? What was wrong?

"I think he's waking up," A soft voice whispered next to him, familiar and calming.

Mom?

"They're weaning him off the sedation, so he should start coming around in the next few hours." Was that his father?

"I should have let James stay, but he was ready to drop." Yep, that was his mother. "He was exhausted."

"No, James needed to go home. We won't know the damage until he wakes. It's better if we know before James. He's been through enough the last few weeks." His father's voice cracked.

"He's going to have a lot of pain for a while." Keith's voice sounded strained.

"The doctor said he would only keep him out for a week," Mike whispered.

Keep who out?

What the fuck was going on, and why was it so hard to open his eyes? He tried again. Slowly his eyes fluttered open, but everything was blurry, and he blinked several times to clear his vision.

"Thank God." Kathleen gasped. "You're awake."

John turned his head toward the sound of his mother's voice, but a sharp pain shot through his shoulder.

"Fuck." John rasped.

His mouth had no saliva, and it was as if someone shoved razor blades down his throat. It hurt to swallow, and his tongue felt as if it didn't want to move.

"Don't move too much, John." his father appeared next to him. "You were in an accident."

What is he talking about?

John squeezed his eyes shut and tried to sift through his muddled thoughts. He remembered Sarah's funeral and leaving Grandda's cottage, but then nothing. When he opened his eyes again, his mother smiled down at him. Dark circles surrounded her watery eyes, and she wasn't wearing her usual makeup. His mother never left the house without it.

"Water." John forced out the word.

His mother disappeared, and seconds later reappeared with a small glass. She held a straw to his mouth, and he sipped greedily.

"Take your time, Honey." It was the same soft, soothing whisper she used when they were sick as kids.

"I hear our patient is awake." the new voice wasn't familiar, and neither was the face.

"Yes, finally." his father blew out a breath.

"It's good to see you awake, John. I'm Dr. Cramer, but most people call me Adam," the grinning man said. "You had us worried there for a bit."

"What happened?" He still found it hard to speak.

"You don't remember?" Adam asked as he examined John's eyes.

John shook his head slowly at the doctor's question. The slight movement made him woozy and sick to his stomach.

"You hit a moose on the highway." His father's voice cracked.

The statement caused the memories to come rushing back. Driving back from the cabin, the dense fog, and skidding into the moose. Everything after that was blank.

"I remember." John turned his head to see his mom.

A tear slipped from the corner of her eye as she explained he had been in the hospital for eight days. The doctor kept him sedated to allow his body to heal. John wanted to laugh. The plan didn't appear to work because everything hurt.

His father listed off the injuries, and with each one, John cringed a little more. John had a cracked collarbone, and two breaks in his leg were surgically repaired. He also had a couple of broken ribs, as well as several cuts and bruises. The thing concerning everyone the most was the concussion.

"My car?" John knew the answer before he'd even asked the question.

"The car is gone, John," his father replied. "You're lucky to be alive."

"You can replace your car, Honey. We can't replace you." His mother squeezed his hand.

John sighed and closed his eyes. The whole thing had to be a bad dream, but the throbbing ache in his head and the agonizing pain across his chest made it real. Taking a deep breath seemed impossible, and his whole chest felt squeezed together. He found out the reason when he moved his hand up to his chest. John felt the cloth of the bandages wrapped tightly around his torso and groaned. The urge to sit up was overpowering, but when he tried, pain radiated through his chest.

"Fucking, Christ," John croaked.

"I'll get you something for pain, John." Dr. Cramer nodded and left the room.

A few minutes later, a young nurse came in and injected something into the IV attached to his hand. In seconds, John's eyes felt heavy, and his body relaxed. It was as if he floated away from the soft beeps and muffled voices of his family. He couldn't fight it, and he didn't want to.

Over the next few weeks, the pain became tolerable, but the longer he stayed in the hospital, the more aggravated he became. The nurses with their friendly smiles and *how are you todays* pissed him off. The physical therapists thought they knew what was best for him and continued to annoy him by telling him he'd never get better if he didn't follow their instructions.

John didn't like them, and depending on others did not improve his mood. He knew what was best for himself, and it was to go home so he could wallow in his miserable existence.

To top it off, his brothers were a pain in the ass and got on the last of his already frayed nerves. They tried to reason with him, but none of them had a damn clue how he felt. None of them had to think about the possibility of not returning to a normal life. None of them worried about losing their careers.

"I don't give a fuck what the doctor said. I want to get the fuck out of here." John clenched his fists as much as he could without causing himself pain.

"You can't go home until you start doing the therapy," Ian shouted.

"They can't keep me here against my will," John yelled as he shoved the blankets off and tried to get out of the bed.

"Stop being a fucking asshole and do what you're supposed to be doing." Aaron stepped next to the bed.

"Fuck you, A.J.," John roared.

"John Thomas O'Connor, watch your mouth." His mother and Nanny Betty stomped into the room. "We heard you when we got off the elevator. Now stop acting like a two-year-old. We're working on something to get you home, but you've got to stop this foolishness."

Leave it to his mother to make him feel two feet tall. Before he could argue, both women had him back in the bed and covered to the waist. The whole while, Nanny Betty gave him the look.

"Now laddie, ya listen ta yar Mudder or I'll duff yar arse." Nanny Betty pointed her finger in his face.

"I want to go home." He was a total ass, but John was pissed, and he squeezed his eyes closed to calm himself.

"And ya tink actin' like a youngster is gonna help," Nanny Betty snapped.

"No." John knew better than to say anything else.

Especially when he noticed his father at the foot of the bed with arms folded across his chest and eyebrows furrowed. His father feared Nanny Betty's stern glares, but Sean O'Connor had his unique version of *the devil's glare*. It was what John and his brothers called the *keep-your-mouth-shut* face, and John did just that.

"Now, if you want to start acting like the gentleman, I know you are, then I'll tell you what we're doing." His mom sat next to him on the bed and gave him a comforting smile.

While his mother explained the family's plans, he tried to keep his opinions to himself. Aunt Cora hired someone to complete his therapy at home, but the idea of a stranger in his house didn't sit well with him. Instead of voicing his complaint, he kept it to himself, because if it meant he could get out of the hospital, he would agree to anything.

While his mother continued, John glanced at Ian and Aaron. The smirks on their smug faces made him want to smack them. Their reaction concerned him, and he had a feeling his mother wasn't telling him all the information.

All John knew was he hated hospitals, and if the plan worked, he'd be home in his comfortable bed. He would have nurses and doctors poking him all day long. He'd have peace.

John moved to sit up and cringed when a muscle spasm shot through his shoulder and down his back. Most of his injuries healed, but the muscles in his back continued to spasm, and it was hard to put weight on his leg most of the time. He'd never admit it to anyone, but the therapy was probably necessary.

An hour later, when he thought everyone had gone, John lay in his uncomfortable hospital bed, flipping through the channels on the television. Just as he thought it was safe to relax, he heard his aunt Cora walk into the room.

"You need to listen to the therapists, Johnny." She stepped next to the bed.

"I know, Aunt Cora. I don't need any more advice." He groaned as she fixed the pillow behind his head.

"We're all worried about you, Doll." Cora cupped his cheek.

"I know, but I'm frustrated, and I hate being here," John snapped.

"You won't be here much longer. I've got an amazing therapist on staff who'll get you back to your old self and make you a very happy man." She sat next to him on the bed, but something

68

about the glint in her eye worried him. "I'm here to warn you. Do not fight against it and do everything she tells you."

"I'll try," he replied, but no treatment was going to make him better.

"You better, or I'll set Nanny Betty on you." Cora winked, and he smiled because nobody wanted to be on Nanny Betty's wrong side.

"Wouldn't want that." John snorted.

"You know we love you, Johnny. I'll let you get some sleep. Brian is waiting for me in the car." Cora leaned down to kiss his cheek and left with a wave.

Cora and Brian were more like another set of parents instead of an Uncle and Aunt. They had one daughter, Pamela, and she worked in Alberta. John couldn't remember the last time Pam was home.

John hated to call the nurse because the drugs fucked with his head, but his discomfort turned into pain again. He didn't want to become dependent on the medication, but it was the only way he would get any sleep. After he tried for a few minutes to ease the pain on his own, he gave up and pressed the button next to his bed.

The cute nurse left once she injected the pain medication into his hip. It made his brain fuzzy, which was why he refused it all day long, and only took it at night. John closed his eyes, and his mind drifted to the only thing helping him relax since all this shit happened.

Stephanie.

The memory of her beautiful face gave him a sense of peace. Thoughts of her got him through the worst times of the last few weeks. He would never see the woman again, but the memory of her calmed him. His mother always said people came into each other's lives for a reason. Maybe he met Stephanie to help him get through a difficult time in his life. She'd never know what those fifteen minutes meant to him.

The medication started to do its trick again, and he whispered her name as he fell into a drug-induced sleep.

Chapter 6

Stephanie was in her second month at Nightingale's and loving every minute. It was refreshing not to be stuck in a building all day long, and her clients were fantastic. They welcomed her into their homes with open arms and made her job easy.

Everything was great, but she worried something would bring it down. Marina informed her earlier in the week she wanted to move in with their parents. Her sister wanted to finish her degree, and it was difficult to do with a baby. Since their mother recently retired, she agreed to babysit Danny. Stephanie was left with a house she couldn't afford by herself. Of course, she could put an ad out for a roommate since it was the original plan, but now, the thought made her shudder.

Stephanie got a message from Cora early in the morning asking her to drop by the office before she started with her first client of the day. She was nervous someone might have complained. Stephanie didn't have any issues with her patients, and all the families had been friendly.

It rained overnight and into the early morning. The dreary weather made Stephanie want to stay in her bed with the covers over her head. If only she could. On the drive, her brain formed all kinds of scenarios of how the day would end. All of them ended with her jobless. By the time she pulled into the parking lot, the rain had eased, but her stress had increased.

When Stephanie walked inside the reception area, Cora stood next to Casey, the receptionist. Both women looked up and smiled as Stephanie approached, and it eased her stress level, but only a little. Cora was a tiny woman with an overpowering presence, but she always treated everyone as if they were her best friend. What worried Stephanie was Cora's smile didn't reach her eyes.

"I'm so glad you could come in today. Follow me." Cora motioned toward the conference room.

Uh oh.

"It wasn't a problem." Stephanie's heart thudded against her chest, and her palms began to sweat.

Cora stopped before she entered the room. She stared at Stephanie for a moment, almost as if she needed to confirm something. When she seemed confident in her decision, she nodded and entered the room. Something had to be wrong. Stephanie took a deep breath then followed Cora through the door.

Cora sat in a chair next to a large table, but she wasn't alone. On the other side of the table, an older couple sat with three younger men. Cora pointed to the seat closest to her, and with shaky legs, Stephanie managed to get to the chair without tripping. That would have made a great impression, and be utterly humiliating, especially if the people around the table weren't pleased with her work.

Stephanie scanned the other people at the table. The couple appeared to be in their early fifties, and the man held the woman's hand, while the three younger men sat next to them. Without trying to look conspicuous, she took in each of the men. One sat with his arms folded over his chest, and the second rested his forearms on the table. The third brother sat eased back on two legs and hands linked behind his head, making it obvious he was the cocky one.

The men had varying shades of light brown hair with hints of auburn. Two of the brothers had longer hair, and the third had a shorter cut. All three were easy on the eyes, and it was evident they got their looks and blue eyes from the older man. Even as she took each of the men in, something nagged at her. They reminded her of someone, but she couldn't put her finger on it.

"Stephanie, this is Sean and Kathleen O'Connor." Cora motioned to the older couple. "This is James, Nick, and Ian, three of their sons."

"It's nice to meet you." James smiled as he shook Stephanie's hand.

"It's nice to meet you too." She almost blurted out the words, *Who wouldn't want to meet you?*

"Sean and Kathleen's other son was in a terrible car accident almost two months ago." Cora's voice cracked, and Stephanie couldn't help but think these people were more than just another client to Cora.

"I'm so sorry to hear that." Stephanie's heart went out to them.

"He'll be leaving the hospital next week. His family wants someone with him at all times until he fully recovers." Cora continued.

"I understand." Stephanie nodded.

Cora covered her face with her hands, and Stephanie heard a soft whimper. Sean reached across the table and touched Cora's shoulder. Cora dropped her hands, and he nodded.

"Okay, let's be completely honest here. Sean's my brother, and my family needs my help. I asked for you because you're the only person for my nephew." Cora smiled. "You see, he isn't dealing with his recovery well. He's fighting everyone in the hospital, and he's angry all the time."

"And you think I can help him with his anger?" It sounded as if the man needed a phycologist, not a physical therapist.

"Stephanie, in the past couple of months, I've received excellent comments about you from clients. They tell me you don't take any crap, and you're tough when you need to ensure your patient gets well quickly." She smiled. You're also sympathetic and sweet."

"Sometimes people are angry because they can't do the things they normally do." Stephanie fidgeted in the chair. "They need someone to listen and not let them give up."

"Exactly. This is why you're perfect for him," Cora said.

"He won't listen to any of us." Kathleen sniffed, and Sean wrapped his arm around her shoulder.

"I'm sure he's frustrated." Stephanie tried to assure them. "I understand your concern."

The relief of not being fired eased Stephanie's tension, and the confidence Cora appeared to have in her, made her sit a little straighter. Her boss had so many more therapists who worked for the company longer and were equally as qualified. The fact she chose Stephanie meant Cora had a lot of faith in her.

As Cora described her nephew's injuries, Stephanie winced. He had a cracked collarbone, a broken leg in two places, and several fractured ribs. No wonder the man was angry. Even when the breaks healed, his muscles were going to be stiff and tight.

"I know your sister's moving in with your parents. It's why this is such a great situation for you. There's a one-bedroom apartment in Johnny's house. Sean and Kathleen want you to take the apartment, so you'll be available when you're needed." Cora slid papers in front of Stephanie. "This contract is for twenty-four-hour care. You'll have two days off a week, and his family will take over for those days. You can choose which days."

The sound of being responsible for a client for twenty-four hours a day sounded overwhelming. It would also kill any attempt at a social life. Not that she had one.

"You'll be paid very well, Stephanie, but I don't trust anyone else to do this job but you. You'll be his attendant, make his meals, and make certain he eats. He can go to the bathroom on his own, so you won't have to worry about that sort of thing. You'll also be his physical therapist. This is the file from the hospital." Cora spoke so fast Stephanie had trouble keeping up with all the information Cora threw at her. "You're the best thing in the world for him." Cora took both Stephanie's hands and squeezed them gently.

"I don't know what to say." Stephanie glanced at the others around the table.

When Cora finally released her grasp, Stephanie picked up the contract and flipped through the pages. She wouldn't have a better offer if she waited a thousand years. The apartment was no charge, and she'd be paid for five days a week, twenty-four hours a day. Anything she required, Cora supplied without question. Her duties included cooking, cleaning, some personal care, and physical therapy. It was a lot, but the company would pay her well.

"If Aunt Cora thinks you can help, we've got no doubt you're the one to give my brother the kick in the ass he needs," James said.

"James, watch your language in front of a lady." Kathleen chastised, and James rolled his eyes.

"Mom, she's going to hear worse when he realizes what we're doing." Ian snickered.

"Well, I better not hear him using foul language in front of this lovely girl." Kathleen's expression reminded Stephanie of her own mother when she was in mom mode.

"Stephanie, I know you're the only one who can make him happy again." Cora smiled.

These people depended on her, but Stephanie knew if someone didn't want to get better, no amount of pushing would help.

She was apprehensive, because if the man wouldn't listen to the hospital workers, chances were he wouldn't listen to her either.

"Cora, I'll do everything I can, but I can't make any promises." Stephanie wanted them to understand she wasn't a miracle worker.

"Once he gets a look at your beautiful smile, it might give him some inspiration." Nick winked at her, and she remembered her initial impression of the attractive man.

"I'm sorry, my dear, my boys are habitual flirts." Kathleen shook her head but smiled. "But they're harmless."

The door burst open before she could respond. A tiny older woman hurried into the room. Sean jumped to his feet and pulled out a chair for her. When he took her arm to help her into the seat, she slapped it away.

"I can sit down witout ya helpin'," The woman huffed.

The other three men tried to stifle their amusement when their father sighed and sat back down. Even Kathleen covered her amusement when her husband shook his head at the older woman's attitude.

"Is dis de lass dat's gonna give our Johnny de kick in de arse he needs?" The woman tilted her head and stared at Stephanie.

"Mudder," Sean groaned, and Stephanie pressed her lips together to stifle a giggle as the little woman glared at Sean.

"Stephanie, this is my mother, Betty O'Connor." Cora chuckled.

Stephanie reached across the table to shake Betty's hand, but before she knew what happened, the older woman grabbed Stephanie's hand. Stephanie got dragged around the table and pulled down into the chair next right next to Betty.

"Yar a tiny scrap of a ting aren't ya." Nanny Betty squeezed her hand. "But dat don't mean yar not strong."

"Yeah, Nan's the toughest one around and look how small she is." Nick laughed but quickly stopped when Nanny Betty glared at him.

"Ya look like a good girl, and my Cora says yar de one fer our boy." Nanny Betty gave her a huge smile.

"I'll do everything I can to get him back on his feet," Stephanie confirmed.

"Yar gonna make him a happy man." Nanny Betty reached up and stroked Stephanie's cheek, then dropped her hand.

"So, Stephanie, will you do this?" Cora asked.

"A' course she will." Nanny Betty didn't give Stephanie a chance to answer. "Now, I gotta get ta da grocery store." The little woman jumped to her feet and was out the door before anyone else could respond.

"Um, I guess I don't have a choice," Stephanie replied once she got over the shock that was Nanny Betty.

"You don't want to cross Mom." Cora laughed.

"The hospital is releasing him on Monday," Cora informed her. "He won't know you'll be living there until he gets home."

"Why?" She didn't want things hidden from her client.

"As we told you, he's fighting everything, and if he knows you'll be living there, he might kick up a fuss," Kathleen explained with concern etched on her attractive face.

How could she decline the offer? This family seemed as if Stephanie was their only hope, and since she not only needed to keep her job, she also didn't have to stress over finding a place to live. It was perfect, and she accepted.

By the end of the week, Stephanie was moved into her new place, and she'd dropped off the list of supplies she needed to start her job. Sean volunteered, or voluntold, his other six sons to help her move. She had to admit it was a pleasure to watch the six men lift and squat in jeans and tight t-shirts. They were a fine-looking bunch.

On the drive home, the sun started to break through the clouds. Stephanie took it as a sign she'd made the right decision, and it would change the course of her life. She also wouldn't have to move back in with her parents. Stephanie loved them, but moving back home would be taking a step back in life. Cora didn't know how much she helped Stephanie keep her independence.

Stephanie pulled out her phone to call her parents once she pulled into the driveway of the house. They were worried but had faith Stephanie could do the job. If only she had as much confidence in herself. Cora certainly did, but Cora had to know not everyone would get better. Whether it was because of their injuries or because they lost all hope. From what the family said, it seemed it was what happened with Cora's nephew. She didn't mind dealing with a difficult patient, but she worried it would be a challenge of a lifetime.

Chapter 7

"Are you all fucking crazy?" John shouted.

A strange woman lived in the apartment attached to his house without anyone even asking him. This lady was supposed to get him back on his feet, and according to Cora, she was a perfect choice. His family had utterly lost their minds.

"John, watch your language." His mother's reprimand made him feel as if he was eight years old again, and he shifted uncomfortably in the wheelchair, causing pain to shoot through his shoulder.

"I'm sorry, Mom, but I don't want a stranger living in my apartment free of charge." John tried to keep his voice calm.

"It's part of the contract with Aunt Cora, and this woman is a lovely lady." His father said as he helped John remove his jacket.

If his dad was on board with this, John was fighting a losing battle. To top it off, his brothers were sporting huge grins, and he wanted to smack them off their faces. When his parents left, they were all getting shit for letting this happen.

"I don't want a stranger in my house, Dad." John grimaced as his father pulled the jacket a little too hard on his injured shoulder.

"Oh, I don't think you'll mind." Nick winked. "I certainly wouldn't."

"Yeah, she's going to give you the kick in the ass you need." Mike smiled.

John wanted to punch them so hard. His glares toward them did not affect their teasing. If he ever got back on his feet, he would make them pay dearly.

Fucking assholes.

"So, where's this miracle worker who's going to make all my God damn problems go away?" The anger made his body ache even more.

Since the accident, the pain became the norm. He couldn't move without something hurting. The therapists told him he needed to work harder, but John gave up two weeks into the therapy and demanded to go home. John was sick of being poked and prodded. If one more person at the hospital told him he needed to work the muscles to get the strength and mobility back, he probably would have snapped.

"She'll be here shortly." His mother smoothed her hand over the top of his head right before she disappeared into the kitchen with his dad behind her.

His brothers huddled together, talking in hushed tones, and John waited until his parents were out of earshot before he confronted them. They were his brothers and should be on his side.

"Okay, assholes. What's all the fucking whispering and smirks about?" John kept his voice low.

"Jesus, John. Why don't you calm down and go with this?" Keith sounded annoyed. "What harm could it do?"

"I don't want some old woman forcing me to do stuff I know is gonna give me more pain," John snapped.

"Maybe you should give it a go. You haven't given anything else a chance." James returned. "You've been sitting around since the cast came off cursing everyone and being a shit."

James stalked closer and leaned down to eye level with him. For the first time since all this happened, John saw the dark circles around James' eyes. He hadn't shaved in a while from the look of it, and his hair was longer than John had ever seen it before, but his tone surprised John the most.

"You're acting like a fucking asshole, and we're tired of it. If you want to sit around and feel sorry for yourself, then go ahead, but for the love of God, give this a fucking chance for Mom's and Dad's sake." James' voice cracked even with the harsh way he spoke.

John turned away from James and stared at the fireplace. It was easy for James to say. James wasn't the one who would never return to work because of a freak accident. John wanted to scream and tell everyone to get the hell out of his house. Doing that would make his mother cry, and it would kill him.

For over an hour he waited for his live-in babysitter to arrive. His family's excitement over this woman played on the last of his patience. Why should he tire himself? She worked for him, right? To hell with it, he was going to his room. John was about to ask one of his brothers to help him, but he heard the front door open. Aunt Cora's voice floated through the house, and John rolled his eyes.

"Boys, can you get the equipment in the truck and bring it into the spare room." It was almost laughable how six grown men jumped and ran whenever the women in his family spoke.

All of the females were not much bigger than five feet tall, but they ran the big burly men with iron fists. Himself included.

Wait, what did she say?

What equipment? John didn't have a spare room in his house. He had his bedroom and his home gym. He figured it out before he had to ask, and his temper started to flare. What the hell did they do to his gym?

"Johnny, it must be good to be home." Cora gave him a quick kiss on the cheek as she glided next to him.

"What's all that stuff?" He growled through gritted teeth as he watched his brothers carry box after box into his house.

"Oh, Steph thought it would be a good idea to set up a therapy room in your house." Cora covered his hand with hers and gave it a gentle squeeze.

"Oh, that's what Steph thought, is it?" He didn't try to hide his sarcasm. "And who gave her the authority to make changes in my house." John knew his blood pressure must be through the roof because he could feel his face burn. "Who the hell does she think she is?"

"Now jus' one minute, young fella." Nanny Betty's stern voice stopped his tirade before it got off the ground. "We've had enough a yar self-pity. If I hear ya as much as speak a word outta line ta dis young one, I'll show ya exactly who I am."

John glared at his grandmother, but she could out glare anyone. It still didn't help him feel less irritated, and he clenched his teeth together to keep from making a comment Nanny Betty would find rude and grab his ear until he apologized.

Disrespect was something nobody in his family tolerated. His parents had drilled manners into him from the time he was a little boy.

"We're tryin' ta help ya, and sparing no expense ta do it because we want ya back ta yar old self. Dis man ya are now, I don't like him very much." She reached out and cupped his cheek. "Johnny, we love ya, and we're doin what's best for ya. Ya best treat dis young lass wit respect, or you'll have me ta deal wit. Do ya understand?"

"Yes, Nan." John agreed, only because his grandmother had a way of making him feel like a child.

"There you are." His mother reached for someone in the foyer. "I'm sure you heard Nanny Betty's lecture, so John will behave himself."

John was about to meet his babysitter. He glanced up as his mother walked into the room, pulling someone with her. The woman his mother pulled from behind her made John's heart flip in his chest. His gaze met those green eyes, and he couldn't breathe. The name should have given him some clue. It was her.

Stephanie.

Chapter 8

Nanny Betty didn't sound happy. Stephanie smiled shyly at the six men lugging the equipment from Cora's van as she eavesdropped on Nanny Betty's rant.

"There you are." Kathleen linked an arm with Stephanie's. "I'm sure you heard Nanny Betty's lecture, so John will behave himself."

Stephanie wasn't so sure about that. From what she overheard from James, Ian, Keith, Mike, Nick, and Aaron, their brother wasn't a happy camper. They depended on her to change it. This sweet family put all their hopes on her.

Wait, John?

Kathleen steered her toward the living room where Sean stood behind a man in a wheelchair. Nanny Betty gave her a triumphant smile as she hurried out of the living room. Kathleen gently squeezed Stephanie's arm in support.

"John, this is Stephanie," Kathleen chirped.

She knew the name, but it couldn't be. When he looked up, she gasped.

Officer Hunky.

Stephanie never had to ask what the J in J. O'Connor stood for because Cora called him Johnny. She hadn't made the connection because she never knew *Officer Hunky's* last name. How did she not know Cora's nephew was the same man she couldn't get out of her thoughts or her dreams?

"Are you okay, my dear?" Kathleen put her arm around Stephanie's shoulder.

"Yes." Her voice squeaked. "It's just... well...I ahh."

"Mom, we've met before." The deep rasp of his voice made her stomach flutter.

"You have?" Cora entered the room.

Sean glanced back and forth between John and Stephanie as the noise of the men walking behind her in the hallway stopped. It was as if they were waiting for a bomb to drop. She shoved her hands into her jeans pocket because she had no idea what to do with them.

"I pulled her over a few months back for running a red light." The corner of his lips quirked up, and her cheeks heated.

"Oh dear." Kathleen chuckled.

"Well, my sister was in labor, and she was screaming, and I freaked because it was happening so fast and ...." Stephanie slammed her lips together because her rambling did not help the situation.

"John, you didn't give the poor girl a ticket, I hope." Kathleen wrapped her arm around Stephanie's shoulder and gave her a gentle side hug.

"No, Mom." John shifted in the chair.

Stephanie's cheeks burned hotter by the minute, as he explained. It was hard to wrap her head around the fact that the strong, confident police officer she'd met was the same man in the wheelchair. He'd lost weight, and his eyes didn't have the light in them she'd seen the first time she met him. He looked so broken and beaten.

"He was very understanding." Stephanie wanted him to know how much she appreciated what he did that day. "And he was sweet to my sister." His gaze met hers, and her stomach fluttered.

Butterflies. Really?

No man ever affected her with just a smile. It all started to make sense now. Why his brothers seemed so familiar, and the blue eyes and dimples were family traits.

"I guess you can stop complaining about the stranger taking over your house now, huh, John." A voice came over her shoulder.

"Shut up, A.J.," John growled as his gaze moved over her shoulder.

The chorus of laughter and the expression on his face made her giggle. When he met her eyes again, she pressed her lips together. He made it pretty clear when she walked into the house that he didn't approve of her living in the apartment.

"You know, John; she doesn't look bad for an old woman." One of the brothers shouted behind her, and the laughter got louder.

Stephanie started to giggle, but when he glared at her, she covered her mouth with her hand. The last thing she wanted to do was piss him off. He already looked ready to kill.

"Aren't you guys supposed to be moving stuff?" John grumbled.

It wasn't hard to see the tension written on his face, and the dark circles under his eyes made it clear he didn't sleep well. The information Stephanie received proved he had a lot of anger built up. Who'd blame him? Nobody wanted to be dependent on other people. Especially strangers.

"I'm going back to the kitchen to finish supper." Kathleen gave Stephanie a quick side hug. "Sean, you want to help?"

Sean followed his wife out of the room, and Nanny Betty seemed to have disappeared as well. His brothers went back to bringing in boxes from the van, and Cora followed them, leaving Stephanie alone with John.

"You're welcome to take a seat." John motioned to the large armchair in the corner of the room, and she was glad he offered because her legs were a little shaky. "I have to say, I'm surprised."

"Why?" Stephanie sat straight and clasped her hands on her lap.

"I didn't know you were a physical therapist and a personal care attendant. You must be good because not everyone impresses my aunt." He said.

"One just led into the other, and Cora is a wonderful boss." She told him.

John didn't say anything as he watched his brothers walk in and out of the house. It seemed as if he wanted to help them carry in the equipment, and she could see the distress on his face.

"You know they care about you," she said

She wanted him to realize why they were doing all this hard work. Her statement caused him to drop his head and grip onto the arms of the wheelchair. He lifted his head again and met her eyes.

"I know, but I'm just worried they're doing all this for nothing." John's voice sounded strained with emotion.

"What do you mean?" Stephanie knew she found the root of his issue.

"What if none of this works?" His voice cracked. "What if I can never do the things I've always done? What if I can't go back to work?"

She saw the tears in his eyes, even if he did try to blink them back. John was ready to give up, and it broke Stephanie's heart. She couldn't let him and she wouldn't. She got up from the chair and crouched next to him.

"John, listen to me." Stephanie laid her hand on top of his. "I've read your file inside out. I've spoken with your doctor and the therapist in the hospital. You don't have any permanent damage. Your issue now is, all the muscles and tissues were compensating for the injuries. It's going to take some time to get those muscles back in shape."

When he tilted his head, she knew she had his attention. It could have been because his neck was stiff, but she continued to

90

make sure he knew she wasn't going to let him give up. She couldn't.

"It's not going to happen overnight, and it's going to be a lot of work. It's going to hurt. I won't lie to you, but you will get better if you're willing to work hard. I know you can do this, your family knows you can do this. They told me you're not a quitter." She smiled.

"I never used to be." John closed his eyes and sighed.

"John, I'm going to make you a promise." She squeezed his hand, and he opened his eyes. "You're going to curse at me, and probably hate me, but if you do everything I tell you, I promise, you'll be able to do everything you could do before the accident."

"I don't know if I believe that." He pulled back and rolled his neck.

"Believe me, please." Stephanie knew she was right, but convincing him wasn't going to be easy.

"I'll try." John sounded so defeated.

"Okay, we start right now. You need to rest." The confusion on his face made her smile. "You haven't been doing much for several weeks, and today's been a long day. You need to lay down for a while." She stood up and put her hands on her hips, and without giving him a chance to respond, Stephanie called to one of his brothers.

"What can I do for you, Beautiful?" Nick sauntered toward her.

He was hot, and he definitely knew it, but his attempt at flirting just made her mentally roll her eyes. Nick was young, and obviously didn't have issues with women, but as much as she wanted to deny it, there was only one O'Connor brother who had her attention.

Stop it.

"Can you stop hitting on the girl long enough to help me into my room?" John snapped, and Nick chuckled as he pushed John to his bedroom.

John's bedroom wasn't large and minimally decorated. A double bed centered along one wall with a dresser next to the bed. There was just enough room to walk between them. The side table held a lamp and an intercom so he could call her apartment in case John needed her during the night.

She steadied the wheelchair as John pushed slowly to his feet. It was sweet how Nick stood close in case John lost his balance or needed help, but John seemed annoyed by it. Nick left the room with a wink at Stephanie once John sat safely on his bed. She didn't miss the roll of John's eyes at his brother's little flirtation. It seemed to piss him off, but it was probably because it was unprofessional.

"Now, get some rest." She helped him ease back on the bed and only left when he insisted he was comfortable.

With John settled, Stephanie decided the next thing to do was speak to his family. Nobody could argue the fact they were a close-knit bunch, especially since everyone gathered for John's homecoming.

There was no doubt they expected her to perform a miracle, and it made her stomach knot. John wasn't about to get better overnight, and they needed to know. She didn't want to disappoint any of them. It bothered her more than she cared to admit. The hardest part of the whole process would be to make John realize he would get better as long as he worked hard at his recovery.

Stephanie entered the kitchen as Nanny Betty slapped Mike on the hand when he snatched something from a platter. He leaned down to kiss his grandmother's cheek but grabbed more from the plate. The woman didn't miss it and used the large spoon she was holding to slap him on the butt.

"Now ya get, Mikey." She shook the spoon at him, and he gave Stephanie a playful wink as he hurried out of the kitchen.

"Would ya like a cuppa tea, Dolly?" Nanny Betty offered and had it poured before Stephanie answered.

"I'd love one, thank you. I want to talk to all of you as well. If now is a good time?" Stephanie eased into one of the kitchen chairs.

"Is something wrong?" Sean's face tightened, and she immediately felt awful for putting the concern in his eyes.

"No, not at all. I wanted to explain John's treatment with all of you while he's resting. I'll go over it in detail with him when he's rested and hopefully more receptive." Stephanie smiled at Sean, and he relaxed.

It was apparent John, and his brothers resembled their father for the most part. He was about her parent's age, and his hair was a little darker than his sons, but there were flecks of gray through it. Of course, he had the dimples and the same deep blue eyes.

Nanny Betty scurried out of the kitchen and returned with John's brothers. All their focus was on her, and she suddenly wished the floor would open up and swallow her. It must be how a teacher or public speaker felt, and it was unnerving.

"Now, tell us everything, ducky." Nanny Betty sat across from Stephanie at the table.

James, Ian, Keith, Mike, Nick, and Aaron stood around the room while Sean and Kathleen sat at the table with Stephanie and Nanny Betty. Cora stood next to her and placed a supportive hand on Stephanie's shoulder.

"John's muscles are weak, and he has a lot of stiffness around his neck. I'll need to complete a full assessment of him to see how much of his body was weakened by the injuries before I can give you a better idea of everything, but as of now, I'll adjust the therapy to work on each injury separately. One day we'll work on his neck and back. The next day we'll work on his leg." Not one of the family interrupted and kept their attention on her.

Before she continued, she glanced over her shoulder at Cora. Her boss beamed and nodded in support as she motioned for Stephanie to continue.

"If you want, I can write a full report with a detailed explanation with weekly updates on his progress, but I'd have to make sure John was okay with me giving you the information." He was an adult, and if he didn't want them to know anything, she couldn't betray his request.

"Dat's not necessary. We know yar gonna make Johnny happy." Nanny Betty pushed back from the table and proceeded to carve the rest of the giant turkey on the counter.

"He's going to be frustrated. He's going to get angry, but that's normal," Stephanie continued.

"What you're saying is this could take months." James crossed his arms over his chest.

Of all the brothers, he seemed to be the least vocal, and always had a hint of sadness in his eyes. She knew he was John's twin, and he'd lost his wife a few days before John's accident. The man had every right to be gloomy.

"It all depends on John, and how he takes to the therapy. It also largely depends on how much effort he puts into everything." Stephanie met James' eyes.

James and John were not identical, but James was attractive as well. God blessed all of John's brothers with swoon-worthy looks, but she didn't feel the pull toward any of them the way she did to John.

"I understand. It's just…. John doesn't seem like he wants to get better." James squeezed his eyes closed and opened them again. "It's like he's giving up."

James' voice sounded strained, and when she glanced around the room, there wasn't any doubt the entire family felt the same way.

"He may very well be, but I'm a drill sergeant when it comes to my clients. If he thinks I'll let him off easy, he's in for a rude awakening. I'm no pushover." Stephanie smiled. "I'm sure you know all about drill sergeants."

"I sure do." James laughed for the first time since she'd met him, and the mood in the room seemed to lighten.

John needed to get back on his feet. Not just for himself but for his family as well. They would be devastated if John didn't recover, and so would she.

"I've got his program all worked out, and if he follows it, he'll start to see improvement in a month or so." She sipped the tea Nanny Betty had placed in front of her.

"Can we be here when you start yelling at him?" Aaron sounded way too excited.

"I don't yell." Stephanie chuckled. "Well, not unless I have to."

"How do you know what to start with?" Aaron sat in the chair his grandmother had vacated.

"We start slowly to strengthen his weakened muscles. I'll also have to work with him to increase the mobility of his joints since he's been favoring them for several weeks." It made her happy to see interest in what she'd be doing. "I'll do massage therapy to help to loosen any muscle stiffness."

"I'd like that last part." Aaron wiggled his eyebrows.

"Shut up, A.J.," Keith grumbled. "Sorry, he's a dog."

"Aaron Jacob, that's enough," Kathleen chastised her son. "Go on, my dear."

Stephanie stifled a giggle when Aaron crossed his arms over his chest and pressed his lips together. Mom had spoken, and she had as much power as Nanny Betty.

Stephanie showed them the weekly schedule she'd put together. The only one to stand back was James. He still seemed unsure about everything. It must have been tough to bury his wife and wonder if he would have to do the same with his brother.

"My Cora told us ya were da one fer Johnny, and she's never wrong." Nanny Betty interjected. "Yar gonna make da lad happy again."

Nick, Mike, and Ian rolled their eyes, and Keith shook his head. Aaron's snort made her wonder if she missed some family inside joke. Kathleen, Nanny Betty, and Cora lost count of the number of times they said she would be the one to make John happy. She figured he'd be glad to be on his feet again. Was there more?

"He'll be back to his old self before you know it." Stephanie ignored the statement and told them what she knew they wanted to hear.

"Havin' ya around will make him better." Nanny Betty scurried to the stove and began to stir something.

When the brothers turned their heads, she could see they were covering their laughter. She seemed to be the only one not in on the joke.

97

"Am I missing something?" Stephanie asked as Mike sauntered out of the kitchen.

"You don't want to know." Mike smiled, and she glanced up at Cora.

"Mom just has a lot of faith in my opinions." Cora squeezed her shoulder and busied herself with setting the table.

Stephanie sat back in the chair and studied the remainder of the family as they moved around the kitchen. They chatted with each other and worked together as if they did it every day, and they probably did. They were a close family, but why did she feel as if she was the only one not getting the punch line of a joke?

Chapter 9

The chatter from the kitchen was both comforting and irritating. John lay on his bed and tried to put things into perspective.

She was here. Dreams of her helped John through all the frustration in the hospital. She would be with him every day until he was back on his feet. He scoffed because he'd never be back to himself. Sure, all the bones healed, but he was weak and useless. He cursed the day he made that drive.

Anger began to bubble up and made him want to explode. How could he be so careless? He'd driven on the highway more times than he could count and in weather worse than the day of the accident. One stupid second.

John grabbed the pillow under his head, and as he was about to put it over his face to roar into it, she laughed. It was as if a huge weight lifted off his chest, the anger subsided, and he calmed almost instantly.

"How the hell is she doing that?" John closed his eyes.

John could picture her beautiful face like it was in front of him. Her green eyes sparkled with flecks of gold, and she took his breath away. Was she going to be the one who saved him from himself?

A light knock on his bedroom door jolted him out of his sleep, and the sudden movement caused him intense pain. For the life of him, he couldn't tell exactly where it came from, because it seemed to be everywhere. He clenched his teeth together as he waited for the pain to subside. With slow deep breaths, it gradually eased to a tolerable level.

When James opened the door and entered the room with a strained expression, and John worried about his brother. James was different. Losing a spouse would make anyone change, but all the rage seemed directed at John.

"Supper's ready." James' tone was short and clipped.

"Okay, do you want to tell me what's wrong, or do I have to guess?" James helped John up to a sitting position.

"Nothing's wrong." James supported John until he sat safely in the wheelchair.

"Bullshit," John shouted and fisted James shirt collar, but James managed to pull from the grasp.

"Nothing's wrong," James grunted and stepped back.

"Don't fucking lie to me, James. Nobody knows you like I do." He gripped the arms of the chair and roared.

James glared for a few seconds, and John thought for a moment his brother would shout back at him. Instead, James closed his eyes and inhaled slowly. When he opened them, they glistened with tears.

Fuck.

"You want to know what's fucking bothering me." James' voice remained low, but there was anger in his tone. "I miss my fucking brother. The one who didn't wallow in a heap of self-pity. The one who gave me the strength to go on after my wife got sick. The one who stood by me the day I buried the love of my life." James spun on his heel and stomped toward the door.

"He died in that accident," John yelled behind him.

James stopped in the doorway and turned around slowly. His body shook, and James' face flushed crimson. John never saw his twin so furious.

"No, John, he didn't die, but he might as well have because the guy I see, he's not the brother I grew up with," James screamed as he pounded his hand against the door jamb. "I buried my wife that day, John. For hours, I thought I would have to bury my brother too. My twin brother. You know, the one who was with me from conception?" A tear spilled out of the corner of James' eye and trickled down his cheek. "Do you know how that made me feel, John?"

Shit.

John opened his mouth to answer and then closed it again, because what could he say? As close as he and James were, John couldn't come close to knowing how it must have felt.

"I was never so scared in my life. Sarah's death was the worst thing I've ever dealt with in my life, but as hard as it was, the thought of losing my brother about sent me over the edge." James plowed his hand through his hair. "When they said you were going to make it, I fell to my knees and thanked God, but I thought I was getting John back, not this asshole full of self-pity. Where is he, John? Where in the fuck is my brother?"

John dropped his head to hide the tears burning his eyes. The last thing he wanted to do was hurt his brother. Especially considering how much James had already suffered.

"I want my brother back, John. We all do, and I hope to God you let that beautiful lady out there bring him back because if you don't, it's not only going to kill me, but it's going to kill Mom." James stomped out of the room and left John alone.

There wasn't any way the rest of the family didn't hear James. Half of Hopedale probably listened to the shouting. John couldn't leave his room now, especially with tears in his eyes. The last thing his mother needed was to see him lose it. As he turned back to his bed, movement from the doorway caught his eye.

Stephanie.

Without a word, she glided over to him and placed a box of tissues on his lap. It didn't bother him that she'd seen what happened.

"It's okay to be emotional, John," she whispered.

"Not for me." He rubbed his hands down over his face.

"I didn't know you weren't human," she quipped.

"I'm the oldest. I've always been the strong one. The one there for everyone." His voice cracked, and he swallowed the lump in his throat.

If he looked at her and saw pity in her eyes, it would kill him. He kept his gaze lowered, but she didn't let him get away with it. She put her finger under his chin and forced him to look at her.

"So, now it's their turn to be there for you. To be strong for you, and from what I've seen, they're more than willing to do it." Her smile was beautiful, and he couldn't look away.

Her whole face was stunning, but it wasn't her looks bringing a sense of peace for him. She seemed to be able to reach into his soul and make him feel everything would be okay.

"James is pissed, and probably the rest of my brothers, too." He picked a piece of invisible lint off his shirt. "I'm not used to it."

"I guess you better start doing something about it." Stephanie knelt, and he grasped her hand.

The warmth of her touch radiated through his body. The numbness he'd felt since he woke up seemed to fade, and although he still had pain, it didn't make him want to give up.

"I'm terrified," John admitted. "I've never been so terrified in my life." Why did he pour his heart out to a stranger, when he wasn't able to tell his own family his fears?

"The first step is to admit it." She gave his hand a gentle squeeze. "It's normal after everything you've been through over the last few weeks. Your family is scared too."

John felt as if he was on autopilot as he lifted his other hand and touched her cheek. She tensed but didn't pull away.

"You're an angel. Aren't you?" He smiled for the first time in ages. "An angel sent to save me from myself."

Before he could make a stupid mistake, Stephanie stood and stepped back from him. She nervously glanced around the room before she focused back on him again.

"I'm no angel." She laughed, and he could hear the nervousness. "But I'm here to help. Your nan sent me to tell you supper is on the table. So, get your butt out in the kitchen, Mister."

John laughed and saluted her as she pushed him from the room. It hurt to laugh, but it helped relieve some of the tension he felt after his conversation with James. It was another thing he needed to fix, and as if a switch flicked on, John realized he needed to start there.

His mother and Nanny Betty placed massive plates of food on the table, and the aroma of roasted turkey made his stomach rumble.

Nothing tasted as good as Jigs Dinner cooked by his grandmother and mother. Hospital food was from hell, and even with his family permitted to bring him food from outside, it didn't taste the same as a freshly cooked meal.

Stephanie pushed him up to the table and turned to leave. Panic began to build, but before he said a word, Nanny Betty caught her by the arm.

"Yar eating wit us, ducky." She pointed to the open chair next to John.

It seemed Stephanie figured out it would be pointless to say no to his grandmother. He was pleased about it because when Stephanie sat down, he calmed. The connection with her was foreign to him. The physical attraction was evident the day he pulled her over, but the effect she had on him confused him.

Heaven was the only way to describe the meal he'd practically inhaled when his grandmother placed it in front of him. Around the table, several conversations took place at the same time. Nobody treated him any differently than before, but James hardly spoke a word.

When James was angry, he stayed quiet, but John always felt his brother's emotions. His mother told him all the time he and James had a more profound connection because they were twins. It didn't matter that they were fraternal, because they were with each other from day one.

"Before your mother serves the wonderful dessert she made, I want to make a toast." His father stood and held his glass out in front of him. "It does my heart good to see all my sons sitting at one table." His gaze moved to John. "It's good to see you out of the hospital, my boy. We weren't sure if we would ever do this again, but someone up there was watching over you, and kept you from leaving us."

His father choked out the last part, and John had to look away to keep his emotions under control. He glanced at his mother, but it didn't help. His mom wiped a tear from her cheek, and it began to dawn on him, they must have gone through hell after his accident. The one thing he never doubted, was how much his parents loved him, and to think about the fear they must have gone through, made his heartache for them.

"To family, and all the people who helped us get through this terrible time." Sean raised his glass, and the rest of them followed his lead.

A baby's muffled cry grabbed John's attention. James jumped up and hurried out of the kitchen. John hadn't seen his nephew since his accident, and he was ashamed to admit he hadn't asked about him.

His mother and Nanny Betty did inform him Mason was growing like a weed, and when James re-entered the room with the chubby little boy, John could see they hadn't exaggerated. Mason giggled as James tickled the little boy's belly, and John noticed was Mason had inherited the O'Connor dimples and blue eyes.

"Wow, he's a bruiser." John chuckled.

"Yeah." James sat down and put the giggling baby on his lap. "He eats like a horse."

For one short moment, James seemed happy. Mason was probably the only one who could make James smile. The baby did resemble Sarah even with the O'Connor traits, but Mason still favored his mother.

"He wouldn't be an O'Connor if he didn't." His dad laughed.

"All of ye eat like yar starved to det." Nanny Betty placed a plate of blueberry cake in front of his dad.

John glanced at Stephanie. She smiled at the baby and laughed when Mason spit out the food his brother was feeding him. Baby food dripped down the front of James' shirt, and Mason grabbed the bowl before James could pull it away. The youngster was faster than his father and knocked it into James' lap. The whole scene was hilarious, and John burst into a fit of laughter. His ribs were still tender, and he had to hold them.

"You think this is funny, bro." James grabbed the cloth Nanny Betty held out to him. "Next time the mess comes out the other end, I'm bringing him to you."

"No thanks. I don't do diapers." John held up his hands in surrender.

"Well, it's certainly good to hear you laugh." Kurt appeared in the doorway of the kitchen.

Kurt O'Connor was his father's younger brother and John's boss. Kurt gave John shit every time he'd visit the hospital, and he didn't want or need another lecture from his uncle.

"Being home makes me happier." John shook his uncle's hand.

"Maybe it's this lovely lady next to you." Kurt extended his hand. "You must be Stephanie. I'm Sean's brother, Kurt."

"It's nice to meet you." She smiled, and her cheeks turned pink as she shook Kurt's hand.

"You're late." Nanny Betty snapped Kurt with the dishtowel she had in her hand.

"Sorry, Mudder." Kurt kissed her cheek. "Duty calls."

Those two words made John's stomach turn. Would he ever be able to make that statement again? He wanted to leave the table, but he didn't have the strength to push the wheelchair himself without pain.

Fuck.

"I want to go to the living room." John motioned to Keith.

Before his brother could move, Stephanie pulled him away from the table and guided him to the living room. It was humiliating to have someone push him around. He could force himself, but he was in a little more pain than usual. Of course, refusing to take the pain medication didn't help.

Nanny Betty and his parents cleared the table while everyone else settled around the living room. It felt like old times for a little while. Arguments over which hockey teams would make the playoffs, or which players should get traded floated around the room. It was an ongoing feud between his family and Kurt's.

John was glad his cousins weren't there, because when Kristy, Jess, and Isabelle got going there was no stopping them. Kurt's girls were die-hard Montreal Canadian fans, while he and his brothers cheered for Toronto Maple Leafs. When his brothers and cousins got into it over hockey, it got loud.

The conversations faded into the background when John noticed Stephanie had disappeared. His stomach clenched with some sense of loss, and he could feel a wave of panic bubble up. Jesus, he was pathetic.

"If you're looking for your sexy therapist, she went to her apartment." Nick had a panty-dropping grin on his face.

"I wasn't looking for her," John lied.

"Seriously, John, how are you going to concentrate on your therapy with a woman like her around?" Aaron wiggled his eyebrows up and down.

"Shut the fuck up, A.J.," John growled.

Nobody ever called Aaron by his name. The story of how he got the nickname everyone knew. When Nick started to talk, he couldn't say Aaron and began to call the younger brother Aday. Somehow turned into A.J., and the name stuck. The only time anyone referred to him as Aaron was when he was in trouble.

"Come on, bro, you can't say you haven't looked." Mike grinned. "If you haven't, then I'm worried."

John shook his head. There was no way any of these horndogs were ever going to settle down.

"If you aren't interested, I wouldn't mind taking her out," Nick teased.

"You stay the hell away from her," John responded a little louder than he meant, and his brothers started to laugh.

"See, there's my big brother." Aaron gave him a thumbs-up, and John wished he had the strength to punch his youngest brother.

"Yeah, he needs to protect her against all you horny bastards," James interjected as he changed Mason.

Great.

John wasn't the only one attracted to his therapist, and it didn't sit well with him. He felt possessive of her. He didn't have a right to, because she was not his girlfriend. The thought of her with anyone else made his stomach churn, especially Mike, Nick, and Aaron. They had a reputation of bed-hopping.

"Don't worry, John; I'm pretty sure she's not interested in any of them." Keith plopped down on the lounge chair next to him.

Keith was the typical middle child, always the mediator between the three older brothers and the younger three. His calm demeanor never wavered, and he'd put himself in the middle of fights more often than John could count.

"Besides, she seems too smart for those three." Ian dodged a punch from Mike.

It didn't matter if she was interested in one of his brothers. He didn't own her. She was there strictly in a professional capacity. So why did the thought of her in the arms of one of his brothers, or any guy make him want to vomit?

Everyone slowly left to go home, and he felt relieved. He couldn't take any more of the suggestive comments from Aaron, Nick, or Mike. It's why he was so annoyed when Nanny Betty gave him a stern warning to treat Stephanie with respect. His brothers were the assholes.

John didn't want to mistreat anyone, but when he thought about it, he wasn't exactly pleasant to be around in recent weeks. He was a proper asshole, but it wasn't on purpose. He'd been active his entire life, and it terrified him to think he'd never be able to do it all again.

John eased back in the wheelchair and closed his eyes. He loved family dinners, but the noise could be loud. His body ached from being sat in the chair for too long. The doctor prescribed painkillers, but they made him too dizzy, and it wasn't a good feeling.

"I see everyone's gone." He opened his eyes at the sound of Stephanie's voice.

"Yeah." John forced a smile. "They can be overwhelming, but they mean well."

"I think it's great to have such a big family." She moved to the couch and sat down. "It was just my sister and me, so our house never had much activity."

She smiled, and it hit him straight in the heart. The magnetic pull he had toward her was foreign to him. So was the way her presence seemed to calm him.

"I love having a big family, don't get me wrong, but sometimes it's nice just to be by yourself," he said, but the truth was he wanted to be alone with her.

"Oh. I'm sorry. I thought you might need help getting to bed." Stephanie shot to her feet. "You can call out if you need me."

"No. Don't go," John squawked. "I didn't want you to leave."

He rolled his neck back and forth. He'd sat in the chair most of the afternoon, and it started to affect him. He needed to change the position before the spasms started.

"Is your neck bothering you?" She tilted her head and seemed to study him.

"A little," John responded.

"You need to tell me when you have any discomfort. There's no need for you to be in pain." Stephanie stepped behind his chair. "I'm going to try to loosen the muscles a little, and then I'll put some heat on it."

Her hands touched him, and he tensed because the coolness of her soft hands on his neck felt euphoric.

"I'm sorry, my hands are a little cold." She started to press her thumbs into the tense muscles across his shoulders.

"It's okay." John swallowed hard.

Her cold hands weren't the problem. A zing of heat thrummed through John's body and shot right to his groin. That was the dilemma. John closed his eyes because he needed a distraction fast. It was tough to think of anything as her talented hands worked across his shoulders and up the sides of his neck. It did help with the upper part of his body, but another type of stiffness raged inside his pants. It was fucking hell and heaven at the same time.

"This will help loosen the tissues, but they'll be tender for a while, Tomorrow, I'll see how much mobility you have," she explained.

Even as she spoke, all he could think about was the growing tension in his crotch. Her hands slipped under the neck of his t-shirt, and he was almost at the brink of insanity when she spoke again.

"We'll do full back massage a few times a week so we can loosen those muscles. We'll work on your leg as well."

That did it. John reached over his shoulders and grabbed her hands. Pain be damned, if he didn't stop her, he'd probably have shot off in his pants. The fucking dog that he was.

"Jesus, stop," he gasped.

"Did I hurt you?" She pulled her hands away.

"No, I'm just exhausted." John needed to get to his room before he made a fool of himself.

Pushing the wheels of the chair killed his body, but he needed to put space between them. He couldn't tell Stephanie he ached, but not where her hands were. John enjoyed her hands on him way more than he should.

"John, what's wrong?" If she knew where his mind was, she'd run for the hills.

"I need to go to bed," John snapped. "I'm tired."

Nanny Betty would kick his ass for the shitty attitude toward Stephanie, but he couldn't help it. John hated to be out of control, and he was about to lose it.

"Okay, I'll help you." She stood behind him in his room.

"No," he growled.

Stephanie jumped back, and he wanted to kick his own ass for the look he put on her face. She had to think he was a complete jerk. His family hired her to care for him, and she was only doing her job.

"I'm sorry, I need to be able to do this myself." John ran his hand over the top of his head in frustration.

"John, it's going to take time. It's why I'm here." Yeah, she was here to help, not to be a personal fantasy come true.

"I know, but right now, I don't think it's a great idea for you to help me get ready for bed." John squeezed his eyes shut and sighed before he opened them again.

"John, I'm here to help." She stood with her hands on her hips. "Massages can sometimes cause an erotic reaction for men."

Damn it. She knows.

"I'm sorry it's just. ..." Was he supposed to tell her she made him horny as hell?

"Look, it's a normal reaction," she explained as she pulled the comforter down for him.

"I'm sure it is." John squirmed in the chair and tried to keep his gaze from her ass.

"I can help you if you want." She spun around as her cheeks flushed pink. "Okay, that didn't come out the way I meant it. I meant I could help you get into bed. Not help you with ... ah..." She stopped talking and blew out a puff of air.

"My normal reaction." John raised an eyebrow and grinned when she dropped her head. "Okay, you can help me get this shirt off, and then make sure I don't fall on my face while I move to the bed. I'll get my jeans when I get in bed. Deal?" He held out his hand.

"Deal." She shook his hand, and John squeezed it softly before he released it.

The shirt came off with little effort than he expected, or maybe it was because Stephanie showed him a simpler way to

114

remove it. The issue arose when he sat back on the bed too hard, and pain radiated through his back.

"Damn it." He sucked in a breath.

"Do you want something for the pain?" She picked up the bottle of pills on the nightstand.

"No, I just need to lay down." He held onto her hand as he eased back on the heating pad she'd placed on his bed.

Stephanie explained the pad would turn off after twenty minutes, so if he fell asleep before it was fine. The heat was heaven, and an angel stood over him. He was reminded that part of his body wasn't relaxing. The erection pressed against his zipper uncomfortably, and he lifted one knee in an attempt to hide it.

"I'm okay now. I can finish undressing." Her eyes flicked to his crotch, and his cock twitched.

"If you need anything during the night, there's an intercom on your nightstand. I have one next to my bed," she said as she headed out of the room, but before she left, she turned.

John couldn't take his eyes off her, and for a moment he didn't think she was going to leave. That didn't help his situation. It did put his imagination into overdrive, but a second later, she said good night and left.

John unbuttoned his jeans and pulled down the zipper to relieve the pressure. Somehow, he managed to slip out of his pants and kick them to the floor. Between the heat from the pad on his back, and the memory of Stephanie's hands on his skin, he got harder by the minute. He needed to relieve the pressure before he went insane. He certainly wouldn't sleep in his condition. John's hand slid inside his boxers, and he grasped his thick cock. As he stroked himself, he allowed his fantasy to take over.

"Fuck," he groaned a few minutes later.

John used his boxers to clean himself and tossed them to the floor. As he grabbed the corner of the blanket and pulled it over himself, Stephanie was his last thought before he drifted off into a deep sleep.

Chapter 10

Stephanie trembled as she leaned against his bedroom door. After the realization of why he pulled away, she didn't know how to get out of the situation. Most men got turned on by massages. It never bothered her before, but the familiar pull in her belly made her realize she liked John being turned on by her.

You're a professional.

John might have been inactive for a while, but his body was as sexy as hell. He'd lost a little weight, but the muscle definition was still there. For a man who had been inactive for weeks, he still had well-defined arms and a distinct six-pack. What turned her on was the dusting of light brown hair across his chest, and then tapered down his stomach to disappear beneath the waistband of his jeans.

Stephanie tiptoed down the hallway to her apartment. Her place was small but comfortable. The living room and kitchen were all in one, with a small island separating them. Inside her bedroom, a patio door opened to a deck on the back of the house. It was perfect for her.

Stephanie slipped off her clothes and pulled on her comfy Hello Kitty pajama bottoms and a pink tank top. It was nice to relax and get comfortable. She wasn't the least bit tired, and it was only a little after ten. She'd make herself a cup of tea before she called it a night. Stephanie made her way to the kitchen and stared out the window while she waited for the kettle to boil.

The memory of John lying shirtless in bed was etched in her brain. Although by now, he probably had his jeans off, and possibly his underwear. She had to stop that train of thought. Why couldn't she be drawn to one of his brothers? They were hot. John was her client, and Stephanie needed to control her attraction, but it would be harder than she thought.

She'd poured herself a cup of tea and was about to take a sip when her cell phone rang. She snatched it from the counter and turned the screen to see Marina's picture. Her sister wasn't going to believe Officer Hunky was her new client.

"Hey, Rina." Stephanie flopped on her couch.

"Hey," Marina returned

"Wadda ya at?" She used the common Newfoundland expression, which meant, what are you doing?

"Nothing much. I just wanted to see how things are going?" Marina asked.

"Ok, I guess." Stephanie settled herself and pulled the fleece blanket over her legs.

"That doesn't sound good." Marina chuckled. "Is he in bad shape?"

"No, he's frustrated with everything." She also wanted to jump his bones. "You'll never guess who he is?"

"Who?" Marina inquired excitedly.

"Remember the cop who pulled us over the day Danny was born?" Stephanie smiled at the memory.

"Officer Hunky?" Marina gasped.

"Yeah." Stephanie laughed at her sister's nickname for John.

"Is he still hot?" Marina sighed.

"Rina, I'm here to help him get back on his feet, not size him up." She couldn't vocalize what she thought.

It wouldn't be appropriate to shout, yes, he's still sexy as hell with six hot brothers, but the only one she wanted to ride was her client. It was unethical.

"That didn't answer my question." Marina knew her so well.

"Oh my, God, Rina. Yes, he's still hot, with six hot brothers." Stephanie laughed.

"Wow, this could be interesting." Her sister snickered.

"You're terrible." Stephanie smiled because Marina seemed to be slowly getting back to her old self.

"How do you like living out of the city?" Marina knew Stephanie wasn't sure about living so far from the city.

The house was about fifteen minutes outside of St. John's. It was a small outport called Hopedale. A beautiful seaside town with ocean views no matter where you were in the community. Most of John's family lived nearby, except the three youngest brothers and cousins. One cousin lived in Western Canada while the others lived in St. John's.

"It's nice. Quiet." Stephanie enjoyed it more than she thought. "And it's not far from town."

There it was already. When people lived in St. John's, they would say they lived in the city, but when you lived in the outside communities, everyone referred to St. John's as *town*. It was weird.

"I guess not." From the sound of Marina's voice, Stephanie knew something was on her sister's mind.

"So, what's up?" Stephanie could read her sister very well.

"I called to give you some news." Marina paused before she continued. "I got a new job, and I start in two weeks."

"That's terrific, Rina." Considering the great news, Stephanie didn't understand the lack of enthusiasm in Marina's voice. "So, why do I get the feeling you're not happy about it?"

"The job's in Ottawa." Stephanie's heart felt as if it dropped out of her chest.

"Ottawa?" The lump in her throat threatened to strangle her.

"I need to get out of Newfoundland, Steph." Marina's voice cracked.

"Is that bastard bothering you?" If Marc was harassing Marina, he was going to be one sorry son of a bitch.

"No. I need a change of scenery, and the contract is only for two years, but it'll give me the experience I need to get an executive position when I come back." Marina didn't sound convincing.

"What about Danny? Who's going to watch him while you work?" The thought of not seeing Marina every day made her ill, but even worse, she'd miss watching Danny grow up.

120

"There's a daycare, and it doesn't cost anything for employees," Marina explained.

"I'm gonna miss you, Rina." The catch in her voice was hard to hide.

They were inseparable since the day her parents brought Marina home from the hospital. They had other friends growing up but were always each other's best friend. The only time they drifted apart was the last few months of Marina's marriage, but even then, they talked every day.

"I know, and I'll miss you like crazy, but we can talk on the phone and Facetime, so you'll see Danny." Marina's attempt at sounding upbeat was not fooling Stephanie.

She said Marc wasn't bothering her, but he still lived in St. John's. There was always a chance Marina could run into him, and if he started using again, he'd be crazy enough to do anything.

They talked for almost an hour and made plans for a family get together and a couple of shopping trips before her sister left. With her new job, the only days Stephanie could go were on her days off. It wasn't a typical nine to five. Cora would probably accommodate Stephanie if she asked, but the thought of someone else with John was not pleasant.

After her phone call with Marina, Stephanie grabbed her laptop to check email. She wanted to throw up when she saw another email from Brad. She'd been receiving emails from him on and off over the last few months, but usually forwarded them to her lawyer without reading them.

However, the subject line of this email had Stephanie curious. Marc typed the word regret in all capital letters. She hovered her mouse over the email. Did she want to know what he had to say? Did she want to open that can of worms? She clicked the email and watched it load.

Stephanie

> *I guess you're not going to let this go. I got a letter from your lawyer. If you think this is going to work, you're sadly mistaken. I don't owe you anything, and I'll fight this to the end. You don't know who you're dealing with. I assumed you knew I would not roll over and give you MY money. This is going to end badly. Really badly. This is the last warning I'm going to give you. Call off the lawyer, or you will live to regret it.*

> *Bradley*

Was he kidding? Did he think threats would stop her from trying to get back what was hers? Brad didn't scare her in the least, and she'd be damned if she called off the lawyer. Brad was the one who cleaned out their joint account. All of the money was hers. He was the one who screwed it all up, and since when did he go from being Brad to Bradley? He hated it when anyone called him Bradley. Stephanie realized she didn't know him as well as she thought.

The nasty email was saved and forwarded to her lawyer. It wouldn't look good on him if she produced threatening emails. A cold chill ran down her spine. What if he was like Marc? Brad never seemed the violent type, but then again, she didn't think he would cheat either. He wanted to scare her, but he'd never do anything to hurt her physically. Would he?

"My tea. Damn it. It's probably cold by now," Stephanie groaned. "I should probably get to bed anyway."

God only knew what time John would get up. The massage therapy definitely would be hell. Stephanie forgot how to breathe being so close to him. What was wrong with her? She just ended a disaster of a relationship, and here she was thinking about John in ways she shouldn't. The job started to sound like a bad idea.

Those thoughts drifted around her brain, and she knew sleep wouldn't happen. Stephanie popped her tea in the microwave and gazed out through the kitchen window. The sky was clear, and she could see the ocean in the distance. June wasn't always warm, but the large wicker chair on the back deck beckoned her. Hot tea and a bedroom blanket in hand, she opened the patio doors and headed outside to the patio.

John's garden wasn't large, but he'd landscaped it beautifully. The deck ran the entire length of the back of the house, and another set of patio doors lead into John's kitchen. Scattered around the garden were solar lights giving the garden a soft glow. Two large maple trees stood in opposite corners next to the fence, and she could see the waves crash on the beach between them. The view took her breath away.

She liked it out there. Once John was finished with therapy, she could discuss renting the apartment. Of course, she didn't know how long his recovery would take and didn't know him well enough to ask.

Was he sleeping? He refused to take the medication. Some people disliked the way painkillers made them feel. Luckily, she never had to take anything stronger than Advil. She was aware John was stubborn, but it could be a good thing if he put his mind to getting back on his feet. Hopefully, she could get him to do just that.

It was incredibly relaxing to lay her head back against the chair, close her eyes, and listen to the sounds of the waves. A cold shiver made the hair on her neck stand up, and her eyes snapped open. It was as if someone was watching her, but she didn't see anyone. The sound of someone clearing her throat brought Stephanie's attention to the next garden. A woman pulled a hose from the rack attached to the house next door.

"I'm sorry. Did I scare you?" The woman approached the fence.

"A little. I didn't expect to see anyone out here this late." She seemed pleasant enough.

"I always water my flowers at night. It helps keep the moisture in longer." Glancing at the beautiful garden, it was clear whatever she was doing was working. "I'm Sandy Churchill."

"Stephanie Kelly." She walked to the fence and shook Sandy's hand.

"Are you John's girlfriend?" Her inquiry made Stephanie uncomfortable.

Of course, she wasn't John's girlfriend, but everything in her screamed that she wanted to be. She was sure her desire was written all over her face.

"No, I'm his Physical Therapist and Personal Care Assistant." She couldn't look Sandy in the eye.

"How's he doing?" Sandy turned and proceeded to water her flowers.

"I'm not sure how to answer that, because it's obvious he's frustrated, but I think he's convinced himself he won't get better." Stephanie probably shouldn't discuss John's condition with his neighbor.

"It's got to be hard on him." Sandy continued to spray her beautiful garden. "He's always been very active."

Sandy seemed to know John a lot better than Stephanie thought. Maybe Sandy could be a way to get insight into John from someone besides his family. It wasn't because she didn't trust what they told her, but they were too close to the situation.

Unfortunately, the only information Sandy could contribute wasn't beneficial. John bought the house about six years earlier, and his last relationship didn't end well. Sandy didn't go into detail.

The idea of John having a girlfriend made her stomach churn. The thought of another woman touching or kissing him made a very ugly green-eyed monster appear out of nowhere. She didn't have a right to be jealous because she wasn't romantically involved with John.

Sandy quickly changed the subject. Stephanie found out John's neighbor worked with computers, but when Stephanie asked more about it, Sandy changed the topic again.

The last subject was relationships. Sandy was single and loving it, according to her. Stephanie didn't want to talk about Brad, but for some reason, she found herself describing all the details about her doomed relationship. Sandy easy to talk to, and Stephanie enjoyed their conversation.

"I hope John gets better soon." Sandy rolled up the hose and put it back on the hook. "I've missed our little chats out here."

"If I can help it, he'll be back on his feet in no time," Stephanie said. "I can be your chat buddy until then."

"That's great. I love Hopedale, but sometimes it gets a little boring in the evening." Sandy chuckled.

"I bet, but it's so much better than the city." Stephanie glanced at her watch.

She would probably have an early rise and decided to call it a night. After a quick goodnight to Sandy, Stephanie made her way inside. The reports on John and his family's words were floating through her head. He fought all the therapists in the hospital, and she witnessed some of his anger earlier in the day. Bringing out her inner bitch may be required if he was resistant to the therapy. It wasn't how she liked to do things, but it was necessary sometimes. If John wanted to play that game, she knew precisely how to handle it.

"I'm a professional. I can do this." Stephanie crawled into bed and pulled the blankets over her. "I'm a professional. I can do this." She repeated the mantra until she drifted off to sleep.

Chapter 11

John jolted upright in the bed. Nightmares of the accident continued to haunt his sleep. He didn't remember everything from the crash, but he relived it in his dreams almost every night. His body was still at war with his will, but it wasn't anything new. Over the last couple of months, it became the new norm.

The clock on his nightstand read six-fifteen. Too early to disturb the beautiful blonde, a button push away. It was time to do some things on his own. He'd had enough embarrassment the previous night. His morning wood would be just as humiliating. Plus, it would give him some form of independence.

John could hold his weight on his injured leg, but it was weak, and everyone warned him about it. Since the accident, people thought he was a complete idiot. Maybe partially because of his behavior.

The one thing he could do was sit. It seemed easy enough to say, but the actual attempt made him clench his teeth. After a couple of deep breaths, he had done it. He turned slowly until he sat on the edge of the bed.

"That wasn't too bad." He sighed as he tried to ease the tension in his body

The great part about his room was it wasn't huge, and he could maneuver himself dressed without too much movement. Stephanie explained he'd start his road to recovery later. Comfortable clothes were probably the best. Track pants and a T-shirt was the outfit of the day.

The struggle to pull on his clothes pissed him off because he needed to stop several times before he'd fully dressed. His neck and back made it very difficult, but determination, and let's face it pure O'Connor stubbornness helped him get there. He had pain, but he couldn't let it stop him anymore. His days of being a disagreeable asshole were over.

The wheelchair on the other side of the bed mocked him. How would he get better when he couldn't walk? The chair was the first thing he needed gone. Being pushed around made him feel like a ninety-year-old man, and it didn't do much for his pride. Yes, John had an ego. The hospital gave him a cane to use at home, but he didn't have enough strength to handle it alone. Using the cane was better than the chair and would make it easier to get around in the house. A quick scan of his room told him that plan was out of the question.

Somehow, he managed to maneuver the chair out of his room and make his way to the kitchen. *Push the wheels. Curse. Breathe. Push the wheels. Curse. Breathe.* With that pattern, he made it to the kitchen but suffered because of his determination. He probably did more damage, but to hell with it. He'd get his independence back if it killed him.

The kitchen was the best part of his house, with its million-dollar view. His home wasn't huge but big enough for a bachelor with no prospects of a family in the near future. When the house first went up for sale, John jumped at it since it was in Hopedale, and close enough to the city, it only took fifteen minutes to get to work.

The only thing it needed was a few coats of paint, and he smiled at the memory of the first few weeks after he'd bought it. It took three weekends, with his brothers' help, to have the place looking brand new. The only extra cost was to hire a contractor to close off one side of the house for a rental apartment, but thanks to Keith, he got a reasonable price.

It still amused him when he thought about the day his mother came to inspect the place. She didn't like his home gym or the fact he closed off some of his home for the apartment.

"Not much room for children here." She sighed, but John ignored the comment.

"I like it because he lives closer ta da family," Nanny Betty had interjected and made his mother smile.

John slowly pushed his way to the counter and the coffee maker. Not only was hospital food terrible, but the coffee sucked too. How did a place full of sick people end up with shitty food served to them?

"Who had the stupid idea to store the coffee on the top shelf?" John grumbled, knowing it was his idea.

John put the brake on the chair and pushed himself up on his feet. Standing wasn't difficult, and he was proud to do it on his own. John managed to keep his balance, but trying to lift his arm was another story.

"Fucking shit," he swore at the fact he couldn't even make a pot of coffee for himself.

"Whoa there, Mister." Her voice startled him, and he grabbed the edge of the counter to keep himself steady. "What are you doing?"

It was comical the way she stood in the doorway, hands on her hips and tapping her foot. The problem was he didn't feel like laughing.

"Trying to make coffee." John turned back to the cupboard.

"And overreaching, which will strain your shoulder. You were supposed to page me when you woke up," she chastised, and John sighed as he eased down in the chair.

The scent of vanilla filled his senses as she walked beside him. Like a soldier, his dick started to salute. He'd always had a healthy libido, but Stephanie seemed to put it into overdrive, and in his condition, it was not welcome.

"I was only getting coffee, not building a house," John snapped, but immediately wanted to punch himself for being an asshole.

"It might not seem like much, but if you fell, you could do a lot of damage." Stephanie reached for the coffee in the cupboard.

John groaned inwardly. Her shirt pulled up, exposing the smooth skin of her back, and her ass clenched as she stood on her toes. Sir Brainless Head came to a full salute. Track pants were a horrible idea.

"Why are you up so early?" John needed to use a distraction technique.

"It was hot in my room." She started the coffee pot.

It would have been scorching if I was in there.

"Damn it," John growled.

"You okay?" She turned around.

"Yeah." Sure, he was great.

His body was falling apart, but his dick worked better than ever. Thinking about something else, anything else, was close to impossible with the way those black leggings clung to her firm round ass, and her pink tank top hugging her ample breasts. Were they as firm as they looked?

Dead puppies.

"How long do you think it'll take to lose this chair?" John tried to keep his eyes above her neck when she put a cup in front of him.

She had her hair pulled back into a ponytail hanging over her shoulder in a thick braid. She was stunning, and John couldn't stop his gaze as it dropped to her lips.

"Once you get the strength back, but don't rush it." Stephanie didn't seem to notice as she sat across from him. "I know it's frustrating, but this isn't going to happen overnight, John. You'd probably be out of it if you'd done the therapy in the hospital."

"I know. I know. I was an ass, but I want to get rid of this thing." John sighed, but he hadn't expected to hear the *I told you so* from her. "I need to get rid of it."

"If the chair is your goal, we'll start there." Her beautiful smile made his heart jump in his chest. "Let's get you some breakfast, and then we'll go over everything."

"I'm not hungry." John took a sip of his coffee.

"I don't care if you're hungry." She placed her hands on her hips again, and it was sexy as fuck. "You'll eat breakfast because you need nutrition and energy. Plus, this may be the first day, but it will be a tough workout."

John choked on his coffee because something else was hard too. She was a demanding little thing, and it turned him on more than he ever thought possible. He wanted to make his own requests.

Criminal codes. Criminal codes.

Twenty minutes later, John had breakfast placed in front of him. Scrambled eggs, turkey bacon, and whole-grain toast, but the constant twitch in his groin every time she put the fork to her mouth, made it hard to enjoy his meal. John closed his eyes to try and picture anything else. When he opened them, she was staring at him.

"Are you in any pain, John?" How was he supposed to answer that question?

"No," John answered.

The pain wasn't his issue. The only problem he had was the swollen member causing him discomfort because he couldn't relieve it.

"Are you sure? You seem tense." Her concern made him feel terrible because of what was going through his mind.

"I'm fine. I'm ready to get the ball rolling," he lied.

She was there to help him, not to be the lead in his overactive sexual fantasies. His lie worked because as soon as she had the table cleared, she wheeled him into his home gym.

Stephanie moved some of his regular equipment to the side. An exercise ball and some small free weights sat on a foam mat in the center of the room. He assumed it was part of his therapy, and he scanned the room for anything else new. On the left side, stood a large white table with a hole in the top. It looked like a torture device to John.

"It's a massage table," Stephanie said as if she was reading his thoughts. "You'll need massage therapy at least three times a week, for the first little while."

She confirmed it was a torture table, and he resisted the urge to groan at the thought of her hands on his body. He turned back to Stephanie and watched her tap the screen on her iPod.

"What's that?" He shifted in the chair.

"An iPod." She was a bit of a smart ass.

"I can see that." John chuckled.

"It's motivational music." She smiled.

"Huh?"

"Music to help motivate you." And there was her smart mouth again.

She pointed to the mat. Getting to the floor was a bit of a struggle, especially since he tried to keep the semi in his pants hidden. Her demonstration of a couple of different exercises amused him. How the hell would basic leg lifts help?

"When I start the music, I want you to do two sets of five." She sounded enthusiastic.

John didn't have the heart to tell her this wouldn't work. He had the same arguments with the therapists in the hospital, which was why he refused to do them. Before the accident, John did three sets of twenty of the damn things with weights. He couldn't resist her request, and when the first song started, he met her amused expression.

"Eye of the Tiger." John laughed. "Really?"

"Come on. Let's see that leg moving, Mister. You're stalling." She snapped her fingers.

After the first set, his leg ached, and he couldn't believe it. Halfway through the second set, sweat started to roll down his back. John began to wish he hadn't been such a dick to the therapists in the hospital, but then Stephanie wouldn't be next to him.

Familiar voices floated in from the hallway, and a few seconds later, Aaron and Nick sauntered into the room like they owned the place. When Stephanie smiled at the two fools as they sang and jumped around to the song, he bit his tongue. They were always good for a laugh, but now they pissed him off. Jealousy was not a good look on him, and before he could say a word, the music stopped.

"Aww, I was getting into that." Aaron gave her his fake pout that got his little brother into many unsuspecting girls' panties.

"Wow, you guys can sing," Stephanie gushed. "You should start a band."

John and his two brothers laughed at the statement. The perplexed expression on her face was priceless. He rested his back against the wall, mostly because he needed the break.

"They already did." John snorted.

"What? I'm confused." She glanced between John and his brothers.

"A.J., Nick, Mike, and some friends started a band a couple of years ago. They help raise money for different charities around the province. The band's name is *Rockin' the Law* because all the members are either lawyers, police or law students," John explained.

"That's great." She seemed awestruck, and it pissed him off.

"You neglected to tell her we've been missing a member of the band for the past couple of months, bro." Nick lifted an eyebrow.

"Yeah, the groupies miss ya, big brother." A.J. winked, and the urge to beat his youngest brother lifted its ugly head again.

"Really? You sing too?" It gave a little boost to his ego because he impressed her.

"Yeah, he usually plays the keyboard, but there's a couple of ballads he does that make the ladies swoon," Aaron teased.

"Shut up, A.J.," John growled because the last thing he wanted was to think he was the type of man who jumped from woman to woman.

"I've noticed you say that to him a lot." Stephanie giggled.

"I know, and I'm starting to get offended." Aaron stuck out his bottom lip.

That fucking pout again. Nothing offended Aaron. He moved closer to Stephanie, and John felt a little calmer when Stephanie rolled her eyes.

"Are you here for a reason, or is it only to irritate me?" John grunted.

"Well, irritating you is always fun, but the old man asked us to come over and do some yard work for you before it gets out of hand," Aaron explained as he scrolled through the songs on the iPod.

He didn't think it was possible for him to feel less of a man, but Aaron managed to help him. John couldn't even mow his lawn.

"Hey, you got some excellent music." Aaron smiled at Stephanie, and something in John's stomach twisted.

Aaron wasn't acting any different than he did with his cousins' friends, but John knew if Stephanie showed his brother the tiniest hint of interest, he'd turn the charm on high.

"The beat of the music always helps me when I work out." Stephanie put the iPod back in the dock.

"It works. Very well." Aaron's eyes slowly moved from her face down her body and up again.

"And there it is," John barked.

"What?" Aaron was genuinely confused.

"You've been here all of ten minutes, and you're hitting on the woman." John shook his head.

"It's a gift." Aaron gave his panty-melting smile.

"No, it's a sickness," John snapped.

Stephanie smiled at Aaron, and John wondered if he saw interest. The thought made his chest constrict and gave him a sudden urge to kick his brother's ass.

"We should probably get out of here and start the yard before Mr. Grump starts throwing things." Nick winked at Stephanie and pulled Aaron out of the room.

"They're habitual flirts," John grumbled.

"I've been told they honed their skills by watching their big brother." Stephanie knelt next to John on the mat.

"Yeah, Mike is pretty bad." John was a bit of a flirt himself, at least he used to be.

Stephanie playfully poked him in the stomach, and he grabbed her hand. His gaze met hers, and those emerald green eyes intoxicated him. No woman had ever affected him in the way Stephanie did. When her gaze moved to his lips, he tensed. Was she feeling something too? She had to be able to hear how hard his heart pounded. When her eyes met his again, she jumped to her feet.

"No more slacking off." Her voice sounded shaky.

She practically ran back to the iPod and tapped the screen. When *Man in Motion* started playing, he chuckled.

"Get to work." She winked

"Yes, ma'am." John saluted her.

By the end of the hour, John realized all those little exercises he thought were so stupid, were pure hell. The stretches were a bit painful, but Stephanie helped. She teased his libido, but what was a man to do when a beautiful, sexy woman had her hands on him? He was at the brink of insanity. The poor girl didn't have a clue what she did to him. She was gentle and encouraged him. It would have been sweet if his hormones stayed in check.

"That's enough for today. I'm going to have to ice your shoulder and leg. Your muscles did a lot today, and I don't want you getting sore." Then she pointed to the massage table.

"Tomorrow, massage, and then the next day the same as today." She motioned to the table, and John swallowed hard.

The thought of her hands on his skin left him speechless. John felt as if he needed to get away from her and was about to get up from the floor, but Stephanie stopped him. She left the room, and John wasn't sure what happened until she returned a few minutes later with Aaron and Nick.

"What are you two still doing here?" John almost forgot his brothers dropped in.

"We were finishing up, and Steph asked us to help get you on the table." Nick sauntered across the room to where John sat on the floor while Aaron flirted with Stephanie.

"Didn't you come in here to help me?" John fisted his hands and glared at Aaron.

"Will this therapy help with his grumpy mood?" Aaron teased as he and Nick helped John to his feet.

"I wasn't grumpy until you got here." Of course, he was pissed because Stephanie didn't seem to mind the flirtation.

Nick held John's arm until he settled back on the table. Aaron sidled up to Stephanie while she prepared the ice packs. He turned away and realized Nick had followed John's gaze.

"Feeling a little jealous there, bro?" Nick nudged him with his elbow.

"No." John would never admit he was jealous.

"You know A.J., he can't help flirting with beautiful women." Nick chuckled.

Nick was one to talk, because it was a toss-up on who was the biggest flirt, but for some reason, Nick seemed to keep it in check with Stephanie.

"Yeah, well, he needs to control it with my therapist." John eased back on the table and pressed his eyes closed.

"If you ask me, I don't think you've got to worry. I've seen how she looks at you when she thinks nobody's looking." John's eyes snapped open to see his brother walk away.

Nick grabbed Aaron's arm and dragged him out of the room, leaving John alone with Stephanie again. Was Nick crazy, or did he see something John missed? When he looked in her direction, she was staring at him.

"How do you feel?" Stephanie asked as she placed the ice packs on his shoulder and leg.

140

"A little sore, but okay," John admitted.

"This will help calm the muscles, and I'll give you some Advil to help with inflammation." Stephanie stared down at him for a moment, then left the room.

Twenty minutes later, she returned, removed the ice packs, and helped him sit up. When her eyes met his, everything around him disappeared, including the pain. He felt the urge to pull her into his embrace, but when he grasped her arm, the doorbell rang.

Son of a bitch.

Stephanie didn't seem to notice anything different as she helped him to his chair, but as she stumbled back from him, he saw something in her eyes. Before he could say a word, the doorbell rang again, and she hurried from the room.

What the hell was he going to do?

Chapter 12

Stephanie's heart raced as she hurried to answer the door. The doorbell saved her from making a colossal error in judgment. She'd almost kissed John. Something about the way he gazed at her caused her to lose all common sense. She needed to get a grip on herself because no matter what she felt, he was her client. It went against all the professional ethics she pushed on herself to get involved with him. The doorbell rang again, and she yanked the door open.

"Who the hell are you?" A blonde woman growled.

"Stephanie." What else was she supposed to say?

"You must be the new flavor of the week. No wonder he dumped me." The woman narrowed her eyes and glared at Stephanie.

"If you're referring to John, I'm not his flavor of the day, week, or year. I'm his physical therapist." Why was she explaining anything to this rude woman?

"Kim, what the fuck are you doing here?" The tone of his voice startled Stephanie, and she shuddered when she witnessed how he glared at the guest on his step.

Whoa.

"Your family wouldn't let me visit you in the hospital. When I heard you were out, I came to see how you were. I missed you." Kim almost knocked Stephanie as she pushed through the door.

When Kim knelt in front of John and touched him, Stephanie wanted to scream. The woman was obviously involved with John at some point, and it was possible John broke it off because of his condition. Maybe he'd take this woman back once he was back on his feet.

"Jesus Christ, Kim, how often do I have to tell you it's over? No second chances. Over." John wheeled his chair back from her, and his face was hard with anger.

"I'm just going to leave you two alone." Stephanie turned to enter her apartment.

"No, Stephanie. Kim is leaving and not coming back." John's voice sounded harsh and full of rage.

"You're really ending things," Kim whined, but John didn't answer, and after a few seconds, Kim spun on her heel and tossed her hair over her shoulders. "Fine, but you'll live to regret this, John O'Connor."

Kim jerked the door's handle and glared at Stephanie. When Stephanie didn't flinch, Kim stomped through the door and slammed it behind her. The whole house shook, and for a moment, there was an awkward silence. Without a word, Stephanie clasped her hands in front of her and headed toward the kitchen. John grasped her arm as she passed by his chair and stopped her.

"I'm sorry about that." His expression softened.

"It's none of my business." She gently pulled her arm free and continued on her way.

She poured a glass of juice and leaned against the counter to drink it. The anger on his face made it clear John didn't want to be with Kim. Part of Stephanie was relieved, while another part of her wondered if he'd treat her the same way. A few seconds later, John appeared. She didn't know what to say in the situation, but the sadness in his eyes almost broke her heart.

"I want to explain what happened out there." He rubbed his hands down his thighs.

"You don't have to. It's none of my business, John." She wasn't sure if she wanted to know.

"I know, but I feel I have to explain. She cheated on me," John blurted out, and Stephanie understood betrayal.

"I'm sorry, I know how it feels." When she'd discovered Brad's cheating, her heart ached for weeks.

Stephanie skipped meals and lost more sleep than she cared to admit. At one time, she thought Brad was it for her, and even toward the end, when she had doubts, she fooled herself into believing it.

"She just doesn't get it." John blew out a breath. "No matter how many times I tell her it's over, she doesn't get it."

"It's hard when a relationship ends." It took Stephanie a lot of tears to figure it out.

"I guess, but we weren't dating very long." John closed his eyes.

"Maybe you should get some rest." She didn't want to hear about his short relationship with the scorned blonde, because the thought of him with the woman made her jealous

Stephanie pushed him into his bedroom and positioned the chair next to his bed. After applying the brake, she finally looked at his face. His eyes showed intense pain, but it wasn't physical. The woman hurt him more than he admitted. Her stomach retched to think about him with Kim. She met his eyes, and they glistened with unshed tears. Without thinking, she cupped his cheek.

"You're an angel." His voice was barely above a whisper, and he covered her hand with his

"I already told you. I'm no angel." She tried to pull her hand away, but he held it tightly.

"I know an angel when I see one." He took his time easing down to the mattress. "Thank you."

Three weeks of intensive physical therapy and sexual frustration, but Stephanie managed to keep things professional. John worked hard to where he no longer needed the wheelchair and only used a cane when he left the house. John progressed much better than she initially thought, and it was the problem. The stronger he got, the less he needed her, and Stephanie wasn't sure how she felt about it.

John's family was great, and she got to know all his brothers pretty well. Not a day went by where one of them didn't drop by for a short visit. Most nights, she and John spent time in the garden and chatted with Sandy. It was easy and natural to talk to John.

The tough thing in her life was his massage sessions. Although it was supposed to be strictly clinical, when she rubbed her hands over his muscular body, it drove her insane with desire. After every session, her body would be on fire.

Later in the day, he had another session, and her neck and shoulder muscles were tight with tension. She debated with herself over the previous week to ask Cora to have another massage therapist, but then her stomach would churn with the thought of another person touching him. The idea got tossed away before it even had a chance.

"You need a boyfriend," Stephanie groaned and covered her face with her hands.

"No, you don't." She squeaked at the sound of his deep velvety voice. "Sorry, I knocked, but you didn't answer."

John leaned against the door jamb with his lips quirked up in a sexy grin and those damn dimples ever-present. He crossed his arms over his chest, and his biceps stretched the short sleeves of his t-shirt. Her only thought was it should be illegal for a man to look so good.

I'm totally screwed.

"I... I didn't hear you." Stephanie stood and pulled her shirt down over her hips.

"I noticed, but why exactly do you need a boyfriend?" John smirked, and his blue eyes twinkled with mischief.

146

"I... I don't need one." She avoided his amused expression. "Are you ready for your massage?"

"If you are." Those words almost seemed strangled, but there was no change in his expression.

"You can go get on the table. I'm just gonna put this in the dishwasher." She held up the cup that only contained water, but it gave her a minute to calm her libido.

Stephanie blew out a breath when he nodded and disappeared from her doorway. She'd taken to leaving the door to her apartment open during the day, but since he didn't need her as much in recent days, it would probably be better if she closed it. At least he wouldn't overhear her awkward conversations with herself.

John was face down on the massage table when she entered the room. The soft music she used during the session played low, and as usual, her eyes went straight to where the thin sheet covered his firm muscled ass. What she wouldn't give to grab his ass while he was...

Whoa, stop that.

Those thoughts needed to stop, but the man was so freaking hot. The more time she spent with him, the more she enjoyed his company. When she sighed, John lifted his head from the table with a gin on his full lips.

"Something wrong?" He propped his chin up with his fist, and it gave her a view of his well-developed pectoral muscles.

He's your client.

"No." Did her voice sound breathy?

Stephanie turned to prepare the heating pad she used before she started the actual torture to herself. She could feel his eyes on her as she killed time with the oils she applied for the session. Almond oil with a little lavender was her favorite to use. Hopefully, the scent would help her calm herself as well.

"Maybe you need a massage." The comment caused her to almost tip the bottle.

"What?" She turned around.

"You seem tense." He laughed.

"Oh," she said. "No, I'm a little tired. I haven't been sleeping very well." *All because I keep thinking about having my hands all over you, and you have your hands all over me.*

"I see." Why did his voice sound so sensual?

Stephanie motioned for him to turn over, and she placed the hot pad on his back, mostly because she didn't want him to see any signs of her undeniable attraction. She could hide it most of the time, but when he was practically naked under a thin sheet, it was not as easy.

"Maybe you need to go out for a night," he suggested.

"Maybe," she mumbled mostly to herself.

After ten minutes, Stephanie began to work the muscles of John's upper back. She needed to get out and put some distance between her and John. All the time spent with him played havoc with her brain. At the moment, all she wanted to do was lick every inch of his hard, hot body.

"I don't think you've been out since you started working with me." The vibration of his voice rumbled through her.

"I go to my parents on my days off." Her hands slid down the center of his back, using the heels of her hands to work deep into the muscles.

A small moan from him made her squeeze her legs together, and she wanted to moan herself. Instead, she continued to work the area that had him make the sounds she imagined he made during sex. Why did she torture herself?

"We could probably go to a movie or something tonight," he said, but she wasn't sure she heard correctly.

"Me and you?" Stephanie's hands stilled.

"Yeah. I haven't been out either, and I'm starting to get cabin fever." He sounded casual with the suggestion. "I mean, I do consider you a friend, and what's wrong with two friends catching a movie."

"Nothing, I guess." She tried not to sound disappointed, but she was.

"You don't have to if you don't want to, but I think it would be fun." John turned his head and glanced over his shoulder at her hands. "Are you finished?"

"I think a movie would be great." Stephanie smiled and pushed his head down. "And no, I'm not finished."

She tried to force herself to concentrate on what she was doing because he'd only suggested a movie. *Wait.* Did she agree to go out with John?

She paced the floor in her apartment and debated with herself. Should she go or tell John she had to cancel? He was her client, but he did say they were friends. There was nothing wrong with friends going out for a movie. How pathetic was it that her first real date in months was going to be with her client?

Hopedale was not very large, and it only took about fifteen minutes to drive around the whole town. Besides a couple of convenience stores, every other business in Hopedale stood on one side of Harbour Street. The other side of the road was Hopedale Harbour, which was where the fishing boats docked.

Hopedale Cinemas stood on the corner of Harbour Street and contained a total of two theaters that played mostly old movies. Stephanie didn't mind. Why would she? She got to spend an evening with John.

"How about this one?" John pointed to Theater A.

Stephanie saw the action movie a while back and enjoyed it. It was safer than the love story in Theater B. The last thing she needed was to sit through hot sex scenes with a man who made her want to create her own with him.

"Looks good to me." Stephanie reached for her wallet, but before she had a chance to pull it from her purse, John pressed a ticket into her hand. "Hey, I was paying for that."

"Too late. You snooze you lose, Cupcake." John winked.

Cupcake?

Did he realize what he'd just called her? It was stupid, but the use of the endearment gave her a warm feeling through her chest.

150

Of course, she couldn't let him see how much she enjoyed it, so she narrowed her eyes.

John chuckled as he sauntered toward the food court, seemingly proud of himself. She realized he didn't have his cane, and his limp was barely noticeable. The sight of it made her smile, and her eyes filled with tears. She was sure she felt the way a parent did when they watched a child take their first steps.

"What are you smiling at?" John raised an eyebrow and smiled.

"You're walking without your cane." She swallowed hard against the lump in her throat and was slightly embarrassed by how emotional she felt.

"Yeah, and my leg seems to be fine." His smile widened.

She was so excited she almost missed how he'd eased into the line to get at the concession stand. John scanned the menu, and Stephanie used the distraction to jump ahead of him in the lineup.

"Hey, you skipped me." John slid up behind her.

"You snooze, you lose, Cupcake." She winked, and John threw his head back and laughed.

Once they entered the theater, Stephanie decided it would be better to take a seat further from the screen to prevent any strain in John's neck. He didn't seem to mind, and he motioned to two chairs in the center of the back row. The memory of her teen years flashed through her brain and the times the boys wanted to sit in the back to make out. The thought made her shiver with desire, and her cheeks felt hot.

The movie started, and John remained a complete gentleman once the lights dimmed. Stephanie wasn't sure if she was relieved or disappointed, but she was concerned with the way John started to shift around in his chair as if he was in pain. It had to be difficult for him to sit in the same position for too long, even with the progress he made. The old theater seats weren't exactly the most comfortable.

"Are you ok, John?" She whispered into his ear and immediately became concerned when he groaned. "Are you in pain?"

"No." It sounded like a cross between a groan and a growl.

"Are you sure, because you look uncomfortable." If he was in pain, they were leaving.

"I'm fine." He leaned back and placed the popcorn bucket between his legs.

She'd known him long enough to know something was wrong. His stubborn nature came out a few times over the past few weeks, and he'd push himself until Stephanie saw the strain on his face. The same way it looked now. She glanced at him several times to see if she could read him, but he smiled, and her stomach fluttered the way it did every time he turned on his charm. She was hopelessly smitten.

Chapter 13

Concentrating on the movie became more difficult by the minute. The seats were closer than John remembered, and anytime Stephanie moved, her thigh would brush against his. When her warm breath blew across his ear, it almost sent him over the edge.

He leaned forward, but it made his jeans more uncomfortable. When he sat back, it would be obvious why he squirmed around so much — *the popcorn*. John grabbed the bucket and placed it between his legs to cover his growing problem.

"Are you sure, because you look uncomfortable?" Her scent made him clench his teeth together, and his dick throbbed.

For the last three weeks, her scent drove him crazy every time she was within a foot of him. It was so bad that when Mike brought him a French Vanilla coffee two days earlier, John got a hard-on.

"I'm fine," he answered.

Sounding casual wasn't easy, especially when all he wanted to do was tell her he had a raging erection and wanted her to ride him until they were both too exhausted to move.

It was getting ridiculous. John couldn't sleep because his dreams were full X-rated images of him and Stephanie naked in every position imaginable. Wet dreams were supposed to be for teenagers, and he was no teenager.

John also enjoyed her company, which only increased his attraction to her. Stephanie was funny, sarcastic, compassionate, and intelligent. When they talked, it was easy and natural. John never had that with any other woman in his life, and it terrified him.

By the time they left the theater, his problem had deflated a little, but he untucked his shirt to cover that part of his body anyway. As they walked outside, he glanced across the street at the fishing boats. The lights reflected off the harbor as a gentle breeze swirled around him.

"It's gorgeous here," Stephanie said, but John didn't know if she meant to say it out loud since it was barely a whisper.

"It's my favorite part of living in Hopedale." He turned to her. "Would you like to get a cup of coffee at Aunt Alice's pub?" He motioned to *Jack's Place* two buildings down from the theaters.

"If your Aunt Alice owns it, why is it called Jack's place?" She asked as they walked toward the pub.

"Uncle Kurt and Aunt Alice opened the place about four years ago. When they originally tried to find a name for it, Grandda suggested naming it after him. He was joking, but Alice loved the idea, and it became *Jack's Place*." John pulled open the entry door to the diner.

Alice divided the place into two businesses. The diner was on one side and the pub on the other. When the restaurant closed after supper, the pub would open. Alice insisted the restaurant was for family, and she wouldn't have alcohol served until all underage kids were gone home. Luckily, they'd gone to the first movie and made it to the diner before it closed.

"I like the name." Stephanie glanced around and almost bumped into Cora and his uncle Brian.

"Aww…. Look who it is, Brian. Are you too having a date night?" Cora linked an arm with her husband.

"No," John and Stephanie answered in unison.

"Oh? Too bad. Maybe soon." Cora nodded and gave John a huge hug. "Johnny, it's good to see you up and around. Stephanie certainly is good for you."

"She's an excellent therapist." John wasn't lying, but he eyed his aunt suspiciously because he could tell she was up to something.

"Brian, you remember Stephanie," Cora gushed.

"Yes, I do. It's lovely to see you again, my dear." Brian nodded at Stephanie and then turned to John. "John, my boy, you've got a lovely lady here." Brian patted him on the shoulder.

"They're not dating." Cora raised an eyebrow. "Yet."

Cora kissed John's cheek and left the pub. For a few seconds, John stared after his aunt and prayed this didn't have anything to do with Cora's Cupid thing.

"Umm. What was that all about?" Stephanie stammered.

155

"I have no idea. Aunt Cora is unique." John motioned to a table near the window with a great view of the harbor.

John sensed Stephanie's discomfort and wondered if they should have gone home. Cora's comment about John and Stephanie out on a date made him uncomfortable, so he could only imagine what Stephanie thought. He wouldn't mind dating the woman across from him because there was a spark, at least on his end.

The stories of his aunt over the years were legendary. She had a special gift for knowing when people belonged together. He and his brothers always considered it a load of bull, but his mother was convinced. So was Nanny Betty and his aunt Alice.

Cora had introduced his mother and father and Kurt and Alice. She even introduced James to Sarah. When Cora met Kim, she told John she wasn't the one. There was no way this Cupid thing was real. John chuckled

"What's so funny?" Stephanie stared at him.

"Just thinking about Aunt Cora." John smiled. "She's a character."

"Yeah." Stephanie dropped her gaze.

"Look who we have here." Alice smiled.

Aunt Alice was always in the diner or the pub. Lately, his uncle had convinced her to take some time to herself, but it didn't work very well. John's cousins would work there when they got the chance as well.

"Hi, Aunt Alice." John stood up and kissed her cheek.

"John, it's so good to see you out, and you too, Stephanie. I've only seen you in passing and never got a chance to have a chat." She reached out to shake Stephanie's hand.

"It's nice to see you too." Stephanie smiled at Alice, and his heart flipped.

"You're definitely the woman who's going to give John the life he deserves." Alice took Stephanie's hand in hers and squeezed. "You make him smile."

"Aunt Alice, could I have a coffee and a piece of your coconut cream pie." He motioned to Stephanie to order and to distract his aunt.

"Ummm... I'll have a cup of tea, please." Stephanie smiled.

"I'll get that in a jiffy." Alice nodded and hurried away from the booth.

"Did you like the movie?" Stephanie appeared more relaxed than earlier.

"Yeah, it was good," he lied, because he couldn't remember much of the movie.

"I love Sandra Bullock." She stopped when Alice returned with their order, winking at him as she walked away again.

"She's great." John swirled the coffee in his cup.

Every time she put the cup to her kissable lips, his jeans would get a little tighter. He wanted to kiss her, feel her body writhe under him, and hold her in his arms until they both fell asleep.

John winced as he tried to adjust himself inconspicuously. He jabbed the fork into the pie and practically shoveled the whole piece into his mouth in a few bites. He was relieved she hadn't ordered any, because if he had to watch her mouth wrapped around a forkful of the pie, it would probably kill him.

"John, are you in pain?" Not the kind of pain she meant.

"No." He mentally kicked himself for being such a horny bastard.

"Are you going to tell me what's wrong with you, because you say you aren't in pain, but you look as if you want to scream?" She placed her hand on top of his, and as he met her eyes, he couldn't put two words together. "Did I do something wrong, or is there something you want to know?"

"I'm not in any pain." He pulled his hand away and sat back in the chair. "And you didn't do anything wrong."

"Then why are you acting like a cat on a hot tin roof?" She asked, sounding a lot like his grandmother.

"I really can't say." He gazed out of the window.

"John, I thought we were friends?" Now he hurt her feelings.

"We are friends." His gaze moved back to her, and hell if he didn't get tongue-tied again.

"Then you can tell me anything." How could he tell her what he felt was more than friendship, and he wanted to kiss her until they were both too breathless to speak?

"I can't tell you, Stephanie." He closed his eyes and ground the heel of his hands into them.

"John, there's nothing you can say that'll make me stop being your friend." Stephanie pulled his hands away from his face, and when he looked into those green eyes, it was over.

"I like you," he admitted.

"I like you too." She glanced around the diner as if she was afraid someone would hear her.

John sighed, she didn't get what he meant, and maybe it was a good thing. He reached across the table and ran his finger down her cheek.

"I don't think you understand." John dropped his hand, stood up, and threw a twenty-dollar bill on the table. "Ready to go home?"

The drive back to his house was quiet. John glanced at her a couple of times. Stephanie sat with her hands between her knees and stared out the window. At least it was only a five-minute drive to his house which was a good thing because being so close to her made it hard to think

She saw them as friends. Stephanie said it herself. The attraction was one-sided, and it was as if his heart cracked. The only women he seemed to attract were ones who ended up hurting him. He found it hard to believe he'd imagined the connection between them. It was as if she calmed him and excited him at the same time. He'd never felt anything like it. What was he going to do? It hit him like a punch in the gut. He had an idea.

Chapter 14

Stephanie tossed and turned the whole night as she tried to tame the constant fantasies about John. The lack of sleep did not do her mood any good either. John wouldn't tell her what bothered him the previous night and went to bed without even good night to her. The more she thought about it, the more it pissed her off.

She leaned against the counter and sipped her tea. Why would it be a good thing she didn't understand? She'd enjoyed herself the night before. Maybe too much, and under different circumstances, it could have been a date, but it was unethical to think anything with John. He was her client.

"Why do you have to keep reminding yourself of that?" She whispered into the cup.

Stephanie couldn't understand why she felt so annoyed with him, but she was. She was a pretty easy-going person, and it took a lot to tick her off, but when she looked up as he appeared in the kitchen, she wanted to punch him.

"Good morning," he greeted her pleasantly.

Oh. He wanted to be a cheery morning person now. During the first week she was in the house, John was anything but pleasant in the morning. Now she was irritated, he wanted to be chipper. No. Damn. Way.

"Yeah, morning." Stephanie put her cup in the sink and moved to leave the kitchen.

"What's wrong?" He stepped aside as she motioned for him to move out of her way.

"Nothing's wrong with me." She stomped out of the kitchen and made her way to what she now referred to the therapy room.

As angry as she felt, she still had a job to do. The schedule for the day would start with wall push-ups to test how he could tolerate the pressure on his shoulder. He had regained more mobility, but he needed to increase his muscle strength.

Stephanie had some space cleared next to the wall when John walked into the room. She pretended not to notice as she moved weights and equipment out of the way.

"Are we rearranging the room today?" He stood in the doorway with his arms crossed over his chest and a sexy grin on his gorgeous face.

"No. *We* aren't doing anything," she said a little ruder than she meant. "You're gonna do two sets of five wall push-ups."

"I see." John smirked.

Every time she'd work in a new exercise, John thought it would be easy. Each time he'd admit he struggled, and she knew this would be the same. Before all of this, he probably did a hundred push-ups a day, but it would probably take some time to get to that point again.

Stephanie pointed to a spot in front of the wall she'd cleared away. As she explained what she wanted him to do, she demonstrated the exercise. When he laughed again, she spun around.

"Am I amusing you?" She glared at him.

"Kind of." He was not supposed to grin at her when she was so pissed.

"I'm so glad you're amused." She crossed her arms over her chest. "Now, get to it."

"Yes, Ma'am." John saluted and positioned himself facing the wall as she instructed, but when he started, she stopped him immediately.

"Your hands need to be level with your shoulders, John." She stepped between him and the wall.

Stephanie pulled his hands down, so they were parallel with his shoulders. She turned to face him to ensure he understood. John's eyes locked with hers, his hands were position on either side of her head. Her breath caught in her throat, and her heart pounded, but when his gaze moved to her lips, she swallowed hard.

"John ..." He stepped closer and pressed his body against hers.

"Stephanie." He lightly brushed his mouth across hers. "Your lips are so soft," he whispered as he did it again.

Stephanie's brain said she should stop him, but her feet wouldn't move. His lips touched hers as he threaded his fingers into her hair. John tilted her head as if he needed a better angle to her mouth, and she groaned as his tongue slid between her lips. Desire coursed through her body, but she fisted his shirt to push him away. They needed to stop, but when he moaned, Stephanie pulled him closer. Every hard muscle of his body molded against her, and she relished every inch of it.

John seemed to have some mental capacity because he pulled his lips from hers. John panted heavily, and his warm breath blew across her cheek. Her brain and body reeled from being kissed so thoroughly. Nobody ever devoured her mouth like John did, and it was tough to remember how to breathe

"I've wanted to kiss you since the first time I saw you," He whispered.

"John, this isn't a good idea." Her brain started to remember why this was all kinds of wrong. "I mean, you're my client. Your aunt is my boss."

"I know, but I can't help it, Stephanie, I want you more than I've wanted anyone in my life." He caressed her cheek with his knuckle.

"I feel it too." She needed to breathe, and she couldn't with his scent all around her.

"Why do I feel a but coming?" John rested his forehead against hers.

"You're my client." She could barely hear her own voice as she repeated the words. "I've got to remain professional, and what just happened wasn't professional."

"I understand. Really, I do." John pulled away and ran his hand through his hair. "It's not going to be easy, but until I've completed my therapy, I promise we'll keep it professional."

John turned and left the room without another word, and her legs buckled. Stephanie slid down the wall to the floor and tucked her legs against her chest. She needed to get out of the house. The way his body pressed against hers and his kiss muddled her brain.

It had been weeks since she'd seen Donna, and longer since they hung out together. They texted all the time, but between Donna's schedule and hers, they never got a chance to see each other. She picked up her phone and tapped Donna's name.

"Please, let her be off today," Stephanie whispered as she put the phone to her ear.

"Hello, stranger," Donna answered on the second ring.

"Hey." Stephanie practically shouted the word.

"Okay, what's wrong?" Donna knew her almost as well as Marina.

"I'm getting cabin fever. Want to go out for tea?" The sentence seemed to come out like one long word.

"I'd love to. I've been cleaning the house all day, and my roommate went away for the weekend. So, a nice little drive to Hopedale would be great." She sighed. "I'll pick you up."

"Sounds terrific. See you soon." Stephanie ended the call.

She quickly changed into jeans and a T-shirt and waited on the front step. It was a beautiful day, and she noticed the car John had been using was not in the driveway. John left without a word, and it stung a little.

John didn't even say goodbye, but he probably headed to his parent's for supper. Kathleen asked her to join them all the time, but she always declined. She didn't want to get too attached to the family.

Stephanie was lost in her thoughts when she heard someone call her name. Sandy waved from the other side of the driveway as she headed down her front steps. They'd become good friends over the past few weeks, and a thought hit her. Sandy knew John pretty well, and maybe it would be a good idea to get her thoughts on the situation. What would it hurt?

"You looked like you were off in another world." Sandy chuckled as she walked up to her.

"Yeah, I have a lot on my mind." Stephanie met her at the fence

"Do you want to talk about it?" Sandy's expression turned serious.

"It's about John." Stephanie sighed.

"Oh, Mr. Hot and Sexy." Sandy laughed. "Wait, he's not here, is he?" The sudden panic on Sandy's face made Stephanie laugh.

"No, he's gone out, but I'm extremely attracted to him, and I'm pretty sure he's feeling it too, but he's my client, and I'm struggling with the whole ethical issue. I called my friend Donna to get her opinion, but you know him well, so maybe you can help. I don't know what to do, and my sister is away, and oh, I don't know." Stephanie took a deep breath and dropped her head.

"You do know you ramble when you're stressed." Sandy snickered.

"I know." Stephanie covered her face.

"He's a great guy, and obviously, I've noticed his hotness level is off the charts, but all the O'Connor brothers are hot. Have you ever looked at Ian?" Sandy sighed.

"Yeah, it's a real problem, and am I sensing a little interest there?" Stephanie giggled, but before Sandy could answer, a car pulled into the driveway, and Donna stepped out.

"You want to come with us to town for tea?" Stephanie motioned toward Donna

"Sure. Just let me grab my purse and lock the door." Sandy jogged back to her house.

"Who was that?" Donna hugged Stephanie.

"My neighbor. I hope you don't mind, but I invited her to come with us." Stephanie walked to the passenger side and opened the door.

"Not at all." Donna shrugged and hopped back in her car.

"I need some major girl talk." Stephanie sighed as she plopped down in the car seat.

"Well, tea isn't going to do it. We're going to *The Pier*." Donna grinned as Sandy got in the back seat.

At *The Pier*, Stephanie followed the hostess to the table, and the three women took their seats. Stephanie did introductions in the car, and they decided the conversation would wait until they arrived at the restaurant, if she could figure out where to start.

"Okay, spill it." Donna slapped her hands on the table, making Stephanie and Sandy jump.

"I don't know where to start." Stephanie groaned.

"Maybe I can help. Did you know she rambles when she's stressed?" Sandy asked Donna.

"Don't I know it." Donna rolled her eyes.

"Bite me, Donna." Stephanie narrowed her eyes at her friend.

"I'm guessing you know she has the hots for John, but she's having an issue with whether it's ethical to get involved with him because he's a patient." Sandy summed everything up in one sentence, and Stephanie wished she knew how people did that.

"This is the same cop who pulled you over a few months back, right?" Donna rested her chin on her fists.

"Yes." Stephanie nodded.

"The same cop Marina nicknamed *Officer Hunky*?" Donna laughed.

"Yes." The worst thing she ever did was tell anyone about the stupid nickname.

"I say ethics be damned and jump his bones." Donna wiggled her eyebrows.

That was Donna's answer to everything. If the guy was hot, jump him. Stephanie loved her friend dearly, but Donna was a little too promiscuous. One of these days, some guy was going to knock her on her ass.

"Not helping." Stephanie exhaled as Sandy and Donna continued to tease her.

"Maybe if you did, it might help the stress." Sandy joked.

None of this helped her, and the two women at the table with her told her to go for it only made it worse. Stephanie could only look at the grins on her two friends, and she was about to say something when Sandy's smile disappeared.

"Oh shit," Sandy groaned.

Stephanie glanced up at the waitress and wanted to vomit. John's ex-girlfriend stood next to the table with a hateful expression. She was the last person Stephanie wanted to see.

"Nice to see you too, Sandy." Kim's sarcasm was evident.

"Wish I could say the same, Kim," Sandy replied.

Donna furrowed her brows as she looked back and forth between Sandy and Kim. There was no way to explain the situation until Kim walked away.

"So, has John got in your pants yet?" Kim narrowed her eyes.

"I'm his physical therapist," Stephanie answered, but Kim seemed to think John was only after one thing, but was she right?

"Sure, you are. Anyway, can I take your order?" Stephanie wasn't sure she was hungry anymore.

Thank God for Sandy. The girl didn't miss a beat and ordered for all of them. When Kim spun on her heels and stomped away from the table, Stephanie blew out a breath.

"What was that all about?" Donna leaned across the table and whispered.

"It's a long story." Sandy sipped her water and set the glass back down.

Sandy seemed to have a strong dislike for Kim, but Stephanie didn't know why. At first, Stephanie thought her friend might be interested in John and was jealous of his ex, but after the way she sighed over Ian, it was evident Sandy was into John's brother.

"Kim is John's ex-girlfriend. I knew her before John dated her. She'd get pissed when he worked, and when he was off, he had to spend all of his time with her. A few months ago, I heard them arguing in the driveway. Of course, I had to find out what was going on." Sandy shrugged. "John found out she screwed around on him, and he kicked her to the curb. She has been trying to get back with him ever since. I don't think he was serious about her."

"Which means they weren't sleeping together." Donna pointed her finger at Sandy.

"How the hell do you figure that?" Stephanie hoped it was the case.

"Easy. John is hot. She fucked someone else, which means she wasn't getting it from him." Donna sat back in her chair and looked as if she just solved the biggest mystery of life.

"Your logic is astounding." Stephanie rolled her eyes.

"But seriously, should we trust her with our food?" Donna whispered and then glanced over both shoulders.

They stared at each other for a moment, and they broke into a fit of laughter. They probably shouldn't eat any food Kim brought them.

As luck should have it, another waitress brought their food. Kim probably didn't want to serve them after the way Sandy spoke to her.

"Look, if you're interested, there's nothing wrong with pursuing it. Especially if he's interested," Donna said as they started to eat, and Sandy nodded.

After the kiss Stephanie shared with John, she didn't doubt his interest. She did, however, worry about her job. It wouldn't look very good to her boss, especially since Cora was John's aunt.

The food was incredible. Stephanie hadn't realized how hungry she was until she saw her empty plate. It was Sandy who suggested dessert, and of course, girl time wouldn't be complete without a little sweet treat. While Stephanie and Donna visited the ladies' room, Sandy ordered.

"I like her," Donna expressed as she washed her hands.

"Me too." Stephanie agreed.

The dessert was on the table when Stephanie and Donna returned. Sandy was halfway through hers and had a look of pure pleasure on her face as she savored it. Stephanie was on her third fork full when a voice made her blood run cold.

"Hello, Steph." Brad stood next to their table with his fake blonde bimbo clung onto his arm.

His voice was sugary sweet, and the chocolate cake she'd eaten suddenly made her want to throw up. How could he talk to her so sweet considering the email he sent?

"Brad." Stephanie tried not to let her fury show.

"Donna, nice to see you." Brad smiled.

"Too bad I can't say the same, asshole." Donna's hands clenched together, and her knuckles turned white.

"Was that necessary?" He pouted, and Stephanie rolled her eyes.

She used to think it was cute once, but now it looked stupid. She couldn't say how often Brad used the same face to get his way. Stephanie could never understand how Brad continued to act like a spoiled rich brat when he grew up in a low-income part of town with a single mom who worked two jobs.

"Yep, now go away and take Barbie with you." Donna waved her hand at him.

"I wanted to say hi, and introduce you to Erica." Brad grinned. "Enjoy your night."

Stephanie made a fist under the table. The blonde Barbie wannabe, or Erica, as Brad called her, smiled back, and tucked herself under Brad's arm.

"Argh, what is it? Asshole day here." Donna grumbled as she shoved a forkful of her dessert into her mouth.

"I don't feel well. I need to go home." Stephanie couldn't understand why seeing Brad made her feel physically ill, but she felt awful.

"The meal is on me." Sandy grabbed the bill off the table.

Stephanie didn't have the energy to argue because she wanted to go home. Her stomach clenched, and her heart raced. She started to think if she didn't leave soon, she would throw up all over the table.

The drive home was anything but pleasant. Her stomach was cramping, and a couple of times Donna had to stop for her to get sick. It couldn't be the food because Donna and Sandy weren't ill. She just needed to get home and go to bed. It was probably a virus she picked up somewhere.

Chapter 15

John sat on the couch next to his father and tried to stay involved in the conversation going on around him. It didn't work. His thoughts kept returning to Stephanie. According to her, things had to remain professional, but there was one problem. It started to become painful, and now with the memory of their kiss at the forefront of his thoughts, it was worse.

"Everything okay, John," his father asked.

"Yeah, Dad." The last thing he wanted to do was talk to his father about his constant hard-on for a particular therapist.

"You look tense." His dad turned to face John.

"Just tired." It wasn't a lie because he was tired of trying to control his feelings for Stephanie.

His therapy couldn't end soon enough. Physically, he felt stronger and even started to work out more. Stephanie kept him to a minimum but encouraged him to try a little extra every day, and he didn't tell her, but he did more on his own at night.

"Tired, bro. Something, or should I say, someone keeping you up late?" Aaron chuckled as he held out a beer to John.

"Have you been told yet today?" John growled.

"Told what?" Aaron plopped in the armchair and propped his feet up on the footstool.

"Shut up, A.J.," John snapped.

"You know one of these days you guys are gonna say that to me, and I'm going to stop talking," Aaron whined.

"God, let it be soon." Keith put his hands together as if in prayer

"Can you imagine how quiet it would be?" Mike sighed.

"Dad, do you see the way they treat me?" Aaron grumbled.

"I've got a feeling you bring it on yourself, my boy." his dad chuckled, and a chorus of laughter echoed in the room.

John enjoyed time with family, probably more than he used to. They didn't spend as much time together since they'd all moved out on their own. There were still the monthly family suppers, and every couple of weeks, his brothers would get together at *Jack's Place* for some brother bonding, although John hadn't participated in a while.

"Seriously, how are things going with the sexy therapist?" Aaron wiggled his eyebrows.

"Her name is Stephanie," John returned as he tossed a cushion at Aaron. "And my therapy is going fine."

He didn't like how Aaron referred to Stephanie. John knew she was sexy. Damn sexy, but he didn't want Aaron or any of his brothers to get any ideas. He didn't worry so much about the older three, but the younger three were dogs in heat most of the time.

"Jesus, John, he's only joking." Nick chuckled.

"I think John has some unreleased... shall we say... tension." Mike laughed.

"I can't say I blame him, living with a girl like her." Nick moved his eyebrows up and down.

"God damn it. Do you guys ever think about anything else?" John jumped to his feet and stomped out of the room.

He made his way to the kitchen and tossed his empty beer bottle in the recycling bin. In his heart, John knew neither of his brothers would make a move on Stephanie if they knew John was interested in her, but it was difficult to let it go when they teased him about her.

"Ya gonna tell me wat's boderin' ya?" Nanny Betty sat at the kitchen table, sipping her tea.

He hadn't seen her when he stomped into the kitchen and knew it would be impossible to hide things from her. Nanny Betty always knew when they were sad, happy, angry, or just needed a hug.

"It's nothing, Nan." John sighed.

"Johnny, ya may be able to fool some people, but ya can't fool me." Nanny Betty pointed to the chair next to her.

"Yeah, it's hard to fool you." John kissed her cheek and sat down.

"Tell me wat's got ya so bloody contrary." She pushed the plate of cookies toward him.

"I'm frustrated. I hate not being back to work." John didn't exactly lie, because he wanted to go back to his job.

He certainly wasn't about to discuss his sex life or lack of one with her. It made him cringe to think about it. The last thing he would do was tell her how he woke up every morning with an erection because of dreams about Stephanie.

"Dat may be part of it, ducky, but dat's not all of it," she said, and he knew she could probably read his thoughts.

"Nan, I don't want to talk about this." John cringed as he hung back his head and squeezed his eyes closed.

"Oh, I see. I'm guessin' Nicky wasn't far off da mark." John's head snapped up.

"Is there anything you can't figure out?" John felt the heat rush to his cheeks.

"No, and da sooner all a' ye figures dat out, da better off ye will be. Now, do ya want a little advice?" She pat his thigh and John nodded. "I tink ya need to follow yar heart. I've seen da way ye look at each other. Who wouldn't be attracted to one of my handsome grandsons? Cora says she's the one for ya, and my Cora is never wrong, but ya need to face yar feelins' before ya go any further." Nanny Betty stood up and left the kitchen.

John was grateful for how Stephanie helped him, but in his heart, John knew it was more. Talking to her was comfortable and natural. When they were together, he didn't want to be anywhere else. When they weren't together, she was always in his thoughts. It hit him like a slap in the face.

"I guess it's true. It hits you when you least expect it." He'd fallen in love with the woman and never realized it.

"What hits when you least expect it?" His mother's voice startled him.

John turned around as his mother placed a cup in the sink and joined him at the table. The last thing he needed was his mother getting excited about him being in love. She'd have a wedding planned ten minutes later.

"Nothing, just thinking out loud." John smiled.

"Don't you lie to me, young man." She poked John in the shoulder. "Besides, I can tell by the faraway look in your eyes."

"Mom." John threw his hands up in the air.

"If you love her, tell her. Don't waste time. Life is too short." His mother wrapped her arms around his neck and kissed his cheek.

"How do you and Nan know these things?" John hugged her tight.

"It's a mother thing." She pulled back and winked. "I like her, and she's good for you."

"Mom, we haven't even been out on a date," he said, remembering their movie night had been a mess.

"There's a reason Cora gave Stephanie the job with you." His mother raised an eyebrow.

"Yeah, I know. I needed a physical therapist." He laughed.

"That was part of it, but you know Cora has a gift, and when she met Stephanie, she knew. She's the one for you, John." His mom cupped his face between her hands.

"Mom, I love Aunt Cora, but I find it hard to believe she can tell someone is meant to be with someone else just by looking at them." John rolled his eyes.

"She's never been wrong. The first time I met her, she walked up to me and told me I was going to marry her brother." She stared over his shoulder as if lost in a happy memory.

It was pointless to argue with his mother about Cora's gift. She was a true believer, and as far as John knew, Cora had never been wrong. At least with his family.

The house was dark when John arrived home shortly after eleven. John was disappointed to see the apartment was also dark. He'd wanted to see Stephanie before he went to bed, if only for a minute. Maybe she wanted to avoid him.

With the containers of leftovers his mother forced him to take home put away, John headed to his bedroom. A faint sound made him pause outside his room. A whimper? A groan? What was it? The hair on the back of his neck prickled, and he knew something wasn't right.

John scanned the living room, but nothing was out of place. He checked the gym room, but everything seemed fine. He strained to hear the sound again as he walked down the hallway toward the apartment door. It was open slightly, and he knocked. Nobody answered.

"Stephanie," he called as he pushed open the door and entered the apartment, but she didn't answer.

Her car was in the driveway, which meant she had to be home. John left in such a hurry earlier in the day he hadn't even asked if she wanted to go to his parents for supper. All he wanted to do was put some space between them before he screwed up any chance he had with her.

"Stephanie," John called again as he walked into the bedroom.

There was no sign of her, and he was about to leave when he heard a thump from the bathroom. John pushed the bathroom door open and found Stephanie on the floor. Her hair hung over her face.

"Sweet Jesus, Stephanie." John fell to his knees and pushed her damp hair back.

Stephanie's eyes barely opened, but before he had a chance to speak, she pushed him away and hung over the toilet. John didn't hesitate to call one of the best doctors he knew.

"Hello." His father answered.

"Dad, can you get over here quick? I just found Stephanie on the bathroom floor in her apartment." John tried to remain calm, but this was Stephanie, and she didn't look right. "She's throwing up."

"I'll be right over," His dad returned.

John shoved his phone back in his pocket and searched the bathroom for where Stephanie put her towels and facecloths. He found a cloth in the small linen closet just outside the bathroom. John ran it under cold water and dropped to his knees next to Stephanie.

"Here, honey, put this on your head." John pushed back her hair from her face and pressed the cloth against her forehead.

"I can't stop throwing up." Her voice was weak.

John felt her head, but she didn't have a fever. Her face was ghostly white and soaked in sweat. Stephanie hunched over with her hands wrapped around her stomach and groaned.

"I'm going to help you to bed." John grabbed the bucket next to the toilet and helped Stephanie to her feet.

She couldn't stand on her own, so John hoisted her into his arms and made his way to her bed. His heart thudded in his chest as he gently placed her on the mattress. All John wanted to do was hold her until she felt better, but instead, he sat next to her and pressed a cold cloth to her head.

"Thanks," she sighed and rolled onto her side.

"I called my dad. He's on the way." John pushed her hair back over her shoulder.

"I think I ate something that didn't agree with me." She bolted upright, snatched the bucket from the nightstand, and started to retch again.

John rubbed his hand up and down her back in an attempt to help soothe her. She might have had food poisoning, and it's why he checked the fridge to make sure he got rid of any of the spoiled food.

"You need to drink some water, or you'll get dehydrated," he said as soon as the wave of vomiting stopped.

John checked both his fridge and hers, but he didn't find anything that could have made her so sick. He grabbed a couple of bottles of water from her fridge to bring it to her. He hurried back to her room and found Stephanie in the bathroom again. John knocked on the door.

"No. Don't come in." She gagged through her retching.

"I've got some water for you." he tried the door, but it was locked. "Sweetheart, open the door."

"No. I'm... uhh... please, give me a minute." She groaned.

Vomiting wasn't her only issue, and she was probably embarrassed. John fixed the blankets on the bed while he waited for her to return. A few minutes later, she walked out with her arms wrapped around her stomach. He managed to get her to sip some water before she climbed back into her bed.

Ten minutes later, his father walked through the door, and John left the room, so his dad could check her over. What the hell was wrong with her?

John paced the hallway after he searched the fridges a second time. He didn't find anything suspicious, and it concerned him. It seemed as if his dad had been in with her for hours, and when he was about to burst into the room, his father walked out of the room.

"Is she going to be okay?" John ran his hand through his hair.

"I'm pretty sure it's food poisoning, but I took some blood to confirm." Sean pulled a bottle out of his pocket.

"So, she'll be fine?" John tried to stay calm.

"Yes, but you should probably keep an eye on her tonight. Make sure she gets plenty of fluids into her." His father dropped his hand on John's shoulder. "She's going to be fine, son."

"I'll keep an eye on her." John sighed with relief.

"You should probably stay with her." His dad handed him a bottle. "Give her two spoonfuls every four hours for the next twenty-four hours."

"Thanks again, Dad." His father hugged him and headed out the door.

Thank God he had a doctor in the family. Actually, two doctors, but it would have taken Ian a lot longer to get to his house from town. His father only lived down the road.

John tiptoed into Stephanie's bedroom and dragged the chaise lounge next to the bed. Before he got comfortable, he grabbed a few more bottles of water and placed them next to her on the night table. He tucked her in bed and then switched off the lamp.

John made himself comfortable in the chair, or as much as he could. The moon illuminated the room and allowed him to see her face. She was a little pale, but still the most beautiful woman he'd ever seen.

"Sleep well, sweetheart." He set the alarm on his phone to wake him in four hours and then eased back on the chaise.

When the alarm went off, he woke with a start. He fumbled with his phone to shut it off and sighed when the loud buzz finally stopped.

"Why is your alarm going off at three in the morning?" Stephanie's voice croaked.

"Sorry, but Dad said you needed to take this medication every four hours. It's supposed to help settle your stomach." He measured out the dosage into a medicine cup and handed it to her.

"Oh. Thank you." She sat up.

"How do you feel?" He gave her the small cup of medicine and waited for her to swallow it before he handed her the bottle of water.

"Like I died." She groaned. "Why are you sleeping in my chair?"

"Dad said it was possibly food poisoning, and I needed to keep an eye on you." She pulled the blankets back and started to get up. "Whoa, where are you going?"

"I've got to... um... nature calls." She stumbled over her words.

"Oh, okay." John helped her stand up, and while she was in the bathroom, he fixed the blankets.

"You need to get some sleep. You're doing so well with your therapy, and you don't want to be exhausted in the morning," Stephanie complained when she returned from the bathroom.

"I don't think we'll be doing any therapy today." John stared into her eyes and knew those eyes were going to be the death of him. "You're going to be resting."

"I'll be fine tomorrow. Or today. Or... forget it. You know what I mean." She lay back and sighed.

"Dad said you needed to rest for the next twenty-four hours. So, you'll be staying in bed all day, Missy." John tucked the blankets around her.

"Hey. You're the client here, not me." Stephanie pointed her finger at him, and without thinking, he covered it with his hand and kissed the tip.

"Not for the next twenty-four hours, Honey." John made himself comfortable on the chaise and closed his eyes, but a minute later, she sighed. "What's wrong?"

"It's not good for your back to sleep on a chair." she sat up. "You're too big to be laying there all night."

"Are you calling me fat?" John feigned shock.

"Yeah, you are oh so fat." Stephanie rolled her eyes.

"I'll be fine for one night. Now go to sleep." John reassured her.

"If you insist on staying in here, at least lay in the bed. I can move over." The very time she asks him to sleep next to her, and she's sick.

"I'm fine here." His voice was tight.

"You're going to be cramped up in the morning if you sleep there." Stephanie wasn't going to go back to sleep unless she thought he was comfortable.

"Will you lie down and go to sleep if I lay down on the bed?" She might sleep, but he certainly wouldn't.

"I'll feel better if I know you aren't doing yourself more harm than good." She was going to drive him out of his mind.

"If it'll get you to got to sleep like you're supposed to do." He chuckled as Stephanie moved over, and John lay on top of the covers. "Happy now?"

"I'd be happier if it didn't feel as if a trunk ran over me. Are you sure I didn't get hit by a truck?" She grunted as she turned over on her side.

"I'm sure. Get some rest." John closed his eyes.

Hopefully, he could get some sleep too. The panic he felt when he found Stephanie on the floor finally eased, but it killed him to see her so sick. John had been in several situations where most people would panic, but he kept his wits about him. To see Stephanie on the floor, terrified him, and he turned his head to gaze at her. She'd gone to sleep quickly, so he closed his eyes again and prayed she'd be better in the morning.

How did he know something was wrong when he got home? Nanny Betty always said people could sense when something was wrong with someone they loved. When he opened his eyes again, Stephanie was watching him.

"I told you to get some rest," he whispered.

"You're awful bossy." She rolled her eyes.

"Payback's a bitch," John snorted as he rolled over on his side to face her.

"Thank you, John." She met his eyes, and as usual, his heart raced.

"You're welcome. Now go to sleep." He chuckled as she rolled her beautiful eyes once again.

John couldn't remember when he fell asleep, but he was so damn warm. He tried to move to get out of the sun, but there was a heaviness on his body, making it hard to move. Stephanie's head lay against his chest and her hand on his abdomen. It was wonderful to wake up with her in his arms. Her breath was hot through his T-shirt, and it heated his whole body. It felt right to lay next to her, but then she moved.

"Good morning." John felt a sudden loss as she pulled away from him.

"I don't know about good, but it's morning," she grumbled.

"Do you feel any better?" John quickly got up and measured out the medication.

"A little, I guess." Her hand trembled as she grabbed the small cup.

"You're spending the day resting, so anything you need, let me know." John held out a bottle of water to her.

"I can't spend all day in bed." She pulled back the covers and attempted to get up.

"Sorry, sweetheart, you don't have a choice." He pulled the covers back over her. "Doctor's orders."

She opened her mouth, then closed it again as she glared at him. He hid his grin as she propped her back against the headboard and crossed her arms over her chest.

"You want to try to eat? I can make you some toast or something." John made his way to the door of the bedroom.

"Maybe some dry toast. I still feel a little queasy." She didn't have the energy to argue.

"Okay. Do you want some tea?" He was a little suspicious as he left the room because she'd given in almost too easy.

John entered the room with a tray. Stephanie walked out of the bathroom and crawled back into the bed. She sat up as she yanked the blankets back over her, and he hid his grin. Stephanie was not happy to be stuck in bed.

He placed the tray on her lap as he studied her. Stephanie's face was still ashen, and she was still weak. His dad may need to make another house call before the day was over.

"Thanks for taking care of me, John." She glanced up and smiled.

"You've been taking care of me for weeks." He smiled. "I don't mind one bit. Besides, it was the best night's sleep I've had in weeks."

"Sorry about the crowding, I tend to navigate to the left side of the bed." Her face flushed, and she wouldn't look at him.

"I didn't mind." John knelt next to the bed and lifted her chin with his finger.

His thumb brushed across her lower lip. A small sigh escaped, and it went straight to his groin. He was a bastard to think about sex when she was barely able to bite into a piece of toast.

"Okay, how much longer do I need therapy?" He winked.

"John." She giggled.

"The last day of my therapy, woman, we've got a date." John kissed her forehead and left the bedroom to phone his dad.

The call to his father resulted in a voicemail message. While he waited for a return phone call, John grabbed a couple of bottles of water and went back to Stephanie's room. She was asleep, and it bothered him because he wasn't able to make her better right away. He couldn't imagine the pain it caused James to see Sarah fade away and not be able to fix it. It killed him to watch Stephanie with a stomach bug.

He was channel surfing when the doorbell rang. John raced to the door, so it didn't disturb Stephanie because the more she slept, the faster she would get better. Sandy stood on his step when he opened the door.

"Hey, Sandy." He motioned for her to come in.

"Hey. Is Stephanie around?" Sandy smiled and stepped inside.

"She's actually in bed. She got sick last night," he explained. "My dad thinks it was food poisoning."

"Oh, my God. We had supper together last night at *The Pier*." Sandy covered her mouth with her hand.

"You and Stephanie?" He asked.

"And her friend Donna. We all had the same thing." Sandy tilted her head in confusion.

"You look fine. I wonder if Donna is sick." He hadn't met Donna.

"I can call her. We exchanged numbers yesterday." Sandy pulled out her phone, and John waited as Sandy spoke to Donna.

If the three women had the same thing to eat, why wasn't Sandy sick? Sandy shook her head as she ended the call, which told John, Donna was fine.

"Maybe, it was the combination of having Kim serve us and her ex showing up with his girlfriend." Sandy raised an eyebrow.

"Her ex?" It was as if Sandy punched him in the gut.

"Yeah, his name is Brad, but he was kind of a jerk from what she told me. She turned pale and wanted to leave right away," Sandy explained.

"Did Kim say anything to her?" He would deal with Kim if the woman upset Stephanie.

"She asked Stephanie if she had gotten into your pants yet." Sandy rolled her eyes. "But Stephanie didn't seem fazed by it."

Stephanie may have been upset, but there was no way seeing both of their exes would make her so sick. He plowed his hand through his hair.

"I hope it didn't upset her." John glanced over his shoulder toward the apartment.

"I've got to run, but tell Stephanie I hope she feels better, and if you need anything, let me know," Sandy told him after she looked down at her phone.

John made his way back to Stephanie's bedroom. He found her stood next to the bed with her hands braced on the mattress. When she saw him, she sighed.

189

"Where are you going?" John leaned against the doorframe.

"I was going to get my laptop, but my legs are a little shaky." She plopped back on the bed.

"I'll get it, but first I've got a question." He needed to find out about her ex.

"Okay. What?" She leaned against the headboard.

"What happened at the restaurant last night?" He placed her laptop on the bed as he sat next to her.

"Nothing." She wouldn't look at him as she reached for her computer.

"Sandy just left and told me you saw your ex, as well as mine." He pulled the computer away from her.

"It's nothing." She pushed her hair behind her ear.

"That's not what Sandy said." He crossed his arms over his chest.

"Sandy has a big mouth." She rolled her eyes and held her hand out for her computer.

"Tell me." John wouldn't give in until he knew everything.

"Will you give me my computer if I do?" Stephanie groaned.

"I will." John placed it next to her.

"It's no big deal. I dated Brad for four years. I assumed we'd eventually get married." She sighed and then continued. "The last six months our work schedules clashed, and we didn't spend much time together. He's a fireman. One night I got off early and came home to surprise him, but he wasn't home. I picked up my cell to call him, but I heard the key in the lock, and he came through the door with a woman. They were all over each other. He didn't see me at first, and they were half-naked before he realized I was there. I couldn't speak; I was in shock."

"It's okay. You don't have to tell me." He never wanted to hurt someone so bad in his life, and it tore his heart out to think she'd been hurt.

"No. I need to get this out. I did manage to scream at him to get out. He left, but when I got home from work the next day, I knew he was back and cleared out all his things. He also cleared out the account we had for our bills. He took every cent." She narrowed her eyes in anger.

"Can you prove who put the money in the account?" John would gladly arrest the asshole.

"Right now, the lawyers are hashing it out." She sighed.

"I'm not a hundred percent sure, but I think if you lived together for more than six months, everything goes fifty-fifty." John had seen enough domestic situations to know some things about cohabitation situations.

"I know. That's what my lawyer said." She ran her hands through her hair.

"Well, let the lawyers deal with it, and don't worry." He covered her up and left the room.

He couldn't believe how pissed he felt over the way her ex mistreated her. He left the room because she didn't need to be upset by his anger.

John sat down in the armchair and rested his head against the back. He closed his eyes for a moment as he took several deep breaths and let them out slowly. It was a trick Stephanie taught him in the early days of his therapy to help ease his tension when he was frustrated.

The worst thing about Stephanie's trick was most of the time, he fell asleep, or he was so relaxed everything around him disappeared. He didn't even realize he fell asleep until his phone vibrated in his pocket and startled him. He pulled it out, and his father's picture showed on the screen.

"Hey, Dad." John sat up and yawned.

"How's Stephanie today?" His father asked.

"She seems better. No more vomiting, just tired." She'd been asleep most of the day.

"I'm not surprised." His father cleared his throat. "John, her blood work showed traces of Ipecac in her system."

"What's that?" Panic coursed through his veins.

"It used to be used to induce vomiting, but not anymore. What worries me is, I know people with Bulimia and Anorexia who use it to make themselves sick." Okay, his father was crazy, because Stephanie was too health-conscious to be making herself sick.

"Dad, there's got to be a mistake," John insisted.

"There's no mistake, but I'm going to come over and talk to her," his dad said. "There wasn't a lot in her system, but I'd like to know if she took it herself, or if someone slipped it in her food or drink."

192

There was no way John believed Stephanie would take something to make herself sick. The thought of someone slipping it to her made him furious. The muscles that were so relaxed a few minutes earlier were now so tense it was almost painful.

He ended the call with his father and made his way to her room. She was still asleep, and he needed to make sure he was right about her. He knew deep down she'd never do something to harm herself.

John quietly walked into her bathroom and searched the medicine cabinet. *Nothing.* Under her sink. *Cleaners.* What the hell was he doing? He didn't believe she took anything. John left her bathroom and stopped when he saw her sat up in the bed. It made him feel two inches tall to have doubted her.

"Feeling better." Hopefully, the casual tone he tried didn't show the guilt he felt.

"A little." she tilted her head and stared at him. "Is there something you're looking for in the bathroom?"

He couldn't lie to her, but he didn't want to accuse her either. Since the first day Stephanie arrived, she'd preached about the right food to eat. They spent a lot of time together, and John never heard her throw up or refuse to eat until he returned home the previous night.

"John, is something going on?" Stephanie asked.

"I've got a question to ask you." He sat next to her on the bed.

"You're making me worry. What is it?" She wrapped her arms around herself.

"Have you heard of Ipecac?" He knew Stephanie would never do something to hurt herself.

"Isn't it some sort of syrup used to induce vomiting?" She knew what it was, but it didn't mean she was using it.

"Yes." He watched her face for any sign of nervousness.

"That's a weird thing to ask." She furrowed her brows.

"Your blood work showed you had Ipecac in your system," John explained.

For a moment, she stared at him, but then her eyes grew wide, and her mouth dropped open. The shocked expression proved she had not taken it herself.

"How would it get in my system? I'd never take that." Stephanie looked as if she would burst into tears.

"I don't know, but from what Sandy told me, the only thing you ate before you got sick was the food at the restaurant." There wasn't any way she'd ingest it accidentally.

"You think someone deliberately tried to make me sick?" She pressed her fingertips against her temples.

"Not sure, but it seems a little suspicious, especially since you ran into Kim and your ex at the same restaurant." John hated to accuse people of things without proof.

"Brad wouldn't. I mean, he's a jerk, but I really can't see him doing something to hurt me." She didn't sound sure.

194

"I wouldn't think Kim would either, but I've seen a lot of people do things you'd never expect," he said

As a police officer, John knew too well people could be capable of horrible things when pushed too far. Love, obsession, and anger could make a person lose all reason and turn into a dangerous individual.

"I'm calling Uncle Kurt to see what he thinks. He might want to talk to Brad and Kim." John wanted to question them himself, but he would never be permitted to do it.

John's dad dropped by later in the evening to check on her. He told John she would be fine, but she should still take it easy for the rest of the day. After his father left, John ensured a frustrated Stephanie remained in bed for the rest of the day. She was stubborn, but since she still felt weak, he won the war of wills.

While he waited for Kurt to call, John wasn't optimistic they could find who poisoned her. If there wasn't proof, nothing could be done. He was tempted to have a chat with Brad and Kim himself, but Kurt insisted it wasn't the wise option.

"How's our girl?" Nanny Betty barged through the front door.

John jumped to his feet and grabbed the containers his grandmother balanced in her arms. The visit shouldn't have surprised him because when someone was sick, Nan cooked up a storm, and then she'd deliver it as quickly as possible. Nobody ever questioned if his seventy-two-year-old grandmother should still drive, mostly because everyone valued their lives.

195

"She's doing better, Nan." John kissed her cheek. "What are you doing here?"

Nan pushed him aside and headed for Stephanie's bedroom with John behind her. The fact she came to deliver food didn't mean she wasn't going to check on Stephanie. He wasn't going to stop her, not that he could.

"I'm here ta check on our girl." Nanny Betty scurried to the side of the bed and put her hand against Stephanie's forehead. "At least dere's no fever."

"She was stomach sick." John stood in the doorway arms full of the containers.

"Don't jus' stand dere heat up some a' dat turkey broth and bring it here for da girl. She needs her strength." Stephanie's eyes opened, and she stared at Nanny Betty. "Go on wit ya."

John shook his head as he turned and left the room. He probably should have stayed with Stephanie, but when Nanny Betty took over, she was the boss. It's why he did what she told him.

Chapter 16

She'd been stuck in bed for two days but finally started to eat solid food. Mostly because Nanny Betty insisted, and Stephanie couldn't say no to the woman. It amused her to see how the tiny woman bossed John, Sean, Kurt, and John's brothers around as if they were little boys. Even Cora, Kathleen, and Alice jumped when Nanny Betty spoke.

Stephanie was concerned that the days she was forced to stay in bed would set John back in his therapy. When she asked Kathleen about it, John's mother chuckled and explained Nanny Betty made sure John did his daily exercises. Earlier in the morning, when John wanted to take a day off of his therapy, Nanny Betty grabbed his ear and tugged him out of Stephanie's room.

"Just because she's sick, ya don't get no time off." Nanny Betty lectured as she left with John.

John didn't argue, but Stephanie could see he wanted to say something. Stephanie was fine with John taking a break from the therapy for one day. Especially since he'd started to do a scaled-down version of the exercise routine he'd done before his accident.

The only problem for Stephanie was John was closer to not needing her anymore. The thought made her heart hurt.

The other issue was Kurt had Kim and Brad questioned, but neither of them had any idea what happened. There was no way to prove either of them did it either. Kurt had contacted the manager of the restaurant and explained the situation, but he insisted it had to be an isolated incident or someone's idea of a joke. John and Kurt didn't think it was the least bit funny; neither did Stephanie. The only option was to forget about it and move on.

The next four weeks flew by so fast, Stephanie could barely believe it. John only had therapy one day a week, but Cora still paid Stephanie the same as she did in the beginning. When she mentioned it to her boss, Cora insisted she continue until the end of her contract.

Since Marina moved away, Stephanie and Sandy spent a lot of time together. Donna would drop by a couple of times a week, and on her days off, Stephanie would go to her parents' house. The rest of the time, she was with John, and she loved it.

They watched movies, played cards, or talked. Sometimes she caught John looking at her, and it would take her breath away. His massage sessions were not any easier, but she discovered if she concentrated on the tattoo on his left shoulder, it went much better. John told her the tattoo was their family crest, and all his brothers, his father, mother, cousins, uncles, and aunts had the same one. Even his grandmother and grandfather had both gotten the tattoo as well.

However, John had joked Nanny Betty would never tell anyone where she had gotten hers.

John was supposed to have massage therapy but asked to change it. He'd made plans to spend the day with his brothers, and then they'd be back to John's house to watch a hockey game. So, she was free the entire day but alone. Sandy had plans, and Donna had a shift. Her parents were gone to visit Marina and Danny in Ottawa.

She'd cleaned her apartment all morning, but it only killed a little over two hours. She scrolled through Facebook several times, but it was depressing because so many of the posts were about parties. She had just turned on the television when she heard a light knock on the apartment door. Her heart jumped with excitement, fully expecting to see John. To her disappointment, when she opened the door, a pretty brunette, with bright blue eyes, stood there with a huge smile on her face.

"Hi." Stephanie was polite, but the little green-eyed monster crawled up onto her shoulder.

"Hi, Stephanie." The girl reached out and shook Stephanie's hand. "I'm Kristy."

"Nice to meet you." Stephanie hoped her smile looked genuine.

She hated the sick feeling she got thinking the pretty woman was the reason John canceled his therapy. She seemed a little young for John, but something seemed familiar about Kristy. Stephanie's thoughts raced as she tried to figure out how she knew the girl.

"Okay, I can tell by the look on your face, you've got no idea who I am." Kristy chuckled.

"I'm sorry, but no." Stephanie dropped her shoulders in relief because the girl didn't seem offended in the least.

"I'm John's cousin. Kurt and Alice are my parents." Stephanie had seen her picture on John's wall. "I just moved back from Nova Scotia, and James invited my sisters and me over for the game."

"That's cool." Stephanie didn't want to be rude, but Kristy only made her feel worse about her night alone.

"Anyway, Mike told me you were here, and I wanted to meet you. I also wanted to thank you for helping John. He's back to himself. So anyway, since John's too stupid to invite you over for the party, I decided to invite you." Kristy put her hands on her hips. "But your invite depends on which hockey team you like, Toronto or Montreal?"

"Montreal has always been my favorite." Stephanie was almost afraid to answer, but she couldn't lie.

"Woohoo." Kristy grabbed Stephanie's hand and pulled her to John's living room. "This is one intelligent girl."

"Please don't tell me you're a Habs fan." John narrowed his eyes, but she could see the hint of a smile.

"Sorry, but Montreal is my team." Stephanie giggled as Kristy dragged her to the couch.

"I used to like you," John grumbled.

"You still do." A girl sat on the floor, elbowed John in the leg. "I'm Jess, and much to the boys' dismay, a Montreal fan." She grinned.

"Is it started yet?" the only cousin she'd met entered from the hallway.

"Isabelle took the night off from her restaurant to be here tonight." John leaned toward her, and his warm breath blew across her neck, making her shiver.

"Hey, Stephanie." Isabelle sat on the arm of the couch next to John. "Too bad you couldn't cure his hockey team." John shoved her with his elbow, almost knocking her to the floor.

"Asshole." Isabelle smacked John's arm.

"You want a beer or something?" Mike carried a large tray filled with bottles.

"She's a Montreal fan, bro." Ian grabbed a bottle as he put a fake grimace on his handsome face.

"Get out." Mike pointed toward the door.

"You shut up, jerkwad. She's a smart woman." Kristy grabbed two bottles and handed one to Stephanie.

"Sorry, guys, but Montreal is a better team." Stephanie clinked bottles with Kristy.

"No wonder Aunt Cora hired her," Keith scoffed. "For some reason, all the women in this family cheer for the Habs."

Keith's lips quirked up into a small smile as if he had some huge secret. He was the middle brother, but he didn't talk much. She

201

hadn't seen him smile much either, but when he did, it could melt a woman's heart.

Stephanie tried hard to concentrate on the game, but being sat next to John played havoc with her hormones. His thigh pressed against hers, and his muscles flexed every time his team came close to scoring. Anytime Montreal scored, a deep groan would come from his throat, and Stephanie's mouth would go dry. It wasn't meant to be sexual, but it sounded that way to her.

"You guys are so screwed." Kristy squealed as Montreal scored their fourth goal.

As the Toronto player raced toward the opposing net, John leaned forward. Stephanie stiffened when his hand grabbed her knee. He probably didn't realize it, but the closer the team got to the net, the tighter he squeezed. It should have been painful, but all it did was make her entire body vibrate.

"Go. Go. Go," John and his brothers yelled at the television as the girls screamed at the goalie, but Stephanie couldn't speak.

"Damn it." John flopped back, and his arm dropped across the back of the couch, grazing the back of her neck. "I can't believe you're a Habs fan."

"I only cheer for winners," she teased.

"I didn't know you were so mean." John narrowed his eyes, and then a sexy smile spread across his face.

"No, just smart." She giggled when he poked her side. "Hey."

She grabbed his hand, and he tightened his grip. She turned and met his gaze. She felt as if she couldn't breathe, and her heart pounded. For a short moment, she thought he was about to kiss her, but a shout from the girls drew his attention toward the television.

"You owe me twenty bucks, A.J. I told you they'd win." Isabelle held out her hand, and Aaron slapped a twenty-dollar bill into Isabelle's hand.

The television went off, and everyone started to wander around the house. The girls gloated, and the boys tried to come up with a good excuse for their team's loss. John didn't move, and even though they were the only two sitting on the couch, she still sat pressed against his side.

"I hope they didn't turn you off of hockey," John asked, and when she turned, he tucked a piece of her hair behind her ear.

"Not at all. I had fun." His eyes burned into hers, and she couldn't look away if she tried.

"I'm glad you joined us." His eyes moved to her lips. "Really, glad."

His strong masculine scent enveloped her as he leaned closer. She had no idea what kind of soap he used, but it made her want to bury her nose in his neck and inhale.

His lips brushed against hers, soft but unsure, and she swallowed hard as she leaned into him. His lips teased hers as he slid his hands into her hair and deepened the kiss. She opened her mouth to his tongue, and John plunged it into her mouth. His taste was addictive, and she needed more. Her fingers tangled through his hair to pull him even closer. She'd almost completely forgotten there were nine other people in the house until she heard someone clear their throat. Stephanie jumped back and glanced toward the voice.

"Umm... sorry to interrupt. I'll come back later. Carry on." Nick grinned as he disappeared back into the kitchen.

Her cheeks were warm, along with another part of her anatomy, but it was a different kind of hot. She covered her face with her hands and groaned.

"I didn't mean for that to happen right now," John whispered into her ear.

"It's okay. I'm sure it didn't mean anything." She stood, but he shot to his feet and grabbed her hand.

"I didn't say it didn't mean anything." John put a finger under her chin and forced her to look at him. "I didn't plan on doing it with a house full of people." His thumb brushed across her lips.

"I wasn't paying attention to the people." She gazed into his eyes.

"Me either, but right now, I want to kick them out," he whispered as he pressed his forehead against hers.

"I'm sure they wouldn't be happy about you throwing them out." Stephanie lay her hand against his chest.

"I don't care." He kissed her cheek and then moved his lips lightly across hers.

"Hey, bro. Oh. Shit. Sorry." Another voice behind her, and she closed her eyes.

"Get out, A.J.," John growled over her shoulder.

"Okay. Yep. I'm gone." Aaron whistled as he left the living room, and John feathered his lips against hers again.

"I think we should probably stop right now." Stephanie sighed as his tongue ran across her bottom lip.

"I don't want to stop. Since the first time I met you, all I wanted to do was kiss you," he whispered into her ear. "Along with other things, but you're right. I should get rid of everyone first."

"I think we need to talk before other things," she replied.

"We do. I've got a lot I want to say." He backed away from her and winked.

Stephanie had lots to say as well. She hoped what John had to say was something she wanted to hear.

Chapter 17

He'd finally kissed her again, and he could thank his family and the little bit of liquid courage. He'd gotten a taste of her again, so there was no going back. First, he needed to get his brothers and cousins out of his house. The want in her eyes after he kissed her made his jeans uncomfortable, and he couldn't adjust himself while she stood in front of him.

"I better see why they keep interrupting." He backed away from her and entered the kitchen.

John ignored the blatant stares from everyone as he grabbed a beer out of his fridge. Nick or Aaron wouldn't keep what they saw to themselves, especially since they teased him about it constantly. John leaned against the counter as he popped the cap off his bottle.

"What?" He shoved one hand in his pocket and sipped his beer.

"So, how's therapy going?" Keith was the last person he expected to speak.

His quiet brother's lips twitched, and if John had made a bet on who would be the first to start with the digs, Keith would have been his last choice.

"Fine." John crossed his ankles.

"I bet it is." Mike wiggled his eyebrows.

John glared because he knew exactly what Mike thought. From the glances he got, they all had the same thoughts. He certainly wouldn't mind getting hot and sweaty with Stephanie, but for him, it was much deeper than a sexual attraction.

"I like her." Jess linked her arm into John's and lay her head on his shoulder.

"Me too." Kristy agreed and then poked Nick after he made a comment John didn't hear.

"I think John does too." Ian chuckled.

"What did you asses want?" John cleared his throat.

"Some of what you were about to get." And there it was, Aaron's perverted thoughts.

"We've been asked to perform for a fundraiser. You know the one the NPD throws every year for the Janeway?" Nick shoved Aaron and almost knocked the youngest brother off the chair.

The NPD or Newfoundland Police Department threw a major fundraiser every year for the local children's hospital. The Janeway was the only children's hospital in the province and was one of the major charities the police supported.

"The guy filling in for you is good, but it's not the same. We miss you." Mike winked at him.

John lifted the bottle of beer to his lips to cover his grin. To find out they missed him made him feel good, and he did enjoy it when they all played together.

"We were wondering if you're feeling up to it." Nick picked up where Mike left off.

The band was more of a hobby for them, but it was something the brothers shared. Ian, Keith, and James didn't perform publicly but helped with backstage things and moving equipment. The other two guys in the band were friends of Nick and Aaron, but they'd become adopted brothers.

"When is it?" John asked.

"Saturday night," Aaron said.

"This Saturday?" It was only three days away. "It's not much time to practice. I haven't played or sang in months."

"Like you need to practice." Isabelle snorted.

"Come on. If it doesn't interfere with your therapy, we can rehearse here for a couple of days." Mike started to beg. "It's not like we'll be playing anything we haven't done a thousand times."

"Friday night we can do a short rehearsal at the ballroom." Nick had a look he gave his parents when he wanted something as a kid.

He wasn't the only one. Kristy had her hands clasped together as if she were saying a prayer. Isabelle kept nodding, and Jess kept repeating the word *yes*. The hopeful look on their faces was comical.

"For fuck sakes. Stop with the puppy eyes." John rolled his eyes. "I'll do it."

The group erupted in cheers, and they surrounded him. They all spoke at once, and all he could hear was how happy they were to have the group was back together.

"Good to have you back, bro." James shook his hand.

One by one, his brothers and cousins left, and each one advised what he should do about Stephanie. Aaron's advice was X-rated, and Nick offered to take John's place if he was too tired. He loved his brothers, but sometimes John wanted to pretend they were not related.

John expected to see Stephanie waiting once everyone left, but he walked into the living room, and it was empty. After their kiss, she was not going to get away from him so easily. He knocked softly on the door to her apartment and waited. Maybe she changed her mind, and until she opened the door, his stomach was in knots. He was relieved she didn't run for the hills.

"Hi." He braced his shoulder against the door frame.

"Hi." She smiled at him, and his heart rate increased. "Is your family gone?"

"Yes." John gazed into her eyes.

"Did you want to talk?" She leaned her cheek against the door, and he was suddenly jealous of the door.

"Yes." He nodded.

Stephanie stepped back and motioned toward the couch. John walked into her apartment and sat down, but she seemed reluctant to move from the doorway.

"If all you want to do is talk, I'm okay with talking. I'll be glad to spend time with you." John held out his hand.

Stephanie sat next to him and clasped her hands in her lap. John chuckled because she seemed as nervous as he was. John hooked his finger under her chin to turn her face so he could see her eyes.

"Just talking, Honey." He reassured her.

"I'm sorry. I don't know why I'm so nervous." She smiled and relaxed.

"I don't want to make you feel uncomfortable." He wanted her to be comfortable with him.

"John, I..." She stopped and looked down. "I'm attracted to you. Really, attracted."

"That's good, sweetheart, because, in case you haven't noticed, I'm attracted to you too." He covered her hand with his.

"Are you sure this attraction isn't because I've helped you get back on your feet again?" She didn't pull her hand away, and it made him feel as if he had a win there.

"Is that what you think?" John asked.

"It's quite common for patients to fall for their nurses, doctors, therapists, and so on." She stared at him, and John put his finger to her lips.

"Stephanie, I'm extremely grateful for what you've done for me. I don't think I could've done it otherwise." She lowered her head, and he ducked his head to see her eyes. "But these feelings I have for you have nothing to do with that. From the day I pulled you over, I felt something, and to be honest, when I found out you were my therapist, I was happy but embarrassed. I didn't want you to see me so broken and out of shape."

"There was nothing wrong with your shape." Stephanie giggled, and her cheeks flushed.

"I wasn't exactly at peak form." John ran a finger down her cheek. "Those rubdowns were hell."

"I know they hurt at the beginning, but it's because your muscles were so tight." Her expression filled with concern, and her smile faded.

"Not what I meant. There was one stiff muscle, but you weren't paying attention to it." John raised an eyebrow, and for a moment, she stared at him.

"Oh." The color in her cheeks made her even more beautiful.

"It was difficult to relax when all I wanted was to pull you down on the table." John allowed his gaze to travel across her face and studied every feature as he spoke.

"I didn't mean to put you through that," she returned.

"I know you weren't trying to torture me." He ran a finger down her jaw. "It was amazing torture."

"It wasn't easy for me either, you've got an amazing body," she whispered as he brushed his thumb across her lower lip, and a small sound escaped her mouth.

"Stephanie, I want to kiss you again, but if I do, I won't be able to stop with a simple kiss, and I want to do this right." John stared into her eyes because if he focused on her lips again, he wasn't going to be able to keep from devouring her mouth. "I want a date."

"You do?" Her smile lit up her face.

"I don't want this to start the wrong way. I care about you." John took her hands in his.

"I care about you too." She linked their fingers.

There was an issue with their date. John promised to perform with his brothers for the fundraiser. Which meant being tied up for the next three days, and the closest thing he could think of was the fundraiser.

"I'd like you to be my date for a fundraiser on Friday, but I won't get to spend much time with you." It certainly wasn't a dream date.

"Is it formal?" She caressed his finger with her thumb.

"It's black tie." He was practically holding his breath as he waited for her to answer.

"I'd love to go." She gave him the biggest smile he'd ever seen on her, and John grinned as he mentally pumped his fist in the air

They sat together on her couch while he gave Stephanie all the details about the Janeway fundraiser. He rambled on because he didn't want the night to end. Unfortunately, when she covered her mouth to stifle a yawn, John knew it was time to leave.

John walked her to the apartment. He didn't want to walk away from her, but he wanted to do things right. John saw his future when he looked at her.

Chapter 18

To say Stephanie was thrilled would be an understatement.
When he kissed her, it made her toes curl and set her body on fire
with desire. If she was truthful, she felt it in other places as well.
She'd never had a kiss affect her so much, and it amazed and
terrified her all at the same time. Stephanie had fallen hard and fast
for John, and if things went wrong, it would shatter her.

Oh, brother.

Sleep was not her friend, and after a restless night, Stephanie
gave up. Which meant she was up at five in the morning to see the
sunrise over the ocean. How many people could look out their
window to see such beauty?

The rest of the day, she cleaned her apartment, which took
about thirty minutes since she'd cleaned like a lunatic the previous
day. To make matters worse, it was her day off. It meant there
wasn't a reason to go into his half of the house, but she desperately
wanted to see him.

John wouldn't need much more therapy, which made her feel
sad. He seemed to regain nearly all his strength and mobility. When
he worked out, she didn't have to be in the room, but she would not

miss out on a chance to see his muscles ripple with every push-up or sit up.

"Grrrr... this is insane. Stop thinking about him." She groaned.

Stephanie grabbed her iPad and forced herself to sit down. It was time she got started on the numerous books she'd downloaded. Reading always killed time.

Deep into a murder mystery, she was startled by loud ringing from the phone. Her arms flew up, and the iPad tumbled to the floor. Stephanie cursed under her breath as she glanced at the screen to see a blocked caller. Who would block their number? *Marina.* Her sister got a new phone number since she'd moved away, and she made sure it was unlisted. After she answered, the voice on the other end made her muscles tense, and her teeth clench.

"Where's my wife and son?" Marc screamed into her ear.

"First of all, she won't be your wife much longer. She already filed for divorce, Marc, or are you so high you don't remember." Stephanie shook because she never thought she could hate anyone so much.

"Listen here, you self-righteous bitch, my marriage is none of your fucking business," Marc shouted. "I want to know where she is. Right now."

"I wouldn't tell you where they were if you were on your death bed, asshole," she raised her voice and gripped the phone tighter.

"If you don't tell me right fucking now, you'll be in for a world of hurt, little girl." His voice sounded sinister, but Stephanie wasn't afraid of him.

"Fuck off, and drop dead. I'm not afraid of you. Marina's where you can't hurt her, or Danny, so move on with your pathetic life and don't ever call me again." Stephanie ended the call and tossed her phone on the couch.

She pressed her fists into her eyes and roared as she shook with rage. Stephanie never felt so angry in her entire life. Marc put her sister through hell, and if he thought he would get information from her, he was sadly mistaken.

She needed to calm herself. Stephanie closed her eyes and took several deep breaths as she sat back on the sofa. Her body muscles started to relax, and she felt the horrible hatred dissipate until a knock made her jolt upright.

Jumpin' Jesus.

"Come in," she squawked, but when the door opened, her heart skipped.

"Is everything okay, sweetheart?" She cringed as she saw the concern on John's handsome face.

"I just got a call from my soon to be ex-brother-in-law," she explained as John sat next to her. "He wanted me to tell him where Marina and Danny are, and I'm not telling him anything. It's a long story, and I don't talk about him because he makes me so bloody angry."

216

Stephanie pressed her lips together because she'd started to ramble. As much as they had talked over the last few months, Stephanie still hadn't told John about her sister's situation. The only thing John knew was Marina's marriage was over, and her ex-husband was out of the picture.

"Is he dangerous?" John couldn't hide the police officer in him if he tried.

"Not to me, but he put Marina through a lot, and she's finally getting back on her feet. She's away from him, and I'm happy she is." She swallowed against the lump in her throat because she knew Marc was the main reason her sister left Newfoundland.

"If he starts bothering you, let me know." It was comforting to know John wanted to protect her.

"I'll be fine." she smiled. "Was there something else?"

"I just wanted to let you know; it's gonna be a bit loud here for a few hours. My brothers are here to rehearse." As he spoke, she could hear the sound of footfalls outside her door.

"Can I watch?" The words were out of her mouth before she could stop them.

"Sure, but most of the music we do isn't recent stuff. Mostly the oldies, the sixties, seventies, and eighties stuff. We do some country too. We also play some Newfie tunes, but it depends on the venue." He was obviously proud of their group.

"I grew up listening to that music. My parents listened to all kinds of music." Her mom and dad always had music around the house, and long road trips meant what she and Marina used to refer to as *old people music,* but she'd grown to love it.

"Mine too. I guess it's why we started to play it." John stood and headed toward the door. "We're getting the equipment set up. Should be ready in about an hour."

John opened the door but stopped. He turned and stared at her for a moment. It seemed as if something was on his mind, but he didn't know if he should say it. He closed the door again before he spoke.

"Are you sure you're okay? If you need me to help with this, I can shut this rehearsal down and go report this guy?" John motioned over his shoulder.

"I'm fine. Really. He doesn't worry me," Stephanie assured him, but it made her feel so incredible he wanted to protect her.

John seemed to contemplate her answer before he disappeared through her door, but not before she got a glimpse of his snug jeans hugging his ass perfectly. The man was sex on a stick; there was no question about it. Stephanie flopped back on the couch with a sigh.

Her thoughts returned to Marina. She wondered if she should contact her sister and let her know Marc called. Marina would worry if she thought Marc wanted to cause trouble. Marina was happy now, or at least seemed to be. She was over two thousand kilometers away, and Marc wouldn't be able to find her.

Stephanie closed her eyes, took a couple of deep breaths, and the tension in her body eased. The faint sound of music drifted in from the house, and she listened. She didn't recognize the song, and she strained to hear it. She grabbed her phone and headed to the door, but as she pulled it open, she almost ran into Kristy.

"I was coming to get you." Kristy laughed. "They're ready to start, and the guys have a surprise song for John."

"Oh?" Stephanie followed John's cousin into the living room.

"Something about motivational music, but the guys hope he'll think it's a good addition to their list." Kristy grinned.

The room no longer looked like John's living room with the furniture pushed back to the corners. The center of the floor contained a set of drums, two microphone stands, and a keyboard near the window, next to a couple of guitars.

"You know, that part of the family got all the talent." Kristy grabbed Stephanie's hand and dragged her over to the couch.

"Why don't, Ian, Keith, and James play with them?" Stephanie noticed the three brothers appeared to have other jobs.

James leaned against the doorframe with an iPad in his hand, discussing something with Nick. Ian sat on the arm of the chair with a clipboard in his hand as Keith checked the equipment and made sure everything was plugged in.

"Trust me, they have pipes, but they never enjoyed being in the spotlight. Especially Keith," Kristy said. "They stay on the sidelines like me and help set everything up, but honestly, James is an amazing singer. Ian can sing too, and Keith can play pretty much any instrument you put in front of him."

"Do Isabelle and Jess help out?" Stephanie had gotten to know the three sisters and liked them a lot.

"Isabelle doesn't have time. The restaurant is pretty much her entire life. Jess, well, let's say Jess doesn't want to be around the members of the band who are not related. Well, at least one of them anyway." Kristy motioned to the two other men.

"I was wondering who they were." Stephanie sat back on the couch.

"The drummer is Cory Fleming, and he went to high school with A.J. They are in the police academy together. The guitar player is Jason Brenton. He went to law school with Mike," Kristy explained.

"Which one is the reason Jess isn't here?" Stephanie asked.

"That would be Jason. Jess used to date him, but something happened, and now they can't even be in the same room together. Jess hasn't told anyone what happened, and apparently, neither has Jason." Kristy shrugged.

"Not good," Stephanie said, and Kristy nodded in agreement.

Once John walked into the living room, her conversation with Kristy was over. Even with the abundance of gorgeous men around, he was the only one to cause her breath to hitch. His jeans hung low on his slim hips, and a grey T-shirt clung to his defined chest and abdominals.

John seemed to search for her when he entered the room. His eyes found her, and her cheeks warmed. It appeared when he entered a room it was as if nobody else existed to Stephanie. It was just her and him, but Kristy broke the spell when she nudged Stephanie's shoulder.

"I think my cousin might have a little crush on you," Kristy teased.

Stephanie was a little smitten herself. Who was she kidding? He completely bewitched her, but she couldn't tell Kristy, because if there was one thing she learned, Kristy was a bit of a blabbermouth.

"Before we start, we've got a song we want to play for John." The sound of Aaron's voice echoed through the room.

He motioned for John to sit on the stool James moved behind him. John narrowed his eyes as he hopped up on the seat and waited. He seemed a little apprehensive about what his brothers were up to. Especially with the way Aaron grinned.

When the music started, Stephanie recognized it right away. *Eye of the Tiger.* She glanced at John to see his reaction. He shook his head, but there was a big smile on his face.

"This is for you, bro," Aaron shouted before he began to sing.

Stephanie had to admit, it sounded great. Aaron had a fantastic voice, and she was impressed. She glanced at John, and he nodded along with the music with a grin on his handsome face. When the song ended, John slid off the stool and approached Aaron.

"I know you're attempting to poke fun, but it sounded great." John slapped Aaron on the shoulder.

"I want to do it, though. This beautiful woman I know said it could be motivational. A lot of those sick kids need motivation, and

221

maybe it can motivate people to donate more." A small lump formed in her throat, and she noticed Aaron's typical mischievous grin was gone.

Aaron was sincere, and she could see even with his playboy ways, he had a heart of gold for the kids. Stephanie's eyes filled with tears as John ruffled his younger brother's hair.

"You're right, A.J., motivation helps, and we should do it." John turned and winked at Stephanie.

She knew her face probably glowed red, but she didn't care. When John looked at her, it took everything she had not to run across the room and jump his bones. Luckily, she had some willpower and stayed next to Kristy to enjoy the music.

For the next few hours, they played dozens of songs. Some Stephanie recognized as favorites of her parents, but others she didn't know. Ian wrote down each song they agreed to add to the playlist on his clipboard. James and Keith stepped in to play instruments when one of the other guys stepped away. For a bunch of guys who only did this as a hobby, they were impressive. They were better than a lot of bands she heard on the radio.

"Hey, John, what about, *You are the Woman* by *Firefall*? It's one of Mom's favorites, and she expects you to sing it every time." James glanced over at Stephanie and grinned. "I think you've got the inspiration for it in front of you."

Stephanie didn't recognize the band or the song, but with the way everyone kept looking at her, she had a feeling it was probably a love song.

"Come on, John, let's see if you still got it, big brother," Nick teased.

Ian pulled the stool next to the microphone, and John sat with one foot on the rung of the chair and the other on the floor as he adjusted the microphone. He glanced up at her and winked when the music started, but she still didn't recognize it. It didn't matter to her, because as soon as he began to sing, his eyes never left hers.

"*You are the woman that I've always dreamed of, I knew it from the start.*" John's voice was low and husky, but he had a perfect tone.

At least it sounded perfect to her. If someone told her to look away or she'd die, Stephanie would've died then and there. Everything about the way he sang entranced her. It was as if nobody else was in the room; all she could see and hear was John.

The end of the song came way too soon, Stephanie could've listened to him all night. When the room erupted into a chorus of hoots and hollers, it startled her because she'd forgotten they were there. John lowered his head, and when he lifted it again, his gaze found hers. His eyes sparkled, and when he smiled, she knew she was in love with him.

"I guess having a beautiful lady in the room gives John the inspiration to sing with all his heart," Kristy teased as she pushed Stephanie with her shoulder.

"Inspiration is everything, cuz." John winked at Stephanie.

Stephanie was a little disappointed when the rehearsal finished. She enjoyed it, but she knew John would be tired once everyone left. While John spoke with his family, Stephanie slipped around the people in the hallway to get to her apartment. She had reached for the door when John grabbed her hand.

"Did you have fun?" John grasped both of her hands as the last of his family left the house.

"Yeah, I did. You guys are incredible." She swung their hands between them.

"Thanks." He glanced down to their joined hands.

"I've never heard that song before." The song made her realized she was head over heels for the man in front of her.

"It's an oldie but a goodie." He chuckled. "My dad sang it to my mom when he proposed. It's her favorite."

"That's sweet." Stephanie gazed into his eyes. "I guess you get your talent from him."

"Yeah." John's eyes lowered to her lips.

"You've got an amazing voice. The band is terrific." Why did her voice sound so breathy?

"Thanks." His voice was low.

For a moment, his focus moved back to her eyes, and she swallowed hard. She couldn't think with the way he stared at her, and it seemed like the last thing he wanted to talk about was the band. Stephanie forgot all about the group when John lifted his hand and ran his finger down her cheek.

"John," Stephanie whispered, and she was surprised he heard her.

"I don't want to say good-night right now." His thumb glided across her bottom lip.

"What about going slow?" Rushing into things never worked.

"I just want to spend some time with you." John tucked her hair behind her ear.

"We can watch a movie," Stephanie blurted out because it would be a great distraction.

At the moment, the only thing she could think about was stripping him naked and licking him from head to toe. Maybe a movie would help her cool down.

"Sounds great. We'll watch it in your apartment because all the equipment is in the way. You pick a movie, and I'll make some popcorn." Before she could say a word, John ran off to his kitchen.

Stephanie plopped down on the couch and scanned through Netflix. She finally settled on a horror movie she wanted to see, mostly because it would be safer than the romance movies she usually watched. Ten minutes later, John returned with a massive bowl of popcorn in one hand and a couple of sodas in the other.

"What are we watching?" He put the bowl and sodas on the table as he glanced at the screen and grinned. "You like horror movies?"

"Love them." She didn't really, but it would keep things in the PG zone.

"Me too, but I never met a girl who did." John sat back and placed the bowl in his lap.

He popped a few pieces of popcorn in his mouth, and his tongue darted out to lick the butter off his lips. The motion caused Stephanie to press her legs together to try and calm the sensation building between them. Thoughts of his tongue sliding over her skin made her stomach flutter, and the heat of his leg pressed up against hers made it very hard to concentrate. She was at a point she couldn't remember why they needed things to go slow. She was never so sexually aware of anyone in her life.

They made it about halfway through the movie, and Stephanie felt as if she would spontaneously combust. John leaned forward to put the bowl back on the table, and the muscles in his arms flexed. Was he doing this on purpose? Did the man know she was ready to explode? He leaned back and wrapped his arm around her shoulder and began to play with a strand of her hair. It seemed purely innocent, but it made her crazy. His other hand rested on his thigh, and all she could think about was how sexy his hands looked. Thoughts of how his strong hands would caress her entire body while he pressed against her made her mouth go dry, and she shuddered.

Stop it.

"Are you cold, sweetheart?" He must have felt her shiver.

"Not really." Her body was on fire.

John placed his finger under her chin and tilted her head up. There was no choice but to look into his eyes. Would he see the desire in her gaze?

"What's wrong? You seem about to jump out of your skin. Is the movie scaring you?" John chuckled.

"What movie?" Her focus moved straight to his lips, and his grin disappeared. "John, kiss me, please."

"Baby, you don't know how much I want to kiss you, but I don't know if I could stop with just kissing." She wasn't the only one to feel the electricity between them.

"Kiss me. Now." Stephanie pressed against him.

John's eyes dilated and seemed a deeper blue. She moved until her lips almost touched his, and placed her hand against his chest. She felt his heart pound as hard as hers. John stared into her eyes, and for a moment, she thought he would pull away.

"Stephanie," he growled her name as he tangled his hands in her hair and pressed his lips against hers.

Stephanie grabbed the front of his shirt into her fists and pulled him closer as his tongue penetrated her mouth. She couldn't hold back the moan deep in her throat as John slid his hands down to her waist and lifted her into his lap.

Stephanie straddled his legs and felt his erection press against her core. A sound somewhere between a groan and a growl vibrated in his chest. John kissed his way down to the nape of her neck and nipped the sensitive skin making her shiver. When he cupped her ass and pulled her hard against him, she placed soft kisses across his jaw.

"John," Stephanie whispered into his ear and nibbled her way down the side of his neck, and goosebumps formed on his skin.

227

"Stephanie, I want you so bad." John scooped her up into his arms and stood.

She wrapped her legs around his waist, not wanting to break the connection between their bodies. She found his mouth again and thrust her tongue inside. John moaned as his tongue swirled against hers, and he pulled her tighter against him.

"Baby, I'm almost at the point of no return." John pulled his lips from hers and panted the words into her ear. "You've got to tell me now because once I get you in my bed, I won't be able to stop."

His hot breath against her skin sent shivers through her body, and she threaded her fingers through his thick hair. Stephanie felt as if she were on fire.

"Take me to your room," Stephanie whispered against his neck.

"You don't have to tell me twice." John growled.

Seconds later, she lay flat on her back in his bed, and John hovered above her. For a moment, she thought he'd changed his mind, but then he dropped his head and covered her mouth with his. His tongue plunged between her lips, and when she sucked on it, he groaned.

Chapter 19

Every sound she made vibrated through his body and made him harder than he'd ever been in his life. John had to slow down, but it was difficult. He'd wanted Stephanie for months. Longed to feel her soft skin against his and have her writhe beneath him. He couldn't wait for her to come while he was buried deep inside her.

John tore his mouth from hers and gasped for air. He gazed into her eyes and could see his own desire mirrored there. Her cheeks flushed, and her lips swollen from their kiss. It was the most erotic thing he'd ever seen.

They still had way too much clothing between them. John ached to feel her skin against his. He yanked his T-shirt over his head and threw it to the floor, and her sweater followed it. Her nipples pebbled behind the thin fabric of her bra, and the sight alone almost did him in.

John kept his eyes locked with hers when he lowered his head and covered her taut nipple with his lips. When he gently rolled it between his teeth, she arched off the bed as she lightly scraped his naked chest with her nails.

"I need you naked," John growled against her breast.

He didn't know or care where her clothes went, but to his relief, Stephanie lay under him beautifully naked seconds later. Well almost. The only exception was a sheer pink thong barely covering her sex. John hovered above her with a hand on either side. He let his eyes devour her body

"God, you have to be the most beautiful thing I've ever seen," he whispered with reverence.

"Can you stop talking and get the rest of your clothes off." She grinned and giggled when his eyes met hers again.

John didn't want to move from her, but the rest of his clothes had to go, and fast. He eased off the bed and quickly dropped his jeans and boxers in one swift movement. His erection stood pointed upward to his stomach, and as he watched her eyes lower to his member, it throbbed for her touch.

He didn't have to wait long, because Stephanie moved to her knees on the edge of the mattress. Her long blonde hair fell over her shoulders and lay against the top of her round firm breasts.

"So much better than I imagined," she purred, and her finger lightly circled the tip to spread the moisture around the sensitive head.

His dick jerked, but for a few seconds, he allowed her to explore his shaft. It was all he would be able to handle, or he'd embarrass himself. John grabbed her hand as she started to lower her mouth to the tip. There was no way he could last if her lips wrapped around his dick.

He crawled onto the bed as she backed up to the middle. He pulled her against him and slowly caressed the soft silky skin of her back and ass. John pressed his erection against her, and he could feel her heat through the sheer material or the thong.

"Jesus, Stephanie, you're driving me crazy," John growled as her nails dragged lightly down his back.

John eased her to the bed and kissed the hollow of her throat. He covered her breast with his hand as he gently pinched her nipple. She arched against him again as he dragged his tongue down between her breasts while he continued to tease her hard bud.

"So fucking beautiful," John whispered against her skin.

Her body quivered when his lips wrapped around the hard, pink tip and sucked it into his mouth. She squirmed under him as his hands slipped down her body. John grinned against her breast because she wanted him as much as he wanted her. His tongue trailed down her body while he hooked his finger in her thong and slowly pulled it down her legs.

John dipped his tongue into her navel as his finger slid against her wet folds, and her scent surrounded him. It intoxicated him, and his erection throbbed with the need for release. He needed to calm down, or he would lose it before he could bury himself inside her.

Her body trembled under him, as he pressed his thumb against her clit and made small circles against the sensitive nub. Stephanie whimpered when he slid a single finger inside her. His tongue found her wet sex, replacing his thumb with his tongue, and she cried out in pleasure. As he lapped at her, he inserted another finger into her tight wet heat.

"Open for me, baby," John whispered. "I want to taste every inch of you."

Stephanie spread her legs wider. John watched her as he flicked his tongue against her swollen clit and slowly pumped his fingers in and out. The sounds she made had his dick dripping. He wanted so badly to plunge inside her, but her taste was addictive.

Jesus. Fuck.

John thrust his fingers in and out as his tongue flicked her hard bud. Her hips rose to meet the rhythm of his fingers as he sucked her clit into his mouth, and she clenched around his fingers.

"That's it, baby, let go," John encouraged and sucked her clit into his mouth once more.

"John. Oh, John. Yes," she screamed as her body shuddered.

"Beautiful." John thrust his tongue inside her and lapped up her release. "You taste delicious, sweetheart."

John watched her as he brought her to another orgasm. More intense than the first, and her body convulsed as she shouted his name. It was the sexiest thing he'd ever seen.

John crawled up and hovered above her. When he ground his erection against her, she opened her eyes and pressed her hips against him. It was difficult to hold his control and clenched his teeth. As he lowered his head to kiss her, she licked her lips, and he groaned at the sight of her pink tongue.

232

John covered her lips with his and drove his tongue inside her warm mouth. He loved the taste of her, but he needed to feel her body take him inside. Feel her squeeze his dick when he brought her over the edge with him.

John reached for the drawer of his nightstand and grabbed a condom. He silently prayed that he still had some. When his hand wrapped around a foil package, he mentally sighed with relief. Before he had a chance to open it, Stephanie pulled the condom out of his hand.

"I want to put it on," she purred with a seductive grin on her beautiful mouth.

She pushed him until he lay on his back, and she straddled his legs. John gripped her hips while she held the condom package in her teeth and lightly ran her nails down his chest.

"Baby, you're killing me here." John clenched his teeth.

Her sexy wink made him realized this woman liked to tease, but she stopped and pulled the condom package from between her teeth. She lay flat on top of him and trailed her tongue along the side of his neck.

"What's the hurry?" She whispered as her lips moved up to his ear.

"I need to be inside you before I spontaneously combust," John rasped when she pulled his earlobe between her teeth.

Stephanie sat up and opened the square package. John had to grip the sheets as she slid the condom slowly down the length of his cock. He needed to calm himself, or he wouldn't last more than a minute when he pushed inside her. He closed his eyes and took several deep breaths. It seemed to help the intense urge to come, but not much, especially when she lowered herself down over the length of him.

"I hope you're close, cause I don't know how much longer I can last." John tried to think about something to hold himself off longer, but nothing could distract him from the incredible feeling of having her heat around him.

They fit together perfectly. John cupped her breast and teased her nipple with his thumb as she slowly rode him. His other thumb rubbed small circles over her clit, and Stephanie whimpered when he increased the pressure. He knew she was almost there again when she started to quiver above him.

"That's it, baby, I want to feel you come around me." John panted.

John was close, but he couldn't leave her behind. The familiar tingling sensation starting through the tip of his cock meant he was almost at the point of no return, and he pressed against her clit harder.

"John," Stephanie roared as her pussy squeezed around him.

His name coming from her lips in the throes of orgasm was the last straw for him. John gripped her hips and thrust deep inside three times, and it was all it took. His cock jerked inside her, and every muscle in his body shook. It seemed to go on so long; he didn't think it was going to stop.

"Fuck. Stephanie," John gasped as she fell against his chest.

It was heaven to hold her soft body against his. John didn't want to let her go and knew he would never be able to. He kept her tightly wrapped in his embrace while they both enjoyed the afterglow of their lovemaking.

"Wow." She lifted her head.

"My sentiments exactly." John rolled them both over until she was on her back.

He gave her a quick kiss before he moved off the bed and headed to the bathroom to dispose of the condom. When he returned, she curled up under his quilt, and he crawled under the blanket with her.

Stephanie snuggled into his side and rested her head against his chest. For a few minutes, he didn't say a word because he wanted to enjoy the feel of her in his arms and his bed.

Her giggle broke the silence, and she pushed herself up on her elbow. John smiled at her, but he had no idea what she found so funny.

"I'm sorry, I seduced you. I couldn't help myself. You're one sexy man, John O'Connor." She winked.

"I'm not sure about the sexy, but I know I was about to go insane." He laughed as he pushed a stray piece of her hair away from her face. "It's not easy going around with a constant hard-on, and I hate cold showers."

"I don't know what it is, but there's something about you, John." Her smile faded, and her expression turned serious. "I couldn't stop thinking about you from the first day I saw you."

There was nowhere he'd rather be than with her. The stories about love at first sight used to make him roll his eyes. He never believed it could happen. Nobody could fall in love with someone with one look. Now he knew. The intense urge to be with someone special, and dreams about a stranger were crazy, but it made sense the minute he kissed her. It wasn't only sexual. Stephanie made him feel as if there was nothing he couldn't do.

"Why are you looking at me like that?" She raised an eyebrow.

"Because I still can't believe how beautiful you are." He grazed his knuckles against her soft cheek.

He couldn't tell her about the thoughts in his head. Did she feel it too, or was he the only one? John doubted if someone could kiss the way she did without any attraction at all. John wasn't ready to admit it, but deep down, he knew how he felt about her.

Stephanie lightly pressed her lips against his as her tongue darted out to trace the outside edge of his bottom lip. John plowed his fingers through her hair and covered her mouth with his before she had a chance to move. He couldn't get enough of her taste, her scent, or her touch. The only reason he pulled away from her lips was to breathe.

"I've got a feeling it's going to be a very long night." Stephanie grinned as her hand slipped under the blanket and wrapped around his shaft.

"Me too," he murmured.

John would be exhausted for rehearsal the next day, but he didn't care. He wanted to spend the rest of the night making all his dreams a reality.

Chapter 20

Stephanie opened her eyes and surveyed her surroundings. At first, confusion set in, but then the memories came flooding back. Her lips curled into a wide smile. She couldn't stop it if she tried. She and John made love so often she'd lost count, and afterward, she curled up in his arms and had the best sleep of her life.

Stephanie scanned John's room as she stretched. The walls were a light taupe and accented by forest green drapes hung over the two large windows. The matching green comforter covered her, and she could tell it wasn't store-bought.

The sun peeked through the small opening in the drapes, and she could see it was a lovely day. It was undoubtedly a beautiful night. She turned to the other side of the bed, where John still slept.

One hand tucked under his head, and the other rested against his flat abdomen. The quilt lay below his navel, and her cheeks warmed as she thought about what was under the blanket. She rolled on her side and tucked her hand under her cheek. Even in sleep, John oozed sexiness with his light brown hair mussed and lips slightly parted. It was the first time she noticed the light auburn highlights.

With John's eyes closed, she could study the features of his face without the distraction of his smile and those intense blue eyes. His long dark eyelashes fanned under his eyes, and all she could think was, some women would kill for his lashes. A long straight nose and a strong jaw completed his handsome face.

She scanned down to his muscled chest with a light dusting of hair a little darker than the hair on his head. She shivered as the memory of how the hair tickled her breasts as he pumped into her. When her gaze moved up at his face again, his eyes were open, and he had a wide grin.

"See anything you like?" He wiggled his eyebrows up and down.

"I like everything I see," she purred. "And the things I can't see."

John turned on his side and pulled the blanket down, exposing her breasts. He wiggled his eyebrows as he slowly ran his index finger down her neck and between her breasts.

"I like everything I see too." He leaned down and flicked his tongue against one of her nipples.

"Oh no. Not again. Did you see the time?" She playfully slapped his hand and pulled the blanket over her nakedness.

"Nope. I'm not worried about the time right now." He lifted the blanket to give her a full view of his erection.

"Does he ever go down?" Stephanie giggled when he pulled her against him.

"It's only been this way since I met you." John buried his face in the crook of her neck and teased her with soft kisses.

"What time is everyone supposed to be coming?" She moaned, but before John could answer, a deep voice echoed from the hallway.

"John, get your lazy ass out of the sack," James shouted.

John continued to tease her with kisses and nips down the side of her neck, and as much as she wanted to go on, the fear of James outside the room gave her the strength to push him away and tug the blanket up over her head.

"John, get up before he comes in here," she whispered.

"I can get a bucket of water, bro," James shouted, and all Stephanie could do was pray John's brother didn't come busting into the room.

"I'm up for Christ's sake," John yelled at the door. "In more ways than one," he whispered and grinned down at her.

"John," Stephanie whispered and gave him a playful shove.

John had the cutest pout on his lips, and it made her giggle. She covered her mouth in panic and prayed James wasn't outside the bedroom door.

"Remind me later to take the house keys from my family," John whispered as he gave her a quick kiss and then jumped out of bed.

"You have to distract him. I need to get out to my apartment," Stephanie begged, because the last thing she wanted was for James to find her in John's room.

"I'll get him into the kitchen." John winked as he dressed and hurried out of the bedroom.

Stephanie jumped out of bed and ran around the room snatching her clothes off the floor. *Bra.* Where the hell was her bra? She searched under the bed and pulled back the comforter. *Damn it.* There was no time. She needed to get to her apartment before James knew where Stephanie spent the night.

She pressed her ear against the door and listened. She wasn't ashamed of what happened between them, but John's brothers would tease them mercilessly. Plus, it would look unprofessional for her to sleep with him when technically he was still her client.

Stephanie opened the door a crack and heard the voices in the kitchen. Hopefully, she could slip out of the room quietly and make it to her apartment before James could catch on. She kept her focus on the kitchen door as she tiptoed down the hall. As she turned into the foyer, she came face to face with John's father.

"Oh, God," she gasped.

Sean's lips quirked into a grin, and she could see where John got his mischievous grin. Her cheeks felt as if they were on fire, and she thought it would be an excellent time for the floor to open up and swallow her.

"Good morning, Stephanie," Sean greeted her with a wink.

"Um… Hi… Mr. O'Connor," she stammered and looked everywhere but at him.

What was she supposed to say? *Oh yes, Mr. O'Connor, it is a good morning because your son and I spent the night naked and screwed until we were exhausted.* Well, that would be crude, but what could she say to Sean after she tiptoed out of John's room?

"Are my boys in the kitchen, or is John still sleeping." He raised an eyebrow.

Yep, John favored his father. Stephanie felt a little tug in her belly as she thought about how John would look when he was in his fifties.

"They're in the kitchen." She squeaked.

She hoped that would be the end of the conversation because then she could run to her apartment and die of humiliation in peace. Thankfully, John's father took pity on her. He smiled as he gave her arm a little pat, stepped around her, and made his way to the kitchen. She heard him ask John how he slept the previous night, and she practically tripped over her own feet.

Stephanie ran into her apartment and leaned against the door. She'd never been so embarrassed in her life. The next time she came face to face with Sean O'Connor, it was going to be awkward. There was no way John's dad missed her coming out of his son's bedroom. He didn't seem angry, but she knew some people could hide their emotions. He'd probably lost any respect for her, and the feeling made her sick to her stomach.

After a long, hot shower and fresh clothes, she felt a little better. She didn't know if she could ever face John's father again. Stephanie flopped down on the couch and pressed one of the decorative pillows against her face. She wanted to watch John and the band rehearse again, but if Sean stayed, it would be uncomfortable. At least it would be for her. As she was putting herself into a frenzy, her phone chimed with a text.

John: Are you coming to watch?

Stephanie: I'll be out in a few minutes. Is your dad still there?

John: Yeah. LOL, he said he saw you in the hallway.

Stephanie: Don't LOL me. He saw me coming out of your room.

John: He won't say anything. I promise.

Stephanie: It's embarrassing.

John: Don't worry, baby.

The endearment made her sigh, and because of it, she couldn't disappoint him. She glanced at herself in the mirror to verify her cheeks were scarlet with the thought of facing Sean. She wanted to lock herself in the apartment, but her phone chimed again.

John: Stephanie, I promise he won't say a word.

Stephanie: Fine. I'll be right out.

Before she opened the door, she took a deep breath. Voices floated out from the living room, telling her Sean and James weren't the only ones in the house. She took another deep breath and pulled open the door.

The rest of the guys had arrived and were tuning the instruments. Stephanie turned toward the couch, and all the air whooshed out of her. Sean sat on the sofa with Kathleen next to him. She didn't want Kathleen to know and prayed Sean hadn't said anything.

She was about to run back to her apartment, but before she could escape, Kathleen motioned her to come closer. *John is dead.* She moved slowly toward the woman as if she was on her way to the gallows. Stephanie smiled and eased down next to John's mother.

"We can't go to the fundraiser, so I wanted to see my boys do a few of my favorite songs." Kathleen squeezed Stephanie's knee.

"They're excellent," Stephanie admitted as she spotted John behind the keyboard, and he winked at her.

"How are you and John getting on?" Stephanie's heart jumped in her chest, but Kathleen didn't even look at her.

"Umm... great. He's almost done with therapy," Stephanie stammered as she stared down at her hands.

"I see." Kathleen turned to her. "Has he asked you out yet?"

Stephanie's heart thudded in her chest as she glanced back and forth between Kathleen, Sean, and John. Was this a trick? John seemed oblivious to the conversation between Stephanie and his mother. John was in the middle of a chat with Keith.

"He... ah... the fundraiser... he asked me to the fundraiser," Stephanie stammered.

"Oh, for heaven's sake, that won't be romantic," Kathleen complained. "Sean, you need to talk to your son and teach him how to be romantic." Kathleen pinched Sean's cheek.

"Sweetheart, I think John's doing fine, all on his own." Sean leaned forward and winked at Stephanie.

Oh. Dear. God. Kill me now.

Her face had to be glowing red. Would it be wrong to jump up and leave? She wanted to scream and run out of the house like a crazy person.

"We watched a movie last night and ate popcorn," Stephanie said quickly. "It was nice."

She glanced toward John, and for the first time since she met him, she wanted to slap the grin off his face. Stephanie narrowed her eyes, and when he laughed, she shook her head. Yep, she wanted to hit him. Hard.

Stephanie squirmed on the couch as if she was on pins and needles. Where was Kristy? Why wasn't she here to save her today? She adored John's parents, but Sean knew where Stephanie slept the previous night. His expression didn't show disgust, but she was supposed to help John recover, not to jump into bed with him.

The longer she thought about it, the more paranoid she became. Was everyone staring at her? She scanned the room. Aaron, Nick, Mike, John and the other two guys in the band were busy practicing. James was off to the side, tapping his foot to the music, Ian's head was down reading something on the clipboard, and Keith seemed entranced with something on his phone. John's parents weren't even paying any attention to her. She glanced back at John to see him watching her. He smiled, and all her tension dissipated.

When the rehearsal ended, they started to load the equipment into the back of a large box truck parked in John's driveway. Stephanie offered to help, but Kathleen axed the idea and escorted

Stephanie to the kitchen for a cup of tea. As with Nanny Betty, it was impossible to say no to John's mother as well.

"One thing you need to learn, my dear. Let the men do all the manual labor." Kathleen linked into the crook of Stephanie's arm and steered her toward the kitchen.

As soon as they entered, Kathleen released her and proceeded to the cupboards. She talked casually about her day as she pulled two cups down. The whole time Stephanie waited for Kathleen to say something about what Sean had seen.

"Cream and sugar, Dear?" Kathleen turned on the electric kettle.

"Black, please." Stephanie climbed onto one of the barstools next to the island in the center of the kitchen.

Kathleen continued and explained why she and Sean couldn't go to the fundraiser, but for the life of her, Stephanie didn't have a clue what the woman said. Sean hadn't exposed Stephanie, and she relaxed a little. Kathleen probably wouldn't think very highly of her if he had.

"Are you okay, Stephanie?" Kathleen placed two cups on the counter and sat on the stool beside her.

Kathleen's eyes were full of concern, but there was a sparkle in her grey-blue eyes. The same shine Stephanie saw in her own mother's eyes. There was no doubt, Kathleen O'Connor was indeed a happy woman.

"I'm fine. Just tired." Stephanie picked up her cup to sip her tea.

"That'll happen when you're up late." Kathleen tipped her cup to her lips.

Stephanie almost dropped her cup at Kathleen's statement, but she managed to recover and lay it safely on the counter.

"Pardon," Stephanie squeaked.

"Stephanie, I hoped John would see what a beautiful and intelligent young lady you are. Cora knew you were the one for him." Kathleen took Stephanie's hand. "When Sean told me, he saw you this morning. Well, you've got to know. I was thrilled."

Stephanie was sure she looked like one of those cartoons where the character's eyes bulge out of their head. She shook her head to make sure she didn't imagine what Kathleen had said.

"Don't be embarrassed, my dear, I'm so very happy for you and John." Kathleen kissed her cheek and turned back to her tea.

"Thank you... but... Cora...What do you mean Cora knew I was the one for John?" Was she having this conversation, and how the hell would Cora know?

"Cora has a special gift since she was a little girl. Cora knows when people are meant to be together." Kathleen sat back, her lips curled up at the corners. "When Cora meets someone, she can tell instantly when they have love issues. The way Cora explains it is her heart will race, and she becomes really warm. Then a face will flash in front of her, or she sees it in her mind." Kathleen took another sip of her tea and continued. "Cora's nickname is Cora the Cupid, and she's never wrong."

What could Stephanie say to such a crazy story? There was no way Kathleen was serious about any of what she said. Any minute Kathleen was going to burst out laughing. Stephanie stared at John's mother, but the woman was completely serious.

"I can see you like my son a lot. Cora was right again." Kathleen covered Stephanie's hand and squeezed it gently.

"John is a wonderful man." Stephanie didn't know how else to respond to everything Kathleen said.

"It's hard to resist those O'Connor men. I could tell you stories about Sean that would curl your toes." Kathleen winked, and Stephanie burst out laughing.

"I'm sure you could." Talking with Kathleen reminded Stephanie of chats with her mom.

Kathleen turned their conversation to stories of John when he was a little boy. Stephanie couldn't help laughing as Kathleen told her about how John wore a Batman costume for the entire summer. Anytime Kathleen had to wash it, John would sit in front of the dryer until it stopped. It was the cutest story Stephanie ever heard, but she couldn't hold back the giggle when John walked into the kitchen. She covered her mouth as Kathleen sat up straight.

"I'll give you the recipe the next time I come over." Kathleen turned in her stool. "Oh. Hi John, did you get the truck all loaded?"

"Yes, and what stories have you been telling Stephanie, Mom." He folded his arms across his broad chest and raised an eyebrow at his mother.

"Now what stories would I have to tell about you, John? You were a perfect angel." Kathleen fluttered her eyes innocently, and Stephanie couldn't hold in the laughter.

"I love it when you lie to me, Mom." John leaned down and kissed Kathleen on the cheek.

Why did the sight of John showing affection to his mother make her want to sigh out loud? Maybe because her mother always told her to watch how a man is with his mother because it showed how he would treat his wife. As she practically melted in the chair when John smiled at her, Sean walked in and immediately wrapped his arms around Kathleen.

"Are you ready to go home, darling." Sean kissed her temple.

"I am, but you're cooking supper tonight." Kathleen smiled up at him.

"We'll stop into Isabelle's restaurant on the way home." Sean chuckled.

"You're such a smart man." Kathleen affectionately touched Sean's cheek.

They were too cute. Even with all their years together, they were still deeply in love. She saw the same thing every day with her own parents and hoped one day she'd find the same connection.

"I've sent the rest of the boys home, so you two have the rest of the night to yourselves." Sean winked as Kathleen hugged her, but Stephanie didn't miss the glint in John's eye, and it made her shiver with desire.

John walked his parents to the door, and Stephanie cleared the cups away. She wiped down the counter and turned as John entered the kitchen again.

"So, what stories did my lovely mother tell you?" John wrapped his arms around her.

"It's a secret." Stephanie winked as she melted into his embrace. "I am a little surprised, though."

"Why?" He asked

"Your mom and dad didn't seem the least bit outraged about me coming out of your bedroom this morning, and your mom told me she could curl my toes with stories about your dad." Stephanie giggled.

"My parents are pretty liberal, but sometimes they share a little too much information about their relationship." John shuddered. "When we were teenagers, lots of times we came home and caught them in…." John stopped to re-evaluate what he was going to say. "Let's say a compromising position."

"Oh dear. That sounds like my parents." Stephanie wrapped her arms around his neck. "It must be something with their generation."

"Maybe we can take a lesson from them." John nipped her ear, and Stephanie shivered. "What are we going to do for the rest of the evening?"

"We could play checkers," she sighed when John sucked her earlobe into his mouth.

"I'm sure we could come up with something a little more exciting." His hands eased under her shirt.

"Oh yeah, like what?" His warm touch against her skin caused goosebumps to come out all over her body.

"Well, there's this." He brushed his lips against hers.

"That's nice," she sighed.

"And this." John trailed small kisses across her jaw and up behind her ear.

The warmth of his breath against her skin was like an electric surge, and she tilted her head to give him better access to her neck. John lifted her on to the counter and stood between her legs. He made small circles on her back with his fingers and continued to tease her with feather-like kisses up and down her neck and shoulder.

"I. Can't. Get. Enough. Of. You." John kissed across her jaw with one kiss for every word.

Stephanie whimpered and closed her eyes as she wrapped her legs around his waist to pull him against her. His lips pressed found hers, and as his tongue plunged into her mouth, a loud pounding on the front door echoed through the house, startling her.

"Who the fuck is that?" John snapped as he pulled away from her and stomped out of the kitchen.

Stephanie hopped down from the counter and followed him. She enjoyed the seduction in the kitchen and was a little annoyed at the interruption. Whoever knocked better have a damn good excuse for disturbing them. John opened the door as Stephanie entered the foyer.

"Thank God, you're here." Sandy panted as she pushed into the house, and Stephanie could see the woman was distressed over something.

"Sandy, what's wrong?" John closed the door.

"I was coming back from the grocery store, and I saw someone come out from behind your house. He was dressed all in black and a hood over his head. I couldn't tell if it was a man or a woman, but I'm going to say he, because it's easier. When he saw me, he ran up the road," Sandy practically shouted, and Stephanie's whole body tensed.

"Which way did he go?" John yanked open the door.

"Up toward Main Road." Sandy pointed to the end of the road.

Before Stephanie could protest about John going off by himself, he grabbed his keys and ran out the door.

"I'm so glad you two are okay." Sandy turned to Stephanie.

"I'm glad you saw whoever it was," Stephanie admitted. "Who knows what they were up to?"

She motioned for Sandy to follow her into the kitchen and gave her a glass of water. Sandy still appeared shaken and sat on one of the stools as she held the glass with two hands. Stephanie sat next to her and placed a comforting hand on Sandy's shoulder.

"I heard the band earlier today," Sandy said after she placed the glass back in front of her.

"They're rehearsing for a fundraiser for the Janeway." Stephanie glanced out through the kitchen door in hopes to see John come back.

"The one at the Delta?" Sandy stood up and put the glass in the sink

"Yeah." Stephanie leaned on the counter.

"I'm working at that event." Sandy smiled.

"I guess I'll see you there." Stephanie spun around when she heard John's voice.

"Yes, you will," Sandy replied.

Stephanie wasn't sure what Sandy did for work, but she did remember her saying she did odd jobs for catering companies once in a while. Sandy didn't talk a lot about herself, and when they chatted, it was mostly about books or John's therapy. The only other thing she knew was Sandy had a sister, her mom passed away a few years earlier, and her father was not in her life.

Stephanie couldn't imagine not having her parents in her life. Sandy told Stephanie she missed her mom, but she seemed indifferent about her father. It was probably the only thing Stephanie was able to pull out of the woman. Sandy was a nice person, but very private.

"I don't know who it could be. Sandy said she couldn't tell if it was a man or woman." John's jaw clenched as he held the phone to his ear. "I'll let you know, but I don't think it's necessary to send anyone over."

Stephanie had no idea who John was speaking to, but from the way he rolled his eyes, he didn't like what the person was saying.

"Uncle Kurt, I may not be back to work, but I still remember how to take a statement." John shook his head as he listened to his uncle for a few seconds. "Fine, I'll get her to stay here until you get here."

John tossed his phone on the counter and slammed his hand down next to it. He was pissed about something, and it was the first time Stephanie had seen his anger since the first few months she'd been at his house.

"What's wrong?" Stephanie touched his arm, and he blew out a breath.

"Uncle Kurt's coming over to take a statement from Sandy. I'm still on medical leave, so I can't take her statement," John grumbled.

"Maybe Kurt just wants to make sure you're okay," Sandy said, obviously seeing John's irritation.

"I go back to work in two weeks." John threw his arms in the air in frustration.

"Jesus, John, calm down. It's protocol." James' voice startled Stephanie.

She hadn't heard the front door, but James stood in the doorway of the kitchen. Either John didn't lock the door, or James had the key.

"What're you doing here?" John leaned against the counter and crossed his arms over his chest.

"Uncle Kurt called. I wanted to make sure you guys were okay," James explained. "Hi, Sandy."

"Hi, James." Sandy plopped down in one of the kitchen chairs.

"We're fine," John snapped.

Stephanie was surprised by the way John spoke to his brother. He sounded like a complete ass, and when she caught his gaze, she narrowed her eyes at him. John's shoulders drooped, and he sighed as he appeared to understand the look she gave him.

"I'm sorry. I didn't mean to snap at you, bro," he apologized to James.

"I know," James said as he joined Sandy at the kitchen table.

Kurt arrived a few minutes later, and John's frustration returned when Kurt ignored John to listen to Sandy. James stood silently next to the counter as John paced back and forth like a caged animal. She didn't understand all the fuss. The person was long gone, and with no real description. Sandy did her best to give Kurt as much information as she could.

"It might be some kid looking to find an empty house." James shrugged his shoulders.

"Maybe, but it makes me nervous to know someone was lurking around looking into windows." Sandy wasn't the only one.

"This kind of thing doesn't happen here. Could be some kids from town coming here thinking it's an easy mark," Kurt suggested. "You should probably give the neighbors a heads up. Just in case."

"Come on, Sandy. I'll make sure you get to your house safely." James motioned to the door.

"Thanks, James." Sandy hugged Stephanie then followed Kurt and James through the door.

John closed and locked the door when they left and let out a ragged breath. He turned around and held out his hand to her. Stephanie took his hand and stepped into his warm embrace.

"Are you okay?" She asked.

"Yeah. I overreacted." John sighed.

"It's creepy to know someone was sneaking around your house. I can understand your reaction." She wrapped her arms around his neck.

"It's not that." He sighed. "I guess; I just miss work." John held her against him, and he seemed to relax.

"Only twelve days left." She smiled and pressed her lips against his chest.

"Yeah, but right now, I wanna pick up where we were so rudely interrupted." John cupped her ass and pulled her against him.

She loved the way his brain worked. Stephanie's hands slid under his shirt, and she traced the muscles of his chest with her fingers. Every muscle hard and defined. Her gaze never broke from his as she glided her fingers down to his jeans and popped open the button. John seemed to hold his breath as she took her time lowering the zipper. His eyes fluttered closed when her hand dipped into his boxers and wrapped around his erection.

"You're trying to torture me, aren't you?" He groaned.

"You started this." Before she could say anything else, he swung her into his arms and stalked toward the bedroom.

"Damn right I did," John growled as he kicked open the bedroom door. "Are you complaining?"

"Oh... Ah... no... never," Stephanie moaned as he stripped her and teased her with his tongue. "Now who's torturing who?"

She sighed when his fingers glided up the inside of her thighs. The gentle caress of his knuckle against her skin caused her body to hum. Stephanie yanked off her shirt with hopes his hands would continue the sweet torture further up her body. She was disappointed.

John grasped her hands and pulled her up until she sat in the middle of the bed. The disappointment faded when he yanked off his shirt, and his jeans followed. John stood in all his beautiful masculine glory with his erection straining against his boxers. His thumbs slipped into the waistband, and he slid them down over his hips. He knelt on the bed between her legs and wrapped his hand around his swollen member. It was the hottest thing she'd ever seen.

"You like watching?" He slowly stroked himself, and when Stephanie licked her lips, he growled. "God, when you do that, all I can think about is having those lips around my cock."

He must have read her mind because the same thought went through her head. Stephanie pushed him back on the bed and positioned herself between his legs. As she lowered her mouth above his straining erection and flicked her tongue against the swollen head, she kept her gaze locked with his.

"Jesus, Stephanie." He took a quick intake of air.

She wrapped her hand around him and licked down his hard shaft. When she took him into her mouth, John cursed and cupped the back of her head. Stephanie's lips moved down his length then slowly up again. John's muscles contracted with every stroke her lips made.

"Baby, I'm gonna come. So, if you don't want to..." He didn't finish the sentence because she took him entirely into her mouth.

The warm salty liquid slid down her throat as he groaned, and he gripped her head between his hands. She slowed her mouth as his body convulsed, and he murmured her name.

"You taste so good," Stephanie whispered as she slid up his body.

For several minutes, he held her on top of him as he tried to catch his breath. Stephanie rested her head on his chest and smiled at the way his heart thudded.

"Let's see if you still taste as good as you did last night," he whispered once he could speak again.

John flipped her onto her back, then hovered over her as he glided his hot, wet tongue down her body. He made several stops as he licked lower. A quick flick of his tongue against each nipple, then his tongue continued to slide down her body as he caressed her breasts with his hands. Her hips raised as she tried to get his mouth where she wanted him the most.

John's tongue finally slid between her wet folds, and he was relentless. Her hips lifted off the bed to give him better access to her throbbing sex. He could take her to the point of no return so quickly that it surprised her, and she was so close. All she needed was a little more pressure on her clit. John's tongue assaulted her sensitive nub, as a finger sank deep inside her, and she arched off the bed.

"Ahh...Yes." She gasped.

When a second finger pushed inside her, he used them to massage the front wall of her opening. It was a strange but fantastic sensation she'd never felt before. Between the stimulation inside and her clit, her body shook. The orgasm hit her fast, and her hips lurched off the bed, her muscles clenched, and her body quivered. He didn't stop the pressure inside her, and within seconds another slammed through her.

"Ah... John," she shouted and fisted the sheets because it felt as if the wave of pleasure would never stop.

"Mmm... The sounds you make drive me insane." John moved over her, bent down, and kissed her lips as he pressed his fully engorged cock against her opening.

"I feel something is awake again." She hummed when his lips traveled across her collarbone.

"It just took a cat nap." John flicked his tongue against each of her hard nipples, but she noticed him pull a condom from above her head. "I need to be inside you."

Stephanie giggled as John tore open the condom and rolled it on. His eyes never left hers as he pushed inside her with slow, deep thrusts. It was different from the night before. It was as if he couldn't get close enough to her, and she could hardly catch her breath as he devoured her mouth.

"I can't hold it anymore." John pulled his mouth away to bury his face into her neck. "Stephanie. Fuck. Baby. Yes."

John's body shuddered, and Stephanie could feel every muscle in his body tighten. When he started to relax, he didn't speak. He rolled them over and disposed of the condom in a bucket next to his bed.

Stephanie curled up against his side and rested her head on his chest. The gentle beat of his heart soothed her, and her eyes closed as she listened to the steady rhythm. There was no conversation for several minutes while they held each other in the post lovemaking haze.

"You're amazing, Stephanie Kelly." His voice rumbled through his chest several minutes later.

"You're pretty amazing yourself, John O'Connor," she whispered, and his thumb lifted her chin for her to see his face.

"I mean it, sweetheart." His expression turned serious. "Nobody has ever made me feel like this."

"Feel like what?" She blurted out the words because she had to know it wasn't only her.

"I know this sounds crazy. We haven't known each other long, but…" John stopped and swallowed hard. "Stephanie, I'm in love with you."

The words swirled around her head as she stared at him. Did she hear him correctly? Was she dreaming? Her eyes became painful because they were open so wide. Okay, her heart was about to jump right out of her chest. John O'Connor loved her.

"You look like a deer in the headlights, Love." He chuckled as he touched her cheek. "The last thing I want to do is scare you, but I've always been told to say what's in my heart."

"You love me?" The lump in her throat made it hard to speak.

"I love you." He caressed the side of her face with his finger as if he was trying to memorize every contour of her face.

Stephanie knew the first time John kissed her she'd fallen in love with him. It was hard to believe it could happen so quickly, but it did, and as much as she tried to deny it, she couldn't.

"I didn't think I could fall in love so fast. I thought I imagined it." She cupped his cheek. "Are we crazy? This is crazy. Isn't it?"

"I don't know if it's crazy, but I've never been so sure of anything in my life." He kissed the top of her head as he wrapped his arms around her.

She knew John was a good man. She'd become cynical about relationships over the last year, and with reason. Between her relationship with Brad, and the hell Marina lived through, it seemed impossible to find love. She always wanted a relationship as close as her parents. Nobody would ever doubt her parents were madly in love. John's parents had it too

"You're quiet," John whispered against her temple.

"Sorry." She sighed.

"Don't be sorry, but if there's anything on your mind, you know you can talk to me." He pulled his head back when she lifted her head. "That's a serious face."

"I'm scared," she admitted.

"Of what?"

"It's too fast," she whispered. "My sister had a whirlwind romance, and she's raising a child all on her own. She had to move away from home to get away from the memories of her relationship, and my ex turned out to be a cheating ass, who left with every cent I had, and I know we feel this now, but is it real or…"

John pressed a finger against her lips and smiled. She did it again. Why did she ramble when she was scared, nervous, or excited? She sighed against his finger, and he laughed.

"Stephanie, I've never cheated on anyone in my life. If the guilt didn't kill me, Nan would. I'd never in a million years do anything to hurt you." He turned so they lay face to face and gazed into her eyes. "You know that, don't you?"

"Part of me knows, but I haven't had much luck with relationships in the past." She took a deep breath and slowly released it. "Neither has my sister." Tears formed in her eyes.

"I don't know what I'd do if I had a sister and someone hurt her. Nobody should be treated so violently, but I do know if my brothers or I ever did anything so vile, my father would kick our asses all over Newfoundland, and then Nan would do it all over again." John pulled her into his arms and held her against his chest.

"I can see your grandmother doing that." Stephanie giggled.

"I understand you're apprehensive about all this, hell, it scares me, but I don't want fear to keep me from seeing where this goes." His lips were pressed against the top of her head as he spoke softly.

"Me either." She snuggled against him as his hand gently caressed her back.

"Sleep, beautiful," John whispered.

"Good night, John," she whispered just before she drifted off in the warmth and safety of his arms.

The next morning Stephanie stretched, and the pleasant ache of her muscles made her smile. She reached for John, but his side of the bed was empty. Stephanie scanned the room and saw the bathroom door open. She reached for her cell phone and realized she'd left it in her apartment.

The sun peeped through the curtains, but she had no idea of the time. Technically, she was still on the payroll for John's therapy, but she was in his bed while he was probably in his gym. Guilt showed its ugly head.

Stephanie sat up as the bedroom door opened, and John sauntered in dressed in Athletic shorts and nothing else but sweat. Was there ever a time he didn't look like an erotic God? He wiped the sweat off his face and smiled at her. His smile made her turn to jelly.

"Why didn't you wake me?" She complained.

"You looked so peaceful. I didn't want to disturb you." He leaned down to kiss her cheek.

"John, I'm supposed to make sure you don't do anything to hurt yourself again." She sighed.

"I'm fine, besides I told Cora you're doing an amazing job." John wiggled his eyebrows up and down as he stripped out of his sweaty shorts.

"John," she squeaked. "I shouldn't get paid when I'm not doing my job."

"You did your job, and you're still under contract, but Cora did say she has some new clients lined up for you when my contract ends," he told her.

John headed into the bathroom, and her eyes followed his perfectly toned ass. This man would probably drive her insane, but what bothered her was he seemed indifferent to her contract ending. She wouldn't live in such close proximity anymore. If Stephanie remembered the date correctly, she had a little over a week left. Stephanie needed to get on the ball and look for an apartment. She snatched her clothes up and hurried to her place.

Showered and dressed, Stephanie lay her laptop on her legs. She hated to look for an apartment because it was such a pain in the ass. Maybe she could find one in Hopedale, but she needed to find one she could afford. She did have a good salary working for Cora, but nice apartments could be pricey. As she was scrolling through Kijiji, John knocked on her door.

"Come in," she called to him.

"Hey, whatcha doin, sweetheart?" John plopped down on the couch.

"Looking for an apartment." He stiffened next to her.

"Wait... what... why?" He stammered.

"My contract ends next week." She glanced at him and then back to the screen.

"What does that have to do with you looking for an apartment?" He sounded terrified.

"Because the apartment was part of the contract." Her tone should have been followed by duh.

"But it's my house, and I want you to stay." He waved his hands around the room.

"I wouldn't feel right keeping the apartment, John." she sighed.

"Why?" He pulled the laptop from her and took her hands in his. "The apartment will be vacant if you leave, and then I've got to find another tenant, and I haven't had the best of luck with previous tenants." He looked into her eyes. "I don't want you to leave."

"I don't know, John. I feel like I'm taking advantage of the situation." Stephanie didn't want to leave.

"Please, don't leave." John's voice was desperate, and she met his eyes again.

"I don't want to leave, but won't people think I'm taking advantage of you?" Stephanie was more concerned with what Cora and John's family would think.

"I don't care what people think." He cupped her cheek

"I do. Cora's my boss, and God knows what she'll think when she finds out about us." Stephanie's stomach turned because she could probably lose her job.

"She knows, and I never heard Aunt Cora so excited in my life." John laughed. "Her exact words were, *I was right again. I amaze even myself.*"

"What?" Stephanie squeaked. "Are you serious?"

"Yeah." John lifted her into his lap. "She's been trying to match all of us in the family. She introduced Sarah to James. When Aunt Cora was younger, they used to call her Cupid and still do." John chuckled. "She introduced mom and dad too."

"Your mom told me Cora had a gift for matching people." The conversation with Kathleen came back, and she narrowed her eyes as she played with the collar of his shirt. "Did you know she was doing this?"

"When you first got here, it was the last thing I was thinking about. I wasn't in the best state of mind. I return to work in eleven days, and I've got you." John cupped her cheeks and held her gaze. "I do have you, don't I?"

"You've got me," Stephanie whispered against his lips.

The kiss was slow and tender. Not like the kisses they shared the night before. It was a promise telling her he belonged to her, and John O'Connor had her body, mind, and soul.

"Do you two ever come up for air?" A voice boomed from the doorway.

266

"A.J, do you ever knock?" A deep groan vibrated through her mouth before John released her lips.

"If I knock, people know I'm coming, and they may not let me in." Aaron chuckled as Stephanie tried to move off John's lap, but John wrapped his arms around her. "Hi, Stephanie."

Aaron's lopsided grin made her giggle. Aaron was like a playful child, and she could see why girls swarmed to him. With the O'Connor charm and good looks, he could be lethal to a woman's heart.

"Hi, A.J." Stephanie smiled.

"What do you want?" John grumbled in annoyance.

"I was looking for some advice, and Uncle Kurt told me what happened last night. I wanted to make sure you guys were good." It was the first time Stephanie saw Aaron with a serious expression since the day she met him.

"I'll be right out." John nodded to his brother.

"Thanks, bro." Aaron winked at Stephanie and disappeared from the doorway.

"So, we've decided you're staying, right?" John held her face between his hands, and with the hopeful look in his eyes, it made it impossible to say no to him.

"I'm staying." She smiled.

"Thank, Christ. One crisis averted." John chuckled as he placed a quick kiss on her lips, and before he disappeared out of her apartment, he blew her another.

Stephanie did have to talk to Cora, though. Whether the woman knew or not, it wouldn't be professional if she didn't face the music. Stephanie wasn't nervous about the call to her boss and smiled as she tapped Cora's number.

"Cora the Cupid strikes again." Stephanie snickered.

Chapter 21

Aaron leaned against the counter, gazing through the patio door. The happy go lucky bundle of energy who annoyed the shit out of everyone looked nothing like himself. John's little brother appeared to have the weight of the world on his shoulders.

"You want a beer or something?" John opened the fridge.

"No thanks." Something was wrong if Aaron turned down a beer.

"What's up?" John poured himself a cup of coffee and held the pot up, but again Aaron shook his head. "Spill."

"Were you always sure you wanted to be a cop?" His youngest brother shoved his hands in his jean's pockets, and for the first time, uncertainty spread across Aaron's face.

"I had my doubts in the beginning." John had struggled with the same thing after he graduated from University.

"How'd you decide?" Aaron turned away from the door and stared at him.

There was something in Aaron's eyes. Something John hadn't seen since Aaron was a little boy. His brother was scared.

"I always wanted to help people, and there are only a few ways I could do it. Medicine was not an option for me. Ian is the only one who got those brains. The only option I could think of was law enforcement. Even during training, I wavered. Then I got to go on a ride-along with Uncle Kurt. A young girl had been missing for a couple of days, and her family was sick with worry. Uncle Kurt got called to a house where someone had called about being held against her will." John remembered the day he knew for sure he wanted to be a police officer vividly.

John sipped his coffee and made his way to the barstool. Aaron followed and leaned his elbows on the counter. The ride-along with Kurt wasn't something he talked about, but it was a pivotal moment in his life.

"To make a long story short, it was the missing girl. Her boyfriend kept her locked in his apartment. Something about her wanting to break up with him, and he didn't like it. The asshole got thrown in jail, and Uncle Kurt brought the girl back to her family. A.J, it was amazing to know you helped bring two terrified parents back their daughter. I wanted the same kind of joy in people's lives." John watched his brother for a moment.

"Cool," was all Aaron said, but he seemed to be searching for something else to say.

"I love my job, A.J., and sure it's not always a bed of roses. Hell, most of the time you're arresting pricks you want to smack up the side of the head, but even getting them off the street makes a difference. You're keeping people safe." John was proud to be a police officer.

"I'm terrified, John. What if I'm not good at this?" Aaron plowed his hands through his hair.

"I'm not going to tell you what to do, A.J., but I truly believe you'll be one of the best. Being scared is normal. You're only twenty-two years old. Hell, I still get scared." John would say he'd been scared about his feelings for Stephanie, but it would give Aaron the perfect opening. "If you change your mind, you still have lots of time to decide on another career choice."

"You want to know why I decided on this career." Aaron blushed.

"If you want to tell me." John squeezed his shoulder.

"Because I look up to you and James." Aaron looked down at the floor. "As much as I bug the shit out of both of you, I think you're the best guys in the world."

"I'm honored. You need to think long and hard about whether this is what you want to do." John threw his arm around Aaron's shoulders. "I honestly think you'll be a great addition to the department. You've got the heart and the compassion for the job. Even if you're a pain in the ass sometimes."

"Fucker." Aaron shoved John and laughed.

"Maybe you can talk to James and Uncle Kurt too. Maybe get their take on it." John wanted to make sure Aaron had all the information he needed to make an informative decision.

"I'll do that. I do feel better. Thanks, bro." Aaron gripped his hand.

"Anytime." John had no doubt his little brother would be a great cop.

"How are things with you and Stephanie going?" Aaron asked.

"Great." John couldn't stop the smile. "She's great."

"How great?" Aaron grinned as he lifted an eyebrow, showing the Aaron he knew and loved.

"None-of-your-business great, you pervert." John playfully pushed him, and Aaron let out a hearty laugh.

"What about the prowler last night. Have you heard anything?" Aaron followed John into the living room, and they settled in front of the television.

"No, I'm trying not to worry, but something doesn't strike me right about it." John shook his head.

In the small town, he knew almost everyone, and Hopedale was a safe, quiet place. Hell, people couldn't go to the bathroom without neighbors knowing. James could be right, and it might have been a teenager up to mischief, but something in the pit of his stomach told John it was more.

Aaron stayed for a couple of hours, and John was glad. It wasn't often he had one-on-one time with Aaron. Usually, seven of them would hang out together. At least they used to.

James started to back out of things at the last minute. It wasn't him. John and James used to spend hours watching a game or shooting the shit. His twin seemed to be distant in recent weeks. Almost as if he wanted to avoid John, and when James did drop by, he never stayed for more than a few minutes.

Growing up, John and James were always in each other's pockets. They enjoyed all the same things. Hockey, baseball, action movies, and at times, they could almost read each other's minds. They both went through the police academy together. James did better in some elements while John excelled in others, but the one thing they were both great at was working as one. Their co-workers couldn't understand how they always knew what the other was going to do before he did it. They'd always explained it as a twin thing. John wished he could access the twin thing because he didn't have a clue what was going on with James.

Stephanie left for a meeting with Cora, and Aaron headed back to town. John wanted to figure out what was going on with James, and his brother wasn't going to brush him off this time.

John stepped outside his door and glanced around. Hart Street was one of the smaller roads in town and ran off Main Road. Only four houses stood on the tiny street. Sandy lived in the first, and James' home was the last. The two in between belonged to John and Mary Ray.

Mrs. Ray was a widow in her mid-sixties and lived in her home for as long as John could remember. She used to babysit John and his brothers when they were children and had nine kids of her own.

"It's good to see you up and around again, Johnny." Mrs. Ray waved to him from her front step as he passed her house.

"It's good to be up and around, Mrs. Ray." Besides Nanny Betty and Cora, Mrs. Ray was the only other person who called him Johnny, and as much as he hated the name, he had to respect his elders.

"On your way to see Jimmy?" She shouted, and John chuckled.

"Yeah, and my nephew." John was almost to the end of her property.

"That boy needs to get out more." Mrs. Ray nodded her head toward James' house. "Poor sweet Sarah wouldn't want him to keep himself locked in the house."

"I'm hoping I can change some things with my visit." He waved to Mrs. Ray and continued down the road. "You take care of yourself, Mrs. Ray."

The driveway to James' split-level house looked bare, and a lump formed in John's throat. The house was a little bigger than his with a larger front garden. James bought the house when he and Sarah got married. The front yard was well-manicured, but usually, flowers lined the walkway to the front door. This year there were no flowers because Sarah wasn't there to plant them. The house looked naked without her special touch. Sarah was gone.

John opened the door and shouted to James. Nobody answered. James SUV was parked in the driveway, which meant he had to be home. John called out again but still no response. He closed the door and walked up the few steps to the main landing, but the house looked deserted. John started to head to the top level to see if James had laid down for a while, but a noise from the kitchen drew his attention.

The patio door leading to the backyard was open, and the vertical blinds flapped against the wall as the breeze flowed through the door. John stepped outside and spotted James on the grass holding Mason in front of him. The youngster was growing so damn fast, and John laughed at Mason's contagious giggle.

"James," John yelled from the back deck.

"Hey, what're you doing here?" James stood and made his way toward the house with Mason in his arms.

"I knew you were off today, and Steph had some work stuff to do." He'd never had to explain why he showed up unannounced before.

"I was just about to go and get the big guy some lunch." His brother tickled the baby's belly, and Mason giggled as he grabbed onto his father's hand.

"Big guy is right." John laughed. "What the hell are you feeding him?"

"He eats like A.J." James chuckled.

"You better look for another job to feed him when he gets older." John followed James into the house. "I can't believe how big he's gotten."

"I know. Can you believe he'll be a year old in three months?" James placed the baby in a high chair.

Mason slapped his hands against the tray and squealed. When John sat in the chair next to the highchair, Mason stared at him with a big sloppy grin.

"You're having a party for him, right?" John wanted to kick himself right after he asked the question.

Maybe it wasn't a good idea to have a party. It had been less than six months since Sarah died. As John glanced around, he could still see so much of his sister-in-law. John didn't know if he would be able to stay in the house in the same situation.

"Mom insisted we have it at their house." James moved around the kitchen as he prepared lunch for Mason.

"What do you want for your big birthday, little man?" John asked.

Mason slammed his hands against the high chair's table again, and bubbles of saliva ran down the baby's chin. John tapped his hand on the tray of the high chair and Mason did the same

"Oh. A set of drums, huh," John said to his nephew.

"And we can keep them at Uncle John's. You can play them when you go to visit. Right, buddy?" James placed the bowl down in front of Mason.

Without hesitation, the little boy plowed his two hands into the bowl and shoved a fist full of food into his mouth. John shook his head in amusement, but this was as good a time as any to get to the root of James' distant behavior.

"James, can we talk?" John asked.

"That sounds serious." James poured two cups of coffee.

"Are we okay?" John leaned forward in the chair and rested his elbows on his knees.

James stiffened for a moment and then plowed his hand through his brown hair. John knew from his brother's movement. James was about to clam up, but John wouldn't give in to it.

"We're fine, bro." The tone confirmed John's suspicion.

John sat back in the chair as Mason tipped the bowl of food onto the tray of his highchair. He knew if he pushed James too much, it would be a huge argument, but he wanted his brother back. If James needed to talk, John wanted to be there for him.

"It doesn't seem like it. You hardly call, you rarely come over, and you seem pissed with me." John turned to see his reaction.

"I'm not pissed with you." James sighed. "I was pissed with you, yes, but I was angrier with myself."

"What? Why would you be mad at yourself?" Now he was baffled.

"The day of the funeral, you asked me to go with you. Mom was going to keep Mason for the night. I was so wrapped up in my grief. I didn't want to go anywhere." James turned to the window. "It's my fault you had the accident. If I'd gone with you, we would've stayed all night, and the accident wouldn't have happened."

John leaped up from the chair. James had a death grip on the counter, and his jaw clenched. John quickly realized why James stayed away, and it had nothing to do with work or Mason. James blamed himself for what happened to John.

"Hold on a second, bro." John grabbed James by the shoulders and turned him. "None of it was your fault. It was a moose, bad weather, and dumb luck."

"I should've gone with you." James's voice cracked.

"You'd just buried your wife for Christ's sake. I don't blame you. I probably would've crawled in a hole if I were in your shoes," John admitted. "I wouldn't be able to keep things together the way you did."

"That's just it, John, I'm not keeping it together." Tears filled James' eyes. "Sure, when people are around, I put on this brave front, but I feel lost. Empty. The only thing keeping me from falling apart is Mason."

John's heart broke as tears streamed down James' face. Everyone thought James had dealt with Sarah's death so well, but he'd held it all inside.

"Why didn't you talk to me? Or mom and dad. Hell, you could've talked to Ian, Keith, or Mike. For fuck's sake, even Nick and Aaron would've listened." John knew his family would have been there in a second if James needed to talk.

"I couldn't. Everyone was so worried about you, and the last thing they needed was to worry about me too." The guilt hit John in the gut like a sledgehammer.

"So, you just tried to deal with all this yourself." John shook his head. "Well, you don't need to anymore, James. You shouldn't have tried to do this on your own. I'm here for you. Even if it's just a couple of hours to yourself or someone to sit and have a few beers."

John pulled his brother into a hug and felt all the tension dissipate from James. He had six months of unshed grief to release, and John allowed his brother to let it all out.

"Let it out, buddy," John whispered as he tried to keep himself composed. "Just let it all out."

"Thanks for being here, bro," James choked out.

"Since conception, bro. Since conception," John whispered.

It killed John to know James kept all his emotions bottled up because he didn't want to upset the family. *Jesus fucking Christ.* If the family knew, they would be devastated. James shouldn't have gone through it by himself. Grief was bad enough when you had someone to lean on, but alone, it had to be like smothering.

When James finally pulled himself together, John turned back toward the baby. Mason stared at them with his little head tilted to one side and his face covered with food. John and James glanced at each other and burst into a fit of laughter.

"See, when I'm having a bad day, I've got him to make me laugh." James smiled.

"He's a character." John chuckled, but John knew James still needed to talk to more than Mason's sweet face.

James put Mason down for a nap after he'd practically had to bath him in the kitchen sink. John cleaned up the mess the baby made on his chair and floor. James seemed to have gotten some of his grief out of his system. At least for a little while anyway. It would hit him from time to time. Either way, John was glad to help.

"Did you know Aunt Cora suggested Stephanie as my therapist because of her cupid power?" John said when he and James sat on the back deck.

John and his brothers always referred to Cora's unique gift as *cupid power*. Of course, it was their way to make fun of it. It was a hard thing to believe, but they were also not stupid enough to doubt it.

"Looks like she was right." James chuckled and held out a beer to John.

"Yeah, she was." John nodded.

"I like her." James leaned against the railing. "I'm guessing you do too?"

"I've never felt like this before." Stephanie brought out feelings John couldn't even imagine. "When you told me you were in love with Sarah after a month, I thought you were nuts, but I understand now."

"You love her?" James raised his eyebrows.

"Yeah," John admitted. "She's amazing. She makes me feel...." John stopped.

"Alive?" James finished.

"Yeah." There was the twin thing or did know because of how he felt with Sarah.

"I'm happy for you," James said the words, but there was sadness in his voice.

"You'll find love again." It was probably the wrong thing to say, but James needed to hear it.

Rhonda Brewer

"I don't know, John. I believe there's only one great love of your life, and I lost her." James cleared his throat.

"Didn't you tell us Sarah said she'd send you someone?" John reminded him.

"Yeah, and she was going to send someone for all of my brothers." James pointed the bottle toward John.

"I guess I was first, huh." John clinked his bottle against his brother's.

"I hope the ones she sends for Nick, Mike, and A.J have lots of patience." James laughed.

Those women would need the patience of saints. The three youngest O'Connors liked to play the field, and it mortified his mother. Aaron and Nick had a string of girlfriends a mile long, and none of them lasted more than a week or two. John couldn't remember the last time one of them spent a weekend dateless. Mike wasn't as bad but still tended to jump from one girl to another. John couldn't wait for the day when they were knocked on their asses by a woman. It'll be a sight to see.

Chapter 22

Stephanie sat across from Cora at the café table and went over her schedule for the next couple of weeks. Cora handed her files on four new patients. She was excited, but she had to convince Cora to stop her last two weeks of pay. Stephanie hated to lose the money, but it was wrong to get paid when John didn't need therapy anymore.

"Cora, I don't think I should be paid for the last two weeks of John's contract," Stephanie blurted before she chickened out.

"Why in heaven's name would I not pay you?" Cora gasped.

"Well... Cora, it's... Oh, God..." Stephanie didn't know what to say.

"You're good for my nephew." Cora smiled at her. "Of course, I knew you would be."

"I've heard you've got a knack for being a matchmaker." Stephanie raised an eyebrow and smiled.

"That's me, Cora the Cupid." She sipped her coffee.

It was hard to believe the woman was in her late fifties. Five feet tall and slender, she didn't look much older than forty. She favored Nanny Betty in her petite stature, and her sky-blue eyes were lighter than John and his brothers. Her stylish bob showed a few flecks of gray, but they appeared more like highlights. She had a kind smile, and Stephanie understood why people felt so at ease with her.

"I've been about your nickname." Stephanie sipped her tea.

"I guess by the light in your eyes and the glow in your cheeks, things with Johnny are good." Cora grinned.

"Yes, they are." Stephanie covered her cheeks with her hands, but from the expression on Cora's face, she knew there was no way to hide the blush.

"Kathleen has explained those O'Connor men are hard to resist and damn good in bed." Cora cringed. "I don't need to know about my brothers, but Kathleen and Alice seem to think it's something I need to know."

"Umm, ok," Stephanie stammered as she almost knocked over her cup.

"No need to be embarrassed, Stephanie." Cora laughed.

The whole family had no qualms in bringing up sex. It had to be the generation because her parents were the same way. There were times Stephanie and Marina wanted to run screaming from the room when her mom and dad would tease them.

Toward the end of her meeting, John texted Stephanie to let her know he would be with James and Mason for the afternoon; then, he'd be at rehearsal. Even though they'd only been apart for a few hours, she missed him, but she knew he was worried about James.

Stephanie didn't know James well, but even she could see he withdrew form people. It was tragic. To be thrown a curveball as he had was heart-shattering. Stephanie always believed things happened for a reason, but it was hard to see why someone needed to be taken away so young. There were other plans for James.

The traffic on the way to her parent's house was out of control. She'd gotten so used to living in the easy-going community of Hopedale she'd forgotten what a pain it was to drive around St. John's. By the time she got to her parents' house, Stephanie was ready to turn around and speed back to Hopedale.

Her mom stood outside the front of the house watering the flowers lining the front step. Her mother wasn't one to sit around and do nothing. Stephanie didn't remember a time when her mom sat down and just relaxed.

Her father owned and operated a construction company in the city, and her mom worked there as the receptionist. Her dad told everyone his wife was the heart and kept the company going. Although her mother recently retired, she still went to the office every day to help the office staff. Stephanie couldn't quite understand how it meant she was retired.

"Hi, Mom." Stephanie jogged up the steps and hugged her mother.

"I wasn't expecting you today." Her mom dropped the watering can. "What a grand surprise."

"I had the afternoon off and a meeting with my boss." She linked her arm with her mother as they walked into the house. "She gave me some new patients since John's contract is up in two weeks."

"That's great, sweetheart." Stephanie inhaled as they walked into the kitchen.

The mouth-watering aroma of baking bread filled the air, and she started to salivate. Her mother's homemade bread was the best. Of course, there wasn't much her mother couldn't cook. Stephanie's mom grew up in a small community where her parents owned a bakery.

"Homemade bread." Stephanie sighed when she saw the counter lined off with several loaves.

"Would you like a couple of slices?" Her mom chuckled as she cut one of the hot loaves.

"Definitely." Stephanie grinned.

Warm homemade bread right out of the oven and smothered in butter was one of the things she couldn't resist. Stephanie grabbed a plate from the cupboard, and her mother poured two cups of tea as Stephanie took a huge bite of the fluffy bread. *Heaven.* Stephanie glanced up when she noticed her mother across the table with her eyes narrowed, staring at her.

"What?" Stephanie mumbled with a mouth full of buttery goodness.

"You look different." Her mother sat back in the chair and studied her. "You're glowing."

"Mom, you're crazy." Stephanie took another huge bite of bread and avoided her mother's scrutiny.

"You're seeing someone," her mom gasped, and Stephanie practically choked on her bread.

"What makes you say that?" Stephanie sipped her tea as she tried to hide her smile.

"It's in your eyes." her mother smiled. "Who is he?"

No matter how much she tried to hide things, her mother always knew. It was some sixth sense. Stephanie wiped her hands and sat back in her chair.

"How do you do that?" Stephanie shook her head and smiled.

"It's a gift." her mom chuckled. "Now spill it, young lady."

There was no use in trying to deny it. The woman was relentless when she wanted to know something. Stephanie remembered she and Marina suspected their mother must have been an interrogator in a previous life.

"He's a police officer," Stephanie began. "I know it probably sounds terrible, but it's the client I've been helping for the past few months."

"Oh." She couldn't read her mother's expression.

"He's wonderful, Mom. He's smart, funny, kind, and makes me so happy." Stephanie sighed.

"Is he handsome?" Janet raised an eyebrow.

"Very." Stephanie fanned herself.

"Are you careful?" her mother asked.

"Mom," Stephanie groaned, but her mom was always an advocate for safe sex.

"Stephanie," her mother mocked.

"Yes, Mom, I'm careful." Stephanie rolled her eyes but answered because there was no way the subject would drop until she knew for sure.

"Good." Her mother smiled.

"Where's Dad?" Stephanie decided it was a good time to change the subject, but from her mother's expression, a cold chill suddenly ran up her back. "Mom, what's wrong?"

"Don't start to worry. Your dad went to get a restraining order." Her mom clasped her hands around the teacup.

"What? Why?" Stephanie's heart jumped

"Marc's been harassing us. Wanting to know where to find Marina. For the last couple of days, he's been waiting in the driveway when we get home from the office. Your father just wanted to punch him in the jaw, but I called the police to have him removed from the property," her mother explained. "Your dad is worried he's going to do something."

"Does Rina know?" Maybe it wasn't a good idea to keep the phone call she'd gotten a secret.

"No, and we don't want her to know." Her mother shook her head. "She's happy and content and doesn't need to worry about his issues, and he'll give up eventually."

"I don't know, Mom. He seems pretty determined." Maybe her sister should know because if Marc did anything to hurt their parents, Marina would never forgive herself.

"I don't want to talk about him. Now tell me more about your sexy man." Her mom put her elbows on the table and leaned her chin on her fists.

"Mom." Stephanie giggled.

"Do we at least get to meet him?" she asked.

"Of course. We're going to a fundraiser on Friday. So probably Saturday or Sunday." She should probably ask John if he wanted to meet her parents first.

"The one at the Delta hotel?" Her mother's face lit up.

"Yes." Stephanie nodded.

"Your father and I are going. I guess we'll meet him there." Her mother was way too excited.

"I guess so." Stephanie smiled

Stephanie helped her mother tidy the kitchen and bag the fresh bread. Of course, declaring at least one loaf was hers to take home. As they finished, her father sauntered into the kitchen. Her dad went directly to his wife and kissed her like they'd been apart for months instead of hours.

Stephanie still felt embarrassed when her parents kissed in front of her. Growing up, Stephanie couldn't remember a time her parents spent more than a few hours apart. They had disagreements over the years, but even their worst conflict would be over after a long overnight discussion. Janet had two rules about relationships. Never go to bed angry, and kiss like it's the last time.

"Hi, Dad," Stephanie greeted her father.

"Hey, Princess." He wrapped his big arms around Stephanie and lifted her off the floor.

Her father was a large man, six feet four, and even at fifty-one years old, he was still solid muscle. All his years of working construction kept him in great shape. Although he owned the company and didn't need to do manual labor, he always worked right alongside his employees. It was one of the things Stephanie admired about her father. His thick ash blonde hair had started to turn grey, but he still turned her mother's head, and his deep green eyes sparkled whenever he looked at the love of his life.

"Our baby girl has a new man." Her mother sidled up to him and wrapped her arms around his waist.

"Mom, really?" Stephanie groaned.

"Oh, and who is this new man?" Her dad's deep voice boomed.

"He's a police officer," her mom continued. "He'll be at the fundraiser tomorrow night."

"I'll have to check him out." Her father narrowed his eyes.

"Dad, please be good," Stephanie groaned.

"It's my job to intimidate your boyfriends." His face turned serious. "I wish I'd scared off Marc sooner."

"Dad, it wasn't your fault," Stephanie reminded him. "He fooled all of us in the beginning."

"Let's be glad Marina and Danny are far away from him." Her mother reached up to kiss his cheek. "Did you get the restraining order?"

"They said because of his past violence, it was a good idea to get this." He pulled an envelope from his pocket and handed it to her mom. "You should probably get one too, Princess, before he starts bothering you."

"Dad, I live in an apartment owned by a police officer, and he has a brother and an uncle who are also police officers, plus another brother in the police academy," Stephanie said. "I'm sure he isn't stupid."

"I don't know, but you may want to talk to your new man about it and get his opinion." Her mother was probably right.

Marc O'Reilly didn't worry Stephanie in the least. He'd backed down quickly the couple of times she confronted him. Mentioning it to John would only worry him and his family.

The day with her parents had been fun. It seemed like such a long time since she spent a full day with them. They missed Marina and Danny as much as she did. Probably more. Marina lived with them for the last few weeks before she moved, so they were used to having them around all the time.

Stephanie was about to leave when she received a text from John. He was on the way home and wanted to let her know. When she sent a message to tell him she was on the way back too, his next text made her smile.

John: I missed you today.

"Must be from your man, huh." Stephanie glanced at her dad.

"Yes, it is." She couldn't stop the smile if she tried.

"If he can make you smile with a simple text message, I like him already." Her father kissed her cheek. "You've got to bring him by on Sunday. I want to give him the third degree."

"Dad." Stephanie rolled her eyes.

The drive home seemed to take forever. Mostly because she couldn't wait to see John, it was the first time since they admitted how they felt, they'd been apart all day. She missed him more than she thought possible. He was on the front step when she pulled in the driveway, and Stephanie grinned as she walked up the steps.

"Hi, sweetheart." John kissed her on the lips quickly.

"My parents want me to bring you for Sunday dinner," she said quickly because she was still reluctant to believe they were together.

"Sounds great." John took her hand as they entered the house.

"They're going to the fundraiser tomorrow night, and said they want to meet you." She glanced up at him.

"Why do you look nervous?" John chuckled.

"Because my dad tends to embarrass me, and my mom is just as bad." She sighed when he wrapped his arms around her.

"Isn't that what parents are supposed to do?" John kissed the top of her head.

"I suppose." She rested her cheek on his chest. "I don't want them to scare you away."

"That'll never happen." John squeezed her tightly. "I'm not easily scared."

"Good." She played with the buttons on his shirt. "I enjoyed myself today, but I missed you."

"I missed you too." His voice was barely above a whisper. "But I've finally got everything straightened out with James, and I had a great day with my nephew. I found out Mom and Dad had a change of plans, and they're going to the fundraiser as well."

"That's great," Stephanie murmured when his lips brushed below her ear, sending tingles down her body.

"Now, I'm all yours." John kissed the side of her neck. "Hmm... you smell good." John's warm breath made her shiver.

"You drive me crazy." She wrapped her arms around his neck.

"I know the feeling." He cupped her ass and backed her into the living room.

His lips met hers, and she'd started to unbutton his shirt when the sound of breaking glass and loud pops startled them. John pushed her to the ground and covered her with his own body as glass from the large bay window showered around them.

"John," Stephanie screamed.

"Don't move," John shouted.

"What's going on?" She was too terrified to move.

"Crawl into the hallway," John ordered.

When the loud noise stopped, John bolted to the laundry room and returned with a gun in his hand. He cracked the front door open enough to peek out. His weapon was held in front of him as he wedged himself through the narrow opening and disappeared outside.

Stephanie managed to crawl into the hallway without cutting herself on the pieces of glass all over the floor. She glanced into the living room and scanned the wall where the window used to be. Jagged pieces of glass stuck out around the edge of the large window, and the furniture in front of the window glittered with shards of glass.

What in the hell happened?

"I didn't see anyone." John had his cell up to his ear when he re-entered the house. "How the hell am I supposed to know? Just get over here. Now."

His gun was now at his side, and she shivered at the sight of it. Stephanie was never a fan of them, but John was a police officer, she didn't know he kept his weapon in the house.

John shoved the phone back into his pocket and his gun into the back of his jeans. It almost seemed as if he was afraid to approach her as he knelt in front of her.

"Are you hurt?" He scanned her from head to toe as he helped her to her feet.

Stephanie's legs were wobbly, and she took a minute before she felt steady. As she got to her feet, she glanced up and saw a trickle of blood run down John's face. She gasped and reached up to the side of his head.

"John, you're bleeding," she said.

"I'm fine. It's just a scratch." The amount of blood running down the side of his face seemed to be coming from more than a scratch.

"Let me check it, please," she begged.

John tipped his head down for her to examine. A small gash ran across the side of his head just above his ear. It wasn't big, but it looked deep, and she ran to the bathroom to get a cloth. When she returned, James, Ian, Mike, Keith, and Aaron stood in the foyer like a bunch of avenging angels. She went straight to John and pressed the cloth against the side of his head. As she turned, Nick ran in through the door.

"You should have called Uncle Kurt," James sounded pissed.

"I called him." Nick glared at John.

"What the hell is going on here?" Mike asked. "First, I find out someone was lurking around your house the other night, and now this. Have you checked what broke the window?"

Stephanie assumed it was a rock someone threw at the window. Although, when she looked at John, a chill ran through her body.

"Bullets." John plowed his hands through his hair.

One little word made it feel as if ice started to pulse through her veins. Stephanie's legs gave out, and John grabbed her before she hit the floor.

"A bu… bu… bullet broke the window?" She didn't even realize she'd said the words until John sat her on a chair. "How do you… know it was a… bullet?"

294

"I know the sound of a gun, and I saw it hit the wall." He held her hands as he motioned with his head at the wall opposite the window.

"John, what the fuck is going on? Why would someone be shooting at your house?" James yelled.

"How the fuck am I supposed to know, but I've got a feeling it has something to do with the prowler the other night." John didn't look at James as he rubbed his hands up and down her arms.

"Marc." Her voice cracked, and all eyes turned to her.

"Who's Marc?" Aaron crouched next to her and John.

"Marina's ex-husband?" John practically growled the words, and Stephanie nodded.

"Marc O'Reilly was married to my sister. While she was pregnant, she found out he was on drugs. He hit her, but she refuses to admit he hit her more than a few times. My parents had to get a restraining order against him today because he kept showing up at their house looking for Marina. He called me a few weeks ago and demanded I tell him where she was. I didn't tell him, but he said I'd be in for a world of hurt if I didn't." She knew she was rambling again, but they didn't seem to be annoyed as they listened to her.

"Why didn't you tell me about this?" John cupped her face in his hands.

"I didn't think he'd do something so awful." She trembled so bad her teeth began to chatter.

Nick disappeared at the nod of Ian's head and returned with a blanket. John wrapped it around her shoulders and shoved her hair back from her face.

"Do you know where he lives or any of his family?" Kurt's voice boomed from the front door.

Stephanie slowly glanced up, and for the first time since she'd met John's uncle, he scared her. Kurt always seemed to be friendly toward her any time she'd been in his company, but with the way his brow furrowed, he looked ready to kill someone.

"No. He has no siblings, and both his parents are deceased." Stephanie sat up straight. "Oh my God, John. My parents." She slapped her hands against her pockets in an attempt to find her phone. "I need to make sure they're okay."

"Give me their address. Me and Mike will check on them." Keith nodded toward Mike.

When she retrieved her phone from the floor where it had fallen when the chaos started, Stephanie texted the address to Keith. He disappeared through the door with Mike behind him. Seconds after they left, the house filled with police officers, and John guided her to the apartment out of the way. He helped her to the couch, and she watched as officers tracked in and out of the house. Stephanie continually glanced at her phone for word on her parents. It seemed to take forever for Keith to text her.

"Uncle Kurt will find him, and your parents will be fine." John wrapped his arms tightly around her.

She nodded, but she wasn't sure. Why hadn't Keith texted her? It had been more than forty-five minutes, and she'd about reached the end of her patience. She was about to call Keith when her father's voice drew her attention. She looked up as Ian escorted her parents into her apartment. Stephanie jumped up and ran into her father's strong arms.

"Princess, are you okay?" Her dad kissed the top of her head.

She nodded as she tried to swallow against the lump forming in her throat. Her parents were there in front of her, but the thought of what Marc could have done to them had tears burning her eyes.

"Hi Mr. Kelly, I'm John." He shook hands with her father.

"Call me, Doug, please. This is my wife, Janet," her dad said as he kept Stephanie tightly in his arms.

"I wish we'd met under better circumstances." Her mother's voice cracked.

"Me too, and I hate to say this, but my uncle wants to ask you both a few questions." John motioned to Kurt, who still looked like he was ready to kill someone.

"Certainly." Her dad guided Stephanie and her mother to the couch and sat between them.

Stephanie didn't hear half of the conversation because all she could think about was the bullets that could have killed her or John. Ian had finally convinced John to allow him to check the gash on his head. John seemed annoyed, but he at least allowed Ian to clean it and put some sterile strips on it.

"I never thought he'd do anything like this," Janet sobbed.

"If it's him, we'll find him before he does anything else." Kurt shook hands with her dad and patted Stephanie's hands. "Don't you worry. My nephew will make sure this little lady is safe."

"We're finished, sir." An officer's voice floated in from the doorway.

"Thanks, Simms." Kurt acknowledged the young man. "I know you don't want to upset your other daughter, but I think she needs to know about this. She may be living in Ontario, but finding people is not as hard as it used to be. She needs to be careful just in case this guy manages to get off the island." Kurt nodded at her dad, then left the apartment with the other officer.

Kurt wasn't wrong, Newfoundland was an island, but there were a lot of ways to get to the mainland before anyone knew a person was gone. Stephanie hated the thought of telling Marina, her sister didn't need to be afraid again, but Marina could be in danger.

"You know we're all assuming it's your sister's ex, but we can't be sure until they talk to him." Nick was studying to be a lawyer, and it seemed as if he was in lawyer mode.

"Who else could it be?" John asked. "I don't know anyone else who would do this."

"Neither do I." Stephanie couldn't think of anyone.

Once the police had left, John, James, Keith, and Mike covered the window with pieces of board. She couldn't stop glancing at the small holes in the wall. Bullets that could have killed John. Her stomach lurched, and she had to swallow to keep from vomiting.

She was horrified to think she could have lost him. She shook her head and purposely turned away where she couldn't see the wall.

Kurt sent a police cruiser to watch her parent's house and stationed another in front of John's house. Since Aaron and Nick still lived in town, they drove her parents' home and promised Stephanie they'd make sure they would check inside before they left them. Her father tried to convince her to go with them, but she didn't want to leave John.

A loud knock on the door startled her, and John was instantly at her side. Keith and James stepped in front of them like bodyguards as Ian and Mike stood next to the door. Mike glanced back at John, and when he nodded, Mike opened it.

"What happened?" Sandy rushed in and immediately rushed to Stephanie.

"Someone shot through the window," Stephanie explained, but as soon as the words were out of her mouth, tears filled her eyes.

"Oh, my lord." Sandy's face paled. "Who would do such a thing?"

"We don't know for sure, but the police are looking into it." Stephanie didn't want to say anything about Marc until they were sure.

"Did you see anyone around the house?" John asked.

Sandy glanced at Keith as if she couldn't speak until he gave her permission. When Keith nodded, Sandy turned back to John.

"I've been at work all night. I just got home and saw your window." She wrapped her arm around Stephanie's shoulder.

"Make sure you lock your doors and windows. Keep all your drapes closed too," Ian commanded Sandy.

Ian's face flushed when all eyes turned to him, and he immediately turned away to close the door. Mike smirked, and James grinned as Ian casually leaned against the wall. His eyes looked everywhere but at the woman next to her. Sandy's eyes flashed toward Ian several times with a look of obvious adoration. *Ah ha.* Now it made sense.

"I will." Sandy blushed.

"You'll be safe enough. There's a cruiser outside all night. So, don't worry." John seemed to be hiding a smile.

"I have an alarm system. I'm not worried, but it sure helps to know the police are outside." Sandy shot to her feet. "Anyway, I need to get home, but I'm glad you both are safe."

She nodded at Keith before going to the door. Ian opened it, and Sandy smiled at him. *Yep.* There was a spark. Stephanie wondered if Cora met Sandy.

"I'm heading home, but if you need me, call. Mom has Mason for the night." James followed Ian and Mike through the door, but Keith seemed apprehensive.

"You sure you don't need me to stay, bro?" Keith asked.

Keith was the biggest of all the brothers and built like a brick wall. His arms were large and muscled with tattoos around both biceps. Stephanie sometimes wondered how he fit through the door without needing to turn sideways because his shoulders were so broad. Keith was a construction worker, but he didn't get all those muscles from just construction.

"No, we're good, Keith." John slapped his brother on the back as he walked him to the door.

Keith nodded at Stephanie and left. He always seemed to be so stern, and she'd rarely seen him smile. It was as if he had the weight of the world on his shoulder, and she assumed he'd been hurt either in love or life.

John closed the door behind him and turned. His face was tense, and she could see the concern in his eyes. Things could have been so much worse. A lump formed in her throat as scenarios flashed through her head, and she wrapped her arms around herself.

"Don't worry, baby." He kissed the top of her head as he tugged her into his arms. "Everything's gonna be fine. Let's get some sleep."

John guided her toward his bedroom and tucked her tightly against him. Stephanie wasn't sure she'd be able to sleep and felt as if she was in a daze as she stripped and got into bed. John wrapped arms around her, and she relaxed in his embrace, although she still worried about the shooter returning.

"I love you, John," she whispered against his chest.

"I love you too, sweetheart." He pressed his lips against her temple. "Nobody's going to hurt you or your family. Not if I've got anything to do with it."

Stephanie closed her eyes, and as the adrenaline drained from her body, exhaustion set in. She drifted off to sleep in the arms of the man who'd become her world.

Chapter 23

Sleep was not his friend. The few times John did fall asleep, nightmares of Stephanie bleeding on the floor plagued him. He'd wake and make sure she was still safe in his arms. The third time John woke, he decided to give up.

John grabbed his phone off the nightstand and sighed when he saw it was only a little after five. Stephanie slept soundly next to him, and it took some careful movements to untangled himself from her arms. His heart skipped in his chest when he gazed down at her.

Nobody is ever going to hurt you.

John quietly dressed and headed out to the front deck. The light from the rising sun shimmered on the water as he glanced to the left. A warm breeze blew across his face, and the salty smell of the ocean filled his senses.

It was the end of June, and although it was chilly at night, the days started to get warmer. John's focus moved to the plywood covered window, and his body tensed. He needed to get Keith to fix it as soon as possible because it was only a reminder of what happened the previous night.

Keith didn't do much construction anymore, but he still owned the company and would make sure the window got fixed immediately. The family didn't know Keith had started a high-end security company when he lived in Yellowknife. A few years earlier, he'd moved it to Newfoundland so he could come home to live. For some reason, Keith kept it a secret. The only family who knew about it were John, James, and Kurt. John wasn't sure why his brother changed his career, but he stood behind him.

With a cup of coffee in one hand and his cell in the other, John returned to the front step. He sat down in one of the two wicker chairs and stretched his legs in front of him. It was always quiet early in the morning, except for the distant sound of seagulls and waves on the beach.

John scanned the road in front of his house as a black car drove by. John didn't pay much attention until the vehicle turned around and passed his home again. The car slowed, and John sat up straight.

The windows were tinted so John couldn't see the driver. He stood up, and the car sped off. John wondered if the officer in the police cruiser at the end of the driveway noticed the strange vehicle. John grabbed another cup of coffee from the kitchen and hurried down to the road.

"Hey, John." Rick Avery stepped out of the car.

"Whadda ya at, Rick?" John handed him one of the cups.

"Good, but a lot better in about fifty-four minutes." He chuckled. "It's been a long night."

"I bet." John scanned the road. "Anything strange during the night."

"Nothing out of the ordinary," Rick said. "That car seemed a little suspicious. I ran the plate."

"Probably someone being nosey." John laughed, but he had a strange feeling it was more.

"Yeah, typical small town. Heard you're coming back soon." Rick sipped the coffee.

"Yeah, it's been a long few months," John admitted.

"It'll be good to have you back, John." Rick slapped him on the back. "You've been missed."

"Thanks. It's good to see you again, Rick. I appreciate you keeping an eye on the house." John waved as he headed back to the house.

"No problem. Just keep your beauty safe." Rick winked as he slid back into the car.

It was going to be a long day, and Stephanie was going to need all the rest she could get, so he let her sleep. John went straight to his laundry room and tossed some clothes in the washer. Being able to do things himself again felt good. It was probably a good day to mow the lawn as well, but since it was still before eight in the morning, it was a little early to start the mower.

John's thoughts were interrupted by the vibration of his phone in his pocket. He headed out of the laundry room as he tapped the screen.

"Hello," he answered as he prepared another pot of coffee.

"Hey, bro," Nick responded.

"What's up?" John leaned against the counter and watched the coffee drip into the pot.

"Just wanted to let you know we're meeting at the hotel around five for soundcheck, but if you don't want to leave Stephanie after last night, I understand. We're not starting until eight," Nick said.

"Mike told me last night. I told him I'd rather not leave Stephanie alone." John didn't want to leave her for a minute after what happened.

"Mike told me to call you. He's such a fucking idiot," Nick complained. "How's she doin' today, by the way?"

"She's still sleeping, but she was pretty scared last night." The hair on the back of his neck prickled with the thought of what could have happened.

"You looked pretty scared yourself," Nick said.

Damn right, he was scared. He was fucking terrified, but what scared him the most was Stephanie could've been seriously hurt or worse. It made his blood run cold. What if he couldn't protect her?

"Did Ian pick up the tuxedos this morning?" John changed the subject because he couldn't talk about his fears.

"Yeah, he should be there soon. He dropped off mine and A.J.'s about twenty minutes ago," Nick answered and then shouted to someone.

John was about to say something when the front door opened. Ian's voice echoed from the front hall, and John hurried to the door to make sure he didn't wake Stephanie with his bellowing.

"Hey." Ian held up the garment bag. "One monkey suit for you, sir."

"Thanks." John hung it on the coat rack next to the door. "You want a cup of coffee or something?"

"Would love one." Ian grinned as he followed John to the kitchen. "You're my last drop off."

"Where's the little woman?" Ian moaned as he sipped the cup of coffee. "I needed this."

"She's asleep. Last night took the good out of her." It did for him too, but his brain wouldn't let him relax.

"Do you think her sister's ex could be involved?" Ian nodded toward the living room.

"He's the only one we can think of," John said. "He's known to be violent. I've got to make sure this guy doesn't hurt her."

"I could beat the shit out of guys like him." Ian growled.

John didn't doubt it. Ian achieved a black belt in Karate in his last year of high school, although John wasn't sure what level his black belt was. Their father had insisted they become involved with the sport when they were children. Kurt was a fourth-degree black belt and taught John, his brothers, and all John's cousins. Jess, Ian, and Keith stuck with the sport over the years, but the rest of the brothers and cousins did get as far as brown belts.

It was a toss-up of who was larger, Ian or Keith. Ian seemed to take up working out as therapy when his ex-girlfriend left him. John figured it was better to take his grief out on gym equipment rather than stick his head in a bottle.

"I've never seen you so starry-eyed over a woman before." Ian nudged him with his elbow.

"That's what love does to you, Bucko." John laughed.

"I'm not going there again. Just gonna play the field." Ian chuckled.

Colleen Morgan was Ian's best friend from the time she moved across the street from his parents. Ian was about seven, and Colleen was the same age, and they were joined at the hip right up until high school when they started to date. Everybody assumed Ian would eventually marry the girl.

Then two years earlier, Ian came home with an enormous chip on his shoulder. Nick had made a joke about there being trouble in paradise, and Ian slugged him. John and James had to pull them apart before Ian got another punch in. After a lot of shouting, Ian finally told them Colleen ended things and was moving to Manitoba with her brother. Ian never talked about her again, and nobody ever asked anything else.

"Ah, little brother, it'll hit you again when you least expect it." John squeezed Ian's shoulder.

As much as Ian joked about playing the field, John knew he wasn't one to jump from woman to woman. He also knew Ian had it bad for Sandy. Although anytime he mentioned it, Ian would deny it.

John was pretty sure the feelings were mutual since Sandy blushed anytime Ian spoke to her. Maybe someday they'd get together, but John wasn't about to turn to Cora for answers

Stephanie emerged from the bedroom as Ian was on his way out. She looked well-rested, but when she glanced into the living room, the fear in her eyes was evident.

"Hey there, sleepyhead." John tried to draw her attention away from the damage.

"Why didn't you wake me earlier? It's almost noon." Her eyes darted to Ian, and she blushed.

"He wanted to make sure you have lots of energy for tonight," Ian smiled, and John smacked him in the back of the head. "For the fundraiser."

"You're a pervert." John narrowed his eyes.

"Hey, your mind's in the gutter, bro. Watch him, Beauty. He's got a dirty mind." Ian ducked as John tried to smack him again. "Too fast for you, old man."

"I'm not that old, asshole," John grumbled.

"Seriously, how are you today?" Ian turned to Stephanie.

"I'm fine." She snickered as John glared at his brother.

"Good, we'll catch you tonight. Save me a dance." Ian smirked as he headed out the door.

Stephanie laughed as John took another swing at Ian, but his brother ducked and ran down the front steps.

"Still too slow, bro," Ian shouted.

John got the last laugh. Ian tripped when he noticed Sandy pull into her driveway, but he quickly recovered and gave John the middle finger for laughing. Ian always seemed to be a clumsy oaf whenever he was around John's cute neighbor.

When John turned back into the house, Stephanie stood in the hallway with her arms crossed over her chest, and her shoulder pressed against the wall.

"Did you sleep well?" John walked toward her and kissed her cheek.

"I think I died because I didn't even hear you leave the room." She sighed. "I seem to be sleeping in a lot lately. I've got to start setting my alarm."

"You must've needed the rest. It was a rough night last night." He took her hands in his and pulled her into his arms. "You want something to eat. I was just about to make myself some lunch, but I could make breakfast for you."

"You're too good to be true." She gazed up at him and smiled.

"Trust me, baby. I've got lots of faults." He took her by the hand and dragged her toward the kitchen. "I've been taught to take care of the ones I love."

"I need to thank your mom and dad for teaching you to be so wonderful." She giggled as he pulled her in his arms for a sweet, gentle kiss.

"I've got to thank your mom and dad for making you so amazing." John kissed her again.

The afternoon flew, and Keith dropped in with a contractor who replaced the broken window. The two brothers cleaned up the glass around the room, and Stephanie used the vacuum to make sure it was off the furniture.

John looked up when Keith nudged him with an elbow. Stephanie kept glancing toward the window, almost as if she expected something else to come flying through the boarded-up window. He took the vacuum from her and suggested she take a hot bath.

Kurt called mid-afternoon and informed them Marc was located, but he had an airtight alibi. Marc was in jail at the time of the shooting. He'd been picked up two days earlier for impaired driving. Kurt told John to keep his eyes open for anything suspicious.

The forensics team pulled the bullets from the wall, but so far, nothing showed up in the system. Not knowing who shot at them put John on edge. First, someone poisoned Stephanie, then there was the prowler, and then the shooting. It wasn't random, and he had to find out who was trying to hurt the woman he loved.

Keith assured John he'd help to find out what was going on, although John didn't know how. Keith did seem to have sources the police didn't. John didn't ask questions because he didn't care how they got the information. He just wanted to make sure Stephanie was safe.

John paced the hallway as he waited for Stephanie. He tugged on the neck of his tuxedo because it seemed intent on strangling him. The last time he wore one was at James and Sarah's wedding. How was he going to handle wearing the damn thing all night, if twenty minutes after he'd put on the tie, he wanted to rip it off? He debated on removing it until Stephanie was ready, but the apartment door opened.

Holy Fuck.

John's mouth went completely dry, and he forgot how to breathe. Stephanie's long blonde hair was pulled back from her face and lay over her shoulder in loose curls. She typically didn't wear much makeup, but the understated makeup she wore brightened her eyes, and her lips shined with some sort of lip gloss.

John's gaze traveled down her body. A pale-yellow dress accentuated every sexy curve from her ample breasts to her tiny waist and clung to her full hips. The dress touched the floor, and a slit went up to mid-thigh. On her feet, she wore elegant silver shoes with heels so high he wondered how she could walk. She was mesmerizing.

"What?" She said. "Do I look okay?"

"You're stunning," he whispered when he finally found his voice. "I've never seen a dress look so sexy. I think I'll call James and tell him I'm sick, and we need to stay home." Stephanie giggled as John pulled her into his arms.

"Then my parents or your parents will be here bringing turkey soup. Or maybe your grandmother." Stephanie pulled away from him, and John groaned as she pulled him out the front door.

John scanned the street on the way to the car. He was still on edge but tried his best to keep calm for Stephanie. He wanted her to enjoy herself.

Smartly dressed people filled the large banquet hall. A quick glance to his left and John relaxed. Keith stood next to the door with two large men, and nobody was getting past those three without an invitation. Keith winked at him and nodded to Stephanie.

"Good luck." Stephanie kissed John's cheek and left him to track down her parents.

John didn't need to worry about her, because Keith followed behind her as if he were casually strolling around the hall. If Stephanie knew John asked Keith to keep a close eye on her, she'd probably panic.

The guys were next to the stage on the far side of the room. Ian and James were on the platform setting up the microphones, and Nick organized the instruments. The rest of the band looked uncomfortable in their tuxedos. John scanned the crowd until he spotted her, and as if she sensed him, she met his gaze and blew him a kiss. She pointed to a table directly in front of the stage, and John winked.

"Can you drool over your girlfriend after we finish the first set?" Mike teased.

"With that body, he won't be the only one drooling." Aaron whistled.

"Shut up, A.J., and keep your fucking eyes to yourself." John shoved Aaron toward the steps of the stage, but as he turned back, James motioned for him to the other side of the platform.

"Kurt told me about Marc's alibi." James kept his voice low.

"I think someone is out to get Stephanie," John whispered.

"You're not the only one. Keith and Nick said the same thing. Have you told her it wasn't Marc?" John shook his head. "She might be able to give us another direction. You can't keep it from her, bro."

"I know, and I'll talk to her tonight after we get home." John knew James was right.

How was he going to approach the subject with her? They needed a list of people who may want to hurt her. There could be someone in her past holding a grudge. He needed to know.

After the first hour, John was itching to take a break. He wanted to spend some time with Stephanie, but mainly he wanted to make sure she was okay emotionally. Keith wouldn't let anything happen to her, but he needed to see for himself. As Aaron finished singing, *Crazy Little Thing Called Love.* John stepped back from the keyboard.

"I hope everyone's having a good time." Aaron cheered into the microphone. "We're gonna take a little break, but don't worry, D.J. Cory's gonna keep the tunes goin'." Whistles and applause erupted when Cory hopped down from the drums and made his way to the computer system at the side of the stage.

John jumped down to the main floor and sauntered toward the tables. His parents sat at a table next to Stephanie and her parents. John gave his mom a quick kiss on the cheek and shook his dad's hand on his way to the other table. His eyes met Stephanie's, and she smiled.

"You guys were so great." She stood and kissed his cheek.

"Thanks." John gazed into her eyes, and for a moment, everyone disappeared, but someone clearing his throat broke the spell.

"Hi, John." Doug held out his hand.

"Mr. Kelly, good to see you again." John shook the man's hand.

Stephanie's father was a huge man. He wasn't much taller than John, but he was built similar to Keith. The only difference, Doug appeared to be more intimidating. John was pretty sure the man would probably kill anyone who hurt his daughters.

"Your band is wonderful." Janet linked into Doug's arm.

"Thanks, Mrs. Kelly. We aren't professionals, but perform for events like this," John said. "It's lots of fun, and I get to have a good time with my brothers and friends."

"It's Doug and Janet, my son." Doug chuckled. "My parents were Mr. and Mrs. Kelly."

Janet and Doug sat close together as did his own parents. John was pretty sure he couldn't put a quarter between them if he tried. It was embarrassing when he was younger, but now, he understood.

315

"Stephanie tells me you'll be returning to work soon." Doug placed a bottle of beer in front of John.

"Yes. It's been a very long few months, but this pretty lady made the last couple a lot easier." He squeezed Stephanie's hand.

"You two look so cute together," Janet cooed. "Don't they, Doug?"

"Mom, stop." Stephanie rolled her eyes.

"Okay... Okay." Janet sighed. "You two are coming for supper on Sunday. Right?"

"I never say no to a home-cooked meal." John winked.

The conversation with Stephanie's parents was enjoyable and much less stressful than their first meeting. John's laughter subsided when he felt Stephanie tense next to him. He turned and tried to follow her line of sight, but all he saw was a jungle of people.

"Let's dance before you have to go back up on stage." She pulled him off the chair.

"What are you looking for?" John wrapped his arms around her.

"My ex is here with his new girlfriend." Stephanie gritted her teeth.

"Where?" Every muscle in his body tensed.

"Next to the bar. If my dad sees him, he'll freak." Stephanie glanced over toward the table where they sat.

"We'll keep him away from your dad." John scanned the room for one of his brothers. "Which one is he?"

"Next to the bar with the blonde in the red dress." John's eyes locked with a dark-haired man.

When the man's eyes moved to Stephanie, it made John's body run cold. The old saying, *if looks could kill*, came to mind. The only thing he was worried about was the death glare the blonde gave her.

"Why would he be here?" John asked.

"He's a firefighter," Stephanie whispered into his ear. "Are they part of this?"

The fundraiser was for all public service workers, police, firefighters, doctors, nurses as well as many of the large businessmen and women. It had started several years ago when the former Premier of the province decided it would be a profitable way to raise money for the children's hospital.

"Yes. Stations all over the city and surrounding towns are involved in this," he explained and turned when he felt a tap on his shoulder.

"Sandy." John smiled.

"Hey, guys. You both look incredible. I hate to spoil your evening, but I thought I'd warn you both. Kim is here." Sandy motioned to the far side of the room. "She's here with Stew Michaels."

Stew was a high-profile lawyer in the city. He was known to be a lady's man, but overall, John knew him to be a good person. John thought Kim was a little young for the man since Stew was about his father's age.

317

"Great, both our exes are here," Stephanie grumbled.

"As long as they stay away from us, it'll be fine," John whispered into her ear.

Sandy waved and disappeared through the staff door. He enjoyed having Stephanie in his arms, but he kept his eyes focused on Brad and the blonde. The daggers they were shooting at Stephanie made the hair stand up on the back of his neck. When he felt Stephanie stiffen in his arms, he glanced down at her.

"Kim is heading this way," Stephanie informed him, and he clenched his teeth together, he didn't want to deal with Kim.

John smiled down at Stephanie, and she picked up on his cue as she smiled back. John glanced toward Stephanie's parents and noticed them watching.

"Your parents are watching." He leaned down as if to kiss her cheek, but he whispered in her ear.

"Well, it's about to get awkward. Kim is right behind you." Stephanie smiled as she spoke.

"Hi, John," Kim greeted him.

"Kim." John couldn't believe the woman was so friendly with him.

"I just wanted to say it's good to see you on your feet again, and the band is great as usual." She seemed nervous.

"Thank you, Kim." John didn't want Stephanie's parents to see him be rude.

Kim's eyes moved to Stephanie, and he could see the shadow of something in her eyes. He just wasn't sure what, but the next moment her eyes flicked to the door where Sandy disappeared.

"Is there something else?" He raised an eyebrow.

"Umm… no. Just make sure you take care of your lady." She walked away.

"What was that about?" Stephanie's smile was more forced as they turned on the dance floor.

"I don't know, but we're about to have another intruder." John held Stephanie tighter as Brad walked toward them.

What concerned John was he'd left his girlfriend at the bar. Her face was almost as red as her dress, and John could see tears in her eyes.

"May I cut in?" Brad tapped John on the shoulder.

"No, you may not," Stephanie replied before John could refuse.

"Come on, Steph; we need to talk," Brad said.

"No, we don't," Stephanie snapped. "Now, if you don't mind, I want to continue my dance with John. Would you be so kind as to go back to your bimbo before I forget I'm a lady? I don't think you want to sing soprano."

John bit back a laugh. If anyone saw them from a distance, the conversation between Stephanie and Brad appeared friendly. She smiled while she spoke, but her whole body was rigid.

"Fine, but we need to talk sooner or later." Brad stalked away.

"Remind me never to piss you off." John chuckled.

"What? I was polite," she said sweetly.

John led Stephanie back to her parents' table. It was empty, but Keith appeared and nodded toward his parents. Doug and Janet sat with his family, and the two couples were engrossed in a conversation as John and Stephanie stepped next to them.

"I see you met John's parents." Stephanie stood behind her father and wrapped her arms around his neck.

"They invited us to their table." Janet smiled.

"John, we've got to get back on stage." Aaron walked up behind John.

"This is our youngest son, A.J." Kathleen introduced Aaron as he leaned down to kiss Kathleen on the cheek, and while Aaron kept their attention, John pulled Stephanie aside.

"You sure you're okay." He held her hands in his.

"I'm fine. Brad won't come near my dad." She snickered.

"I don't think I want to piss your father off." James appeared behind them. "He looks like he could put a world of hurt on someone if he were pissed off."

"Dad is a big teddy bear, but when it comes to his family, he can turn into a grizzly bear." Stephanie smiled.

"Good luck with him, bro." James nudged John. "You better not piss him off."

"I don't plan on it," John returned.

From the stage, he could see Stephanie. Keith stood close by, but it made him feel better to be able to see her himself. She danced a few times while he was on stage. One with her dad, and then his father. She even managed to drag Keith out on the dance floor at one point. Between Ian and James, they kept her busy.

He met up with her again at the end of the night, and she looked like she was ready to run. When he walked next to her, she grabbed John's hand and pulled him away from the table.

"Save me," she groaned.

"What's wrong?" John laughed.

"I don't think it was a good idea for our parents to be in the same room when they have alcohol in their systems." She shuddered. "I've found out things I didn't need or want to know about our parents."

"Let me guess; they're swapping sex stories." John rolled his eyes.

"Yes," she sighed. "Oh, and we're not going to mom and dad's for supper Sunday. We're going to your parents."

"Is that good or bad?" He wrapped his arm around her shoulder.

"I'm not sure." She furrowed her eyebrow as his dad's and Doug's laughter boomed behind them.

"I can see why Stephanie fell for John." Janet nudged Kathleen with her elbow. "He's a very fine-looking man."

"Yes, all my boys take after their handsome father." Kathleen pinched Sean's cheek.

"I hope they have my stamina too." Sean winked at his wife.

"Okay, too much information, Dad. I think you all had way too much to drink." The last thing John wanted in his head was how long his dad could last.

"Does everyone have a way home?" Ian stepped next to the table with a clipboard in his hand.

"I'll get them home, Ian." John nodded toward Janet and Doug.

"Nick is driving us home." Sean tossed back the rest of his rum.

"I guess this party is all set then." Before Ian walked away, Stephanie introduced him to her parents.

"You certainly have the recipe for handsome boys." Janet winked.

Ian quickly excused himself and walked away from the table. John shook his head when Ian almost smacked right into Sandy while she cleared off one of the tables.

On the drive home, John laughed as Stephanie filled him in on some of the discussions between their parents. She informed him there would be no more alcohol when the two couples got together.

John's smiled disappeared as he pulled into his driveway. The first thing he noticed was his front door was wide open. He reached across the car at the sound of Stephanie's intake of breath.

"Stay in the car and lock the doors. I'm gonna check out the house." He was confident he closed and locked the door when they left.

John crept up the front steps wishing he had his magnum strapped to him. He scanned the porch and front door as he entered the house.

John pressed his back against the foyer wall and slid along until he could peer into the living room. His heart thudded in his chest, but as he carefully checked the rest of the house, his police training took over. Nothing seemed out of place or missing. The computer, television, and sound system were still there, but something didn't feel right. He started to doubt himself as he questioned if he had closed the door all the way. He'd been distracted by how sexy Stephanie looked when they left, so he could have been distracted.

John did manage to retrieve his magnum on the sweep of his house. Before he checked her apartment, he stepped outside to see if she was okay. He saw her crouched next to her car, and John hurried toward her. The two tires on the driver's side were both flat.

"Someone slashed my tires." She slowly stood up.

John circled the car, and his blood ran cold. All four tires were damaged. John scanned the front yard as he took her hand and towed her behind him.

"Stephanie, come inside, we'll get it fixed tomorrow. This is getting ridiculous," he growled through clenched teeth.

"I'm calling Uncle Kurt." He closed the door and pulled out his phone

"I'm going to get out of this dress." Stephanie opened her apartment door and shrieked his name.

"Stay behind me." John pulled her aside as he entered her apartment.

It was destroyed. Broken picture frames, slashed furniture, and a shattered laptop covered the floor, and her clothes were strewn all over the bedroom. John had Kurt's number called before he made it out of the apartment.

"They have to find Marc," Stephanie whispered.

"It's not Marc." John waited for Kurt to answer.

"What?" Her voice quivered.

John steered her into his living room and sat her down on the couch. She trembled, and he wrapped his arm around her shoulder. All he knew was it wasn't Marc. Someone else was doing this. He just wished he knew who, and why?

Chapter 24

Stephanie's hands shook, and her heart thundered in her chest. Two nights in a row, the police filled John's house. He told her Marc wasn't the one who shot at them. Then who? Brad was angry, but he wasn't crazy. This entire thing was disrupting everyone's lives and putting John in danger too.

Of course, John's family swarmed the house as soon as he called. She didn't want to worry her parents, so she asked John not to call them. At least not until they knew more. Nanny Betty was the first one to arrive after the police. She whirled through the house and sat next to Stephanie.

"Doncha worry, ducky. Kurt and his lads will find out who's up ta dis nonsense." Nanny Betty rubbed a hand up and down Stephanie's back.

She wanted to believe the woman, but fear overpowered her. She wasn't afraid only for herself but for John and her parents. Whoever was out to get her wasn't about to give up, no matter who they hurt.

"I hope so," Stephanie whispered.

"Johnny'll keep ya safe. Dat lad loves ya." Nanny Betty gave her a gentle hug.

Stephanie didn't doubt John loved her, but could he keep dealing with all this? He was back on his feet and going back to work. He didn't need all this shit going on in his home.

As if thoughts of him made him appear, John entered the living room, followed by Kurt. He looked furious and glared at his uncle as if he wanted to punch him.

"Stephanie, can you think of anyone who would want to hurt you?" Kurt was blunt.

"Kurt Patrick O'Connor, who in heaven's name would want ta hurt dis sweet little girl?" Nanny Betty snapped. "What kinda question is dat?"

"Mudder, I have to ask. Let her answer, please." Kurt respectfully spoke to his mother, but Nanny Betty huffed and patted Stephanie's back.

"The only one I can think of is Marc." She shrugged.

"It wasn't him tonight. He's still locked up until court on Monday." Kurt informed her.

"What about Brad?" John's question sent chills down her spine.

Could Brad be capable of all this? He was never the violent type, but the emails she'd received from him and the way he looked at her earlier in the evening, she began to wonder.

"Who's Brad?" Kurt turned to John.

"He's my ex-boyfriend, and we're in a bit of a dispute over money, but I can't see him doing this." Brad was a jerk, but he wouldn't stoop to this level.

Would he?

"That's the guy we questioned when you were drugged?" Kurt asked, and she nodded.

"He was at the fundraiser tonight." Stephanie glanced at John.

"There's nobody else you could think of?" Kurt wrote something on the notepad he held in his hand.

Stephanie was always kind to people and never thought anyone would have a reason to hurt her. If anything, Stephanie was too nice to people, which was something Donna warned her about frequently.

"What about dat trollop ya got rid of, Johnny?" Nanny Betty didn't think too highly of Kim.

"Nan, whoever is doing this is not trying to hurt me. They're trying to hurt Stephanie." John rolled his eyes.

"Does Kim know you're dating Stephanie?" Kurt raised an eyebrow at John.

"Yeah, but…" John plowed his hands through his hair. "I don't know if she'd do this, but maybe you should talk to her too."

Could Kim be obsessed with John? She was at the restaurant when Stephanie was drugged. The lump in her throat felt as if it could choke her. She tried to keep it together, but the tears burned her eyes, and she couldn't stop them as they rolled down her cheeks.

"Sweetheart, don't cry. We'll find out who's doing this." John knelt in front of her and wiped her tears with his knuckle.

"Dat's right, dear, my Kurt is a good police officer, and he'll catch dis son of a gun." Nanny Betty nodded. "Or I'll bust his arse."

Stephanie hiccupped as she laughed at Nanny Betty's comment. She couldn't stop it, the thought of the tiny woman putting John's Uncle over her knee and spanking him was ridiculously funny.

"Mudder, one of these days, you're going to realize I'm not a little boy anymore." Kurt rolled his eyes.

"If I told ya once, I told ya a dozen times. Ya might be bigger den me, but I can still swing up at ya." Nanny pointed her finger at her son.

"Yes, ma'am." Kurt leaned down and kissed his mother's cheek.

"See, he's a good boy." Nanny Betty stood up and headed to the kitchen. "I'll make some tea."

"Nan, I'll get it." John stood up.

"Jesus, Mary, and Joseph. I'm not too old ta make a pot a' tea. Stay and look after da girl," she ordered as she disappeared into the kitchen.

"There's no dealing with her." John moved next to Stephanie and wrapped his arms around her. "We'll find out who's doing this, honey. Nan's right about one thing. Uncle Kurt's one of the best cops in Newfoundland."

Stephanie closed her eyes as she allowed the warmth of John's embrace to bring her comfort. She was exhausted. The voices of the police and John's family swirled around her and slowly began to fade. Minutes later, she felt as if she was floating, and she sank into a soft, warm cloud. Her eyes fluttered open, to see John smiling down at her.

"Sleep, baby. I'll be right here." John's voice lulled her back to sleep.

Two weeks passed, and things were back to normal. Whoever was terrorizing Stephanie seemed to stop, at least for the moment. John was back to work, and she had her new clients.

Stephanie pulled into the driveway of one of her new clients. Frank Carter was a widower and recovering from hip surgery. He was always pleasant with a funny story or joke for her, and he lived with his son Bill and daughter-in-law, Marg.

Stephanie liked him, and Frank worked hard to get his mobility back. The man was in his late seventies and always told her working hard made you live longer. He'd probably never be as mobile as he used to be. Nevertheless, Stephanie could help him at least get to a point where he could move around the house without a wheelchair.

"Good Morning, Stephanie," Bill greeted her at the door.

"Good morning, Bill." Stephanie stepped inside the house. "How's Frank today?"

"See for yourself." She followed Bill into the small living room off the main hallway.

"Hello there, my love." Frank beamed with pride. "Watch this."

He stood next to his wheelchair with a walker in front of him. With a proud grin on his face, Frank gripped the handle of the walker and pushed it a couple of inches. After a couple of steps, he pushed it a second time, then a third.

"That's wonderful, Frank. I see you've been practicing, but I don't want you to overdo it." She moved toward him.

"I won't, but it feels good to be on the old feet again." Frank chuckled as he eased back in his chair.

"I'm sure it does." Stephanie crouched next to him. "Do you feel up to doing some exercises?"

Frank nodded and rubbed his hands together. The man seemed to be ready for anything. She should introduce him to Nanny Betty because she would have him running in no time.

Stephanie was almost ready to leave as Marg walked into the living room with a young woman. She looked to be a little younger than Stephanie and very beautiful. She wore her black hair down, and it flowed in loose waves over her shoulders. Stephanie noticed Marg clung to the girl as if she was a lifeline.

"Stephanie, I wanted to introduce you to one of our children," Marg said. "This is our daughter Belinda."

"It's nice to meet you, Belinda." Stephanie shook the girl's hand.

"It's so great to meet you. You can call me Billie." Billie smiled at her. "Pop adores you from the way he talks about you."

"Your Pop is a wonderful man." Stephanie placed her hand on Frank's shoulder.

"Belinda's working on a bachelor's degree in social work." Frank smiled at his granddaughter.

"Awesome." Stephanie could see the pride on Frank's face.

"I still have a couple of months to get there, but I love it." Billie hugged her grandfather.

"She's going to be the best social worker St. John's has ever seen. Do you know why?" Frank boasted.

"Why?" Stephanie asked as Billie rolled her eyes.

"She cares about people, just like you." Frank grasped Stephanie's hand. "She's working with deaf people now while she's in school."

"Really?" Stephanie smiled.

"It's only part-time, Pop." Billie laughed. "My best friend is deaf, and I've learned sign language from her. She teaches at the school for the deaf."

"I think it's great." Stephanie hoisted her purse onto her shoulder.

"I need to go, but it was nice to meet you, Stephanie." Billie leaned down to hug her grandfather once more and kissed her mother on the cheek.

"I should be going too. I'll see you in a couple of days, Frank." Stephanie followed Billie down the front steps as they waved to Marg and Frank.

"It's so strange to see Pop so immobilized," Billie whispered as they walked together.

"He's doing well. He should be back on his feet in no time." Stephanie could see the sadness in the girl's eyes.

"I know he'll get some back, but with his age, he's not going to be able to do the things he loves." Billie gazed at the house. "I'm just afraid if he can't do those things, he'll start to slip away."

"We'll just have to keep him busy with other things." Stephanie squeezed Billie's shoulder.

"I'm moving to Labrador at the end of the summer. I already have a work term set up there. My mom is worried, and she doesn't want me to go, but I've got to do it. Maybe you could keep me up to date on his progress. My parents tell me he's doing well, but I think they tell me what I want to hear." Billie seemed close to her grandfather, and it was apparent she was concerned about his condition.

"Why don't you give me your number, and I'll call you with updates." Stephanie handed her phone to Billie so they could exchange numbers.

"Thanks, Stephanie." Billie waved as she got in her car. "Maybe we can go for coffee before I go."

"I'd love to. Call me next week, and we can meet at Tim's," Stephanie called out.

"I will." Billie backed out of the driveway, and her first thought was how perfect Billie would be for Mike.

Stephanie laughed at herself as she opened her car door. Her laughter stopped when something caught her attention out of the corner of her eye. A black car stopped at the end of the driveway, and a chill ran up her spine. She clutched her cell phone in her pocket, but before she pulled it out, the car drove off.

"Don't be so paranoid," she mumbled to herself as she hopped into her car.

After an exhausting day of scooting all over the city for clients, the ten-minute drive back to Hopedale was heaven. All she wanted to do was spend a quiet evening at home. Maybe watch television and veg out on the couch. John was on a twelve-hour day shift and didn't get off until seven.

It was a little after five by the time she got home. Stephanie took a quick shower and pulled on a comfy pair of pajamas. There hadn't been any incidents over the last couple of weeks, but she still felt on edge. She was in the middle of pouring a cup of tea when a loud knock startled her. Stephanie hurried to the door and when she opened it, she gasped. Stephanie squealed and wrapped her arms around her sister.

"Steph, you're choking me." Marina laughed.

"I'm so happy to see you. What are you doing here?" Stephanie stepped back.

"The company I work for is opening an office in St. John's." Marina grinned.

"Really?" She motioned for Marina to come inside.

"Yes." Marina glanced around the foyer before she turned her attention back to Stephanie.

"Come into the kitchen. I just poured myself a cup of tea. Well, I spilled most of it when you knocked, but I can get another and get you one too. You need to tell me all about this because I'd be so happy if you moved back home." Stephanie grabbed Marina's arm and led her to the kitchen.

"I see you still ramble when you're excited," Marina teased.

"Yes, I do, and you know you missed it." Stephanie narrowed her eyes and poked Marina in the shoulder.

"Yes, I did." Marina climbed onto one of the stools.

"Now, I want all the details." Stephanie placed a cup in front of her sister.

According to Marina, *Popular People*, the publisher she worked for as an editor, was opening an office in the city. The owner, David Molloy, was from Newfoundland and wanted to move home. David offered Marina a head editor position because she was the only one from the province, not to mention he was impressed with her work.

"So, you'll be moving back home?" Stephanie hugged Marina excitedly and almost knocked over the cup Marina was holding.

"Yes, but I'm worried." Marina looked as if the weight of the world was on her shoulders.

"Why?" Stephanie should have known the reason.

"Dad told me about Marc and how he was harassing them." Her eyes filled with tears. "And he could be the one trying to hurt you."

"Aww... Rina... Don't worry about him." Stephanie pulled Marina into her arms and kissed the side of her head. "We'll make sure he doesn't bother you, and he was in jail when both the shooting and the break-in happened. Besides, I don't think Marc has bothered mom and dad in a while."

"I don't understand why he's looking for me. The last time I spoke to him, he told me he wanted nothing else to do with me, and he definitely didn't want Danny." A tear rolled down her cheek.

"Don't cry over him, Rina. He isn't worth your tears." Stephanie grabbed a couple of napkins off the counter and handed it to her sister.

"I'm not crying over him. It kills me he doesn't care about his son." Marina took a deep breath as she wiped her face with the napkin.

"Danny's better off without him." Stephanie tried to hide her dislike for the man.

How could a father reject his child? Marc was a colossal asshole, and Danny didn't need him as far as she was concerned. Stephanie had her arms wrapped around Marina when she heard a deep male voice. The one that sent shivers of pleasure through her every time he spoke. John walked into the kitchen looking sexy in his uniform.

"Hey. You're home." Stephanie's voice came out breathy.

"Yes, I am." He glanced between Stephanie and Marina.

"John, this is my sister, Marina, when she's not screaming in pain," Stephanie said, reminding him of the first time he'd met her sister.

"Officer Hunky." Marina held out her hand, and Stephanie poked her, making Marina giggle.

"Pardon me?" John raised an eyebrow.

"Nothing." Stephanie glared at her sister.

"It's nice to see you again, Marina." John's eyes sparkled with mischief. "The last time you were digging your fingernails into my arm."

"Oh. Yeah, sorry about that." Marina snickered. "I hope I didn't hurt you."

"I've had worse. I'm sure it was nothing compared to what you were feeling." He smiled and headed to the laundry room.

John had a gun safe in the room, and it was his routine when he got home from work to go in there to secure his weapon. Then he would change out of his uniform.

"My God. He's hotter than I remember." Marina mouthed the words, and Stephanie giggled.

When John returned, he went straight to Stephanie, wrapped his arms around her, and kissed her lips. She beamed up at him. He did it every day when he returned, and it always made her heart do a little pitter-pat.

"Are you home for good, Marina?" He glanced over Stephanie's head at her sister.

"Hopefully, soon." Marina met Stephanie's eyes and smiled.

"Good to hear. I need to get out of these clothes." John gave Stephanie another quick kiss on the cheek and left the kitchen.

"You're glowing," Marina teased.

"He makes me so happy, Rina." Stephanie sighed.

"I can see that. Dad and Mom seem to like him." Marina sipped her tea.

"You know he has six brothers. They're all hot." Stephanie nudged Marina with her elbow.

"Don't start, Steph. I'm not looking for anyone. I've got too much on my plate now with work and Danny," Marina warned.

"And why didn't you bring my nephew with you to see his favorite aunt?" Stephanie folded her arms across her chest.

"If you want to try prying him out of mom's arms, you go right ahead. You'll need a crowbar to get him away from her. She's spoiling him rotten." Marina rolled her eyes and laughed.

John returned dressed in jeans and a black t-shirt. Nothing he wore ever looked bad on him. Even when he woke up first thing in the morning, he had a sexy, mussed look.

"What are you beautiful ladies up to tonight?" John sauntered to the other side of the island and rested his elbows on the counter.

"Just catching up." Stephanie grinned.

"So, you're the reason my sister can't wipe the smile off her face." Marina winked at him.

"I like making her smile." He reached across the counter and squeezed Stephanie's hand. "By the way, who is officer hunky?"

"Shit," Stephanie groaned as she almost spilled her tea.

"This policeman who pulled us over the day I went into labor." Marina winked.

"I see, and who gave him that name." John raised an eyebrow as he met Stephanie's eyes.

"I did," Marina confessed. "But my sister agreed with me."

Stephanie could see by the smirk on John's face he would tease her about it later, but the name suited him, and he'd have to live with it.

"You ready, bro," Nick shouted as he, Keith, and Aaron walked into the kitchen.

Stephanie pressed her lips together to keep the laughter from bursting out when all three brothers blatantly checked out Marina. Stephanie couldn't blame them, Marina was a beautiful woman and had the curves most men enjoyed.

"Marina, these are three of John's younger brothers, Keith, Nick, and A.J." Stephanie motioned to each one of the men.

"Nice to meet you." Keith nodded.

"You too." Marina smiled.

"I see great looks run in your family." Aaron winked at her sister.

"And there it is. We're out of here." John kissed Stephanie and quickly guided his brothers out of the kitchen, and his voice echoed down the hall as they left. "Can't you just say hi to a lady without hitting on her?"

"A.J. is a bit of a flirt." Stephanie chuckled.

338

"They all look like that?" Marina's mouth hung open.

"Yep. James is John's twin. He's a widower, and Ian, Keith, Mike, Nick, and A.J. are all single," Stephanie said as she poured them both another cup of tea.

Marina didn't comment, but Stephanie saw the roll of her sister's eyes. Marina was in no way ready to date again, and it was easy to understand why. Stephanie hoped Marc didn't turn her sister from being open to love in the future.

For the next couple of hours, Marina gave Stephanie all the details of her life in Ottawa. She loved her job and made a few friends at work and a couple she met through her boss. Even though Marina tried to seem upbeat, Stephanie knew her sister wasn't as happy as she wanted Stephanie to believe. It made her hate Marc even more for turning Marina's life upside down.

"Mom told me all about the shit that's been going on." Marina's expression filled with concern.

"Well, nothing in the last two weeks. Hopefully, it's over." Stephanie crossed her fingers. "I wish we knew who it was."

Stephanie had barely finished her statement when a loud pounding startled both her and Marina. They stared at each other for a moment, but before she could move off the stool, loud shouting made her blood run cold.

"I know you're in there, Marina. Open the fucking door," Marc roared from outside the front step.

"How did he know I was here?" Marina's face turned completely white, and Stephanie grasped her hand.

"I don't know, but he won't get in." Stephanie's anger increased when he pounded again.

"Open the door, bitch," Marc shouted.

Stephanie told Marina to stay in the kitchen, and she hurried to the door. John always locked it when he left the house, but she needed to make sure for her piece of mind. At least he couldn't storm in through the door.

"She doesn't want to talk to you, so get the hell out of here," Stephanie yelled through the closed door.

"Oh, she's gonna talk to me," he shrieked, and the door shook as he pounded on it again. "I'll kick the fucking door in if you don't open it now."

"Marc, leave, or I'm calling the police." Stephanie reached into her pocket and wrapped her hand around her phone.

"I don't give a fuck who you call, you fucking little bitch. I'm not leaving until I see Marina and my son." His voice had turned to a sinister growl.

"You're not seeing either of them. Get the hell away from the door," Stephanie shouted as her body shook with rage.

"Fucking whore." She knew by the sound he had kicked the door. "I'll fuck you up."

Stephanie pulled her phone out of her pocket, but she didn't know if she should call the police or John. She hated to interrupt his night with his brothers, and he'd be pissed she didn't call, but when Marc gave the door another hard kick, she decided it was better to call the police.

"Nine-one-one, what's your emergency." A pleasant female voice answered.

"A man's trying to get into my house." Stephanie tensed as the knob rattled and then another kick.

"What's your name?" The operator asked.

Stephanie gave her all the information and tensed as Marc continued to pound harder on the door. The door rattled again, and she prayed the police arrived before Marc broke it down.

The operator told her to stay on the phone until the police arrived. Stephanie stepped back and squeaked when the door sounded as if it cracked after Marc kicked it several times. Maybe she should have called John after all.

Marina had made her way into the living room. She sat on the floor next to the couch with her knees pulled up to her chest, and her hands over her ears. Stephanie hurried to her and fell to her knees. She wrapped her arm around her sister and continued to keep the operator updated on what Marc was doing outside.

"Hurry, please," Stephanie begged the woman.

Marc sounded crazed, and Stephanie worried about what would happen if he got inside. Before she could worry herself into a frenzy, flashing blue and red lights lit up the living room.

"Thank God," Stephanie breathed as she ended the call and tossed her phone on the couch.

Stephanie peeked out through the closed drapes and could see two officers move cautiously toward the house. The pounding stopped, but she heard the muffled voices of the police as they called out to Marc. She still couldn't see him, but her attention was distracted when a second car pulled into the driveway. Two more officers got out of the car, and one had a phone to his ear. It was Kurt.

Chapter 25

John put his darts into his jacket pocket and sat down on his James' couch. It was great to spend time with his brothers and could relax because Stephanie wasn't home alone. Plus, if she needed him, he was only a couple of houses away.

Although there hadn't been any other incidents, he still had a gut feeling it wasn't over. Kurt still had an investigation into what happened, but so far, there were no leads.

"I think we lost our big brother," Mike teased.

"Can you blame him, with two hot women at his house tonight?" Aaron wiggled his eyebrows. "Care to share some of that, bro?"

"It's Stephanie's sister, you fucking pervert." John threw a bottle cap, and Aaron dodged it.

"Hey, sometimes two sisters can be good." Aaron laughed and hitched his thumb over his shoulder. "Ask Ian."

John couldn't hide the chuckle as Ian's face flushed. A couple of months after Ian's ex-girlfriend left him, Ian thought a pub crawl with Mike, Nick, and Aaron would be a good idea. Ian ended up so drunk he hooked up with two sisters and spent the night with them. He never talked about it, but Aaron liked to tease him all the time.

"Fuck you, A.J. Am I ever gonna live that down?" Ian grumbled.

"They're jealous, Ian." John nudged his brother.

Ian was the shy one and wasn't comfortable with the way his younger brothers teased him. He was also the quietest of the bunch and didn't say much, even in his own defense.

"Yeah, A.J. wishes he had your game." James seemed to pick up on John's train of thought.

"I got all the game I need, assholes," Aaron bragged.

John sat back on the couch and took in everything. Aaron and Mike argued over baseball teams and who would win the playoffs. The season barely started, but it was a yearly discussion between them. John couldn't remember any of them ever getting it right.

With Mason at their parents, James looked at ease with a coffee in his hand as he and Keith talked about the property Keith had bought. Nick had coffee as well because it was his turn to be the designated driver. Ian was engrossed in a boxing match on the television. Being together was good.

John stood to grab another beer for himself, but his cell phone vibrated, and he pulled it from his pocket. When he glanced at the screen, he saw his uncle's number. It was odd for him to call so late.

"Hey, Uncle Kurt," John answered.

"John, you need to come home. Now." Kurt's tone meant John wasn't to question his request.

"What's wrong?" John waved his hand in the air to get his brothers to be quiet.

"We're at your house, and a guy is pounding on the door, I'm pretty sure it's Marc. He's yelling to see his wife. Stephanie called nine-one-one, and when I heard your address, I came right away," Kurt explained.

"I'm on the way." John couldn't believe he didn't hear the sirens considering he was two houses down.

John quickly explained what happened and bolted out of the house. He tried to call Stephanie as he ran up the road, but it kept going right to voicemail.

"Fuck. Fuck. Fuck," John growled through his teeth as he picked up speed.

John saw the lights of the cruiser before he heard the shouts. Rage ran through him when he saw the man on his step. If it was Marc, the prick wasn't paying any attention to the police because he continued to kick and pound on the door. John took one step toward the house, but Kurt dropped a hand on John's shoulder and pulled him to a stop.

"What the hell are you doing, Uncle Kurt?" John snapped and tried to pull away.

"Stay out of this, John," Kurt warned. "Let Steve and Cory handle it."

"You need to step away from the door now, pal." Cory's voice was calm but full of authority.

"I want to talk to my wife." There was no doubt it was Marc.

Cory and Steve slowly moved up the walkway toward the steps. Both officers had their guns drawn because Marc could pull out a weapon of his own. John had been in these situations more times than he could count. John knew the rush of adrenaline that surged through a person's body when in a dangerous or possibly volatile situation. Those in law enforcement needed to watch every move the subject made.

"The lady obviously doesn't want to talk right now, and it's probably not a good idea for you to be harassing her at a police officer's home," John shouted and took a step forward, but Kurt held him back.

"Let them handle this, John," Kurt warned.

As hard as it was, John knew his uncle was right. Not to mention, Kurt would probably kick John's ass if he didn't listen. His Uncle was his superior, and you didn't disobey an order from him whether you were on duty or not. John had confidence in Cory and Steve and knew, next to James, they were probably two of the best at deescalating a situation.

Keith tapped John on the shoulder and nodded his head toward the window. Stephanie peeked out through the curtain, and it tore his heart out not to be able to get to her. She had to be scared, and he could only imagine how her sister felt.

John couldn't see Marina, but from what Stephanie told him, her sister was terrified of her ex-husband. The sound of a scuffle tore his gaze away from the window in time to see Marc face down on the step, and Steve handcuffed him. As Marc was led down the driveway, John stepped in his path, but before he had a chance to do or say anything, Cory stepped between John and Marc.

"Let it go, John," Cory cautioned.

"Just check on the ladies." Steve opened the car door and pushed Marc inside.

John didn't hesitate as he bolted toward the house and up the front steps. Stephanie ran into his arms as soon as he opened the door, and John hugged her tightly against him as he let out the breath. Marina stood in the doorway to the living room with her arms wrapped around herself. Her tear-stained face was pale, and John quickly wrapped his arm around her as well.

"It's okay. He's gone." John assured them as he walked them toward the couch.

"He just wouldn't go away." Stephanie's voice cracked.

"I'll make some tea, or would you rather something stronger?" Ian's voice startled him.

When John turned, five of his brothers stood in the hallway. Mike, Keith, Nick, and Aaron were quiet, but John could see they were concerned about Stephanie and her sister.

"Tea is fine." Stephanie leaned forward and grasped Marina's hand. "Are you okay?"

"This is why I moved away. He's never going to give me any peace if I move back home." Marina stood and moved to the window as tears started to run down her cheeks.

Aaron disappeared, and seconds later returned with a box of tissues. He held it out to Marina and then made his way to the kitchen. Stephanie looked at John as if she was begging him with her eyes to fix this. John nodded toward the kitchen to silently ask his brothers for a little privacy.

"You can get a restraining order. He'll probably have charges for disturbing the peace and trespassing tonight added to his record." John informed the two women.

"What good is a piece of paper going to do?" Marina sniffed. "And what will he get for those charges, a slap on the wrist."

"You can stay here with us tonight, and tomorrow we'll go down and get the restraining order." John stood and moved toward Marina, but she held up her hand to stop him.

"Thanks, John. That's nice of you. Really, it is, but I've got to get back to mom's and dad's house. Danny's there." She turned to Stephanie and took a deep breath. "I'm changing my flight to the next one out of St. John's. I can't come back here and be tortured by him."

John didn't know how to respond, and he hated the devastated look in Stephanie's eyes. Marina flopped down on the couch and buried her face in her hands as Stephanie wrapped a comforting arm around her sister.

The front door opened, and John met James in the foyer. He said Marc would probably be locked up overnight and see the judge in the morning.

"Is everything okay?" James nodded his head toward the couch.

"Marina is terrified, and Stephanie is worried about her sister." John glanced at the two women.

"Can't blame them." James shoved his hands into his jean's pockets.

"I don't know what to do, but I doubt Marina is going to stay in Newfoundland after this," John whispered.

"Maybe when everything settles, she'll change her mind." James kept his tone hushed. "What can I do?"

John plowed his hands through his hair and motioned for James to follow him into the living room. He didn't know what anyone could do, but maybe James could think of something to say to Marina. He was always better with words.

"Marina, this is my brother James. I'm going to get him to drive you back to your parents." John lay his hand on James' shoulder.

"I have my dad's car." Marina lifted her head, and James stiffened.

John turned to see his brother's jaw clenched, and there was something in his eyes. John couldn't put his finger on it, and when James took a step back from the women, John swore he saw fear mixed with something else. Desire?

"I'd feel a lot better if you'd let him see you home safely." John continued as he kept his focus on James, who hadn't moved any further away but still looked ready to bolt.

"Rina, I'd feel better if James drove you home," Stephanie begged her sister.

When Marina finally allowed her gaze to fall on James, her expression changed. It was as if she calmed, and her body relaxed. John met Stephanie's eyes briefly, but she didn't seem to notice the change.

"Okay... Ah... If he doesn't mind," Marina stammered.

"I'll get her home safe, bro. I'll drive her in her dad's car, and Nick can follow me to bring me back home." James' eyes hadn't moved from Marina.

"Thanks, James," Marina whispered as she slowly stood up.

John glanced at Stephanie, and she raised her eyebrow. It seemed as if Stephanie saw the spark there as well, but John was pretty sure neither James or Marina was ready for anything romantic.

James, Nick, and Marina left a few minutes later. John watched as James opened the passenger door of the car. He helped Marina into the vehicle, but he managed to touch her as little as possible. When James closed the door, he blew out a breath and hurried around to the driver's side.

"I'll see you later." Nick waved as he jumped into John's truck.

Since Nick's truck was down the road, he took John's vehicle. As he watched them drive away, he felt Stephanie tuck herself under his arm. John wrapped his arms around her and kissed the top of her head.

"I'm so sorry about all this." Stephanie sniffed as she nuzzled against his chest.

"This isn't your fault, sweetheart." He rested his chin on her head.

"I… I… don't want her to go away again, but he's never gonna leave her alone." Stephanie sobbed in his arms, and it killed him to see her so defeated.

"Let me see what I can do in the morning." John tilted her chin up, "Maybe Uncle Kurt can get through to him."

Before she could say another word, Aaron sauntered into the hallway holding two shot glasses. He handed one to John and the other to Stephanie, but she hesitated.

"A good shot of Newfie Screech will help your nerves, honey." Aaron grinned.

It was the same one that irritated John, but he didn't care, because it put a smile on Stephanie's beautiful face. If Aaron's grin could make her forget what happened for a moment, John would keep him there all night with his stupid smirk.

"I've never had Screech before." Stephanie took the glass.

"It burns like hell, but then you feel all warm and fuzzy." Aaron winked. "Almost as good as sex."

Stephanie laughed, and it was the best sound in the world to John. For a moment, she hesitated with the glass close to her lips. After a deep breath, she tipped the dark rum into her mouth. As soon as she swallowed, she held out the glass to Aaron and started to cough.

"Sweet Jesus, I'd say it burns." She blew out a breath.

"Now in ten, nine, eight, seven, six, five, four, three, two, and one. Bet you feel warm and tingly now, don't ya?" He wiggled his eyebrows.

"Yeah, I do. Thanks, A.J." She giggled and kissed his cheek.

For the first time in a long time, John saw Aaron blush. Before he could tease his younger brother, Aaron quickly recovered and opened his big mouth.

"I'm sure John can help with more of those tingles when we leave." Aaron winked, and John's hand instinctively swung at the back of Aaron's head, but he ducked.

"Getting too fast for you now, old man." Aaron backed into the kitchen.

"I swear he's one big walking hormone." John peered at Stephanie.

The smile faded from her face, and she tucked her head under his chin. John was pretty sure Marc wasn't the one responsible for the previous incidents, and his gut told him they needed to examine other avenues.

Stephanie seemed wound up tighter than a drum, and John convinced her to take a hot bath, and he brought her a cup of the herbal tea she liked. Keith, Aaron, Ian, and Mike waited for Nick and James to return before they headed home.

John leaned on the kitchen counter and listened as his brothers went through the list of what happened. Nothing made any sense to them. Marc didn't shoot at the window, and he was nowhere near the restaurant when Stephanie was poisoned. He was also in jail during the break-in. Ian suggested that maybe Marc hired someone, but Kurt always told John to listen to his gut, and it told him it wasn't Marc.

Nick and James returned a short while later and joined the discussion. James agreed with John. Marc was an ass, but it had nothing to do with Stephanie. The asshole's issue was with Marina. Nick brought up Kim, but John didn't believe it was her, and Stephanie was sure it wasn't Brad. Who was left?

John couldn't think of anyone. Stephanie needed to make a list that included her friends, family, co-workers, enemies, and clients. It would probably be a long list, but it was a place to start.

John walked his brothers to the door and thanked them for their help. He knew they didn't mind because it's what they did. When they left, John checked on Stephanie.

She lay on the bed in his t-shirt with her hands tucked under her cheek, and the quilt tucked around her. The bath and tea seemed to help her fall asleep, or maybe it was the shot. Either way, at least she'd managed to rest.

He stood next to the door and stared at her sleeping form. No matter what happened, he'd protect her at all costs. Nobody would ever hurt her on his watch. When she started to stir, John stripped down to his boxers and eased into the bed next to her. She moved into his body, and he wrapped his arm tightly around her.

"I'll keep you safe, baby," John whispered as he pressed his lips against her forehead. "I promise."

The next day John wanted to talk to Kurt, which was why he arrived at the station on his day off. When John walked into his Uncle's office, Kurt was engrossed in a file on his desk, and John cleared his throat to get his attention.

"How are the ladies today?" Kurt pushed the file to the side and pointed to the chair across from him.

"I don't think Marina's going to move back to St. John's after this, and it's upsetting Stephanie." John sat in the chair and propped his ankle on top of his other knee.

"And what about you?" Kurt raised a brow.

"I'm pissed." John linked his hands behind his head. "Uncle Kurt, there's gotta be something we can do to keep that fucker away from Marina."

"He's charged with disturbing the peace, and he's got a restraining order, but it only applies to Janet and Doug Kelly. The girls can get their own order." Kurt leaned back in his chair and crossed his arms over his chest.

"I mentioned it to Marina, but she said a piece of paper wouldn't stop him." John understood her apprehension over it because he'd seen too many assholes completely ignore them.

"But that's not why you're here. Is it?" Kurt leaned forward and rested his elbows on his desk.

"I'm trying to figure out who wants to hurt Stephanie. We know it's not Marc, and I know nothing happened in a couple of weeks, but nobody does this and then suddenly stops." John wondered when the jerk would strike again.

"It's not good seeing someone you love scared." Kurt steepled his fingers in front of his chin.

"No, it's not." John sighed.

"I was starting to wonder if James was the only one of you seven ever going to settle down." Kurt chuckled. "Your dad tells me she's a wonderful young lady."

"She's amazing." John couldn't hold back the smile.

"It seems the only time I associate with her; it's when the shit's hitting the fan." Kurt shook his head.

"I know." John stood up and started to pace.

"Nothing is telling us who's doing this shit, but John, whoever this is..." Kurt stopped.

"Each incident is worse. Whoever is doing this is getting more aggressive." John finished his uncle's statement.

"Yes. She needs to be extra careful. I know you don't want to frighten her, but maybe we should get Ian, Keith, or even Jess to give her some self-defense lessons," Kurt suggested.

"You're probably right. I'll talk to her about it." John turned to leave.

"By the way, it's good to have you back." Kurt winked.

"Thanks, Uncle Kurt. Hug Aunt Alice for me." John left the office.

On the way home, he tried to think of the best way to bring up self-defense classes to Stephanie. Keith and Ian knew what they were doing, but Jess would probably be the best one to ask. She was a third-degree black belt in Karate and taught kids at the community center.

John knew self-defense techniques, but Jess was the better option. Next to Ian, Keith, and Kurt, Jess was the best. It was a running joke in their family, how the little flower child could kick all their asses.

Jess owned a flower shop, and it was hard to believe she could take down someone twice her size. She was probably most even-tempered of all the cousins, and it took a lot to piss her off.

He was almost home when a thought came to him. A nice romantic dinner and a quiet night at home would help take her mind off everything for a while. He made a quick stop at the grocery store and picked up the ingredients for his famous grilled chicken. John wasn't the best cook in the world, but it was one meal he did well.

Two hours later, supper was almost ready. John set the table with candles, turned on some soft piano music, and chilled a bottle of her favorite wine. He checked the time and hurried to prepare a hot bubble bath for her. While the tub filled, he placed several candles on the bathroom counter and in the dining room as well. He checked out the preparations he'd made with pride. Not bad at all. He'd turned off the water in the bathtub and was on his way back to the kitchen when she walked through the door.

"Hey." She smiled, but exhaustion was written all over her beautiful face.

"Good day, my fair lady," John said in a terrible English accent.

He bowed and took her hand in his. When he brought it to his lips and kissed it, she giggled. It sounded like music to his ears because she hadn't had a whole lot to smile about over the last few days.

"Um… okay." She raised her head and sniffed. "Something smells delicious."

"No, my lady. First, I have drawn your bath." John took her hand and placed it in the crook of his arm as he guided her toward the bathroom. "For your comfort and relaxation, my lady."

"John, what did you do?" Stephanie's face lit up, but when she turned back to him, he saw tears in her eyes.

"Oh no, baby. I didn't want to make you cry." John wrapped his arms around her.

"No, these are happy tears. Nobody's ever done this for me." She cupped his cheek and kissed his lips softly. "Thank you so much."

"You're very welcome, sweetheart." He pushed a stray piece of hair from her face. "Supper will be about an hour. So, you can enjoy your bath and relax."

John left the bathroom and returned with a glass of wine for her. When he walked in, bubbles covered her up to the neck, and her hair sat piled up on top of her head. Her eyes were closed, and for a moment, he simply gazed at her. The candles cast a warm glow around the room, and John couldn't remember ever seeing anything so beautiful. Before he could speak, Stephanie opened her eyes and squeaked.

"You scared me." She pressed her hands against her chest.

"Sorry, I was hypnotized by how gorgeous you are," John whispered.

"You're amazing." She leaned her arms on the side of the tub and rested her chin on her hands. "Is the wine for me?"

"Your beverage, my lady." John bowed and placed the glass in her hand.

After a quick kiss on her lips, he returned to the kitchen. Hopefully, she'd enjoy the rest of the evening. The night was all for her, and a distraction from all the shit happening.

John placed both their plates on the table and glanced up as she entered the kitchen. She smiled as she jiggled the empty wine glass in front of her. He motioned for her to sit as he refilled both their glasses.

"John, this is so beautiful." She kissed his cheek as he pulled out the chair for her to sit.

"I wanted to give you a relaxing night." He took her hand and placed a kiss on her knuckles.

"I love it." She met his gaze, and he couldn't look away.

"And I love you. So much."

"I love you, too. More than I ever thought possible." He leaned across the table and placed a quick kiss on her lips. "Now, let's eat."

"This looks amazing." Stephanie put a forkful in her mouth and hummed in approval.

While they ate, they talked about their day. Stephanie told him about her clients, and John listened intently. Stephanie loved her job, and he knew she was good at it. After all, she got him back on his feet when he was a stubborn ass.

Stephanie offered to clean up, but the night was for her. John sent her to the living room with a tender kiss and another glass of wine. The only thing she had to do was relax.

Once he'd put everything away, he turned out the kitchen light and made his way to the living room. It was John's turn to get the surprise. Stephanie turned on the fireplace, and the only other light was several candles around the room. The soft music still played on the stereo, and he recognized the saxophone music. Kenny G, if he wasn't mistaken. She sat with her feet curled under her and tapped the couch next to her.

"Tonight was great." She linked her fingers with his and snuggled into his side.

"I'm glad you enjoyed it because I plan on doing it a lot." He never wanted her to forget how much she was loved and appreciated.

John kissed the top of her head, and she tipped her face up so he could kiss her lips. It was tender, soft, and full of love. When he pulled back from her lips, she sighed.

"You've made this the best night of my life, John." She gazed into his eyes, and it was as if she could see into his soul.

"I'm glad, and guess what else I did to make this special." John grinned.

"What?" She sat up.

"I called all my brothers and warned them they were to stay away from this house, or I'd make them sorry they were ever born." John pressed his forehead against hers.

"That's terrible." She pulled back and playfully slapped his arm.

"No, it's not. I wanted an entire night with you. Alone and uninterrupted." John relieved her of the wine glass, pulled her onto his lap, and started to unbutton her blouse.

"Why Officer O'Connor, are you trying to take advantage of me?" She feigned a gasp.

"Definitely." John growled as he traced the edge of her bra with his tongue.

Her breath caught, and his lips followed the blouse as it slid off her shoulders. John ran his fingers ran up the length of her arms, and goosebumps spread across her skin. He allowed his eyes to travel from her face down to her breasts. A deep moan escaped his lips at the sight of her hard nipples pressed against the fabric of her bra.

"Stephanie, you're so beautiful," John whispered as she pressed against his chest.

John tucked his face against the side of her neck. The vanilla scent from her bubble bath was still evident on her skin, and his dick hardened instantly. John stood with her in his arms and wrapped her legs around his waist.

"I need you completely naked. I want to make love to you all night." He growled when she nipped his neck.

"Sounds like it's gonna be a long night." She grinned as he hurried around the living room, turning off the fireplace and blowing out the candles.

"You're damned right about that." He stalked to the bedroom, intending to fulfill his promise of a long night.

When John woke the next morning, Stephanie was curled tightly against his side. He grabbed his phone from the night table and was surprised to see it was a little after nine in the morning. He usually didn't sleep later than seven, but it was almost daylight by the time they both fell asleep.

Stephanie came into his life when he thought it was over, and she made him want to live again. He never knew what it was like to love someone so much. Stephanie had his heart, mind, body, and soul. Nothing or nobody would take her away from him. John kissed the top of her head and wrapped her in his arms. He closed his eyes for a moment and soaked in the warmth of her body.

The intermittent buzzing woke John from a deep sleep. He couldn't remember drifting off again, but Stephanie was still out. He carefully untangled his arms from her and grabbed his phone. It was his uncle, and John quietly made his way out of the room before he answered.

"Hey, Uncle Kurt." John closed the bedroom door and headed to the kitchen.

"John, did I wake you?" Kurt's gruff voice came through the phone.

"Yeah, but it's okay. What's up?" John started a pot of coffee and leaned against the counter.

"Marc O'Reilly was released today." Kurt sounded almost apologetic.

"I figured he wouldn't be locked up long." John sighed. "What are his release conditions?"

Kurt proceeded to read off the list of conditions Marc had to obey or risk ending up behind bars again. Marc needed to stay at least one hundred meters from John's house or any house where Marina, Stephanie, or her parents resided. He had to stay away from alcohol and drugs and keep the peace and be of good behavior.

"You know how it works if he breaks any of those, he'll be in custody until his court date," Kurt said.

"He's a Meth addict. Does he have to do drug testing?" John had seen orders requiring people to do random testing.

"No," Kurt replied, and John cursed under his breath.

"I hope he obeys it." John knew too many men and women who ended up back behind bars in the first twenty-four hours.

"He better. The report said he had a rough time locked up this round," Kurt told him.

"Let's hope it scared him enough, but he isn't the one who worries me. I wish I knew who tried to hurt Stephanie." John filled a cup with steaming coffee.

"I talked to Jess. She's going to drop over to your house after supper. You should probably let Stephanie know about it." Kurt hadn't given John a chance to ask Stephanie if she'd be okay with learning self-defense.

"I will," he replied as Stephanie entered the kitchen.

"Jess will have her kicking ass before you know it." The pride in his Uncle's voice couldn't be mistaken.

"I have no doubt. Thanks for the info, Uncle Kurt. I appreciate it." John didn't know what he would do without his family.

"No problem, my boy," Kurt answered.

"Good morning, my lady." John winked.

"Don't start that again." Stephanie giggled as she wrapped her arms around his waist.

"I love mornings with you." John pulled her tight against him and kissed the top of her head.

"Me too, but I'm assuming since your Uncle Kurt called, then the call was about Marc." She pressed her cheek against his chest.

He hated to upset her after they'd had such an amazing night, but he knew she wouldn't give up until he told her. John explained everything Kurt said, and from the way she squeezed tighter, he knew the news didn't put her at ease. Who could blame her?

"I just got off the phone with Marina. That's why I was looking for you." She pulled her head back and looked up at him.

"Is she alright?" John kept her secure in his embrace.

"She decided she's not going to allow Marc to ruin her life, and she's not giving up the promotion. She thought about what James said when he drove her home. He said since you and I are together, it makes Marina part of our family, and she'd have your brothers to help if she needed them. She wouldn't be alone." Stephanie smiled.

"James is right. If she ever needs anything, all she'll have to do is ask, and besides, she's a very strong lady. She'll be back home before we know it." John met her eyes, but there was still concern there.

"I know." Stephanie pressed her cheek against his chest.

"There's something else I need to tell you." John hoped she was open to Jess teaching her some self-defense.

"Is it good or bad?" She pulled back and looked up at him.

"Well, it depends on you." John chuckled.

"What is it?" She raised her eyebrow.

"Jess has trained in martial arts since she was a little girl. She's a third-degree black belt and teaches self-defense. Uncle Kurt thought it would be a good idea if she came over and gave you some lessons." John couldn't read her expression, and for several minutes she didn't say anything.

"Is that necessary?" she finally asked as she raked a hand through her hair.

"Uncle Kurt thinks it is, and so do I. I want you to be safe, and Jess is the best." He reached behind her and picked up the coffee pot.

"I didn't know she was into martial arts." Stephanie leaned against the counter as he poured two cups of coffee.

"We all were at one time, but she was the only one of the girls to stick with it. We used to tease her about being the only flower child who could kick ass." John handed a cup to Stephanie.

"I guess it wouldn't hurt." She sipped from the cup.

As long as Jess could show Stephanie how to protect herself, John would be happy. He couldn't follow her around to protect her every day, and she wouldn't let him anyway.

"Are you hungry?" It was time for a change of subject.

"Yes, I'm starving, but I'm cooking breakfast." She poked him in the chest.

"I don't mind cooking, baby." John smiled.

"John, you did everything last night. It was the best night of my life." She cupped his face in her hands. "Let me do this for you."

She placed a quick kiss on his lips as she spun on her heel. Before she could step away, he grabbed her and yanked her against him. He crushed his lips against hers and kissed her with all the love and passion he had for her. When he released her, her dazed expression made him laugh.

"Now, you can cook breakfast." He playfully slapped her bottom. "I'll grab a shower."

John whistled as he left the kitchen. Stephanie was the woman he'd spend the rest of his life with. As he stepped into the shower, his mind raced with ideas for the most romantic proposal anyone has ever seen.

Chapter 26

Monday mornings were the worst. Stephanie slept in and had made an error in her schedule. Her first client was an hour earlier than she thought. While she showered, John made breakfast. Of course, it was partly his fault she'd slept in, but there was no way she could be angry.

It had been a week since he gave her the first romantic dinner, but he still had her practically floating on air. When he worked, he sent little texts making her smile or made her want to rip his clothes off when he got home. When he was off, he would prepare supper and treat her like a queen.

Another positive in their lives was Marc pled guilty to the charges and requested to go to rehab to get his life together. The crown attorney and judge agreed to the plea. As long as Marc stuck to the program, and didn't contact any of her family, he would receive probation. If he wanted to see his son after he completed his rehab, he would need to go through family court.

"I should be home around six," Stephanie called to John as she hurried out the door. "Love you."

"Love you too. Have a good day." He blew her a kiss as she closed the door and was halfway down the steps when she heard her name.

"Stephanie." Sandy hurried toward the fence.

"Hey." She still had a couple of minutes to chat with her friend.

"I hate to ask, but my car won't start, and I've got to be in town in forty minutes. It's the hotel downtown. Would you be able to drop me off?" Sandy never asked for anything.

"My first client is downtown, so it's all on the way." Stephanie would have driven her even if it wasn't.

"I'll even buy coffee. I need to get my things out of my car," Sandy shouted as she ran to her vehicle.

Stephanie hurried toward the end of the driveway where her car was parked. As she got closer, a strong smell caused her to wrinkle her nose. The closer she got to the end of the driveway, the stronger it was. She was almost next to her car when John shouted her name.

"Steph." John waved her cell phone in front of him.

"Shit." She dropped her bags and ran back to the house.

Stephanie smiled as she made it to the bottom step, but before she could thank John, something hurled her forward. A loud explosion erupted behind her, and her ears rang. When she looked up, John grabbed her around the waist and yanked her up from the ground.

"Get in the house. Now," John yelled.

368

When she glanced up at him, his eyes focused on something behind her. She turned, and her heart seemed to stop in her chest. Black smoke swirled into the air at the end of the driveway, and flames engulfed her car.

"My God. Sandy," she screamed as she tried to lunge toward the fence, but John kept a tight hold on her.

"What?" John's voice sounded muffled.

"I was going to drive her to work. Where is she, John?" Stephanie grabbed John's arms.

Her ears felt as if she were underwater, but she managed to hear John yell to Sandy. Stephanie held her breath as John ran to the side of the house and jumped over the fence into Sandy's yard. When she saw him walk back with his arm around Sandy, Stephanie let out a ragged breath at the sight of her friend alive. Stephanie ran toward them to help Sandy over the fence.

"Are you okay?" Stephanie yelled and hugged Sandy.

John's arm wrapped around Stephanie and pushed both her and Sandy back to the house. John said something, but she could barely hear him. He grabbed her face and spoke slowly.

"Get in the house," John said and then put the phone to his ear.

Stephanie didn't let go of Sandy as they hurried inside. Stephanie checked her friend from head to toe, but except for being a little dazed, she didn't seem to be hurt.

"I'm fine. I got knocked down by the force of the blast," Sandy said as Stephanie hugged her.

"Sit down," Stephanie ordered, mostly because her legs felt weak, and she didn't know if she could stand much longer.

"What the hell happened?" Sandy asked.

Stephanie wanted to know too because she wasn't sure she believed what just happened. Was it a dream, or did she see her car on fire? Her brain was muddled, and her ears felt as if something covered them. She tried to put the pieces of what happened together in her mind, but it didn't seem real.

"I don't give a fuck, Uncle Kurt. Someone blew up her fucking car." John shouted.

Her ears might be a little screwed, but she had no issues hearing John raised voice. She thought it was over, but it wasn't, and if she hadn't forgotten her phone, she'd be dead. Tears started to run down her cheeks before she realized she was crying.

"Steph, what the hell is going on?" Sandy wrapped her arm around Stephanie's shoulder.

"I wish I knew. I've got to call Cora and let her know what happened." She pulled out her phone, but her hands shook so badly she couldn't even unlock the screen.

"I'll call her for you." Sandy took Stephanie's phone and found Cora's number.

Everything around Stephanie started to fade into a haze. Why did someone try to kill her? She never did anything to anyone. She was lost in her head and didn't notice John when he knelt in front of her. His lips moved, but she couldn't make out what he said. The only thing she could hear was her heart pounding in her ears.

"Stephanie." It sounded hollow, but she knew it was John.

"I think she's going into shock." She recognized the voice, but for the life of her, she didn't know who it was.

"I'll get a blanket." Another voice.

"She feels clammy." John's voice sounded strange.

"Get her to lay down on her side and cover her up with this until the ambulance gets here." It sounded like James, or was it Ian?

Someone eased her down on the couch, and she looked up to find John above her. Why did he look so worried, and why was she so cold? *So cold.* Oh God, where was Sandy?

"Sandy?" she squawked.

"I'm here, Stephanie; I'm fine. You rest." Sandy knelt next to her and held her hand.

"Yes, rest sounds good. Sandy is fine. I can rest now," Stephanie mumbled as her eyes closed.

Stephanie opened her eyes and sat up in terror. Where was she? The hospital. Why was she in the hospital? Where was John? She glanced around the room as a thousand questions ran through her head.

It was dark, with only a faint light coming from the hallway. John sat in a chair, his eyes closed, and his head slightly hung to the side. She closed her eyes and tried to clear her jumbled thoughts. When her mind cleared, everything came back. The explosion. Her car. Stephanie covered her face, and tears began to flow down her face.

"Shh… honey, you're okay." John's strong arms wrapped around her.

"I smelled gas," she mumbled into his chest.

"What?" John pulled back from her, and she lifted her head to look at him.

"I smelled gas when I was going down the driveway. I didn't know what it was at first, but it just hit me. It was gas." She sniffed.

"Honey, there was a hole punctured into your tank and stuffed with a piece of cloth. Gas dribbled down to the end of the driveway right to the road. We found a couple of matches on the street where the gas trail ended," John said. "Someone saw you head to the car, dropped the matches, and took off."

"John, why… wo….would someone want to ki… kill me?" she choked out between broken sobs.

"I don't know, baby, but we're going to find out." He held her tightly against his chest. "I'm not going to let anyone hurt you."

The next day, the hospital released Stephanie. When John pulled into the driveway, the sight of the scorch marks on the pavement sent a shudder of fear through her body, and she squeezed her eyes closed. John must have sensed her fear because his hand found hers and held it tightly.

She turned her head to the driver's side of the car and opened her eyes. He smiled and nodded toward the house. John's family and her parents poured out through the front door. Before John could get out of the car, her dad opened the door and helped her out. He wrapped his big arms around her and guided her into the house.

Stephanie found it hard to hold back the tears when everyone swallowed her up with hugs. She almost made it to the living room when she heard Nanny Betty order everyone out of her way.

"Now me ducky, ya come in here and sit down. We're all here for ya." Nanny Betty linked into Stephanie's arm and practically dragged her to the couch.

As she made sure Stephanie was comfortable, Nanny Betty sent Aaron and Mike into the kitchen to get tea. She sent James to get Stephanie a blanket and ordered Stephanie's mother to sit on the couch. Stephanie almost choked as she held in the giggles as Nanny Betty turned to Kurt.

"Now, my sonny b'y, I don't know what kinda police department yur runnin' out dere in town, but ya damn well better find dis son of a gun who's tryin' ta hurt our girl." Nanny Betty shook her finger in Kurt's face.

"Mudder, we're doing everything we can." Kurt sounded like a little boy trying to get out of trouble.

"Ya can't be doin' everyting now can ya, or ya'd have dem in jail. Now catch dem." Nanny Betty poked him in the chest and made her way to the kitchen.

"I swear, I should hire that woman for interrogation." Kurt shook his head.

"You really should." Her mom laughed.

"Do you think you could answer a few questions, Stephanie?" Kurt pulled the coffee table over and sat in front of her.

"Is this necessary now, Uncle Kurt?" John sat on the arm of the couch next to her.

"John, you know the answer to that." Kurt glared at John, and she could see how he was the boss. "John told me you remember smelling gas as you walked toward the car. What made you go back to the house?"

"She left her phone on the counter, I called out to her to come back and get it," John answered before she could.

"Stephanie, have you talked to Brad King recently?" Kurt glanced down at a notepad in his hand.

"The last time I talked to him was at the fundraiser." Stephanie shrugged.

"I see." Kurt exchanged a strange look with John.

"Wait... what... You think Brad is doing this?" She glanced between Kurt to John and knew there was something they weren't telling her. "What's going on?"

"He hasn't shown up to work since the fundraiser, and we've tried to contact him at home, but he's not answering. One of our officers went to his apartment, but his girlfriend said he was out of town," Kurt explained. "Do you know her?"

"I just know she's the one he cheated on me with, but I don't know her." Stephanie didn't want to know her.

"Her name's Erica Reid." Kurt flipped through his notepad.

"I only knew her first name." Stephanie sighed.

"Stop harassin' da poor girl, Kurt." Nanny Betty pushed Kurt until he stood up, and she placed a tray on the table in front of

Stephanie. "Now ducky, ya have some a' dis pea soup and dumplin's."

Stephanie wasn't about to argue with Nanny Betty. She picked up the tray and began to eat, but her thoughts swirled around in circles. Where was Brad? Did he go into hiding because he did try to hurt her?

She was tired of the same questions over and over. There were too many emotions, and she started to get a headache from it all. John, James, Keith, Aaron, her father, and Kurt were huddled in the hallway, talking in hushed tones. No doubt about her and Brad. Nanny Betty hovered over her and fed her more food than anyone could ever eat. Her mother and Kathleen were in the kitchen, and Sandy sat at her side.

Sandy could have been killed too, but she sat at Stephanie's side, trying to comfort her. Then again, if Stephanie hadn't forgotten her phone, she'd probably be dead.

Stephanie glanced around the room to distract herself from the emotion welling up inside. Sean, Ian, Mike, and Nick sat on the other side of the living room. Even her friend Donna texted continuously to check on her. It was driving her to the brink of insanity, but a beep distracted her. When she glanced at Sandy, her friend was staring at her cell phone and then suddenly jumped to her feet.

"Stephanie, I hate to do this, but I need to go. It's something with work, but I'll drop in to see you when I get home." Sandy hugged her.

"You really should be resting too, Sandy," Stephanie complained. "You could've been hurt badly."

"I don't have the luxury of resting, but I'll be fine." Sandy waved as she walked away.

Stephanie watched Sandy as she spoke with John, Keith, and Kurt before she left. She waved once more before she disappeared. A few seconds later, Stephanie's cell phone rang, startling her.

"Hello." Stephanie was nervous when she answered it because she didn't recognize the number.

"Is this Stephanie Kelly?" a female asked.

"Yes." She didn't recognize the voice.

"Oh good. This is Kim Newman." Stephanie froze. "Before you say anything, please listen to me."

"Okay." Stephanie glanced toward John.

"I've been told someone is trying to hurt you. I can't tell you who, but believe me when I tell you this person is crazy." Kim's voice cracked.

"You know who it is?" Stephanie gasped.

"I found out at the fundraiser, and I thought it was all verbal diarrhea, but I found out what happened this morning. I need to talk to you about it," she rambled, but Kim sounded sincere.

"You should talk to the police," Stephanie raised her voice so John would hear her.

"I will, but I wanted to talk to you first, and John. I'll text you the address. Please meet me and tell John it has nothing to do with our relationship. It's to keep you safe. I... I have to go." The call ended, and a second later, she received a text with Kim's address.

"Who was that?" John crouched in front of her.

Stephanie told him what Kim said and shown the text she received. John seemed skeptical, but there was something in Stephanie's gut said Kim wouldn't call her if she tried to kill her.

"You don't think Kim could be the one doing this?" Mike stood behind John.

"Until we know for sure, we've got to be careful," Kurt said.

Stephanie glanced at the address and repeated it to herself over and over. It seemed familiar, but she didn't know why. She didn't have time to worry about it.

"Let's go." Stephanie shot to her feet and headed to the front door.

"Hold on there, sweetheart. We need a plan just in case Kim is our culprit." John turned to Kurt. "What do we do?"

Stephanie listened as she continued to get more impatient by the minute. She'd had enough of the worry and fear. Even if it was Kim, she needed to know for sure. This had to end.

It seemed to take forever to formulate a strategy, and Stephanie impatiently tapped her foot as she listened to the plan in detail. John and Stephanie would go to the apartment with James, Kurt, and two of the other officers close by.

The argument started when John demanded she wear a Kevlar vest under her sweater. Unfortunately, she was alone in her refusal to wear it. She had two choices presented to her, wear the vest, or stay home. It was ridiculous and uncomfortable.

The second argument didn't involve her. It started when her father tried to follow them to the vehicles. Kurt made it very clear he wasn't going, and her dad was pissed. It took her mother and Nanny Betty to calm him down. Before he let her go, he hugged Stephanie so tight she thought he would break her ribs.

The entire drive, John kept a tight grasp on her hand. It was almost painful, but she didn't complain. She hadn't paid attention to where they drove until the car pulled in front of the apartment building. A chill ran down her spine as she remembered why the address seemed so familiar. It was the building Brad used to live when they first started to date.

John stepped out of the car and scanned the area before he allowed her to get out of the vehicle. When he seemed comfortable that it was safe, he held out his hand to Stephanie. She took his hand and stepped out as she looked up at the front of the building.

When they were inside, Kurt, James, and the other officers stood around the lobby as John walked her to the elevator. He kept her tucked behind him until the doors opened, and he was sure it was empty. The ride to the third floor seemed to take forever.

"Stay behind me," John urged as the elevator doors opened and they stepped onto the floor.

The apartment was the fourth door on the left. When they were almost in front of it, John pushed her behind him and drew his weapon. She managed to get a quick look and saw the door open. He hooked her hand onto the back of his shirt as he approached the apartment. Her heart pounded as John pushed the door all the way and called out.

"Kim," John shouted and waited.

"Call an ambulance," someone screamed from inside, and Stephanie was sure she knew the voice.

John ran into the apartment with Stephanie on his heels. Her heart was in her throat as they turned into the main area of the small room. Stephanie gasped at the horrific sight in front of her.

Sandy knelt next to Kim's blood-covered body with tears streaming down her cheeks. She had a towel pressed to Kim's chest, but it didn't seem to stop the bleeding.

"Sandy, what the hell are you doing here?" John holstered his weapon and dropped to his knees.

"She's still breathing, call someone," Sandy said through her sobs. "Hold on, honey. Help's coming."

"Sandy, answer me. What are you doing here?" John sounded pissed, but while he waited for Sandy to explain, he radioed James to get help.

"Sh… she's my sis… sister," Sandy choked, and from the expression on John's face, he was shocked to hear the confession.

"What the fuck are you talking about? You knew she was doing this, and you didn't tell me?" John shouted.

Before Sandy could answer, Kurt and James ran into the apartment. They looked confused but hurried around the apartment, checking each room.

"I couldn't tell you," Sandy yelled back.

"Were you fucking helping her?" John's face was red with anger as he grabbed Sandy by the arm and pulled her away from Kim.

"John. Stop." Kurt's voice startled Stephanie, and she stepped back against the wall.

"She knew, Uncle Kurt." John had a death grip on Sandy's arm.

"Jesus, John, she's got nothing to do with this," Kurt roared. "She's one of us. She works for Keith."

Stephanie knew her mouth was hung open, but from the expression on John's face, he was baffled. Stephanie hadn't noticed anyone behind her until she felt a gentle hand on her shoulder. James and Keith stood next to her, and as Keith stomped into the apartment, James guided Stephanie out of the area to make room for the paramedics.

"What's going on, James? What does Kurt mean Sandy works for Keith and is one of you?" Stephanie stared up at James.

"I don't know, but I think we're about to find out." James nodded toward the door where Kurt, John, Keith, and Sandy were exiting the apartment.

John's jaw was clenched so tight she was surprised his teeth didn't crack with the pressure. Kurt and Keith stood on either side of Sandy, and Stephanie's heart went out to the woman, Sandy looked devastated.

"You want to tell me what the fuck is going on here?" John's hands were in fists at his sides as he glared at Keith.

"Sandy works for me and the NPD," Keith spoke with a firm but calm tone.

"She's a cop?" John snapped and glared at his brother.

"Yes," Kurt replied.

"And no," Keith interjected.

"Keith, I need to go with my sister." Sandy sniffed as the paramedics rolled Kim out on the gurney.

"You go with her, and I'll explain everything, but Sandy, we need all the information Kim has," Kurt warned.

"I know." Sandy glanced at Stephanie for a moment, apologized, and then ran after the paramedics.

"You're letting her go." John waved his hand toward the elevator.

"Calm the fuck down before I kick your fucking ass," Keith roared at John.

"Can we all calm down and find out what the fuck is going on." James stepped between Keith and John.

It was the first time since she'd met the family she'd seen any anger between the brothers. Stephanie glanced at Kurt. He stood to the side, eyes narrowed, and arms crossed over his chest, but it didn't seem to faze him that John and Keith looked about ready to come to blows.

"Before I explain, John, you've got to understand; I didn't know Kim was involved in any of this." Keith blew out a breath and continued. "Let's go back to your house. Kurt and I will explain everything."

As soon as the forensics crew arrived, they left to go back to Hopedale. When they arrived home, Kurt tried to clear the family out before Keith explained, but even Stephanie knew, with John's family and her parents, Kurt didn't stand a chance. Especially after Nanny Betty threatened to box his ears if he didn't explain, and explain fast.

"Remember this has to stay quiet," Kurt informed the group.

"Sandy works for me," Keith began.

"I thought she worked with a catering company. You're telling us she's a construction worker?" Nick looked as confused as Stephanie felt.

"Start from the beginning, Keith," Kurt suggested.

"I do own a construction company, but I also own another company that has nothing to do with construction." Everyone's eyes were glued to Keith as he spoke.

"Get to the fucking point." John tossed his hands in the air.

"Watch yur language, Johnny." Nanny Betty swat John on the butt as he paced by her. "Go on, Keithy."

John rolled his eyes, but he did keep quiet. Stephanie covered her mouth to hide her smile because no matter what people in the room thought, Nanny Betty was the only one in charge.

"The reason John is so impatient is because he's one of the few who know I own a high-end security firm called Newfoundland Security Services, or NSS." Keith glared at John.

"Keith's company works alongside the department. His company provides security and investigation services." Kurt picked up where Keith stopped.

"Ok... yes... great. Keith's the man. What the f..." John stopped when he eyed Nanny Betty. "What does Keith's company have to do with all this?"

"Sandy graduated at the top of her class with the police academy in Ontario. There's also nothing the woman can't do with a computer. She has the highest security clearance of anybody in the country and was recruited by the NPD to work undercover when needed, but her main job is with my firm." Keith looked directly at John. "There's no way she's involved with hurting Stephanie. I've known her for a long time."

"You're saying she's kind of the Penelope Garcia of Newfoundland." Aaron chuckled.

"Who's that?" Kurt asked.

"From the TV show Criminal Minds," Mike replied.

"Right. I guess you could say that." Kurt shook his head, clearly annoyed.

"The department can't hire her full time because they can't afford to pay her what she's worth. She's that good. Whenever anyone needs anything, they call me, and I call Sandy." Stephanie wasn't sure if anyone else could hear it, but there was pride in Keith's tone.

"Did you know Kim was her sister?" John raised an eyebrow.

"No, I didn't." Keith seemed almost apologetic.

"Does this mean it's all over?" Stephanie interrupted because she wasn't sure what was going on, but when Kurt and John exchanged a worried look, she knew it wasn't over.

"I need to talk to Sandy." Kurt started for the door.

"I'm going with you." John stomped behind him.

"So am I." Stephanie knew they were going to try and stop her, but when John opened his mouth, Stephanie held up her hand. "Don't dare say no. This is my life, and I want to know what Sandy knows."

Stephanie walked out the front door and waited next to the car with her arms folded over her chest. As adamant as she was to go, she held her breath as she waited for John or his uncle to refuse to let her go. When John opened the car door for her, she finally started to breathe.

At the hospital, a nurse directed them to the intensive care unit. Sandy sat in the waiting room with her head in her hands, rocking slowly. Stephanie had a difficult time wrapping her head around how brilliant her friend was.

"Sandy?" Kurt sat next to her.

When Sandy lifted her head, and Stephanie's heart broke. Her eyes were red, and her cheeks were blotchy. It was apparent she'd been crying for a while.

"How's your sister?" Stephanie sat on the other side of her friend.

Stephanie didn't want Sandy to feel intimidated by Kurt or John, but with the way John glared at the woman, it would make anyone feel nervous. However, it didn't seem to affect Sandy.

"She's stable, but she hasn't woken up. She's lost a lot of blood and has three large stab wounds." Sandy sat back in the chair and wiped her hands across her cheeks.

"So, are you going to tell us what happened?" John snapped.

"John." Stephanie narrowed her eyes at him.

"What?" John didn't seem to know why she was annoyed with him.

"Do you have to be so cold?" Stephanie glared at him.

"No. It's okay. I don't blame him." Sandy took a deep breath, and Stephanie took her hand. "Kim's my half-sister. We've got the same father but different mothers. Our father is Stewart Michaels. Kim has a relationship with him. I don't. He left my mother for Kim's mother, and I haven't had anything to do with him."

"What does this have to do with who's trying to hurt Stephanie?" John grumbled.

"Let her finish for the love of God." Stephanie disliked John's impatient side.

"John, she wouldn't let me tell you we were related. Kim tried to get me to talk to our father. It was a crazy coincidence when you started dating her." Sandy tightened her grip on Stephanie's hand.

"I bet." John's jaw clenched.

"She tried again at the fundraiser, but I refused. Halfway through the fundraiser, she told me she heard a woman in the bathroom laughing about how her boyfriend was going to make his ex-girlfriend's life a living hell." Sandy glanced at Stephanie

"Erica Reid?" Kurt asked.

"Yes, I didn't pay any attention to Kim, but when I got home, I did some research on her. I found out she lived in the same building as Kim. Something told me my sister knew more than she was saying. I called her, and she told me the only way she would tell me anything was if I met with our father. I'm sorry, but I hung up on her." Sandy's voice cracked. "Then I got a text from her saying she wanted to talk to me and it was important. She told me to get over to her apartment right away. She could prove who tried to hurt Stephanie."

"What did she tell you?" Kurt asked.

"Something about a black car, and then she passed out," Sandy said, obviously trying to compose herself. "There was so much blood."

"She must have called me right after she sent the text." Stephanie met John's gaze.

"You should have told me what was going on, Sandy." Kurt was firm but not in an angry way.

"I know." Sandy lowered her head.

"She thought she was doing the right thing. Jesus, leave the girl alone." Ian's voice had everyone turn to the entrance of the waiting room.

Ian walked into the room behind Keith. When Sandy's eyes landed on Ian, she gave him a weak smile. Ian didn't say another word, but it was obvious he was there to support Sandy, as well as Stephanie.

"Ian's right," Kurt said.

Stephanie's phone beeped, and all eyes turned to her. She tapped the screen and froze. There was a text on her cell phone from Brad.

Brad: Stephanie, I need to talk to you. Please, I know who's trying to hurt you.

"John," Stephanie shouted as she shot to her feet and held the phone out to him.

"So, everyone knows who it is, except for us?" John growled through his teeth.

"Text him back and tell him you're on the way." Kurt stood next to her.

"What if it's him?" Stephanie's hands shook as she took back the phone.

"We'll be there with you." Keith placed his hand on her shoulder.

Stephanie sent a return text to Brad and asked him where to meet. Her heart stopped when he gave her the address of the same apartment building where Kim lived.

"He's at his old apartment." Stephanie could barely get the words out.

"There's something else I've got to tell you guys before you go." Sandy slowly stood.

"What?" John snapped.

"Stephanie, you've got to believe me. I didn't know until the fundraiser. Kim told me. Your ex, Brad," Sandy said. "He's also my brother or my half-brother."

"You're telling me, both of our exes are your siblings?" John glared at Sandy.

"John, I don't have any dealings with my father. He's a fucking whoremaster who can't keep his dick in his pants. Fuck, I probably have twenty more siblings I don't know. I hate him. I fucking loathe my father. He's the reason my mother is dead. All the yelling and glares you're giving me couldn't make me feel any worse than I already do. I love Stephanie. She's the closest thing I've ever had to a best friend." Sandy took a deep breath and continued. "I don't want her hurt any more than you do. Yes, I kept this from you, but it wasn't to hurt her, or you. Damn it, John, you're more like my fucking brother than Brad. Can't you see this is killing me?" Sandy shook.

Stephanie was in shock because she'd never heard Sandy curse so much. It was as if she was looking at a stranger. Still, Stephanie stood and wrapped her arms around the sobbing girl, and Sandy clung to her. The whole room was quiet, and the only thing you could hear was Sandy's racking sobs. After a few minutes, John spoke.

"I'm sorry, Sandy," John said. "I know none of this is your fault."

"I just wanted to find out for sure." Sandy wiped the tears from her cheeks. "I was going to tell Keith after I talked to Kim."

"We can figure all this out later. Right now, we've got to see what Brad wants." Stephanie stepped back from Sandy.

John didn't say another word until they returned to the apartment building. He scrutinized the front of the building as if he expected someone to jump out of thin air.

"I don't like this." He blew out a breath as he reached for her hand.

"We've got to find out what he knows." She squeezed his hand and cupped his cheek.

She was tired of being afraid and waiting for something else to happen. Scared the next time she could die, or worse, this person could kill someone she loved.

John took her hand as she stepped out of the car. As they walked into the building, she didn't bother to look for Keith, Kurt, or any of the guys. She knew they were close. She didn't doubt it for a second. John squeezed her hand as the elevator doors opened to the sixth floor. He seemed hesitant as they headed down the hallway toward Brad's apartment.

As they moved closer, John continuously scanned the area. When they stopped in front of the door, Stephanie took a deep breath and knocked. For several seconds she waited, and as she was about to rap on the door a second time, the lock clicked. She glanced at

John as he pulled her back from the door and stepped in front of her slightly. His jaw clenched when the door opened, but Brad didn't answer. Erica appeared in the doorway.

"Stephanie, it's good to see you again." Erica's smile faltered a little when she saw John. "Oh, and you brought your boyfriend. Brad is just in the shower. Come on in."

John positioned himself between Stephanie and Erica as they entered the apartment. John urged her ahead of him as Erica closed the door. Stephanie was about to step into the living room when she heard a grunt. She spun around as John fell to the floor, and she froze. Erica stood next to him with a baseball bat rested against her shoulder.

"What did you do to him?" Stephanie shouted as she tried to step toward John.

"I knocked him out for a bit." Erica's smile changed to a sinister grin, and Stephanie's blood ran cold.

"Where's Brad?" Stephanie backed slowly away from the woman moving toward her.

Stephanie stepped into the small living room and scanned around for some way to get away from her. Dread set in when she realized there was only one exit, and Erica blocked it.

"Oh darling, don't worry about Brad. He's resting." Erica tilted her head to the side and narrowed her eyes at Stephanie. "I've tried everything to get Brad to marry me, but he keeps saying it's not the right time. Do you know why it's never the right time?"

Erica took a step toward Stephanie and dropped the bat down to her side. Her hand still had a death grip on the handle, and Stephanie backed further away from the woman.

"I have no idea why it wouldn't be the right time." Stephanie's heart thundered in her chest.

"He still loves you. When I get rid of you, he'll be free." She sneered at Stephanie.

"Erica, don't do this." Stephanie needed to stall.

She knew Kurt and Keith were supposed to be right behind them. The only thing she was worried about was how she would get around Erica to check on John.

"Brad and I are over; I'm in love with John." Stephanie motioned her hand toward the hallway, where she'd seen John fall to the floor.

"You may have moved on, but Brad is obsessed with you," she growled as she sneered.

Erica looked like an animal about to pounce on her prey. She bared her teeth, and her eyes narrowed as she stalked closer. Stephanie backed up until the back of her legs hit the couch. There was nowhere else to go.

Stephanie tried to move out of the way, but before she could run, Erica launched through the air and knocked Stephanie to the ground. She sat on Stephanie's chest and wrapped her cold hands around Stephanie's neck. Stephanie struggled with the crazed woman, but Erica was bigger and stronger. It was hard to think when she couldn't breathe, and the more she thrashed, the tighter Erica

391

squeezed. Stephanie turned her head slightly, and in her peripheral vision, she saw John on the floor.

The sight of him vulnerable and motionless gave her the adrenalin rush she needed, and she could hear Jess in her head telling her to fight.

Stephanie lifted her knees as if to do a crunch and connected with the middle of Erica's back. The move pushed Erica forward enough so Stephanie could push out from under her and roll away.

Stephanie jumped to her knees, but before she could get away, Erica grabbed her hair and yanked her back. Stephanie fell back against the floor, and Erica was on top of her again. With every bit of strength she could muster, Stephanie balled her fist and punched Erica in the jaw as hard as she could. Erica screamed as she grabbed her face and fell to the side.

Stephanie pushed her away and jumped to her feet. She ran to John and quickly checked for a pulse. He was still breathing, and his pulse was steady. Where in the hell were Kurt or Keith or James?

Stephanie didn't have time to worry, because the sound of Erica's shrieks echoed through the apartment. Stephanie turned in time to see Erica run toward her, and Stephanie scrambled to her feet. She made her way to the door and tried to open it. It was locked, and Stephanie glanced behind her as she fumbled to unlock the door.

"You, bitch," Erica screamed and ran at her.

Stephanie waited until Erica was an arm's length away and did what Jess taught her. She grabbed Erica by the ears and slammed her head into the door. When Erica grunted and staggered back, Stephanie lifted her leg and kicked Erica in the knee. Erica let out a loud shriek and crumpled to the ground holding her injured leg.

Stephanie was pissed. How dare this bitch try to kill her? Stephanie didn't give Erica time to recover. She jumped on top of the crazy woman. With every bit of anger and fear Stephanie dealt with over the last few weeks, Stephanie pulled back her fist and slammed it into Erica's nose. Stephanie missed, and Erica managed to roll over on top, pinning Stephanie to the floor. A fist connected with Stephanie's cheek, and the pain made her see stars.

Stephanie shook her head and used all her strength to push Erica off, but before she could, Erica suddenly sat perfectly still on top of her. Stephanie heard a soft click and blinked her eyes several times to clear her blurred vision. There was a shadow behind Erica, but Stephanie couldn't see who it was.

"Get the fuck up off her. Now." Stephanie recognized the voice. "If you don't, I won't hesitate to blow your fucking head off."
Sandy.

Erica slowly crawled off Stephanie and winced as she grabbed her injured knee. She shuffled backward on her ass away, but she glared at Sandy as if she wanted to kill her.

"Sandy?" Stephanie croaked as Sandy held out her free hand, but her focus stayed glued to Erica as she helped Stephanie to her feet.

"Are you okay?" Sandy asked Stephanie.

Sandy's glared coldly at Erica, and Stephanie shuddered. She was glad not to have the glare directed toward her. The woman Stephanie knew as warm and friendly was gone.

"I'm fine, but how did you get in, I didn't think I got the door unlocked." Stephanie glanced back at the open door.

"The lock is pretty flimsy. Check on John." Sandy stalked toward Erica with the gun pointed straight at her head, and her next words were a snarl. "Where's Brad?"

"What do you care?" Erica shouted, but she continued to back away from Sandy.

"If you've hurt him, I swear I'll beat you within an inch of your life," Sandy said with a cold, dangerous tone.

Stephanie shivered as she dropped to the floor next to John and pulled his head into her lap. This Sandy sounded lethal, but before Erica answered, Keith, Kurt, James, and four other police officers filed in through the door.

"How the hell did you get here before we did?" James glanced at Sandy.

Sandy didn't answer. She didn't seem to be aware James had spoken to her, and it worried Stephanie. When Sandy pressed her gun against Erica's head, Stephanie gasped. If someone didn't stop Sandy, she'd probably kill Erica right there.

Keith knelt next to John and put his finger to John's neck. He looked up at Kurt and nodded. Kurt said something to one of the officers, and the young man ran out of the apartment.

"I think you better get Sandy to lower her gun," Stephanie whispered to Keith.

"Sandy?" Kurt slowly approached Sandy from behind. "I need you to lower your weapon."

"She won't tell me where Brad is." Sandy's voice cracked. "Where's my brother?"

Kurt reached around and placed his hand on top of Sandy's weapon. Before he managed to push it down to a safe position, she managed to push Erica's head back with the muzzle. Kurt holstered his gun and put his other hand on her shoulder.

"Sandy, we got this." Kurt's voice was calm but firm.

James and Keith surrounded her, and as James handcuffed Erica, Kurt managed to remove the gun from Sandy's hand. Erica would probably need to go to the hospital before they locked her up. Stephanie did some damage.

"Thanks, Jess," Stephanie whispered as she wrapped her arms around John.

"You need to find out where he is." Sandy almost fell to her knees, but Kurt walked her to the closest chair.

A line of police made their way through the rooms. Stephanie heard doors open and close as officers cleared each room. James pulled Erica up off the floor; she fought him as she screamed obscenities at Sandy. Another officer had to help James lead her out of the apartment. Erica seemed to have trouble putting weight on the leg Stephanie had kicked.

"Sandy, how did you know to come here?" Kurt was now in supervisor mode, and Sandy shook her head as she seemed to come out of a trance.

"I remembered Erica owned a black car. As soon as I put together what Kim tried to tell me before she passed out..." She sobbed, and Stephanie had to swallow the lump forming in her throat.

"So, you came here?" Kurt asked, but Sandy's eyes went to Stephanie.

"He's my brother. I didn't think. I got in my car and came here. There's a back entrance I use when I come to see Kim. I know I just found out about him, but he's my family." Sandy seemed as if she was begging for forgiveness with her eyes.

It was a silent plea to understand, and Stephanie did. Sibling bonds were strong. She and Marina were best friends, and she would do the same thing if Marina were the one in danger.

"Do you know where he is?" Kurt asked, but before Sandy could answer, an officer shouted from the back of the apartment.

"Sir, there's a male in the back bedroom. He's unconscious but breathing." Sandy pulled away from Kurt and ran in the direction of the voice.

Stephanie gazed down at John and swallowed. He still hadn't moved. It seemed as if he'd been unconscious for a long time, but it had probably not been more than twenty minutes. She looked up when she heard a shuffle next to her. Two young paramedics walked in with large bags on their shoulders and left their stretcher outside the door.

"This is John O'Connor, twenty-nine years old. He's unconscious but breathing and has a strong pulse. We've got another man in the bedroom. Brad King, not sure of his age, but he's unconscious. He's probably drugged." Keith stepped back as one of the men knelt next to John, and the other followed Keith to the back bedroom.

"Is he going to be okay?" Stephanie didn't even realize she'd started to cry.

"He's got a nasty bump, but his vitals are strong. We'll get him to the hospital so they can do a scan. We'll know more then." The man gave her a comforting smile, and Stephanie moved back so he could check John

"Brad's going to be fine." Kurt helped her to stand, but she kept a tight hold on John's hand.

"Miss, we have to get him to the hospital," the paramedic said.

She reluctantly released John's hand and was about to follow behind the paramedic, but she staggered. Kurt grabbed her before she fell, and Keith stepped to her other side.

"I think you better go with these guys." Keith wrapped an arm around her waist, and Kurt released her.

He guided Stephanie out of the apartment and didn't release her until she was in the ambulance with John. Keith nodded to her and smiled as the doors closed. Stephanie turned to where John lay on the gurney and immediately grabbed his hand in hers.

Chapter 27

John's head hurt like a son of a bitch. He couldn't believe he was so careless and turned his back on a possible suspect. Erica could have killed Stephanie while he was in a heap on the floor. To top it off, he was stuck in the hospital again. The doctors wanted to keep him for observation for twenty-four hours, but it was a little easier with Stephanie next to him in the bed.

What bothered him the most was the bruise forming on her cheek and under her eye. He was proud of her, though. According to James, Erica looked a whole lot worse.

John still couldn't believe Sandy worked for Keith as well as the RCMP and NPD. The law enforcement agencies had her under contract as a freelance computer analyst. Sandy also received calls from different government departments to test their network security. The woman was a freaking genius.

It figured Keith would find people who were as brilliant as he was. Keith had an eidetic memory and skipped several grades during his school days. He could have graduated at the age of fifteen, but he begged his parents to stay in school with his friends. They allowed it, but he did extra courses to make sure he didn't get bored.

John leaned his head back against the pillow and sighed. The weight of the world felt as if it lifted off his shoulders. With Erica in custody, it was over.

"Are you okay?" Stephanie cupped his cheek.

"I've got a headache, but not too bad. I'm just trying to get my head around what we found out about Sandy." He shook his head but noticed Stephanie's expression change. "What's wrong, honey?"

"I feel a little hurt because she never told us about Kim and Brad. I thought she was my friend." Stephanie looked about ready to burst into tears.

"I am your friend." John turned to see Sandy walk into his room with Keith, Kurt, and James.

"What are you doing here?" John didn't realize how angry he was until he saw her.

"She's here to explain." Kurt's tone told John he better shut up and listen.

Kurt sat on the chair next to the bed, and James leaned against the window sill on the other side of the room. Keith stood behind Sandy at the foot of the bed with his hand on her shoulder. She seemed to be searching for what to say, and when she looked up, there were tears in her eyes.

"First, I want to tell you both I'm sorry. I never knew Erica was the one trying to kill Stephanie. As I told you, I only found out Brad was my brother at the fundraiser." She glanced at Stephanie. "I don't expect you to accept my apology, but I just wanted to let you know."

"Start at the beginning, Sandy," Keith urged, and Sandy took a deep breath.

"I found out I had a sister three years ago. Kim contacted me when my father told her about me. She's younger, and our father raised her after her mother died. We all have different last names because my father never married any of our mothers. My father wanted a relationship with me and had Kim do his dirty work. I think he wanted to ease his guilty conscience and assumed if Kim made the initial contact, I'd be more willing to meet with him." Sandy paused for a moment as if to let that much of her explanation sink in.

"He was never part of my life and left my mother to raise me on her own. My mother worked two jobs to make sure I had everything I needed. When I was eight, the school told my mom I needed to be in a school for gifted kids. They recommended a school in Ontario. I forget the name now. It was expensive, and my mom couldn't afford it." Keith passed Sandy a box of tissues, and she wiped the tears from her cheeks.

"Being the great mom she was, she swallowed her pride and called Stewart. He told her to take him to court. My mom never contacted him again, and she worked her ass off to make sure I the best education she could afford. She hired special teachers to help me thrive. When I was twenty, she passed away." Sandy swallowed as Stephanie grasped her hand.

"When Keith moved the company here, he told me about the house next to you. He said his brother lived there, but I needed to keep my job with him quiet. I didn't understand, but I did it because

401

he's my boss and friend. Then we became friends. It was hard not to tell you." Sandy took another deep breath.

"You don't have to do all this today," Stephanie told her.

"It's okay. I need to. You dating Kim was just a huge coincidence. I warned her not to tell you she was my sister because of my job. She knows what I do. Then when she cheated on you, I thought you'd hate me if you knew she was related." Sandy squared her shoulders and continued.

"As you know, I found out about Brad at the fundraiser. I remembered him from the restaurant, and when I saw Kim talking to him, I asked her how she knew him. Things couldn't have been more screwed up. How was it possible both my siblings hurt the two best friends I've ever had? I honestly didn't know what to do, and I was afraid to tell you." Sandy turned around to look at Keith, and he nodded.

"Stephanie, I know Brad cheated on you, which makes him an asshole, but he wasn't the one who took the money. He also didn't know about the emails. Erica hacked his email." Sandy explained, and it made more sense because of the wording of the emails.

"She hated me that much?" Stephanie said.

"She's insane. According to Kim, Brad never forgave himself for cheating on you. On the night of the fundraiser, I told Kim about the things happening to you. Stephanie, Kim was hurt because I thought it was her, and she told Brad. He confronted Erica when they got back to his apartment, and she denied it. Then she offered to get him a drink so they could talk some more, the next thing he knew he woke up handcuffed to a pipe in the bathroom. Brad is a strong guy, but she injected him to keep him out. She stole it from her mother."

"Do you want a break, Sandy?" James handed Sandy a glass of water.

Sandy trembled as tears streamed down her face. His heart broke when he noticed Sandy wasn't the only one with tears in her eyes. Stephanie held Sandy's hand and sobbed as she listened to Sandy's explanation.

"No. I need to tell them." Sandy gave James back the cup and continued. "When Kim didn't hear from Brad, she went to the apartment. Erica told her Brad was away on business. Kim didn't believe her and called the fire station. They said Brad's girlfriend called to say he was sick. When Kim heard about the explosion, she knew Erica had something to do with it. After she texted me and called you, she called Erica and told her what she knew. Erica busted into her apartment and stabbed Kim. By the time I got there, Erica was gone, and Kim was... well, you know. I honestly didn't want to see any of you hurt. I didn't know I would get there before you."

"So, you went to Brad's to arrest Erica yourself?" John asked.

"And to find Brad," Sandy returned.

"You did all this to protect your sister and brother." Stephanie tilted her head.

"And my friends." Sandy sobbed, and Stephanie wrapped her arms around their friend.

"I know what it's like to want to see your sibling safe." Stephanie choked.

John knew it too. He would do anything for his brothers, and if he were in Sandy's position, he probably would have done the same thing.

"I'm really sorry, Stephanie." Sandy sobbed.

"I understand, but you've got to promise me one thing before this is considered forgotten." Stephanie pulled back and placed her hands on Sandy's shoulders

"Anything, I don't want to lose you or John as friends." Sandy wiped her cheeks.

"No more secrets. Unless it's work-related, of course." Stephanie smiled at Keith.

"I promise." Sandy hugged her, and then her eyes moved to John.

What was he supposed to say? If Stephanie could forgive her, who was he to hold a grudge.

"No more secrets." John pointed his finger at her.

"No more secrets." Sandy hiccupped.

It was finally over. It was time to move on to the next phase of his life. He was moving on with the woman he loved and making her his wife.

John was sick every time the local news station mentioned Erica's name. It was the top story for over a week, but luckily, Kurt kept Stephanie's name out of the story. Kurt was a big advocate for victim's rights and the right to privacy. It was the reason both Brad and Kim weren't mentioned in any of the reports either. John was glad they were safe and never wanted to see them harmed.

The Crown charged Erica with two counts of attempted murder, four counts of assault with a weapon, unlawful confinement, and a couple of other charges as well. She took a plea deal and sent away for a long time. With any luck, John would never have to hear her name again.

It was early September, and Stephanie's birthday was a week away. John planned a surprise birthday party for her and wanted to propose to her at the party. Before he could, John needed to speak to her parents. More specifically, her dad. John's father always told him and his brothers, a woman's father is the first man to hold her heart. It was a sign of respect to ask for his blessing.

John was a little intimidated by Doug. Not because he'd ever said anything to make John feel that way, but he was a huge man, and fathers didn't take kindly to the man who took their little girls away.

Before John worried about that conversation, he needed to find a ring for Stephanie. In his mind, he knew the ring he wanted for her, but he had no idea where to start. He wasn't a fan of shopping, so he pulled out his phone and called one of the people who thought shopping was a sport.

Isabelle answered on the second ring, and for a few minutes, they chatted about the department and her restaurant. John promised to take Stephanie there for supper soon. Isabelle opened her restaurant two years earlier, and the local news recently featured her business on a segment called *Places to Go with Sharon Snow*. Since then, she had to hire more kitchen staff because she was so busy, but Isabelle was somewhat of a control freak and would be there from open to close.

"You really should hire another chef, cuz. You're going to wear yourself out if you keep working so much." He could almost see her roll her eyes because she heard the comment every time the family got together for family gatherings.

"I know, and I'm looking into it," Isabelle responded the way she always did.

"I'm sure you are." John figured he'd made enough small talk and cleared his throat. "Um… Ah… I've got a question for you."

"Okay." He could hear the curiosity in her voice.

"How are you with picking out rings?" He heard Isabelle stifle a giggle and then cleared her throat.

"Depends on the ring. Would this ring be for someone special?" she teased.

"Okay, little girl, you know what I'm asking." John chuckled.

"John, I've got no idea. Maybe you should be more specific." She wasn't about to make this easy for him.

"You're gonna make me ask, aren't you?" John sighed.

"Yep." She ended the word with a pop.

"Can you please help me find the perfect engagement ring for Stephanie?" John pulled the phone away from his ear when she shrieked. "I'm assuming that means, yes."

"Of course, we will," Isabelle squealed.

"Wait? What? We?" This would not be good.

"You're on speakerphone. Jess and Kristy are here." Isabelle giggled.

"Shopping with three of you? In a jewelry store?" John groaned as he rolled his eyes and suddenly wished he'd just called his mother. "I'm not sure if I'm ready for all of you."

"Too bad. We're all going with you, and you're just lucky Pam isn't back in Newfoundland." Jess laughed.

"Seriously, maybe I should do this alone." John knew shopping with those three would be equivalent to some form of torture.

"We should call Nan and ask her if John should do this alone." He heard the warning in Kristy's snicker.

"Fuck. No Jesus way. Don't call Nan, or Mom, or your mom, or Aunt Cora. How is tomorrow for you guys?" The last thing he needed was to end up dragged from one store to the other with all the women in his family.

"Perfect." They shouted together and were still laughing when John hung up.

"Next step. Talk to Doug and Janet." John blew out a breath as he snatched his keys off the counter and headed to his car.

John pulled his car into the Kelly's driveway. His heart thundered, and he couldn't remember ever being so nervous in his life. He could do this, but it had to be just right.

As he stepped out of the car, Doug waved from where he had just mowed the lawn. He stepped away from the ride on mower and ambled toward John.

"John, this is a nice surprise." Doug glanced behind him. "Where's Stephanie?"

"She's working today." John shoved his hands in his pockets.

His palms sweat, and he managed to wipe them dry on the inside of his pockets. He couldn't shake the man's hands with sweaty palms. As Doug approached, he pulled out one perfectly dry hand and shook the large man's hand.

"Oh? Well, come on in. Janet, look who's here for a visit." Doug bellowed as they entered the house.

John wondered if Doug could hear his heart pounding because it seemed to get louder as he stepped into the house. A few seconds later, Janet appeared in the foyer, and he felt a little more at ease as she gave him a friendly smile.

"John, it's nice to see you. Stephanie isn't with you?" She gave John a gentle hug.

"She's working, but I was wondering if I could talk to both of you about something." He wanted to groan at the tone of his voice.

The words spewed out, so fast he wasn't sure if they even understood what he said. Janet and Doug looked at him quizzically, then looked at each other.

"It's nothing bad. I need to discuss something with you both." Considering what had happened over the last few months, he probably should have started with that.

"Come into the kitchen." Janet turned and went back to the kitchen with Doug behind her.

John shuffled into the kitchen as Janet scurried around the large room. She offered him something to drink, and John accepted a cup of coffee. Once they each had a hot beverage, Janet sat across from John. Doug settled next to her as John built up his courage. Stephanie's parents could make or break his plan to propose.

"Okay, my boy, what do you need?" Doug broke the silence.

"I know Stephanie and I have only been together a few months, but I've never met anyone like her. I want you to know I love her with all my heart." John stopped to breathe and then continued. "My dad always told me, when you find the right woman, you should hold on with both hands."

"Good advice." John saw Doug gently squeeze Janet's shoulder.

"He said before I propose, I should speak to her father and get his blessing." John smiled as Janet gasped and cupped her hands in front of her chest.

"Oh. My. Heavens." Janet gasped. "You're going to propose."

Her eyes filled with tears, and she had a grin from ear to ear. John smiled, but when he turned to Doug, his smile quickly faded at Doug's stone-faced expression.

"You think you're good enough for my little girl, do you?" Doug's deep voice rumbled, and John's heartfelt as if it dropped out of his chest.

"I love Stephanie, and I'll be the best husband I can be. I've had incredible role models who taught me how to have a long and happy marriage," John continued. "My parents are very open and honest with each other. They taught my brothers and me well. I'll always take care of her."

John didn't know what else to say as he rambled on. He was about to speak again when he noticed the corners of Doug's lips twitch, and Janet gave Doug a soft slap on his arm.

"Doug, stop teasing the boy." Janet laughed.

"John, my boy, my daughter couldn't ask for a better man." Doug grinned, and John blew out the breath he was holding as Doug reached across the table and shook John's hand. "What the hell am I doing? Get over here."

Doug jumped up from the table and pulled John into his huge arms. John was sure he'd pass out if Doug hugged any harder. When Stephanie's father released him, Janet pulled John into her arms and kissed his cheek.

"When are you going to propose?" She wiped a tear from her cheek.

Rhonda Brewer

"I'm going to ask her at her surprise birthday party," John explained.

"You keep your mouth shut, Doug." Janet pointed her finger at her husband. "He doesn't keep secrets very well."

"I'll keep this one." Doug held his hand over his heart.

After a couple of more hugs from Janet and a couple more handshakes from Doug, John made his way home. It was as if the weight of the world was off his shoulders. It was one of the hardest things he ever had to do. There were still a couple of hours before Stephanie would arrive home from work.

She'd texted while he was at her parents and told him not to cook, she would bring something home. It gave him time to get some of the plans together for her party.

John called his mother, and she cried as she insisted on the family home as the place for the party. Stephanie wouldn't suspect anything when he suggested going to his parents for supper. Nanny Betty shouted in the background for his dad to get her a pad and pen. Which meant, Nanny Betty was in full menu planning mode. John chuckled as the call ended to Nanny Betty and his mother discussing which finger foods to serve.

He called each of his brothers next, and after they congratulated him, he put each of them in charge of something. James and Keith were on beverages. Ian and Nick were on decorations, and Aaron and Mike would help with the food. John thought about possibly having the party catered, but Nanny Betty would bite his head off for even suggesting it.

411

As John ended the call with Stephanie's mother for the third time, his phone rang right away, but he didn't recognize the number. He ignored it first, but after a second call from the same number, he figured it was important.

"Hello," John answered.

"Is this John?" It was a woman.

"Yes." He wasn't sure if he should admit it was him.

"This is Marina," she replied.

"Oh. Hi, Marina." John should have known by the voice, but he hadn't talked to Stephanie's sister often on the phone.

"Mom told me about the party and the surprise." Marina giggled.

"I thought she might." John chuckled.

"I wanted to let you know, I'm moving home the same week, but since there's going to be a surprise party, I want to surprise Stephanie. I come in the day before the party, and I'm staying with mom and dad. If you need any help with anything, call or text me."

"That's great. She's going to be so happy you're home." John was even more excited about the party.

"Me too. I think the engagement might take precedence, though." He heard the smile in Marina's voice.

"I don't know about that." John knew how much Stephanie missed her sister and her nephew.

He spoke with Marina for a while, and she gave him some great ideas for the party and proposal. John wanted something Stephanie would never forget.

"I'm glad my sister found you, John. I wasn't as lucky in love, but I know she won the jackpot. The only good thing to come out of my relationship was my son." Marina's voice cracked.

"I'm the one who won the jackpot when I met your sister. Look, I know you've had a tough time, but I believe things happen for a reason." John heard Danny babble in the background.

"Maybe. I'm sorry, I've got to go, but keep in touch." Marina ended the call before John could say another word, but he didn't miss the sadness in her voice.

John's heart hurt for Marina. He didn't know her full story, but what he did know infuriated him. At least she still had her family, and if Stephanie agreed to marry him, Marina would have his big, crazy family too. John had noticed a spark of interest between James and Marina the night Marc had shown up at the house. Things happened for a reason.

The next day, John was about to pull out all his hair. Shopping with Jess, Kristy and Isabelle was cruel and unusual punishment. They took him to more jewelry stores than he could count. The painful part was when neither of them could agree on the same ring. John started to regret asking for their help.

The ring he pictured didn't seem to exist. He'd described it to every jewelry store they entered, but nothing came near to what he wanted. As they were about to begin the third hour of torturous shopping, Marina texted, and he figured it was to check his progress. He was embarrassed to tell her he still hadn't found one, but she'd sent him a picture and he opened it.

413

"John, come on," Jess yelled as she entered the shop.

When he opened the text, the picture attached made him want to dance in the middle of the mall. It was the ring, and a huge smile formed on his lips.

"John, you aren't going to find a ring out there," Isabelle complained from the doorway of the store.

"Wait, look at this." John practically ran to where his three cousins stood.

He held up his phone, so they could see the picture Marina had sent. To his surprise, his three cousins squealed, and Kristy snatched the phone from his hand.

"That's it." Isabelle grinned.

"Definitely." Jess nodded.

"It's exactly the way you described it." Kristy handed him back the phone.

"Thank God." John breathed a sigh of relief.

"How did she find it?" Jess asked.

"I sent her a sketch of what I wanted, and she spent all day showing jewelers." John grinned at his cousins as he placed a call to Marina.

He worked out the details with Stephanie's sister, and she told him she'd get it sized, and bring it back with her when she returned to Newfoundland. When he ended the call, he looked at his cousins and grinned.

"Well, girls, it's been a slice, but it looks like we're done." John was ecstatic about the ring but happier not to have to do any more shopping with his cousins.

John had the perfect ring, and in less than two weeks, he'd propose to the most beautiful, kind, and loving woman he'd ever met. Hopefully, she'd say yes.

Chapter 28

John seemed distant for a couple of days. Stephanie wasn't sure why, but she'd walked in on him a few times on the phone, and he'd end the call as soon as he saw her. Stephanie asked him if anything was wrong, but he said it was something with work.

She felt the need to talk to her sister, but when Stephanie tried to call, she couldn't get in touch with her. Her mom told her Marina was probably busy and would call when she got the chance.

John mentioned they would be going to his parents for supper later in the evening, but she didn't want to go anywhere. Her birthday was two days away and the fact she was about to turn twenty-eight, depressed her. Maybe it was because she and John were like two ships passing in the night over the last few days. She missed him.

A week earlier, Stephanie and John sat down with Kim and Brad to bury the hatchet. She didn't want to be enemies with them because they'd started to spend a lot of time with Sandy.

Both Kim and Brad apologized for what they'd done. As much as she and John dreaded the meeting in the beginning, it wasn't bad. Kim had recovered from her wounds, and she told them she was in the middle of cosmetology school. She and a friend of hers were going to open a business together when she finished.

Brad explained he never told Erica he was still in love with Stephanie. The only thing he said was he wasn't ready to get married, and in Erica's crazed mind, Brad wouldn't marry her because he was still in love with Stephanie. Everything in her life seemed to be calm, but she worried it would all come crashing down around her.

Stephanie and Sandy had grown closer since everything happened, and they spoke every day. Stephanie tried to call her as well, but she told Stephanie she was in meetings all day and wouldn't be home until late. Even Donna blew her off.

Stephanie tossed her phone on the counter and grabbed a bottle of water from the fridge. John had something to do for Nick, which meant she had the whole house to herself, and it was lonely.

She and John usually spent his day off together. When he said he'd be gone all morning, she did feel hurt. She didn't tell him because it was stupid and silly.

"Hey, beautiful." John walked through the door as she was headed back to the living room.

"Hey." She probably shouldn't have sounded so depressed, but she couldn't help it.

"What's wrong?" John raised his eyebrow as he wrapped his arms around her.

"Nothing. I missed you all day." She snuggled into his chest.

"You don't have to miss me anymore today." He kissed the top of her head, and she melted into his embrace.

"Do we have to go to your parents tonight?" She loved his parents, but she wanted to be alone with him.

"Well, yeah. I mean, they're expecting us, but we can try to get out early." John tensed and seemed to stammer over his words.

"I guess that would be okay." Stephanie hugged him tighter, and it did make her feel better to be in his arms.

The car ride to his parents' place seemed awkward and quiet. John held her hand most of the way, but he was distracted before they left, and his phone rang every ten minutes. If it wasn't ringing, he was getting a text. It started to piss her off because he was supposed to spend the afternoon with her. Either way, he promised they wouldn't be staying too late.

When they pulled into the driveway, the house looked dark. The only light was the one over the front door, and she found it odd because Kathleen typically had the house lit up.

"Are you sure they're home?" she asked as John opened her door and took her hand.

None of the family's cars were in the driveway. Usually, when Kathleen and Nanny Betty cooked supper, it meant everyone had to be there. None of the boys ever missed a meal.

"I'm sure." John opened the front door and motioned for her to go ahead of him.

Stephanie walked into the living room, and before she could say another word, she was startled by the shouts and sudden burst of light.

"Surprise," John whispered in her ear as she jumped back against him.

"What?" she gasped.

"Happy birthday, sweetheart." He chuckled as he wrapped his arms around her waist.

"Oh, God. This is why everyone was acting so weird." Tears filled her eyes. "I thought everyone was ignoring me."

"Nope. Just trying to pull off a few surprises." John kissed the top of her head.

Stephanie wasn't even sure who hugged her, because as soon as one set of arms let go, another embraced her. She glanced around as much as she could in between the hugs. A banner with *Happy Birthday Stephanie* hung above the fireplace, and balloons and streamers hung from the ceiling and walls.

When she turned to look at John, he stood with his shoulder braced against the doorframe, and a smile on his handsome face. She never had a clue he had planned any of it. She turned at the sound of a whistle.

"Okay, everyone. Let the girl breathe." Aaron stood in the middle of the room. "Before we get this party started, there are two presents Stephanie has to open right away." Aaron pointed to a sheet draped in the corner of the room with the word Surprise written across it.

"Pull it down. Your first surprise is behind it." Nick pointed to the corner.

It wasn't that she didn't trust John's brothers, but she glanced at John. When he nodded, she slowly made her way toward the corner of the room.

"Wait. Is someone going to throw a cake in my face when I pull this down?" Stephanie narrowed her eyes at Aaron and Nick.

"I promise nobody is going to shove anything in your face," Keith assured her, and she trusted him almost as much as John.

Stephanie reached up and gripped the sheet in her hands. She took a deep breath, closed her eyes, and gave it a hard tug. It dropped to the floor, and when nothing hit her in the face, she opened her eyes.

Marina stood in the corner of the room with Danny in her arms. For a moment, Stephanie stared as if she didn't believe what she saw. Seconds later, she gasped and wrapped her arms around her sister and nephew.

"That's why you weren't answering me." Stephanie cried as she pulled back from Marina.

"Sorry, it was a surprise." Marina laughed. "Before we talk, your other surprise is right here."

Marina pointed to three balloons anchored to the table next to her. Each one had a small envelope attached, and she glanced behind her as everyone nodded for her to continue.

"What's this?" Stephanie asked.

"They're numbered. You've got to open them in order and read them out loud." Marina stepped away as Stephanie pulled off the first envelope.

"Happy Birthday, Stephanie, I Love you with all my heart." She glanced around, but John had disappeared.

Stephanie looked at her sister, and Marina nodded for her to continue. Stephanie pulled off the second envelope and opened it.

"Pull off the next envelope and turn around." She grabbed the third envelope and turned around to see John behind her.

"Open it and read it." He smiled.

"Stephanie, you're the love of my life, and although this is your birthday, I want the best present in the world. Stephanie, would you be my wife?" She gasped and covered her mouth with her hand as she lifted her eyes from the paper in front of her.

John was down on one knee with a red velvet box in his palm. He gently grasped her hand and kissed her fingers as he lifted his gaze to hers.

"Will you marry me, Stephanie?" John's voice quivered, and Stephanie couldn't find her voice as tears streamed down her cheeks. "I don't know if crying is a good sign. You're kinda scaring me, sweetheart."

"It's a good sign. These are happy tears." Stephanie pulled him up and cupped his face in her hands. "I love you so, so much, and yes, I'll marry you."

John picked her up and crashed his lips against hers. She pulled back as everyone around them cheered and yelled, congratulations. When he lowered her back to the floor, John slipped the ring on her finger, and Stephanie stared at her hand.

The gold band was simple with a sparkling diamond in the center surrounded by smaller diamonds. Before she could say another word, their family and friends surrounded them.

"Another one bites the dust," Mike roared from the other side of the room.

"We get to have a bachelor party," Nick shouted.

"Strippers," Aaron hooted and quickly turned when Nanny Betty glared at him.

"Can I get everyone's attention?" James shouted.

The crowd quieted as Keith and Ian stepped forward with trays filled with glasses of champagne. Stephanie beamed at John as everyone grabbed a drink and waited for James to speak.

"I'd like to say Happy Birthday to the beautiful birthday girl, and congratulations to my brother and Stephanie. Bro, you've got a gem there. I wish you guys a long and happy life together. Cheers." James held up his glass.

A little while later, Stephanie pulled Marina aside. Danny was in a playpen with James' son Mason, and the two babies eyed each other curiously. They were almost the same age, and Stephanie laughed as Mason passed Danny a block. Danny didn't seem to want it at first, but after a moment took it cautiously. Within minutes the two little boys giggled and babbled as they passed the blocks back and forth.

"When do you go back?" Stephanie didn't want to know.

422

"I'm not." Marina nudged Stephanie with her elbow.

"Really?" Tears filled her eyes, again and she figured at the rate she was going, she'd be dehydrated before the night was over.

"I'm home for good." Marina smiled.

Marina's boss wanted her in Newfoundland to ensure everything was on track. She'd be working from home until the office opened. So, until she found a place to live, and daycare for Danny, she'd be staying with their parents.

"Besides, I missed everyone. I missed home." A tear ran down Marina's cheek.

"I'm so glad you're back." Stephanie hugged her sister.

"Me too." Marina sighed as Stephanie released her.

They talked about when to start planning the wedding, and as they chatted, James walked by. He leaned over the playpen and handed a cookie to Mason and Danny. Stephanie pressed her lips together to stop the giggle when she noticed Marina's eyes drop to James' ass.

"James, you remember Marina?" Stephanie did her best to sound casual.

"Of course. It's nice to see you again." James stood up straight and reached out to shake Marina's hand.

"Marina, you remember James." Marina shook his hand but pulled it back quickly, and her cheeks flushed.

"Isn't he gorgeous?" Stephanie whispered in Marina's ear.

"Aren't you engaged to his brother?" Marina snorted and bent down to kiss Danny's head.

"He's a widower." Stephanie nudged Marina with her shoulder.

"I know, Steph." Marina sighed.

"Not all men are like Marc." Stephanie put her arm around Marina.

"I know, but I'm nowhere near ready for dating. So, please don't start any matchmaking," Marina warned as John walked up behind Stephanie.

"Would you mind if I dance with my fiancée?" John kissed Stephanie's cheek.

"Not at all." Marina wiggled her fingers in a wave as John tugged Stephanie to the dining room.

The dining room furniture stood against the walls to make more floor space. As she scanned the room, she noticed everyone took advantage of the area. Aaron danced with a girl Stephanie never met, but it wasn't hard to tell they knew each other well. One of Aaron's hands were on the girl's ass, and the other seemed to have disappeared under the woman's shirt.

"She must be A.J.'s flavor of the week," John whispered in Stephanie's ear.

"Looks like Nick has a new flavor too," Stephanie nodded toward where Nick slow danced with his date.

"I'm surprised Mike didn't bring a date." John chuckled as he motioned to where Mike and Jess did their best to annoy Nick, Aaron, and their dates.

"Me too." Stephanie snickered as Aaron tried to dance his date as far away from Mike as they could.

"I love you," John whispered into her ear as she pulled her tighter into his arms.

"I love you, too. Thank you for all this, John." She rested her head against his chest, and they swayed to the slow music.

"Thank you for saying yes." John kissed the top of her head.

As the party started to wind down, people began to trickle out of the house and head to their homes. Before Cora and her husband left, she boasted about her being right again. Nanny Betty made Stephanie promise to take care of her grandson. She also got several suggestions from Aaron and Nick on how to celebrate their engagement, but John shut them up with threats of showing some naked baby pictures to their dates.

Stephanie lost sight of John for a few minutes as she was getting ready to leave. She found him with Kurt in the kitchen, and they looked somber. John held a large brown envelope in his hand and was deep in conversation.

"Something wrong?" Stephanie asked as she entered the kitchen, and both men glanced at her.

"I'll let John explain." Kurt leaned over and kissed Stephanie's cheek. "Congratulations, by the way. Welcome to the family."

"Thanks." Stephanie smiled and watched Kurt leave the room.

When Stephanie turned back to John, he held up the envelope and seemed hesitant for a moment. He slapped it against his hand and sighed.

"This was sent to Kurt's office by Marc's lawyer." John stood rigid.

"Do we have to end the night with bad news?" She groaned.

"There are letters in it from Marc to Marina, your parents, and you." John held out the envelope to her.

She stared at it as if it would bite her. Opening it could start a whole lot of drama, and since it was from Marc, it was probably bad news. Stephanie sighed and reluctantly took the envelope.

John wrapped his arm around her as she glanced inside. There was an envelope with her name on it, one for her parents and two for Marina. Stephanie opened the one with her name and began to read it.

The letter was a lengthy apology from Marc. It explained while he was going through recovery, one of the steps required him to make amends to the people he hurt. He hoped Stephanie could forgive him someday for what he did to her sister, and she should know he wouldn't be bothering her family anymore. The last part of the letter made her gasp, and she had to read it several times before it sunk in.

Without a word, she ran out of the kitchen and searched for her sister and parents. She found them with Sean and Kathleen in the living room, and Stephanie didn't even care if it was rude, she shouted to them.

Stephanie explained what John had given her and held out the two envelops meant for Marina. Her sister shook her head and shoved it back at Stephanie.

"I don't want it," Marina snapped.

"You need to read this." Stephanie held out the letter.

"I'm done with him. I don't want to hear anything he has to say." Marina looked as if she was ready to burst into tears.

"Honey, you need to read it." Her mother took the envelopes from Stephanie and placed them in Marina's hand. "We're here with you."

For a moment, Marina stared at the sealed envelopes, and her hands trembled as she slowly opened the smaller one. Marina read the letter to herself while everyone stood silently around her. Stephanie noticed James stood behind her, but his eyes hadn't left Marina's face. When Marina finished the letter, she lifted her head.

"He's not going to bother you again, Rina," Stephanie said. "You'll never have to worry about him coming after Danny either."

"Is this real." Marina held up the papers she'd pulled out of the second envelope.

Stephanie assumed they were the papers to dissolve his parental rights. Marc told Stephanie in his letter that he'd signed them and would send them to Marina.

"Are these papers real?" Marina didn't seem to believe what she had in her hands.

"Mike, come look at this," Kathleen called to Mike as he headed to the kitchen.

Mike specialized in family law and would be familiar with the documents. When Marina handed him the papers, he scanned through them. Marina shuffled her feet as she waited for Mike to finish.

"Is it legal, bro?" John seemed to notice Marina's growing anxiety.

"It's ironclad," Mike said as he finished the last page. "Basically, Marc has dissolved all his parental rights for Danny. The last clause says he can never dispute it."

Marina backed away from the group of people surrounding her and went directly to her son. She lifted Danny out of the playpen where he and Mason had fallen asleep. Stephanie's heart broke with the way Marina hugged her son to her. When Stephanie took a step toward her sister, Marina shook her head.

"I need to go home." Marina weaved around everyone, and when Stephanie tried to run after her, her mom grabbed her arm.

"Let her go, honey." Her mother wrapped her arm around Stephanie's shoulders. "She just needs time to process this."

"I, for one, am glad the ass is out of our lives," Stephanie admitted.

"But you weren't in love with him, or have a child with him." Janet touched Stephanie's cheek. "I'm sure she's happy. It has to be hard to find out your child's father doesn't want anything to do with him."

Her mother's words hit hard. Stephanie had a wonderful man she was going to marry. Marina was a single mother, with a drug-addicted ex-husband who cut all ties with his son. Stephanie couldn't imagine how it would feel. The only thing she could do was wait until Marina wanted to talk.

John pulled into the driveway a short while later. Stephanie made a contented sigh as she gazed at the house she considered home. The house was where her life changed, and where she lived with the love of her life.

"You going to stay in the car tonight?" John chuckled as he pulled open the car door.

"No, I'm going into the house with my fiancée." Stephanie stepped out of the car and took his hand.

"Yes, you are." John tugged her against him and placed a soft kiss against her lips.

"I love you so much, John." Stephanie cupped his face between her hands.

"I love you, too." He brushed her hair back from her face and pressed his lips against her forehead.

"You're the best thing that ever happened to me." Stephanie closed her eyes.

"Sweetheart, the day you walked into my house, you saved me," John whispered against her cheek. "You saved me from living a life of self-pity because everything I did to get better was all because of you. I fell in love with the woman who gave me back my life."

Stephanie smiled. She'd spend the rest of her life with John, and there was nowhere she'd rather be.

Epilogue

Eighteen months later…

It was happening. Stephanie gazed into the long mirror in her childhood bedroom. She didn't recognize herself. The white dress signified the start of her life with the man she loved. The man she couldn't live without.

"Steph," Marina interrupted her thoughts, and Stephanie glanced over her shoulder to where her sister held a long sheer veil.

"I'm getting married today." Stephanie giggled.

"I hope so since over two hundred people are waiting at the church." Marina chuckled.

"Why am I not nervous? I mean, aren't brides supposed to be nervous?" Stephanie asked while Marina pinned the veil in place.

"Only if they're not sure they're marrying the right person." Donna's voice floated into the room.

Stephanie turned as Sandy and Donna entered the room with matching black cocktail dresses. It was the only dress all six of her bridesmaids agreed on.

"I don't think there's any doubt you're marrying the right person." Sandy grinned. "That man adores you."

"I'm pretty sure she adores him too." Jess glided into the room, followed by Isabelle and Kristy.

"Stephanie, you look so beautiful." Kristy gasped and covered her mouth with her hand.

"Kristy, don't you dare make me cry," Stephanie warned.

"It's okay to cry," Kim said as she packed up her makeup case. "The makeup I used is waterproof."

Stephanie and Kim weren't best friends, but they were friends. Stephanie had hired her sister to do everyone's makeup for the wedding. Since Kim was Sandy's sister, they needed to get along.

"Very smart." Isabelle giggled.

"Are you ready, Princess?" Her father stood in the doorway.

He nodded at the girls as they hurried out of the room to give Stephanie and her dad some time before he gave her away. She smiled up at the first man to hold her heart. He showed her how a husband should treat the woman he loves.

"I'm ready, Dad." Stephanie picked up her bouquet and smiled.

"I don't know if I want to give you away." It was the first time she'd heard her father speak so quietly.

"Dad." A lump formed in her throat at the tears in his eyes.

"I know he'll make you happy, and it's the only reason I agreed to this." Doug narrowed his eyes.

"Thank you, Dad. I love you." Stephanie stood up on her toes and kissed his cheek.

"I love you too, Princess." He held out his arm, and Stephanie linked into it.

The bridesmaids slowly made their way to the front of the church, but John shifted back and forth as he waited at the altar. He hadn't seen Stephanie for over twenty-four hours, and he was about to bolt down the aisle so he could see her. Then the doors opened, and she was there. A beautiful vision made his heart feel as if it stopped.

"Don't drool, bro." James nudged him with his elbow.

"I'll do my best." John's eyes locked with hers as she glided closer to him on the arm of her father.

It was as if nothing else existed outside of the angel coming toward him. If he lived a hundred years, he'd never forget that moment.

If anyone asked John what happened during the ceremony, he wouldn't be able to tell them. He'd recited his vows, and his eyes filled with tears as he listened to her repeat them back to him. Then Aaron stood at the podium and started to sing Ave Maria. John couldn't hold the tears back if he tried. He wasn't an emotional man, but after all, they'd been through, he was happier than he could ever imagine.

"How do you feel, Mrs. O'Connor?" John whispered into her ear while they waltzed around the reception hall.

"Thrilled, Mr. O'Connor." Stephanie pressed against him. "And did I mention you look incredibly hot in your tuxedo. I can't wait to rip it off you." Stephanie whispered into his ear.

"Not fair, sweetheart." John groaned as he pressed his lips to hers.

"Get a room," Nick, Mike, and Aaron yelled from the side of the hall.

John saluted them with the middle finger as he pulled his new wife tighter against him. Even his annoying younger brothers couldn't piss him off at that very moment.

James moved through the crowded reception room to where his cousins entertained his son. Mason loved to spend time with Isabelle, Jess, and Kristy, probably because they spoiled him. Of course, what man wouldn't want three women to fuss over him. Even a three-year-old knew that

"Don't tell Daddy I gave you candy." Kristy snickered as James stepped behind her, and Mason giggled.

"I think you're busted." Isabelle pointed toward James.

"Darn cops. Sneak up on you every time." Kristy turned around.

James loved his cousins and was glad to have them in his life. They were like the annoying little sisters he never wanted. He would do anything for them, and he knew they felt the same way.

"He's going home with you." James narrowed his eyes at Kristy as he tried hard to keep a serious face.

"That's fine because we're taking Danny tonight too." Jess linked her arm into his, but James wondered why Jess would be taking Marina's son.

"Yeah, maybe you can make a move since you'll both be childless tonight." Isabelle nudged him.

"Not happening," James snapped as he pulled free from Kristy and reached his hand out to Mason.

The little boy stuck out his bottom lip and put the forbidden candy into James's hand.

"Why not?" Jess said. "You know Aunt Cora says…"

"I don't care what Aunt Cora says," James snapped, then took a deep breath and softened his tone. "I'm. Not. Ready." James sighed and handed the candy back to Mason.

A voice echoed over the speaker to inform everyone it was time for the bridal party dance. James turned toward the dance floor and took a deep breath. If he wasn't ready, then why was the thought of holding Marina in his arms making him hard as steel.

Fucking hell.

When the dance finally ended, James stepped back from Marina and bolted toward the bar. It was rude to walk away from her so abruptly, but he was so damned confused. It had been almost two years since Sarah died, and guilt consumed him for being so attracted to Marina.

Rhonda Brewer

With a fresh beer in hand, James turned around in time to see Aaron grab Marina's hand. James clenched the bottle in his hand so hard it was surprising it didn't break. Aaron pulled Marina into his arms and spun her toward the dance floor. To top it off, the asshole winked at James, and James started to think his brother was trying to get under his skin. Nobody knew how he felt about Marina. James wasn't sure himself.

"She looks really hot tonight." Nick rested his elbows on the bar next to James.

"Didn't you bring a date?" It was hard not to sound irritated with the way Nick seemed to leer at Marina.

"Yeah, but I'm not fucking blind." Nick wiggled his eyebrows as the bartender passed him a bottle. "She seems to be getting a lot of attention in that dress."

Someone would have to be blind not to see how amazing she looked. The thought of another man touching her made his body vibrate with anger. The black dress clung to her, accentuating her full breasts and hips. Marina had curves that could bring any man to his knees, and when Aaron dipped her, James clenched his fists.

"Where's A.J.'s date?" James growled after he slammed back the shot of Screech Nick handed him.

"I don't know, but I don't think A.J. cares right now." Nick laughed as he walked away.

Beating his younger brothers within an inch of their lives at John's wedding probably wouldn't be a good idea. It didn't mean he

435

didn't want to slap Aaron senseless. James wanted her, but neither of them were ready to take that step.

The song ended, and Marina headed straight to her little boy. Danny sat on the floor with Mason and watched everyone dance. The two little boys spent a lot of time together since Marina moved back to Newfoundland.

James smiled when Mason jumped to his feet and wrapped his little arms around Marina. His son seemed to be as smitten with her as James was. To top it off, Marina didn't seem to mind Mason hanging all over her.

"You know she's meant for you." Cora stood next to him.

James was not in the mood to listen to the family cupid put more ideas in his head. Thoughts he knew couldn't come true anytime soon.

"Hi, Aunt Cora." James kissed her cheek.

"Don't ignore me, Jimmy. I'm never wrong, and you know it." She pointed to John and Stephanie. "There's your proof."

James rolled his eyes as she continued to point out the couples she'd predicted were meant to be together. She was the one who told him he was going to marry Sarah, but thinking back, Cora's exact words were, *she's meant for you, for now.*

"Would you like to dance, Aunt Cora?" James hoped the dance could distract her.

Cora wasn't naïve. She narrowed her eyes as she took his hand and followed him to the dance floor. Maybe she was right. Was he ready to move on? Was Marina?

"You're both ready," Cora said as if reading his mind. "Just let it happen."

James looked so God damn hot. Marina tried hard the entire evening to keep her eyes off him. She couldn't get her mind off him either. He was a widower with a child, and she was divorced with a child.

James seemed to be still mourning his wife. Stephanie mentioned several times he hadn't dated since his wife's death. He certainly wasn't going to start with a divorced single mother. Besides, she wasn't sure she was ready either, but it got more difficult every day to fight her growing attraction to him.

It was about to get a whole lot worse. Stephanie seemed to have a lot of family meals lately. Dinners that turned out to be Stephanie, John, James, Marina, and the kids. For some strange reason, the rest of the family always seemed to be busy.

It didn't help that the O'Connor family had their own resident cupid. Cora was under the impression it was her job to get Marina and James together. She sighed when James kissed Cora's cheek and walked off the dance floor. Could she believe what Cora said? Were they meant to be?

Sure, and the moon is made of green cheese. Get a grip.

About the Author

Dreams can come true.

First of all, I'm a wife and mother. I'm also a grandmother. That alone would fulfill any woman's life. To be honest, it does, but I'm also a writer. Someone who loves to tell stories of love, suspense, heartache, and of course, happily ever after. For most of my life, I've written those stories for myself. A type of therapy, I suppose. I love the characters I create. They become part of who I am because there's part of me in them.

So... Now you know this about me. I hope when you read my books; you fall in love with them.

You should also know I'm a Newfoundlander. What is that you ask? Well, we're a proud people who live on an island, off the east coast of Canada. Some people believe Canada ends with Nova Scotia. It doesn't. If you keep going east, there is a beautiful island full of amazing people and magnificent scenery. It's where my stories are set because let's face it. The best stories always come from the places you know and love.

If there is anything else, you would like to know about me

Rhonda Brewer

Keep up to date on all things new.

Follow me on

Facebook

Twitter

Instagram

Sign up for my newsletter and never miss another release.

http://www.rhondabrewerauthor.com/talk-to-me

Coming Soon

O'CONNOR BROTHERS

Book 2

Available July 20, 2016

They have a second chance at love but

Someone from her past could stop it before it starts.

Made in the USA
Monee, IL
03 July 2020